PRAISE FOR SEEKING REDEMPTION: DEVLIN AND GARRICK

"...one of the most talented, vivid writers of romance...Cameron Dane seized my attention from the very first line of *Devlin & Garrick* and didn't let go... Cameron Dane made me not only like Garrick and Devlin, I cared about them. Both men have such distinct, interesting voices that they felt real. And not only did they come to life, they wrapped themselves around my heart; both of them are such good people down to their cores that I absolutely could not resist them... *Devlin & Garrick* is eroticism, warmth, hope, and romance all wrapped up into one perfect package.

—*Shayna from Joyfully Reviewed, a Joyfully Recommended Read*

PRAISE FOR GREY'S AWAKENING

"...Cameron Dane has a very vivid and enjoyable writing style. Dane writes in a way that is descriptive without taking away imagination. This is a story that has both plot and sexuality...I have to applaud Dane for taking a storyline that has been done and making it a world apart from the rest. The characters are highly sexual and damaged just enough to keep it all believable...I found myself getting lost in the romance and lives of the characters...I am happy to say this is not a story that leaves you looking for more because you are left more than sated when you reach the end."

—*Tabatha from The Romance Studio*

Seeking Redemption

Devlin & Garrick

Cameron Dane

ISBN-13: 978-1463711863
ISBN-10: 1463711867
SEEKING REDEMPTION: DEVLIN AND GARRICK

Originally released in e-book format in June 2010 by Liquid Silver Books

Manufactured in the USA

Cover Art by Anne Cain
Print Design and Formatting by April Martinez
Edited by Chrissie Henderson

PROLOGUE

"If you sit there in silence for one more second, I'm going to assume that you fucked him."

Devlin Morgan jerked out of his daydreaming and landed a narrow-eyed glare on the young woman sitting across from him. The words "you fucked him" had registered in his head -- *in his little sister's voice* -- and dragged Devlin back to reality with a shudder. He did not talk about sex with his sister. Especially not in the middle of a diner during lunch hour.

Especially when you're not having any, Devlin added to himself silently.

Maddie smirked at Devlin from the other side of the booth. She pushed her long dark hair behind her ears. "Yep, I thought that would get your attention." Light gray eyes that matched his twinkled with laughter one second and then softened in the next. "I'd say you're allowed to brood and keep quiet all you want, except you're the one who invited me to lunch."

"I was getting a little stir crazy sitting around the apartment," Devlin answered. "I hate that I can't go back to work yet." In performing his duties as a firefighter, Devlin had injured himself while carrying a man out of an apartment building. One month of rehabbing his leg and lower back now under his belt, he still had a few more weeks before he could get back on the job. "I have PT in a few hours, but I needed a change of scenery before I started rearranging the walls with my bare hands."

"Ahh." Maddie nodded, but pursed her lips and gave him the stink eye at the same time. "And here I thought you might finally want to talk about your date."

Darren. The guy was one of only a very few openly gay men in Redemption that Devlin wasn't related to by blood or civil ceremony. The two he claimed as kin were Aidan and Ethan. Aidan was Devlin's brother and Ethan was Aidan's partner. Disgustingly happy as a couple for three years now, they made forever look attainable and inviting. Devlin loved hanging out with them, but the twist of envy that came with seeing them in a successful partnership drove home exactly how far away he was from finding someone himself.

He just couldn't get excited about Darren though. When Devlin thought about what Aidan and Ethan had, a longing for the same constricted his chest, and he couldn't hold back the memories of looking into bottomless green eyes, of gripping thick, wide shoulders, and of gasping for breath the first time another man sank his cock deep into Devlin's virgin ass.

Stop it! Devlin slammed closed a thick metal door on the rest of that picture. *Gradyn is long out of your life. For good.*

"Earth to Dev." Maddie snapped her fingers in Devlin's face, and in doing so yanked him back to the diner again. "Don't make me say the word fuck again."

Devlin shot his sister another pointed glare. "You just did."

"So you hadn't drifted that far away this time," Maddie said as the devil came back into her eyes. "In that case… Your second date with cutie Darren. When is it going to happen?"

Incessant chatter from his first date with Darren still rang in Devlin's ears. "We have something set up for tomorrow night, but I think I'm going to cancel it."

"Really?" Maddie sat up straighter. "He's attractive and I always remember him being a sweetie in school. What's not working for you?"

Maybe that was part of the problem with Darren. His age. Maddie could remember him being a sweet kid because she actually went through high school with Darren not that long ago. Devlin opened his mouth to say so when a shadow crossed their table.

"Maddie." An older gentleman Devlin recognized as a member of the city council paused at their table. "Just the girl I was hoping to find." The man then smoothly transitioned his attention to Devlin and stuck out his hand. "Hi there. Larry

Courtland. And you're Devlin. Correct? How's the physical therapy coming along?"

Devlin had never met this guy in person but figured he must have read about Devlin's injuries in the newspaper a while back. "I'm fine, sir." He shook the guy's hand. "I should be back at the firehouse in a couple of weeks."

"Good. Very good." Larry slipped his hands into his pockets and rocked back on his heels. "The council was speaking with your brother very recently about increasing the budget for the fire department. One of the hardships Chief Morgan cited was when his paid staff gets injured and puts you all down a man."

"It's tough, sir." Aidan was not only Devlin's brother, but also his boss. "We could use a couple more full-time people at the house."

Maddie touched Larry Courtland's elbow and deftly brought his attention back to her. "Did you need me for something, Mr. Courtland?"

"I went by the garage and that new guy told me you were here." With his hands still in his pockets, Larry leaned close to Maddie, as if imparting a state secret. "My baby has a funny hum, and you're the only one I trust to treat her right."

"Ahh." Maddie nodded, and her eyes lit up as she tapped her fingers against her lips. "Do you have her with you right now?"

"Right there." Mr. Courtland pointed, and Devlin followed the line of his finger through the window to a cherry-red classic corvette in the parking lot.

"How's your schedule?" Maddie asked, clearly comfortable as hell, and making Devlin all kinds of proud. His sister was one hell of a mechanic. "Do you have time for me to go take a quick listen right now?" She pulled her hair back into a ponytail and slid out of the booth before the man answered.

"That's why I came in." Mr. Cortland put his hand at the small of her back and gestured toward the exit. "Ladies first."

"Be right back, Dev." Maddie squeezed his shoulder as she walked past. "Knock on the window if our food arrives."

"No problem," he told her, but she was already out the door.

As Devlin watched Maddie cross the parking lot to the corvette, he let his mind wander back to his date with Darren. Compact and wiry, with sandy-colored hair, a mouth that ran a mile a minute, and hands that gestured just as fast, Darren brought to Devlin's mind pictures of chipmunks gathering nuts for winter at a furious rate. That image had popped into Devlin's head over pasta during their first date, and once there, he could not shake it.

Darren. Darren. Darren. Why don't I want you?

The guy was harmless. He really did seem nice enough. God knew he had pretty blue eyes and a full lower lip that should have Devlin wanting to pull it between his teeth and find his way into that mouth for a deep kiss. Devlin just knew Darren's body kicked ass too; he didn't have to see it naked to get a real good sense of its rock-solid shape beneath the too-snug shirts and jeans he often wore.

Everything about Darren should be right, even for just a no-strings tryst, but Devlin couldn't forget another fling, one that left all others pale in comparison before they even happened...

———

...Oh God. This is not me. I shouldn't be here.

Devlin kept his head down and nursed his watered-down beer while techno music blasted in the background and a dozen or so young men gyrated some twenty feet away on a dance floor. An equally small group of guys littered the long line of the bar, although most of them had their backs to the wood. They openly admired the view of dancers swaying so closely together, and Devlin had to wonder if a group orgy might break out right in front of him. Then he figured the club likely paid the hot dancing men to do exactly what they were doing, and that soon a whole lot more customers would trickle in and spend too much money on cheap drinks so they could stare, hope, and maybe even join in the fun, just like Devlin was supposed to be doing himself.

Except, it all felt so impersonal, and Devlin suddenly didn't think he had anything to prove. He was gay. He had wet dreams about random and not-so-random men on a nightly basis and had been noticing masculine bodies and male smells since he'd hit puberty. Just because he'd recently turned twenty-three and still hadn't experienced actual full-on sex with another man didn't mean he had to put-up or shut-up and go straight.

Devlin groaned into his drink. Nearly a thousand bucks on

a round-trip plane ticket, spending money, and a motel for a long weekend in San Francisco, and *now* he had the realization that he should have just stayed home?

Real smart, Dev. You're building yourself a nice track record of leaping before you look.

At least now he knew anonymous sex wasn't his thing. And he felt less guilty for booking the cheap motel rather than the expensive hotel. If it was just going to be him, he didn't need anything fancy. Devlin went ahead and decided he wouldn't spend a whole lot of time in the room anyway. This city had plenty of sights to see that didn't have a damned thing to do with hooking up with men. The trip wouldn't be a waste of his hard-earned money. He could do a hundred touristy things before he had to head home to Maine.

Might as well start now.

"Excuse me." Devlin signaled the bartender before the guy stepped away and strutted his amazing ass down the bar for someone else. The stud looked up at him, and Devlin said, "Can I go ahead and pay my tab please?"

As soon as Devlin got a nod, heat from another source rode his back, drawing a shiver down his spine. Then a voice as smooth as expensive bourbon sank into his ear. "I wondered how long it would take you to ask for the check."

The towering muscular body that went with the deep, rich voice slipped in between the barstools and leaned against the empty one next to Devlin.

"You don't look like you belong here, beautiful," the man

said. He looked right at Devlin and nearly stopped Devlin's heart.

Devlin opened his mouth and was surprised his voice didn't come out as a croak. "Neither do you."

Holy shit. That was the understatement of the year. The man wore a leather jacket with a white T-shirt beneath, faded jeans, and biker boots, but that wasn't exactly what had Devlin swallowing funny. *Not even close.* Indigo colored tattoos that looked almost tribal in design covered part of this man's smooth, bald scalp and went down to a corner of his forehead, around his left eye, over part of his cheek, and down his jaw line to his neck, where the pattern disappeared under his shirt.

"You're right. I don't belong here." The guy answered Devlin's question, drawing Devlin's attention to his sensuous mouth.

The bartender came up right then and slid a credit card receipt and pen in front of Devlin. Devlin added a tip and signed. All the while, every molecule in his being snapped to life and shot to the parts of his body closest to the tattooed man leaning next to him.

Devlin handed the signed receipt back to the bartender with a murmured "Thank you." He said another prayer of thanks when his hands stayed steady. God knew the rest of him shook inside.

"So." The tattooed man stayed on his barstool, allowing Devlin plenty of running room. Fuck, though, his pure green eyes held Devlin captive and made him feel stripped bare right in this techno club. "Do you want to get out of here?" That rich voice slipped into Devlin and infected his blood. "With me?"

"Yeah," Devlin automatically answered. *What the fuck is wrong with me?* Devlin darted his tongue out and wet the edge of his lip as his nerves skittered into overdrive. "I think I do."

The man dropped his focus to Devlin's mouth. It stayed there as he stood and moved in close. He curled his hand around Devlin's neck, pulled him in, and licked right over where Devlin had just dipped his tongue. Devlin jerked; the small contact shot tingles all the way through his body and moved quickly into his jeans. The guy's fingers dug into Devlin's nape right before he murmured a curse and licked Devlin's mouth again, this time drawing a needful little noise of out of Devlin he could not control.

"Damn it." The man's voice suddenly thicker, he let go of Devlin's neck and grabbed his hand. "We have to get out of here right now. Let's go."

"Wait!" Flashing red lights signaled in Devlin's mind, and he tugged against the bigger man's vise-tight hold on his hand. When the guy looked back, Devlin said, "I don't even know your name."

The man smiled, and it went all the way up to his eyes. He let up his death grip on Devlin's hand and instead threaded their fingers together in a gentler, but no less sure, hold. "Gradyn Connell. My mom and my sister call me Denny, and most everybody else calls me GC. What's yours?"

"Devlin Morgan." Devlin grinned back. Couldn't seem to

rein it in. "Some people shorten it to Dev. Doesn't bother me one way or the other."

"Okay, *Devlin*, now we know a little something about each other." Gradyn looked down at their linked hands and then came back up to Devlin's eyes. "Or have you changed your mind about leaving with me?"

"No." *Oh God. This is possibly the stupidest thing I've ever done.* Risky-crazy-stupid or not, something in Gradyn Connell's eyes made everything else that was a little bit scary about him disappear. That green gaze of this man, that didn't waver, kept Devlin's hand firmly in Gradyn's hold when every bit of intelligence he possessed told him this was a bad idea. "I want to go with you."

Gradyn smiled even bigger. Without another word, he pulled Devlin toward the exit.

This time, Devlin didn't fight it…

———

…"Do I have to say that word again?" Maddie whispered in a diabolical tone at Devlin's ear, drawing him away from memories of someone he'd repeatedly promised himself he wouldn't waste time thinking about anymore.

Five years, Dev. Time to forget that weekend ever happened.

Ignoring Maddie's threat, and shaking off his own disturbing thoughts, Devlin asked, "Did you figure out the problem with Mr. Courtland's car?"

"It's not something I can fix in a parking lot. He doesn't

have time to drive it back out to the garage." Maddie dangled a set of car keys off one finger, and Devlin would have thought she twirled a diamond ring. "So he left it for me."

Devlin chuckled as he took another glance at the sweet ride outside. "You have the coolest job."

"Yeah," a little smile added to the life shining in his sister's eyes, "I kind of do. I'm going to need you to drive my truck back to the garage, okay?" Maddie had done the driving, and Devlin's car was back at her work.

He snatched the corvette keys out of her hand and held them above his head. "Why don't I drive the 'vette and you drive your truck?"

Maddie surged up from the booth and grabbed the keys right back with a whip-fast move. She smirked for a second but quickly sobered and pocketed the keys. "Mr. Courtland has a heavy foot and hand, and that makes his car very temperamental to handle. You just got the okay to drive again. I don't need it pulling on you, and you driving it off the road. I'm thinking about your safety more than the fact that it wouldn't be professional of me to let you drive it."

"Fine." Four weeks of limitations and no job to rely on as an outlet turned Devlin's tone somewhat surly. "But don't be surprised if you go to watch last week's *True Blood* and it's mysteriously gone from the DVR."

Maddie snorted and rolled her eyes. "Fat chance. You love that show too much to delete one just to spite me."

"Maybe I've already watched it," he shot back.

"You wouldn't." She didn't even flinch. "Not without me."

That was true. Pathetic and sad, but true. They shared an apartment, and neither one of them dated enough to disrupt any of their routines.

Their waitress breezed to the table right then, just long enough to deposit two plates of greasy food in front of Devlin and Maddie. She offered a quick "Enjoy" before moving on to the next group of customers entering the diner.

"Yeah, all right," Devlin muttered as he picked up his bacon cheeseburger. "Shut up and eat your food."

Maddie flashed him a fast smile and then dug into her mile-high club sandwich.

———

"YOU SHOULD AT LEAST CONSIDER giving Darren another shot," Maddie said as she joined Devlin next to his car in the parking lot of Corsini's Garage. "I don't remember him being a chatterbox. Maybe you're not doing enough talking and he feels like he has to fill in the awkward silences on his own."

Devlin rolled his eyes. His sister had picked up their conversation from the diner as if she and Devlin hadn't driven across town in separate vehicles.

"I'm going to go now, Maddie." Devlin looked at her from over the hood of his piece of crap Corolla that Maddie kept alive with duct tape and prayer, and delivered a look that matched the firmness in his tone. "I'll see you at home tonight."

"No, wait! Come inside with me for a second. I want to

show you something."

"What now?" Devlin didn't move. "I have to get to the hospital for my therapy session."

"You have a few minutes," she answered in a knowing voice. "It's something you might want to consider buying when I'm done restoring it." She sing-songed the information like the Pied Piper from over her shoulder, and Devlin could not ignore the enticing tune.

Devlin jogged and caught up to her side. "What is it?" She knew he hated his car but that he also refused to sink a pile of money into something new that wasn't truly special.

"Just a '77 Trans Am that will have all the interior specs and gleam with shiny black paint and the Pontiac Firebird insignia on the hood by the time I'm done with it."

Shit. "Really?" Devlin used to watch a certain movie over and over when he was a kid, and he had latched onto wanting the damned car like nobody's business.

"Really," Maddie answered. She pushed open the side door to the garage, and Devlin followed her inside the big, cavernous building. "It doesn't look like much right now, but give us some time in between the jobs that pay the bills and Garrick and I will have it looking and running better than the original. Follow me." She circled around two cars. "We have it curtained off and under canvas in back."

They rounded the front end of an Accord and came across a pair of long legs encased in Corsini's standard blue coveralls sticking out from under the car.

"Ooh, stay still, G." Maddie tapped her boot against the boot of the guy under the car. "I think I remember the words to a double-dutch game I used to play when I was a kid." Maddie proceeded to skip in a pattern over and between the man's spread legs, all the while singing an old jump-roping song. At the end, she jumped a foot away with a grand "Ta-da! I did it."

A chuckle drifted out from under the car, followed by a smooth, deep voice. "If you're done skipping rope with my legs, Maddie, can you get me a new light? This one just died."

Holy shit. Devlin trembled as the rich tone of that damned voice washed over his flesh. He knew that voice all the way down to his soul.

Devlin planted his hand against the hood of the Accord so he didn't stumble.

He couldn't fucking believe it.

"Gradyn?" This time his voice did croak.

Chapter One

Gradyn Connell in Redemption. Devlin's mind spun with the information. He could not fathom it. *Holy mother.* Was the man here with his wife?

Maddie shot a puzzled glance in Devlin's direction. "Gradyn? Who's that? Did you mishear me? This is Garrick." She stooped down, squeezed the man's shin, and tugged him out from under the Accord. "He's going to help me restore the Trans Am."

The guy wheeled out on a rolling plank, revealing a fit body, and got to his feet. "Hi." He wiped his grease-streaked hands on his coveralls and then stuck his right one out Devlin's way. "Garrick Langley. Good to meet you."

What the hell?

Devlin went lightheaded for a second time in as many minutes, and he leaned more heavily against the Accord to help hold himself steady. The voice attached to this new mechanic echoed in Devlin's mind as Gradyn. The texture of it rippled through Devlin's being as vividly as he recalled the rough hands of this man learning every inch of his body. He knew the command and tone of that fucking voice. He also still knew the shape and length of this man's cock -- that had taken Devlin's ass with insane slowness and punishing power -- and it had branded Devlin both inside and out while looking at him through green eyes that had pierced right into Devlin's soul.

Only, right this second, Devlin looked into pure blue eyes, not green, and the lack of that connection sucker punched him. Before him stood a lean, sinewy, fit man, not the wide shoulders and thicker bulk Devlin remembered of Gradyn Connell. This man's skin was a handful of shades lighter than the allover tan skin Devlin remembered kissing from top to bottom. This person had raven-black hair, long enough that some of it was pulled back with an elastic band, and the rest looked as if it had worked loose of that band over the course of the morning. And fucking hell, the thing that Devlin couldn't believe with his own eyes -- *fucking shit* -- was that this man didn't have so much as a dot of indigo ink anywhere on his face, into his hairline, or down his neck. Devlin had touched those tattoos; he'd licked them and gotten into a shower with that man multiple times over that weekend in San Francisco. No way had they been surface ink. *What the hell?*

"Dev." Maddie jabbed him in the shoulder. "You're being rude."

"Sorry." Devlin snapped back into the moment and realized the man still had his hand reached out in offering. "Garrick, you said?" Devlin asked. He slid his hand into the warm clasp of this person who *was not* a stranger.

Damned well wasn't any Garrick Langley either, whoever that was.

"Yes, my name is Garrick," the guy said as he shook Devlin's hand. "And I take it you're Maddie's other brother? I've met the chief already."

You've met me too, you bastard. You fucking lived inside me for almost forty-eight hours straight.

Devlin didn't let go of "Garrick's" hand when the man made to pull away. "Yep, I'm Devlin, the other brother," he replied. That *not right* blue gaze shot to his, and the long fingers clasped around his contracted.

"You seem familiar," Devlin pushed. "Are you sure we haven't met?"

"I just moved to Redemption a month ago." Garrick narrowed his stare, as if studying Devlin under a microscope. "I don't think we've crossed paths in town."

Devlin noticed he didn't exactly answer the question. "Where did you live before you came here?"

"DC."

Not San Francisco. Or Oakland. Didn't matter. Maybe Garrick -- formerly known as Gradyn, Devlin damned well knew it -- had moved from one coast to the other with his girlfriend after they got married.

"How's your wife?" Devlin asked.

That got the man tugging against their handhold again, and this time Devlin let him go. "I'm not married." Confusion mapped the guy's tattoo-free features and raised his voice higher. He held up his ring-free left hand, and there wasn't any leftover tan line in sight from something he might have recently removed. "Never have been."

Maddie suddenly pounced and landed a stinging punch on Devlin's arm. "What the hell is wrong with you?" She turned to Garrick and put a hand on his wrist. "G, I'm sorry my brother is being such a jackass. If it makes you change your mind about helping me restore the Trans Am for him, I understand."

"No, it's okay." Garrick waved his hand in a dismissive manner. He crouched back down and sat on the edge of the rolling board. "I obviously look like someone he knows. That has to be kind of weird. No harm done. Nice to meet you, Devlin." The guy looked up at Devlin and held his gaze in silence for a prolonged heartbeat. "I hope I'll see you again." Then he lay back on the board and disappeared under the car.

Devlin rubbed his arm and tried to warm away the goose bumps that had lifted under his skin. For that split second Garrick had stared at him, Devlin had felt naked.

Just like Gradyn made me feel five years ago in that club.

"What the hell, Dev?" Maddie jabbed his arm again, her punch as good as any featherweight boxer. "Come with me before *I* change *my* mind about restoring this car for you."

She grabbed his arm, and Devlin let Maddie drag him across the spacious, open building to the far back corner of the garage. His thoughts remained on Garrick, though, now some fifty feet behind him. Something suddenly hit Devlin. Garrick had forgotten the replacement light he'd initially asked Maddie to hand him. He had slid under the Accord again, under the pretense of working, without a light.

He hid himself under that car. Away from me. He damn well knows who I am. And now he knows I recognize him too.

Question upon question spun in Devlin's head. Why was Gradyn calling himself Garrick now? Or was Garrick real, and Gradyn the lie? Why had he so drastically altered his appearance? Why was he pretending he and Devlin had never met? And why had he come to Redemption?

Devlin had nothing but time on his hands these days, and he intended to find some answers.

DEVLIN STARED AT HIS COMPUTER screen, scanning through the list of e-mails in "Gradyn's" folder. Six months worth of communication, and he couldn't help smiling at some of the subject lines from Gradyn to him. *Miss You, Devlin* and *Horny Tonight* and *Something Cool I Had To Tell You* and *A's Beat Bo-Sox, Suck It* and *I Want Your Cock So Bad*, just to name a few. A handful that dealt with more serious subject matters were mixed in too. *So Sorry About Your Mom* and *Daddy Issues? Heh.*

Can You Have Those If You've Never Had One? and *Lost An Old Friend Today; I Fucking Hate Meth.*

Then Devlin glanced over the ones that had come during the last month of their long-distance relationship, where the subject matter had changed to increasingly benign, until the final one, with the header *I Have To Tell You The Truth.*

Highlighting it, Devlin opened the e-mail, as he'd done a thousand times the first few months after receiving it. Since then, he had avoided it and the stab of betrayal it sent through his gut each time he read the words.

> *Devlin -- I had fun with you, please don't think everything was a lie. I met you at a tough time in my life, a place where I was in transition and had to make some huge choices. I needed to know if committing to my girlfriend was what I really wanted out of life.*
>
> *You're a good guy. I enjoyed experimenting with you, but I see now that was all it was, an experiment. I've been with my girlfriend for a long time, and I love her. About a month ago, I told her everything about us -- the weekend, the phone calls, and the e-mails. We're stronger now than we ever were, and I've asked her to marry me. She said yes, and now it's time to focus completely on my real life.*
>
> *I've been struggling with how to tell you all of this, but I realize that I just have to do it. I won't be calling or e-mailing you anymore, and I won't respond to any attempts to contact me. I'm sorry if this hurts you. When I*

approached you in that club, I didn't have anything but a
night of fucking in mind.
    Goodbye,
    Gradyn

Devlin only winced a little bit as the sensation of a knife twisting in his stomach assaulted him all over again. He forgave himself the shadow of lingering pain, considering he'd just seen the very man a few hours ago. Gradyn or Garrick, lean or thick, blue or green eyes, bald or a head full of hair, tattoos or ink free ... the surface didn't matter. Didn't change the DNA of the man. Didn't change the heart and personality of the person Devlin had somehow fallen in love with over the course of one incredible weekend. Of course, Devlin wouldn't have thought the man he had come to know so well capable of sending this last e-mail -- of Devlin being his dirty little secret -- so what the hell did he really know?

Staring at the words on the monitor now, four and a half years away from reading this e-mail for the first time, it still sounded surreal and like the words of a stranger. This wasn't the style of the guy Devlin had spent a weekend fucking and getting to know, nor like the man he'd traded a hundred other e-mails with, as well as dozens more phone calls.

Unless, as Gradyn had hinted, that man Devlin had gotten to know was a vacation from the life of the real Gradyn Connell. That would make the increasingly distant e-mails during the last month, as well as this final one, the true Gradyn. Or Garrick.

Or whoever the hell this multi-faced, multi-named, multi-lives person turned out to be.

Devlin scrolled back to the first e-mail Gradyn had sent after their weekend together.

> *Hey, Devlin--*
>
> *Goddamn it, man. I told myself I'd be cool and walk away. It was just supposed to be a couple of days of fun. What the hell is wrong with me? I feel so lame right now. If you're laughing at me, I'll fucking come find you and spank your ass.*
>
> *Seriously, though, I want to be real clear about something, and I'm not sure I did a good job of it while we were together.*
>
> *Dev, I think that was the most incredible two days I've ever had in my life. It was because of you. You needed to know that.*
>
> *I don't know what the hell to do next. I miss your voice and I'm pretty sure the next fucking thing I'm going to do is pick up the phone and call you.*
>
> *Still hard,*
>
> *Gradyn*

Devlin chuckled and grinned, just as he'd done when finding this e-mail in his Inbox only minutes after getting home from the airport five years ago. Everything in Devlin's gut, everything in his ability to read people, told him *this* e-mail, not the final one, was the heart and soul of the man he'd gotten to know within the confines of one small motel room in a faraway city…

———

…The motel room door slammed into the wall as it opened. Gradyn, fully in charge, forced Devlin inside and shoved him up against that same wall the second after he kicked the door closed. Both men breathed heavily from the kisses they'd shared on the stairs and in the hallway. Gradyn clutched Devlin's head in his big hands, dipped down, and devoured his mouth all over again.

Devlin held on to Gradyn's waist and opened himself up to a hot, wet taking of his mouth, reveling in the big, male body crowding him into the immovable wall at his back. Devlin licked back with equal fervor, tangled his tongue with this other man's, and fused himself to Gradyn. Gradyn's hard cock pressed deeply into Devlin's lower belly, and Devlin wanted nothing so much as to see it and touch it without two layers of clothes between them.

"Lemme…" Devlin pulled at the man's belt with one hand and through a pair of jeans curled his hand around a thick, solid cock with the other.

Oh shit, it's big.

Gradyn jerked at first contact and then ground himself into the touch. He growled and bit at Devlin's kiss-swollen lips while he snaked his hands down Devlin's back. Gradyn yanked

Devlin's shirt out of his jeans, giving some skin on skin contact that had Devlin moaning for more. The man delved his hands under Devlin's shirt and pushed it off over his head, forcing a break in their kiss.

With a low whistle, Gradyn dropped his attention to Devlin's chest and abdomen, took a backward step into the room, and shrugged out of his leather jacket. "Goddamn it, beautiful." He never took his eyes off Devlin as he reached down and unlaced his boots. "Get those jeans off and show me that pretty ass. I need to fuck you."

Adrenaline flooded Devlin with breakneck speed and had him running to the nightstand next to the double bed. "I have the stuff." He fumbled with the drawer's finicky hinges, wrestled the thing open, and commanded his fingers to listen to the order from his brain to stop trembling. "I don't know what you want," he rambled as he withdrew a large bottle of lube, "but I think I have everything we could possibly need."

He heard the rustling of clothing as it was presumably being removed and hitting the floor, and then Gradyn said, "I have my own condoms, but I'll need your lube." That smooth, deep voice wrapped around Devlin from across the room, shimmering phantom touches over his bare back. "I only have enough slick for one round, and I can already tell that's not going to be nearly enough with you."

Oh Jesus. Devlin sucked in a gulp of cleansing air. *It's really going to happen.* "Okay." Devlin's heart continued to race faster than it ever had, almost burning his chest. He kept his head down and his back turned as he undressed, needing the extra few minutes to gather his nerves. After toeing off his shoes and socks, he finished undoing his belt and slipped off his jeans and boxer briefs.

He breathed, searching for calm again. Shit, though, he'd never been completely naked with a man. Showers in gym class did not qualify as being nude with another guy. At least, not in this sense. It didn't count unless the other guy admired and craved the same things he did.

Suddenly, a furnace of male heat covered Devlin's bare backside. "Fucking incredible," Gradyn murmured at Devlin's ear. His lips grazed Devlin's nape, and a big, calloused hand swept over the hills of Devlin's buttocks. "I knew you'd have a great ass." As Gradyn said that, he slipped a finger into Devlin's crack.

Devlin jumped about a mile into the air and made a very unmanly squeaking noise. He spun and then gasped at the vision before him. The crappy lighting in the room did nothing to diminish the specimen of man just a few feet away. Gradyn's shoulders looked a mile wide, and the definition of muscles roping his arms, chest, stomach, and legs proved that he spent more than a little time working out. The indigo tattoo pattern that started on his scalp and worked its way down the side of his face and neck continued over one shoulder, arm, side, and leg, all the way to mid-calf. That all seemed irrelevant at this point, though.

It was Gradyn's cock -- *oh Jesus, Mary and Joseph* -- it was his cock that got the pinpricks jumping on Devlin's flesh. Fully erect, the thing was thicker than Devlin ever could have imagined, and not without a decent amount of length too. Devlin probably had an extra inch, but he couldn't even get close to the girth of this man. He swallowed. Hard.

Gradyn canted his head and lifted one brow. "You okay, man?"

Devlin jerked his focus up to Gradyn's face. "You surprised me when you came up on me." *I can do this.* He cleared his throat and took a step forward. "That's all."

A flash of wicked smile lit up the sea of green in Gradyn's eyes. "Good." He snagged Devlin around the waist and yanked him up to his front. Devlin grabbed Gradyn's shoulders just as the man dipped down and whispered, "Because I sure as hell didn't want to walk away." Then he took Devlin with another scorching kiss and tripped him right back onto the bed.

Gradyn came down on top of Devlin, and the solid weight of his body rocked a shockwave clear through Devlin's system. Devlin automatically circled his arms around Gradyn's waist, and with the burn of that bare skin, he quickly started moving his hands over more smooth, solid flesh. He frantically traced his fingers over Gradyn's back, buttocks, and legs, unable to stop touching and learning.

"Fuck, I want you," Gradyn said. He groaned for more as he pushed his way into Devlin's mouth with another kiss, brushing a tantalizing hint of tongues. With every lick or jab Gradyn delivered, he rocked his hips into Devlin with increasing intent and made it impossible for Devlin to forget or ignore the man's thick cock. Not that Devlin wanted to but, God, its size and rigidity repeatedly stabbed into the crease of Devlin's inner thigh, and Devlin couldn't stop his passage from clenching each time he imagined that erection trying to force its way into his ass.

Gradyn kept his mouth fused to Devlin's. At the same time, he reached down and dug his fingers into Devlin's hips, gripping him with brutal power and forcing Devlin's legs further apart. He rubbed his hand down Devlin's prick and gave a shivery-nice caress to his balls before delving deeper and fingering Devlin's asshole. A blunt tip teased Devlin's virgin pucker, and Devlin sucked in an unsteady breath.

"Shit." As Gradyn gave Devlin's entrance a little more pressure, he made a low humming noise. "I can't wait another second to feel this ass." He reared up to his knees to grab a condom off the comforter.

With Gradyn poised to rip open the condom packet, Devlin took another glance at this man's penis -- as well as at his clear, unbridled enthusiasm for this coupling -- and Devlin suddenly blurted, "I've never done this before. I've never had a man fuck me."

Gradyn snapped his attention up to Devlin and froze. For a split second, he hung in suspended animation, his dick rearing and nearly ready to go, looking like a predator that could do some serious damage. Then he muttered "Shit" under his breath and shot out of bed. He proceeded to pace the length of the motel room without words. Devlin watched, uncertain but still hard, at the fierceness of this person -- this stranger -- moving back and forth in a precise, deliberate pattern. An oppressive silence coated the air but it was not nearly enough to smother the electricity still sparking off every surface of the room.

The man finally came to a stop. Using his hands, Gradyn braced himself against the dresser, his stance wide and his focus still aimed down at the ugly carpet. The sculpted lines of his beautiful back flexed and strained, making the edges of the tattoo wrapped around his shoulder and side ripple with every move. Devlin imagined that Gradyn wanted to yell down the walls, and that he worked to get his frustration -- and possible anger -- in line.

Devlin could see the front of Gradyn's body reflected in the mirror and took note that the man had not lost a bit of his hard-on. His chest moved in steady waves. Devlin stared openly, and the mirror helped give him a complete view of the singular pattern of Gradyn's body art, showing that it was truly spectacular … and a little daunting. He really did not know this person at all.

Abruptly, Gradyn turned and looked at Devlin. "Come here, beautiful." His voice sounded gentle, and he even offered Devlin a half-grin, which sparked a renewed case of excited butterflies in Devlin's stomach. "Bring your lube."

Devlin crawled out of bed, grabbed the bottle off the nightstand, and shuffled to stand in front of Gradyn. Embarrassment at his inexperience, and that he'd falsely led this man to believe they would have a very different experience tonight, kept Devlin's attention glued to the floor.

I'm such an idiot.

"Look at me," Gradyn said. He took the bottle but didn't say another word. Silence sat heavy between them. When Devlin finally looked up, Gradyn, said, "I'm not mad, okay?" He cuffed his big hand around Devlin's neck and drew their foreheads together. He continued, the edges of his tone now sounding frayed. "But I fucking *need* some kind of connection to another man right now. If you can suck me off, and help me come," he curled Devlin's hand around his erection and helped him stroke the stiff length, "I will bend myself over this dresser and let you have at my ass. We'll worry about patience and going slow later." He held Devlin's stare, and pushed their hands between his thighs. "Think you can handle me?"

Devlin tested the weight of Gradyn's sac. Feeling the man respond against his palm, Devlin reclaimed some of his bravado. "Hell, yeah." He gave a gentle squeeze. "I'll even suck your balls."

Gradyn tunneled his fingers into Devlin's hair and moved them in a massaging caress. "I can live with this kind of negotiation." He brushed his lips against Devlin's, then reached back, took hold of the edge of the dresser, and offered a slow, smooth smile. His cock stuck out big and proud, too weighty to point north. He stared at Devlin, and his eyelids fell to half-mast. "Come on, newbie; show me what you've got."

Devlin leaned in and lifted up on his toes to caress Gradyn's mouth with his. He feathered his lips back and forth across Gradyn's, and smiled against the brushing kisses and grin he got in return. "Give me a chance to work my way there." He chuckled, feeling oddly equal now, and darted the tip of his tongue out for a fast taste. "I think you'll like it."

A rumbling noise vibrated all the way through Gradyn. He pulled Devlin's hair, yanking his head back. "I know I will." He slashed his mouth down on Devlin's and took him with another savage kiss. Devlin soared on this man's desires. Devlin claimed Gradyn just as aggressively, sweeping deep into the wet heat of his mouth, and then whimpered when Gradyn severed the connection. Gradyn fused his forehead back to Devlin's; his eyes burned green fire, and he whispered roughly, "But get there soon or I'm going to fucking crawl right out of my body." The man shuddered, and his fingertips were white with the grip he had on the dresser.

Devlin wasn't a sadist, and he didn't want Gradyn to hurt. "It's like you said," he dropped to his knees, and looked up into the eyes of a person in pain, "patience and slow can wait for next time." Hungry himself, Devlin leaned in and took the thick head of Gradyn's cock in his mouth.

Gradyn hissed above him, and Devlin knew the man's legs trembled in an effort not to shove his full length down Devlin's throat. It didn't matter. Devlin possessed a need to give that more than matched Gradyn's ache for relief. Devlin went down on another inch of Gradyn's shaft and sucked, letting that salty male flavor tingle over his taste buds again. *Oh yeah.* Devlin hummed as saliva filled his mouth and provided all the slickness needed for this task. *So fucking good.* He eased back and used his tongue to spread moisture down and around Gradyn's length, bringing Gradyn to a moan. The man pumped his hips just a little bit, and a shot of thrilling success raced through Devlin's blood, spurring him to do more. He went down again, and this time remembered to wrap his hand around the base, jerking gently in time with the drag of his mouth.

"Oh, yeah ... mmmm ... do it harder." Gradyn covered Devlin's hand with his and forced a tighter grip around his prick. "Don't hold anything back."

Devlin contracted his fingers around Gradyn and dragged up and down the man's dick with a suffocating grip, certainly to a place of near pain. Gradyn went back to clutching the dresser while releasing a deep, low noise that sounded like pure sex to Devlin's ears.

Aggression and lust mingled inside Devlin, taking over every particle of his mind and body, and let him know that he wanted nothing more than to make this man come. He let Gradyn's cock slide from his mouth, pushed it up against his lower stomach, and licked his way down the underside to tongue his lightly-furred sac. Gradyn's balls moved under the protective layer of skin, and he purred with each lapping lick Devlin delivered. Inspired to do even more, Devlin pulled one nut past his lips and suckled.

"Ohhh shit." Gradyn gasped and snapped his hips, his body rolling in a wave as Devlin swirled his tongue around the hairy weight taking over his mouth. "Something about you, beautiful." Gradyn stopped and bit off a curse when Devlin opened wider and eased the second testicle past his lips. Gradyn's back bowed in an arc, and it looked as if he hardly had any strength in his legs to hold him upright anymore. "You're killing me so fucking fast."

Devlin reached up and started jerking Gradyn off while he still had a mouthful of sac. His own prick bounced between his spread legs where he squatted, fully firm with arousal due entirely to what he did to Gradyn right now. Devlin had never been so goddamned hard in his life.

This is who I am. Finally.

Pure, unadulterated acceptance of himself sluiced jet fuel through Devlin's blood and turned his sucking, licking, and foraging more voracious than ever. He whipped his hand up and down Gradyn's prick with rough speed, so much so that his rigorous hand job soon absorbed all the saliva available, and he reluctantly released the feast of Gradyn's balls from his mouth. Devlin batted his tongue against the swinging weight of Gradyn's nuts one last time and then stuck his nose into the man's thatch, inhaling the pungent, heady male fragrance of sex and sweat. He licked his way through the dark fur to the thick root of Gradyn's cock and followed a raised vein to the leaking tip. Murmuring an appreciative sound, Devlin ran his tongue around the crown and across the fat slit to savor all the precum he could get. A hint of bitter whispered across his taste buds and revved him up for more. He took hold of Gradyn's length, opened wide as he moved in, and sucked down half the man's scorching-hot cock again.

Gradyn made deep, vibrating noises that almost sounded like an animal in agony, and he started working his hips with repeated stabs at Devlin's open mouth. He had his stare fixed on Devlin's lips wrapped around his prick, and his fingers still crushed the piece of furniture behind him. Devlin savored every bit of reaction Gradyn gave him. He released Gradyn's cock from his mouth to tease the tender patch under the tip of Gradyn's dick, and it was as if someone shot a thousand volts of electricity straight into the guy's spine. Gradyn roared and yanked his hips back; he grabbed onto Devlin's shoulder with one hand and locked him in a kneeling position on the floor.

His face suffused with color, Gradyn drove his other hand up and down his shaft with piston-fast moves and aimed his cock high on Devlin's chest. "Devlin…" His name turned into a shout as Gradyn shuddered and came, spurting onto Devlin's pecs. Devlin gasped as the first jetting stream of hot seed hit him. Each subsequent milky-white line that marked his flesh licked fiery lust through Devlin's core and rushed a line of need directly to his cock.

Gradyn moaned, and his fingers bore deep into Devlin's shoulder. "Oh fuck." He wasn't steady on his feet, and his erection had not dwindled one bit. "I need more." He grabbed the lube and tore through the protective seal. As he did, he looked up at Devlin and seared a line straight into Devlin's soul with one wild-eyed stare. "Get your condom. You don't need much more than that this time to make it good."

"Yeah, okay." Devlin kept his full attention on Gradyn as he backed up to the nightstand. He tore through the box of condoms, grabbed a rubber, and ripped open the packet. He threw the wrapper on the dresser but didn't get much further than that.

Oh Jesus.

He couldn't look away from Gradyn squeezing a thick dollop of clear lubricant onto two fingers and then reaching around to his ass. The mirror allowed Devlin the perfect view, no matter the shadows the low wattage lights in the room created. Mesmerized, Devlin watched Gradyn lean forward slightly, pull one cheek aside, and rub his own hole. He didn't give himself any time, and instead shoved one finger through the muscle and pushed it in to the second knuckle in one shot. The man gritted his teeth, but he didn't give himself any quarter, and quickly forced another finger into his rectum. He moved them back and forth fast, obviously coating his passage with lube. Gradyn readied himself inside in ways Devlin couldn't see, but the man's lips compressed and his muscles flexed, and Devlin imagined that he scissored and corkscrewed the fingers embedded in his chute to widen the opening.

Finally, without words, Gradyn withdrew his fingers and turned around. He faced the mirror, bent himself over the dresser, and spread his buttocks in a clear offering of his ass.

Saints preserve me. Devlin's mouth went dry on the sight of this man folded over, with the exquisite lines of his muscular body, the firm globes of his ass parted, and his tiny, rosy bud visible and winking. *That's the sexiest damned thing I've ever seen.*

Devlin went to take a step and realized he still had the condom in his hand. Taking a second, Devlin forced himself to look down and pay attention while he rolled the lubricated latex down his shaft.

As Devlin pinched the tip and tucked the end to his root, Gradyn's voice cut through the room with the power of a jackhammer. "Christ, I need you inside me."

Devlin whipped his head up and found Gradyn watching him in the mirror, his gaze dark and piercing in a way that touched over every inch of Devlin's nakedness and made him shiver.

"Get over here, beautiful." Gradyn caressed him again from ten feet away with just his voice and stare. "Come and fuck me right now."

The voice, the body, the eyes, even the tattoos … the entire presence of this man lured Devlin as if it were just the two of them in the whole world, and that it was perfect, and nothing else mattered. It didn't make any damned sense. Devlin didn't know this person, and yet he still walked to him and moved in behind him anyway, only inches away from making them one person for a brief flick in time. Devlin ran his hand down Gradyn's spine, and the man trembled and his asshole contracted visibly.

"Give it to me." Ragged desperation filled Gradyn's voice. He turned his head on the dresser, plastering his cheek against the surface. He pushed back and rubbed his ass against Devlin's cock, and Devlin sucked in air at the heat of first contact. "Please."

Something dangerously near to Devlin's heart lurched painfully. "Shh, baby, shh." He rubbed up and down Gradyn's back with one hand as he fit his member to the man's entrance with the other. The ring pulsed a fast beat against the tip of Devlin's cock, and vibrations from the rest of Gradyn's body shimmered between them. Devlin folded himself over Gradyn and put his mouth to his ear. "Relax for me," he said, and nudged oh-so-carefully against Gradyn's pucker.

Gradyn jerked, and a rough chuckle escaped him. "Giving advice to me now?" His tone remained raw, but his frame did loosen some. When Devlin bumped against his ring this time, Gradyn clenched his jaw and circled his ass back into the pressure on his bud without shying away. "Suddenly an expert?"

Devlin pushed his cock into resistance again, and hid a grin against Gradyn's inked shoulder. "I read a lot about guys fucking." As he made that embarrassing confession, Devlin dipped out his tongue and followed the curve of the tattoo up to Gradyn's neck. "Should come in han…" He bore down again, harder, just as Gradyn pushed back into his efforts, and -- *Holy Mother of God* -- Devlin broke through and his cock slipped inside Gradyn's ass.

Shit. Damn. Motherfucker. Devlin went stock-still as unfathomable pleasure ripped through him in one fiery swoop and then raced back to his penis buried halfway in another man's ass. He bit Gradyn's shoulder as singular words -- *hot, tight, more, hot, tight, more* -- flashed in his head and short-circuited any thought that didn't serve to further that sentiment.

Devlin obeyed his need; he drove his length through a deeper barrier inside the other man, taking him through a grunt and shudder from Gradyn, and didn't stop until he buried himself balls-deep. Scorching heat and clenching walls surrounded every inch of Devlin's cock, killing him with pleasure. As mind-altering good as that was, Devlin pulled all the way out and thrust back into the heaven of Gradyn's ass again, needing to move.

He moaned through the hold Gradyn's body put on his dick, and he pushed through the tightness again. "Oh God," Devlin choked on the sensations, "that's so good." He suddenly reared up and watched himself withdraw and penetrate Gradyn's ass, pushing to the root, and then he forced his weight against the connection, craving even more.

Devlin did it a second time, pulling out and then grinding into that stretched hole as hard as he could. This time Gradyn pulled up, flattened his hands against the dresser, and ratcheted their mating up another dozen notches.

"That's it," Gradyn said. He bumped his hips back in a circling motion and worked himself off on Devlin's cock. "Oh yeah. Do it." His eyes fell closed and he bared his clenched teeth as he took another full hit to his ass. "Fuck me." His channel squeezed in a suffocating hold around Devlin's length.

"Take me hard."

Devlin grabbed onto Gradyn's hips, holding the man to him for a relentless mating. He drove his dick into Gradyn's ass in rapid-fire strokes, creating so much friction and heat he thought he might set them both aflame.

Gradyn gasped but didn't pull away one bit. "Jesus Christ, you get so fucking deep." Ecstasy and pain mapped his face in harsh, beautiful lines. "So good ... forgot." He opened his eyes, found Devlin in the mirror, and a dirty-boy smile made him look downright savage. "Oh yeah ... yeah." Base lust shone in Gradyn's gaze as he jammed himself back onto Devlin's cock with repeated strikes. "Pound me good." He lifted one leg onto the dresser and opened up his ass even more. "Make me come again."

Needing to find his own way to give this man what he needed, Devlin leaned forward and planted his hands on the dresser right on top of Gradyn's, linking their fingers. Gradyn went immediately still, and his focus locked on Devlin's in the mirror. Devlin didn't know how in the hell he didn't move, with the tip of his cock barely tucked inside Gradyn and screaming for more, but he managed it. He nuzzled his face against Gradyn's arm and over his thick shoulder.

"Turn your head," Devlin whispered. He brushed his mouth against the rough stubble breaking through Gradyn's jaw. Gradyn shifted, and their mouths hovered with less than an inch between them. Devlin looked into eyes so close everything should have been a blur, but the green in Gradyn's stare burned bright and clear, and something inside Devlin tightened with recognition, as if he knew exactly who this man was. He didn't know a damn thing *about* him, but everything in his being *knew* this person. Devlin didn't even think as he leaned in half a distance more and whispered, "Kiss me, Denny."

Gradyn moaned and latched onto Devlin with a clinging of their lips. Devlin kissed Gradyn back with equal, guttural need, and at the same time, slowly sank his cock all the way back into Gradyn's ass, taking every damned tight-as-hell inch with deliberate intent, until he couldn't steal a millimeter more.

A tremble trickled through Gradyn, and then he went completely still. The softest, almost surprised-sounding sigh escaped him, and his breath brushed across Devlin's sensitized lips. A second later, while still looking right into Devlin's eyes, Gradyn's pupils flared and his passage contracted in a smother-hold on Devlin's prick, signaling his end.

With their faces so close it felt like they shared the same breath, Gradyn came first, his mouth open but making no sound, and spilled himself against the front of the dresser. Each pulse of his orgasm corresponded with a contraction in his ass, and he sucked Devlin right into coming with him. Devlin's balls drew up against his body. While watching the stark pleasure of release consume Gradyn, Devlin jerked and cried out, unable to fight the inevitable anymore. He shot while still buried in Gradyn's passage, zapping lines of concentrated pleasure to his core, and dumped his seed into the condom.

Exhaustion swamped the men, and they both collapsed

onto the dresser. For long minutes afterward, Devlin remained slumped against Gradyn. He pulled in cleansing air until he could breathe again without his entire body heaving. He still had his cock resting inside Gradyn, still had his fingers locked in a bruising hold over Gradyn's hands, and knew he had enough weight in his six-foot frame to cause someone under him discomfort. Devlin knew he needed to get up and allow Gradyn to unfold from the dresser, but holy hell, he didn't want to separate from this man's body.

In any way.

Gradyn finally grunted and turned his head. "Can I?" He nudged Devlin but didn't shove or force him off. "I have to piss."

Oh shit. "Yeah, sorry." Without thinking, Devlin shot upright, and in the process jerked his cock out of Gradyn none-too-gently. Gradyn hissed as it happened, and Devlin winced at his carelessness. "Fucking shit." He snapped his attention to Gradyn as mortification burned him red from top to bottom. "I'm so sorry."

"It's okay." Gradyn shot Devlin a sideways glance as he moved a little stiffly to the bathroom. "I'll live." He closed the door almost all the way. A moment later, Devlin heard Gradyn sigh as he relieved himself. Devlin peeled off the used condom and found a tissue to wad it into before throwing it away. As the toilet flushed and the water began to run, Devlin grabbed a few more of those tissues and wiped Gradyn's ejaculate off the front of the dresser. No point in trying to clean off what was on his chest; the cum there had already dried to the point that he would need a wet cloth to remove it.

Didn't matter. It was Gradyn's, and Devlin liked thinking about how the man had looked -- so harsh and primal -- as he lost himself and covered Devlin's chest with his seed.

Gradyn emerged from the bathroom with a stretch, lifting his arms toward the ceiling. He moaned a sound of contentment and cracked a few joints as he crossed the room to his discarded clothes. "Goddamn," he rolled his shoulders, "I needed that." As soon as he said it, he glanced up at Devlin with a grin. "The sex, beautiful, not the peeing. I needed the sex."

Devlin felt his cheeks heat, and a thrill shot through him upon hearing this nickname Gradyn had bestowed upon him. "Wasn't anything bad about it for me, either," he admitted, and just went ahead and slipped into full blush again.

Gradyn chuckled as he sorted through his clothes. "You felt damn good in me, that's for sure." He cocked his head, and his jeans and underwear dropped from his hand. "You want to go out to dinner with me? Right now? I'm starving and ... I don't know," he shifted from one foot to the other, and a furrow appeared between his brows, "I want to sit down and have a nice meal with you. What do you say?"

Devlin's heart skittered, and his stomach flip-flopped enough to make him feel a little bit lightheaded. "I would love to." He hoped to hell he wasn't beaming like floodlights in a dark night sky. "Thank you."

"Good." With a fast stride across the room to Devlin,

Gradyn leaned down and stole a quick kiss. "Let's go take a shower." He took Devlin's hand and pulled him to the bathroom. "We can talk about what kind of food you like so I know where to take you."

Devlin let Gradyn lead him into the bathroom, but when he went to turn on the shower, Devlin stopped the man and turned him around. "Wherever we go," Devlin's mouth felt drier than desert sand, "afterward, I want us to come back here so you can fuck me." His ass channel squeezed and his cock twitched just with saying it.

A sweet lopsided smile kicked up the edge of Gradyn's mouth. It whispered through Devlin, exciting him and settling him at the same time, and it made any intimidation he'd felt regarding this man's muscles or body art disappear.

Gradyn brushed the back of his hand against Devlin's cheek. "It's a deal, beautiful."

Devlin swore he almost goddamn purred in response…

———

…Devlin jerked as his elbow slid off the desk, the motion yanking him back to reality. He was rock-hard where he sat in his living room, and a stain of precum darkened his gray sweats. A quick glance at the time on the computer told him his sister would be home soon. *Shit.* Wincing at the stiffness of his erection, Devlin got up and went through his bedroom and into his bathroom for some privacy. He damn well wouldn't be able to talk this thing down; he simply had to take care of it.

He leaned against the wall, closed his eyes, and could see himself back in that motel bathroom sharing a shower with Gradyn. It didn't take anything else to get Devlin stroking his prick and his toes curling into the tile floor as the physical pleasure consumed him.

His mind wasn't entirely in the moment, though. Just a few rubs up and down his dick later, he bit his lip and silently spilled into his hand. And while Devlin did have his mind on Gradyn, the picture that had made him come had not been one of Gradyn back in that shower in San Francisco, but rather one of Garrick Langley, the man he'd seen in Redemption today.

In the aftermath of orgasm, Devlin couldn't help wondering what he would say to Gradyn -- *Garrick* -- when they had another chat.

CHAPTER TWO

I just want to crawl into bed and sleep forever.

It didn't matter to Garrick that it was only six-thirty in the evening and still bright as blazes outside. As he pulled his beat-up truck into the drive, he envisioned stripping out of his dirty work clothes, and falling into bed naked. A shower and food could wait until morning.

He cut the engine and climbed out of his vehicle as stress he couldn't afford to feel pressed heavily on his shoulders and turned his legs sluggish.

"Garrick! Garrick! Garrick!" Shouts from a little boy jerked Garrick fully awake, and he looked up to find a six-year-old blond-headed terror of youthful energy barreling in his direction with no breaking in sight.

"Shawn!" His mother chased him from around the backyard.

A dark-haired girl followed right behind her, yelling, "Slow down, stupid!"

With just a split-second to brace for impact, Garrick caught the boy flying into his arms. Garrick moved half a dozen steps backward with momentum rather than fighting it and saved himself from falling on his ass.

The kid threw his arms around Garrick and planted a big, sticky kiss on Garrick's cheek, all against his mother's and sister's warnings to stop. The boy's open affection had thrown Garrick a bit when he'd moved in a month ago, but damn, the kid didn't have a father, and he clearly just wanted a guy in his life.

Garrick shifted Shawn in his arms and smiled at the other two. "Hi, Grace." He addressed the mother first and then dropped his attention down to Shawn's sister. "How's it going, Chloe?"

The eleven-year-old mumbled something inaudible under her breath as Grace said, "I'm sorry, Garrick. Shawnee heard your truck from the backyard and got away from me before I could grab him."

"He's such a doofus," Chloe said in a snotty voice.

"No I'm not!" Shawn shot up in Garrick's arm and reacted just the way his sister surely intended. "You're a poopy-face and have ugly hair."

Grace stepped in between the sightline of her children and

shot each of them a narrow-eyed glare. "Both of you show me some manners right now or I will start taking away privileges."

Chloe compressed her lips, and her focus lowered to the grass. Shawn shifted in Garrick's hold, looked at him, and declared, "You're gonna take care of us on Saturday."

"Shawn!" Grace's face flooded to full-out red in two seconds flat. She looked to Garrick with a plea in her eyes. "I apologize. I told Shawn I was going to ask you if you were free, not that it was definitely happening."

"It's all right." Garrick kept his voice cool and ignored the fact that Grace looked like she wished the earth would open up and swallow her whole. "What's up?"

"I have an opportunity to show my first houses." Grace kept the books for a local real estate firm, as well as a handful of other businesses, but Garrick knew she wanted to branch out and become a realtor herself. "Unfortunately, the client only has time free on the weekend."

"What time?" Garrick asked as he put Shawn back on the ground.

"He says the morning but it could easily end up taking half the day." She winced and looked at him with a squint. "I hate to even ask but I don't have anyone else."

"It's done; don't worry about it." Garrick didn't have to work this Saturday; he liked these kids, and he remembered how tough it was for his mother to raise two children alone. "You need to be there at nine?"

She nodded, and he said, "Then I'll be here at eight-thirty."

She grabbed his free hand and squeezed. "Thank you."

Chloe pulled her stare off the ground and offered Garrick a wobbly smile. "We were just gonna go inside to make dinner." She shuffled her ballet-flat-covered foot back and forth in the thick grass. "Do you… Would you like to eat with us?"

"Oh…" Garrick hated saying no to these kids but he could also hear his bed beckoning to him from through the walls.

"Yes, absolutely." Grace jumped in. "The least I can do is feed you a good meal in exchange for agreeing to help me out on Saturday. You can't really have anything decent to eat at your place."

Garrick slid his attention to his tiny living quarters above the garage, and he knew that tonight he didn't care about the microwave/convection oven combo or frozen meals in the fridge. The bed, some sleep, and the risk of letting himself fall into oblivion for just a few hours beckoned his exhausted body above all else.

He came back to the various levels of hope in the faces of the Fine family, each not saying a word while they waited for him. Garrick made himself smile. "Sure. Okay. I'm hungry. Let's go."

Shawn hooted and hurled himself into Garrick's arms again. Garrick caught the kid this time without swaying, but at the same time, a shiver of cold trickled down his back and raised the hairs on the back of his neck.

Someone is watching me.

Garrick kept Shawn in his arms, but as he walked toward

the house, he turned in a circle and did a subtle scan of the area. There were not a lot of places to hide in this neighborhood that wouldn't intrude on someone else's property, and doing that would likely get any individual trying to spy quickly caught. Garrick did a visual search of the surrounding houses in reverse anyway and still didn't see any people or vehicles he hadn't already cataloged as belonging on this block. All the same, his skin shivered with awareness, and he knew eyes were on him.

He reached out to Grace and put a hand on her arm, stalling her on the porch. "Have you noticed anything out of the ordinary today?" Garrick worked like hell to keep his tone merely curious. "Did anyone come to the house looking for me?"

Grace immediately shifted her attention to the road. "No, I haven't, and no, nobody came asking about you." She took Shawn out of Garrick's arms and set him down by his sister. "Chloe, take your brother inside. You can help get dinner started by pulling out the big pot in the bottom cabinet. You both can get the spaghetti out of pantry and break it in half for me." Chloe opened the door and let Shawn inside first, and Grace added, "Split the box evenly, please. I don't want to hear any fighting."

As soon as the kids were safely inside the house with the door shut, Grace turned back to Garrick and dropped her voice to just above a whisper. "What's going on? Is something wrong?" She rubbed her hands over her arms as if chilled. "I'm looking around," her focus slowly worked from one end of the street to the other, "and I don't see anything." She kept her gaze on the street, and shivered.

Goddamn it. I overreacted and scared this woman for nothing.

He knew damned well why too. Coming face-to-face with six-feet of dark-haired man who'd made Garrick so hard he'd had to hide under a car at work today. That was why.

Fuck.

Garrick glanced up and down the street one more time, and this time everything inside him remained calm.

"Garrick?" Grace kept her focus on the neighborhood just as diligently as Garrick did. "Do you think someone is watching us?"

"I apologize," he responded, without answering her actual question. "I had a tough day. I'm tired, and maybe that made me twitchy." He clasped his hands behind his neck and exhaled slowly. "I think I need a drink."

"I have a bottle of wine," Grace said. "Will that do?"

"Perfect."

She smiled and swept open the door. "Then follow me."

Garrick couldn't help looking over his shoulder one more time as Grace led the way.

He couldn't completely relax.

He never would again.

———

TWO HOURS OF DINNER, BOARD games, and part of a ball game on TV later, Garrick let himself inside his little apartment above the Fine's garage. He didn't bother turning on the light; he knew the one-room layout by heart, and even if he didn't, the streetlight bleeding in through the shut curtain on his one window provided all the shadows needed to strip out of his clothes.

Unwilling to take the extra minute to unfold his bed, Garrick simply threw himself onto the couch and let his legs hang over one of the arms. The worn-out fabric caressed his flesh with softness, and he wiggled in deeper, settling in. Comfort and exhaustion overrode him, and he let his eyes drift shut on the end of an unexpected day.

A sensation of grittiness irritated his eyes as soon as he closed them, making Garrick curse a string of foul words he should never say around Shawn unless he wanted the kid repeating them to every person he met. Growling like an inconvenienced animal, Garrick got up and treaded to the bathroom with a deftness that defied his mood. He switched on the light, flooded the white bathroom with a shock of fluorescent light, and squinted as he stepped up to the sink. Blinking, Garrick met the stare of the blue-eyed man in the mirror. Then he held his left eyelid open and withdrew a contact lens, quickly did the other, blinked again, and looked into the green eyes he'd kept hidden from the world for almost five years.

Eyes he wasn't sure he could ever show Devlin Morgan again.

Along with a name he definitely could never answer to again.

A man that as far as the world understood, no longer existed.

Gradyn Connell was no more.

Yet this Garrick Langley person, who had to become real, had sat at that dinner table with Grace and her children tonight eating pasta, taking part in the conversation, and smiling in all the right places.

All the while, his mind had drifted to another spaghetti dinner that had been the best of Gradyn Connell's life...

———

...A meal and dessert now complete, Gradyn sipped his cranberry juice and studied the younger man sitting across the table picking at the last of his chocolate cake. Fuck. Devlin Morgan, whoever he was, really was beautiful. Masculine as hell, with an insane body, but somehow beautiful too. Thick deep-brown hair cut neat and trim, but not buzzed in any way, slashing cheekbones, a strong jaw, a wide mouth that didn't lean toward too full or too narrow ... it all spoke to the hungry male living inside Gradyn right now. Devlin's body possessed the same beautiful symmetry as his face; not too much bulk -- the way Gradyn himself was right now -- but not too skinny either. His frame was lean and fucking nearly perfect. He had one of those bodies that lent itself to the belief that God had simply blessed him with great genes.

Devlin Morgan would certainly be at the top of any gay man's fantasy list, yet at the same time, he didn't look like he craved that kind of attention. He definitely hadn't fit in at that techno club, that was for sure. Gradyn didn't get a vibe that Devlin would fit in at any type of bar or club designed for pick-ups -- gay or straight. Something about him said that a simple, basic way of life would suit him like a second layer of skin. When Devlin had confirmed over dinner that he was from a small town in Maine and loved it there, Gradyn put a check in the win column for his ability to read a person.

The cool night air drifted in over the water on the bay and played with Devlin's hair. Jesus, Gradyn could develop a hard-on just thinking about running his fingers through those dark locks. Shit, why stop there? Gradyn could see himself peeling off every piece of Devlin's clothing, laying the man out on that cheap motel room comforter, and licking every inch of his body until Gradyn couldn't stand it anymore and pushed his cock into Devlin Morgan's tight virgin ass.

Fuck, Gradyn nearly moaned right at their table, and had to cross his legs.

He savored another swig of his cranberry juice and admired the view. The night sky and the calm, glassy water of the bay certainly had its beauty in full glory tonight, but Gradyn could not take his eyes off the man sitting across from him. Christ, he'd never been taken with another person in quite this way before, and he wasn't entirely sure he could blame it on forced celibacy.

It had been two and a half years since Gradyn's life had last afforded him an opportunity to be with another man, and he was still horny as hell for more of what Devlin had to offer. Gradyn had stayed away from alcohol tonight so that all of his senses remained sharp for when they returned to the motel. He didn't want to miss a damned bit of the rest of this night by being inebriated in any way. During the course of their meal, Gradyn had noticed Devlin limit himself to one glass of beer and then switch over to water, and Gradyn had to cover his involuntary smile when it happened. Devlin clearly wanted to be just as sober and fully aware the first time Gradyn took him as Gradyn himself wanted to be for that taking. That was a damned good thing for both of them; Gradyn had no interest in having sex with someone who wouldn't remember the event in the morning.

Devlin suddenly shifted in his chair. "Denny, you're looking at me with something in your eyes that's making me a little nervous." His voice held a scratchy quality.

Hunger. The guy had good instincts. And fuck, instinctively choosing to call him Denny rather than Gradyn or GC -- particularly in the throes of fucking -- had grabbed right at the soul of who Gradyn Connell was when he wasn't creating characters for his work or picking up dates.

It struck at the heart of who he was beneath all the labels in his current life.

"Do I scare you?" Gradyn sometimes forgot he had an intimidating exterior right now.

Devlin hesitated for a good long minute, and he studied Gradyn closely enough that the phantom hairs on Gradyn's shaved neck felt like they stood on end.

"No, you don't scare me," Devlin finally answered. "It's just reminding me how little experience I have with men."

The tension eased out of Gradyn at that. Then he went tight all over again as he pictured what they had just come from doing in this man's motel room. "You've sucked a cock or two before, newbie," Gradyn stated, watching Devlin closely. "That blowjob did not have the technique or suppressed gag reflex of a first-timer."

Twinkle-lights running along the restaurant eaves highlighted the dots of color blooming on Devlin's cheeks. "Weelllll, I had this friend in college…"

"Oh yeah?" Gradyn quirked a brow when Devlin didn't immediately go on. "Maybe I should have gone myself after all." He stretched out his legs and linked his fingers against his stomach. "Tell me all about him."

From their secluded corner, Devlin glanced at the other tables scattered around the terrace and then looked over his shoulder to inside the full restaurant. "Shouldn't we go?" he asked as his gaze met Gradyn's again. "We're finished eating. I don't want to take up this table and rob our server of the tips he could be making with other diners."

Irritation nicked Gradyn for a split second; then he reminded himself that this man had only known him for roughly four hours. "Let me ask you something, Devlin. Do I strike you as the type of man who doesn't understand the life of a waiter and wouldn't care if I shafted him just because I can?"

Devlin went back to scrutinizing Gradyn with those intense silver eyes of his. Gradyn found himself holding his breath, knowing it would sting more than it should if Devlin -- a man he hadn't even fucking known existed this morning -- could think him capable of treating others like trash.

"No, I guess not," Devlin replied. With that answer, Gradyn exhaled his trapped breath. "I get the feeling that you know about real life, and that, no, you're probably not some rich, clueless asshole."

With a bark of laughter that surprised him, Gradyn said, "Definitely not rich, and hopefully not clueless or an asshole." Sobering just as fast as he'd found himself laughing, Gradyn held Devlin's stare, and his voice turned thicker than he would have liked witnessed. "I knew I didn't want to feel rushed with you tonight, so when I got up to use the restroom earlier, I told our waiter I would give him a tip that equaled our bill if he let us relax out here without a lot of disruption. I also told the manager that if he agreed, he could put one of his best bottles of wine on the tab and we would take it with us when we left." Gradyn curled his hand around his neck and wished like hell he had hair to grab. "Maybe that's a form of arrogance, I'm not sure, but I knew what I wanted, and all I could do was try to make sure it didn't happen at someone else's expense."

A little smile turned up the edge of Devlin's lips, and something similar lit his eyes. "I like what you did and how you went about it." Slashes of pink crossed Devlin's cheeks again, and his voice dropped to almost a whisper. "I like everything I know about you so far."

Good Christ, it could be Christmas morning the year he got a dirt bike from Santa all over again and Gradyn wouldn't feel any giddier than he did right now.

Fuck. This is bad.

Gradyn didn't care. "You're not bad either, beautiful." Giving in to the urge that had plagued him since they'd sat down to eat, Gradyn leaned across the table and scraped his lips across Devlin's. The man made a needful little noise and took a fast lick at Gradyn's mouth in return, and an innocent excitement that fueled every suppressed base desire clawed inside Gradyn to get free. Gradyn opened up for another taste. He curled his hand around the back of Devlin's head and angled him for a deeper plundering. Silky-soft locks filled the spaces between Gradyn's fingers, and he could fucking practically feel this man's hair brushing up and down his cock and against his balls, tickling his flesh to the point of coming.

Son of a mother. Gradyn's prick swelled to meet that fantasy right where he sat. *Pull away, Connell, before you drag him onto this table and fuck him in front of a crowd of hungry diners.*

Biting down another groan due to the twitch in his jeans, Gradyn eased back into his seat and rewound to where they'd lost track of their conversation. *Oh right.* "So now that you know you have all the time in the world…" Jesus, what he would give to have a cigarette right now, and to hell with the laws and the fact that he didn't smoke. "Tell me about your college boyfriend."

Devlin's eyes were bright, his mouth was appropriately swollen, his hands shook, and it took him a full minute to find his voice again. All of that only made Gradyn want to touch and know him even more.

"Definitely not a boyfriend," Devlin shared, his voice almost normal again. "Just a friend. His name was Kevin -- is Kevin, I should say. He's alive and kicking and lives in Redemption. We're actually still friends."

"Really?" Gradyn swirled his juice in his glass. "This gets more intriguing by the second."

"I wish, but not really," Devlin answered, his smile easy. "Kevin and I sort of knew each other in high school but we didn't hang out or anything. We ended up at our local community college together, sharing a bunch of the same business classes that neither one of us really wanted to be taking."

"Gotcha." Gradyn nodded. "Go on."

"So we're in our second year, and by then we'd become pretty good friends. I had a small apartment; he was still at home so he came to my place most of the time to study or hang out. One night we were half-ass studying, listening to music, watching TV," Devlin raised an eyebrow Gradyn's way, "and also knocking back a few beers."

"Ah yes." With his glass in his hand, Gradyn pointed at Devlin. "The old 'we were drunk and something happened.' An oldie but a goodie."

"Ah yes, indeed, but with a twist." The smile on Devlin's face infused his voice with animated passion. "I can't remember what movie we were watching, but it had one hell of a smokin' love scene. Shit," Devlin laughed, and it made the shots of silver in his eyes twinkle, "I'm not into chicks, and even I thought it was hot. Anyway, by the end of it I was sweating a little from looking at the actor's tight ass and insane body, and Kevin was already full-out hard in his shorts. I'm not sure why, because I guess thinking back it might have been kind of weird, but right after that sex scene, we turned and looked at each other."

Devlin paused again. He put his elbow on the table and dropped his chin into his hand. His smile shifted to something soft, and Gradyn thought the change happened more for Devlin himself than for Gradyn or even anyone else who might happen to glance their way.

"Kevin was suddenly about the sexiest guy I'd ever seen in my life," Devlin shared, that not-so-secret grin still visible. "And when I glanced down, I could fucking see the shape of his erection against his shorts. When I looked back up from gawking at his crotch, he clearly knew I had checked out his junk. He didn't yell or hit me or run away, though. As soon as I processed that something in him might be interested, I threw myself at him. He met me halfway, and then we were kissing, and it was insane. Right away, I grabbed his cock and told him I'd suck him off."

Gradyn made himself more comfortable as he stared and just fucking *absorbed* this man's personality. Goddamn, he already knew he could listen to Devlin talk for days. "Kevin obviously said yes."

"Oh yeah. Enthusiastically." Devlin abruptly sat upright, his face contrite. "In fairness to him, what twenty-year-old guy with a boner is going to say no to someone offering to give him a blowjob?"

Gradyn smiled against the rim of his glass. "Apparently not Kevin."

"Definitely not Kevin," Devlin confirmed. "He shoved his shorts down and, holy hell, I got one look at his prick and knew I was right where I was supposed to be."

His words got Gradyn sitting up straight. "You'd never had a thought about a guy in that way before?"

Devlin made a funny face. He combined it with a half-shrug and a so-so motion of his hand. "Yes, I had done," he said, and went back to playing with his fork and cake. "But at the same time, I don't know…" He looked as if he struggled to find his words. "Here's the thing. I had girlfriends through high school and dated a few women my first year of college. I didn't hate having a girlfriend. I didn't even dread kissing or touching a woman, it just wasn't super exciting or interesting to me sexually. I could take it or leave it, and that made it confusing for me."

Devlin pushed back in his chair, and Gradyn watched him shift his ankle to his knee and dance his fingers over his glass, plate, and utensils.

"Keep going, Devlin." Gradyn reached across the table to still the younger man's nervous fiddling. He locked Devlin to him with his stare and didn't speak again until he felt the battle leave Devlin's hands. "You don't have to be nervous," he said. "Nothing you're saying so far is freaking me out."

"Did you always know?" Devlin asked. "Were you ever unsure or felt like you needed to experiment with a woman?"

"I always knew. I've never had a girlfriend." *Except as part of my job.* "But it's fine if your experience was different. There's not a list of criteria you have to check off before you get approval to join the team. You get here how you get here, at least as far as I'm concerned, and that's cool with me." He squeezed Devlin's hand and finally let go. "Tell me the rest."

"Okay." A smile that trembled a little bit, that Gradyn had now seen on this man at least a half-dozen times since approaching him at the bar, appeared again. Just like all the other moments, it latched on to a soft place deep in Gradyn's core and tugged. Hard.

"Whenever I was with a girlfriend in high school or early college," Devlin started, "I'd do the lean in to touch her breast, the way I thought I was supposed to do. If she let me touch her, okay, cool, I would feel her breasts. It wasn't horrible and it didn't squick me out. I even liked it when she got excited by what I did to her, but it just never worked me up to a place where I had to know more. If I moved in for a touch and she said no, it didn't faze me. I didn't feel like I was missing something that I really wanted. But while I had those girlfriends, at various times during high school, there were also these three boys in particular that I found really fascinating, and I wanted to know everything about them."

Devlin's smile changed the second he mentioned the boys, became something full of light and life, and that told Gradyn as much as Devlin's story did.

Devlin went on, fully animated again. "I never thought 'God, I want to get naked with these guys and do dirty things.' I just liked being near them in the hallway when I could, and I spent a lot of time trying to get close enough so I could smell them. One in particular -- Johnny -- he had this barely-there hint of baby powder smell on his skin in the mornings when he first got to school, and if I got close enough to smell him before my first period class I would think about it all day." Devlin closed his eyes for a minute, and his nostrils flared. Then he quickly put his attention back on Gradyn with hardly a blush. "Anyway, if we were in the same group together for some reason, I always wanted to say something he, or one of the other boys, would think was funny. I wanted to make them laugh so they would think I was cool and maybe they would want to get to know me better. I wanted them to *want* to hang out with me because I *so* wanted to be in their world. You know?"

Gradyn nodded. "I'm with you. Keep going."

"So I had those kinds of thoughts, but I also had a girlfriend. I liked hanging out with the girls I dated, and I enjoyed kissing them. At the same time, I also had these sort of innocent desires for these boys, and so I wasn't sure what all of that information together was supposed to mean. That all changed when I kissed Kevin." Devlin bit his lower lip, and when he blinked and looked at Gradyn, muted heat burned in his eyes. "Feeling his mouth on mine exploded something inside me. I knew that this was how most guys feel when they kiss girls. It was how I should have felt when I was with my old girlfriends, if I were straight. I wanted to tear off Kevin's clothes and learn every part of him in a way I never had with any of my girlfriends. But mostly, right in that moment, on that couch, I wanted to see and touch Kevin's cock.

"There wasn't anything innocent or confusing about what I wanted when I thought about boys anymore; it switched to something raw and real. I wanted to taste Kevin all over; I wanted to suck his prick, and I wanted to see him shoot all over himself and all over me when he came." Devlin shook his head as a soft chuckle rumbled through him. "He held his dick out for me, and I went down on him and went to town. It was sloppy as hell, and I couldn't take much of him that night, but he didn't seem to mind. I did a good enough job to make him come; he shouted as he did it, and I loved it so much I stained my sweats with my own excitement."

Gradyn found himself completely caught up in Devlin's history. "Did Kevin lose his shit when he sobered up and realized what happened?"

"No, he didn't," Devlin answered. "He fell asleep like a minute later, and I admit I chose to fall asleep right on top of him, snuggled up close, rather than pulling away. I wanted to know what holding another guy felt like; I hadn't done that with a girl before. I hadn't even really thought about it, but I wanted to with him. Kevin woke up a few hours later. He did nudge me off him, but he didn't shove or yell. He wiped the drool off his mouth and asked me if I was gay. I told him I was." Devlin kept his head up and his eyes on Gradyn, and strength infused his voice and stance. "Nobody had ever asked me that before, but when he did, I didn't even hesitate. Kevin said that was cool with him, but he wasn't, and that we weren't going to end up boyfriends because of what happened."

"Did you believe him?"

"Oh yeah, totally," Devlin said, without hesitation. "He had this mad hopeless crush on this girl -- Emily Hirsh -- and I knew it was real because I'd seen the way he looked at her a thousand times when we crossed paths. He wanted her so much; it was visible in every pore of him, you know? She didn't know he existed. He was at my place moping one night -- about a month after what happened between us -- and it happened again. We just started kissing and I ended up giving him another blowjob. He told me again that it couldn't turn into anything. I told him I didn't really care, that I just wanted a guy to touch and be near, and that he didn't even have to reciprocate. He never officially agreed, but over the next two months we probably ended up together like that a dozen times."

"Seems a little one-sided."

"Nah, it wasn't." Devlin had a faraway look in his eyes as he answered. "I never felt used or wished for more with Kevin. He always kissed me back, and even though he closed his eyes while I blew him, it wasn't because he was trying to picture someone else doing him. Kevin would put his hand in my hair and hold me to him. He said my name when he moaned about what he liked and what he wanted more of, and he even gave me a handjob in return if I didn't come on my own while I was doing him. He apologized that it wasn't a blowjob but said he couldn't see himself doing more. I didn't mind." Devlin blinked and came back to Gradyn with a sheepish smile. "Hey, it's nice to feel a hand other than your own pulling on your dick every once in a while, you know?"

"Hell yeah, it is." Gradyn flashed a fast grin. "So what ultimately happened with Kevin?"

"He put an end to it. He said he felt like a selfish bastard taking advantage of me, and he was starting to have trouble facing himself in the mirror. He said if he could go all the way for anybody, it would be me, but that it just wasn't who he was, and that as a friend he wanted me to have someone who could get just as excited about sucking my dick as I got sucking his. He said he'd probably kick himself in the ass the next time he had to take care of a hard-on with his own hand, but that it was the right thing to do before someone got hurt or we ended up losing our friendship over what we were doing. I agreed that it was probably a good idea."

Gradyn couldn't help the twist to his lips. "Are you sure Kevin's speech wasn't a line of bullshit?"

"It wasn't." Again, Devlin didn't pause with his response. "Kevin is a good guy, and he didn't avoid me afterward. Shit, he still came to my apartment, alone, obviously not scared that the gay guy was going to attack him. Once we talked about it and agreed that we wouldn't do what we were doing anymore, we didn't. It was tough for me at first; I really did like kissing him as much as I liked sucking him off." Devlin seemed to turn inward again, and he shifted to stare out at the water for a moment before coming back to Gradyn. "The fact that it was so difficult at first told me that stopping was the best thing we could have done. Too much longer and the little crush I'd developed on him might have turned into real feelings that would have made it very hard to stay friends afterward."

"Do you think Kevin still thinks about what you guys did together?"

"I'm sure he remembers it," Devlin answered. "But I don't think he pines for it or has wishful thoughts about our time together, if that's what you're asking. That girl Emily, who didn't know Kevin existed a few years ago? They're engaged now. He's completely in love with her, and she finally woke up and realized what a wonderful person Kevin is too. I don't begrudge him any happiness with her. She is what he wants, and Emily is a good friend of mine now too. So, anyway," Devlin scratched his fingers through his hair, shrugged, and did that hangdog smile thing of his, "that's how I'm not entirely a novice when it comes to blowjobs. You can thank Kevin."

Arousal slammed back into Gradyn with hurricane force. "Remind me to send him an e-mail." He withdrew his wallet and slipped the appropriate amount of money he had promised into the restaurant billfold. "Did you ever find someone who could reciprocate your enthusiasm for sucking cock?"

"No." With that one word, Devlin slid back to a complete blush. "Life got a little hectic after that, and Redemption isn't exactly teeming with openly gay men." He looked as if he swallowed something awful, and then added, "Myself included."

Gradyn moved to Devlin's side of the table and curled his hand against the back of the chair. He put his lips to Devlin's ear and kept his voice low. "Then it's well past time you put your dick in another man's mouth. And you are in luck because I am so fucking hungry for a taste of you." Gradyn drew Devlin to his feet and pressed a kiss to his temple. "Let's go back to the motel."

In a shot, Devlin leaned into Gradyn and slipped his arms around his waist. He burrowed himself right into Gradyn's body and tucked his face against Gradyn's neck. "I like you so much, Denny." Devlin's confession sank into Gradyn and shook him to his core.

With the life Gradyn led, it fucking terrified him to feel the same.

Against his better judgment, Gradyn whispered, "I like you too, beautiful," and led Devlin out of the restaurant...

—————

...Garrick blinked and looked up at the ceiling of his garage apartment to find himself half-hard on the memories of a man he could no longer be.

His chest ached with a familiar pain; his eyes hurt as sleep continued to elude him, and his mind spun with how he would handle this new wrinkle in his utterly stupid impulse to move to Redemption.

All that insanity five weeks ago to get himself safely to Redemption under another new name and life, and not once had Gradyn -- *Garrick now, damn it* -- considered what he would do if Devlin saw through this new name, face, and body to the person he'd spent one weekend with in San Francisco five years ago.

He saw Denny. He saw me.

Gradyn Connell should have anticipated better from the person he had somehow fallen in love with in two days, but Garrick Langley could not afford the impression Gradyn had apparently left on Devlin all these years later.

His life depended on it.

CHAPTER THREE

Devlin dialed his brother's number, and then started pacing the length of his living room, his mind in a thousand places at once.

Primarily in one place, really, and he damn well knew it.

Stop thinking about him, you idiot.

Aidan picked up on the third ring. "What's up, bro?"

"Hey, Aidan, listen; my date has to go into work tonight and called asking if we could switch to tomorrow. What do you say? Can I renege on my invitation to you and Ethan for tomorrow night?" A week ago, Devlin had invited Aidan and Ethan over for grilled steaks. This morning, when Darren had given Devlin the perfect "out" of their date, Devlin hadn't had the heart to break it. "You guys could come over tonight instead. I have everything defrosting."

"It's cool if you need to call off tomorrow night, but I can't do tonight," Aidan answered. "I'm heading into work right now."

"Shit. I forgot." As a firefighter, Devlin knew Aidan's schedule as Chief inside and out. He growled under his breath at the injury keeping him from work. In just this short time away things were starting to slip his mind. "I'll call Darren back and tell him I can't do it. It's not a big deal."

"Don't do that," Aidan replied quickly. "And don't use me as an excuse if you don't want to see Darren again." For a brother who had spent much of his adult life far away from his siblings, Aidan had certainly slipped back into a lecturing tone easily enough upon returning to Redemption three years ago. At least Devlin thought so. "Call Ethan on his cell and let him know the change in your schedule. Unless he's made plans since this morning, he can make it. He mentioned spending part of the evening grading papers, but since it's a smaller number of kids with summer school, I know he can be flexible with that."

Devlin passed by the kitchen and eyed the half-dozen steaks sitting on the counter. "I could do that." *Shit.* That still left a lot of meat he couldn't refreeze. "Maybe I'll invite Wyn too."

Aidan's sharp bark of laughter rang loudly through the phone. "Willing to risk Maddie's wrath, are you?"

Wyn Ashworth was Ethan's younger brother. Maddie had spent a good part of her senior year in high school sending verbal jabs in the older Wyn's direction. Wyn took it in stride and, on occasion, nailed her back. Then, a few years ago, it seemed as if they had called a truce of sorts. Their taunts felt softer, more like teasing -- and maybe even light flirting. Until a couple of months ago, that was. Something had changed, and their friendship turned downright icy. Ethan couldn't get anything out of Wyn about it, and Maddie gave Devlin and Aidan the stone-faced silent treatment whenever they asked her about it too.

With Aidan and Ethan's commitment to each other, though, Maddie and Wyn could not avoid contact. They were just going to have to get the hell over whatever bugs were up their asses and learn to be civil around each other. Devlin had no intentions of refereeing Thanksgiving and Christmas this year or any other in the future. He knew Aidan and Ethan wouldn't either.

"Maddie can learn to deal with it." Devlin forced a bit more bravado into those words than actually beat within him. "This is my apartment as much as it is hers, and I am welcome to invite whoever I want into it. She can do the same."

"It's your funeral."

"Don't I know it." Devlin threw himself down on the couch, and with a groan, covered his eyes with his forearm. "Nothing like one more battle to get my weekend started right."

"Another battle?" Aidan's voice rose in pitch and volume. "What are you talking about, Dev? Is everything okay?"

Damn it. A light pounding started behind Devlin's right eye. "It's nothing. I'm fine."

Devlin heard Aidan sigh. "Now who's keeping secrets?" his brother asked.

"If you'd let me come back to work," Devlin squeezed his eyes shut, "I'd be a lot better."

"As soon as a doctor clears you," Aidan answered, his tone softening. "It's not me. I need you at the firehouse as much as you want to be there."

"I know." Guilt had Devlin swallowing down a second plea. His brother could not treat him any differently than anyone else on his crew. "I'm just being a complaining ass. I'm sorry."

"It's okay. Say goodbye so you can call Ethan. I have to go anyway or I'm going to be late."

"Bye," Devlin said. "Be safe."

"Will do. Talk to you later."

Aidan hung up, and Devlin quickly called Ethan and Wyn, who both agreed to join him for dinner. After he did that, he tossed the phone on the coffee table, and his brain took no time zeroing all of his thoughts in on one thing again. Gradyn Connell -- who had become Garrick Langley.

My Denny.

Devlin couldn't find out much of anything about Garrick Langley. He had not been able to track down a physical address in Redemption for where the man now lived. A search turned up only a local PO Box. No listed phone number either. Devlin obviously knew the guy worked for Mr. Corsini, but then so did Maddie. She practically lived at that garage, which meant Devlin didn't have a chance in hell of cornering Gradyn there to demand answers for why he was masquerading as a man named Garrick Langley. Not without his sister turning on him and demanding answers of her own.

Devlin wasn't ready to share what he knew about Garrick yet. Much in the way he hadn't ever told a soul about what had happened that weekend in San Francisco either, or about what had developed in the six months of e-mails and phone calls that had followed. Devlin had never said a word to anyone about this man who had so completely captured his heart.

A chill went down Devlin's spine right where he sat in his over-warm living room.

Maybe I knew, even back then, that something about him wasn't right.

No, not true. All those years ago, Devlin had trusted Gradyn Connell with his very soul and had believed everything he said.

Today, an Internet search of both Garrick Langley and Gradyn Connell only swirled more confusion into some already murky waters.

Devlin could find very little information about Garrick Langley, which he knew didn't have to mean anything. If someone were to do a search on him, that person wouldn't find much information about Devlin, and he knew he was as real as the day was long. What Devlin had found was a Web site dedicated to a high school in the Midwest. The site had Garrick listed as a graduate for a year that would have put him at thirty-three years old now, and that was within a year of what

Devlin knew Gradyn's age would be today. The Web site had no individual class photos loaded, unfortunately, and nobody identifying himself as Garrick had ever left a comment in the forum there. Devlin could find nothing else about Garrick Langley.

Gradyn Connell was a different story. Or, more accurately, Devlin should say the one piece of information he had turned up trumped a search for anything else.

An obituary.

Devlin went cold all over again just thinking about what he'd read. Everything in that obituary: the age, the place of birth, the surviving relatives of a mother, sister, and uncle -- whose names matched the ones Gradyn had shared with Devlin -- all jived. The obituary hadn't had a photo, but even the job and the city where the deceased had lived were the same as the Gradyn that Devlin had known in San Francisco. The obituary said that man had died in a car accident two months ago.

Only, Gradyn wasn't dead. Or, at least, whomever the hell Devlin had spent a weekend with in San Francisco was still very much alive. Something deep inside Devlin that he could not name recognized that man on a fundamental level. In his gut, he knew he would have felt something inside him hurt two months ago if Gradyn really had died. The draw to that man -- Gradyn -- who was now this Garrick person, felt so goddamned right and real. It pulled at Devlin today with just as much force as it had the night Devlin had given Gradyn his body for the first time all those years ago...

———   ⸱

…Back at the motel room after their late dinner, Devlin leaned in to Gradyn and looked into his beautiful eyes. As he did, their scorching naked flesh and stiff cocks came into full contact, and Devlin sucked in a deep, cleansing breath.

Keep it cool; you can do this.

Their bodies rubbed against one another with greater force, making Devlin gasp again at that searing heat riding his bare front. At the same time, a shudder rocked through Gradyn and went right into Devlin.

Nothing could have gotten Devlin out of his own head faster than that. "You're trembling, Denny." He brushed his fingers down the fierce tattooing that edged Gradyn's face, and then along the rest of the firm, ink-covered skin down his side, paying attention only to the reactions of the man's body and not the way it looked. "You did the same earlier this evening."

Gradyn tilted Devlin's head back and brushed their lips together with the softest caress. "I want this to be as good for you as you were for me. I don't want you to regret your first time." The piercing depth of Gradyn's gaze, and the crush of his hand curled around Devlin's nape, pulled an answering constriction in Devlin's chest. Gradyn scraped their mouths together again, and said roughly, "I don't want you to regret *me.*"

Oh holy hell.

Devlin's knees went a little shaky. He grabbed onto Gradyn's forearm and lifted on his toes until their foreheads touched. "I will never regret you." His blood raced with heady speed as he said those words, and knew he meant them. "No chance of that."

"You are something special, beautiful." Gradyn tightened his hold around Devlin's waist and rocked them in a slow wave. "How are you so fucking sexy and sweet and incredible and bold all at the same time?" He shook his head, as if dazed. "What in the hell made me choose that bar tonight when I fucking hate techno music?"

"Same thing that kept me there longer than I wanted to be." Devlin's throat tightened with a vulnerability he never let anybody see, yet with this person it seemed to flow out of him without any of his usual caution. "I think I knew you would come."

"Christ," Gradyn said, "I'm glad I did." He tripped Devlin's legs out from under him and tumbled them both onto the bed.

The bedsprings squeaked as Gradyn came down on Devlin, and his additional weight created a dip in the center of the mattress. His thick cock dug into Devlin's stomach, just like before, except this time arousal and a strange, incalculable trust in this man overrode the tentacles of fear still whispering inside Devlin over what they were about to do.

Gradyn braced himself on his elbows and brushed the backs of his fingers against Devlin's hair. "Okay?"

Shots of warmth reached into every corner of Devlin's being, and he nudged into the loving touch. "Yeah." He let his legs fall open the rest of the way, and he moaned as Gradyn settled in, filling out the space. "I'm good."

A cheeky, sexy-as-hell grin appeared, and Gradyn lowered his lips to Devlin's. "Glad to hear it." He claimed Devlin's mouth with an exploring kiss that quickly turned voracious, and he sought entry with a lick and tug on Devlin's lower lip. It felt like sparks danced on Gradyn's lips, and Devlin ignited them the second their mouths touched. He eagerly opened up for more, taking with aggression and force.

Devlin writhed under Gradyn. He scratched at the man's back and bit at his mouth, and Gradyn hissed and broke the kiss.

"Slow down, honey." Gradyn wiped his lower lip, and his finger came away clean. Devlin hadn't broken skin. "I like a good bite with my foreplay," the edge of Gradyn's mouth hitched up in a smile, "but we have all night to make this happen."

His skin on fire, unable to remain still, Devlin moaned a hoarse "No." He thrust his hips and dug his bitten-down nails into Gradyn's buttocks. "Please…" He lunged up and tried to pull Gradyn flush against him. "Need you. Oh shit, shit…" Devlin's prick leaked a stream of early ejaculate, and he couldn't stop grinding himself against the solid barrier of Gradyn's stomach. "My cock hurts, and I think my balls might explode." His chest squeezed so tightly he thought he might have a heart attack. "I feel like I could rip you to shreds with my bare hands if I keep touching you."

"Okay then." Gradyn pushed himself into a sitting position. He straddled Devlin's stomach, and Devlin could feel the tension coursing through his limbs. "So maybe you're not feeling so good after all."

Stricken, Devlin surged upright. "I'm sor --"

Gradyn slapped his hand over Devlin's mouth and pressed him back down into the mattress. "Don't apologize. You're not doing anything wrong. A few hours ago, I felt pretty close to what you're feeling right now. The difference is that I can't go at you hard and fast the way you could with me." Gradyn's lips thinned to a tense line. "That's not gonna work for your first time."

Coarse, rough skin abraded Devlin's lips where Gradyn held his mouth closed. Devlin dipped out his tongue, licked at that palm keeping him quiet, and looked up with what he hoped was a plea in his eyes.

With a jolt and a "Damn, I'm sorry," Gradyn whipped his hand away.

Devlin rubbed the tips of his fingers over his mouth and could still feel the tingles and swelling from their kisses. "When I said I was good, I just meant that I'm not scared about what's going to happen, not that I know the right things to do."

Gradyn leaned down and pressed a kiss high on Devlin's cheek. "I'm not knocking your inexperience, honey." He grazed his knuckles up Devlin's jaw, over his cheek, and into his hair. "I promise."

This fierce looking, almost-stranger petted Devlin with

such tenderness Devlin feared he might cry. "It's hard to control myself with you," Devlin confessed. As had happened all evening, Devlin looked into Gradyn's eyes and luxuriated in the feel of their bodies touching one another. This bizarre sense of belonging had him spilling things he'd never dared admit to other potential lovers. "I just want you so much, and every time you touch me, I swear I can feel it all the way down in my goddamned toes. I can't help pushing against you or grabbing for more. Something inside me says that if I don't I'll explode."

Gradyn sat quiet for a moment, drumming his fingers against Devlin's chest in an easy way that put Devlin in mind of longtime partners rather than weekend lovers. Then Gradyn's hands suddenly curled into fists and he straightened fully upright.

"Don't freak out on me," Gradyn prefaced, "but what if I restrained you? Just your arms," he added quickly, before the first wave of shock rolled through Devlin. "And only for this first part."

Gradyn reached back and ran just the tip of his finger along Devlin's cock. Devlin reacted as if someone had put a fully juiced defibrillator to his flesh.

"See that?" Gradyn asked. "I love how you respond to me, but I need to bring you down a few notches so that you can relax and enjoy it when I touch you. Right now, you're strung so tight with anticipation that I know the feel of my hands on you is going to hurt just as much as it makes you feel good."

Only the memory of Gradyn's raw display of need earlier

this evening kept Devlin from pulling a pillow over his face to hide. "Yeah. It's kind of like that."

A small, endearing smile turned the edges of Gradyn's mouth. "Don't get red and shy on me, beautiful." He pressed kisses to each of Devlin's heated cheeks, which apparently the bad lighting in the room had not concealed. "Everything is okay."

Devlin blinked and looked away, befuddled that it had taken a full minute for it to cross his mind that at the first mention of restraints any sane person would have shoved this big man off him and gotten the hell out of this room as fast as his legs could carry him. *This guy wants to tie you up!* Twenty-three years of gathering knowledge and life skills screamed that very thing in Devlin's head. He then pictured his wrists strapped to a bed in a strange motel room, his body at the mercy of this man -- a virtual stranger -- and no alarm bells sounded in his head.

I don't understand it.

Devlin shifted and looked into green eyes that shouldn't be able to speak to him so completely without words so quickly, yet somehow did.

"If I didn't like it and told you to let me go, you would?" Devlin asked.

"In a heartbeat." Gradyn's stare and tone did not waver as he made that vow. "I'd sooner cut off my arm than frighten you. Even for a second. It will only work if you believe you can trust me. If you're tense and scared that I'm going to take advantage of you the whole time, or not let you go afterward, then binding your wrists will only make everything worse."

One little bead of cold tickled down Devlin's spine. "Have you ever bound someone before?"

"No." Gradyn frowned. "But I swear I know enough not to cause you pain or discomfort."

The shot of ice melted, and Devlin let out his held breath. "I wasn't worried about you hurting me. I don't know what made me ask that." As soon those words left his mouth, Devlin wanted to snatch them back. "No, that's not true; I know why." He swallowed through a thickness clogging his throat and forced himself not to look away. "I don't have any right, but I didn't want you to have done this with anyone but me. I didn't want you to have even asked someone else."

The soft, sweet smile Devlin was already coming to know appeared on Gradyn's face again. "I haven't."

"Okay then." Even as his cheeks burned with a second wave of heat, Devlin couldn't ignore the crackling of electricity over his skin or his granite-hard erection that hadn't dwindled one bit during this entire exchange. "Let's do it. Tie me up."

Gradyn dipped down until his mouth hovered so close to Devlin's they shared the same breath. "I get the feeling you're going to like this, beautiful." He stole a fast, hard kiss and then winked. "Be right back."

As Devlin watched Gradyn crawl out of bed, his mind flashed a half-dozen steps ahead to them fucking, and he lunged for Gradyn's arm. "Wait!" He held Gradyn to the foot of the bed, and looked up into his eyes. "I don't want to be tied up when you take me. I want... I need... When you're inside me..." *Fuck, Morgan, stop trying to make this some epic event.* Blown out of proportion or not, Devlin couldn't stop his runaway mouth. "That part has to feel like we're doing it together."

Gradyn took Devlin's hand and squeezed it in a way that felt reassuring. "I want that too. I'll release you as soon as you blow through that first wave of steam. Or at any point when you ask me to. It's completely in your control."

"All right." Devlin watched Gradyn turn in a circle, clearly studying the room, and he tried to control the dizzying racing in his heart. "What are you going to use?"

"We'll have to see." Gradyn walked to the curtains, ran two fingers down the pull cords, but silently shook his head and moved to his discarded clothes. "Like I said, I haven't exactly done this before." He retrieved his flannel shirt and stretched out one of the arms.

Guilt twisted a bundle of nerves in Devlin's belly. "I'm sorry for turning this into such an ordeal."

Letting his shirt fall to the floor, Gradyn strode back to the bed, leaned over, and used his hand as leverage beside Devlin's head. He trapped Devlin with one look, and Devlin felt covered with Gradyn's heat from top to bottom. "Beautiful, this is no trouble." Gradyn stroked his thick, heavily-ridged cock and showed Devlin that he still sported a full erection. "It's entirely my pleasure." While keeping his gaze locked on

Devlin's, Gradyn dropped down and teased his tongue around Devlin's nipple. "I promise."

Devlin moaned, and his nipple twisted. Gradyn delivered a second soft flick, and the barely-there contact reached all the way down with a phantom touch and pulled on Devlin's cock, making it rear toward his stomach.

Please don't come yet. Please don't come yet. Please don't lose control.

The second Gradyn started to suck on the beaded knot of Devlin's nipple, Devlin blurted, "I have some ties." The information slipped out of him in a frantic, desperate bent that matched the screaming tangles of nerve endings running amuck in his body. "They're draped around my suit in the closet."

Gradyn planted a chaste kiss to the center of Devlin's chest, and then walked across the room to the closet. His glorious naked back, ass, and thighs were on full display as he opened the accordion door. The sight of his muscles, that bunched and released with every small or big movement he made, had Devlin stuffing down another groan. The comfort Gradyn exhibited in his own skin fed Devlin's desire to know more about this man, and it pulled him to find a connection to Gradyn that went deeper than a night of fucking.

Don't fall in love, Morgan. It's just sex.

The sound of a zipper sighed across the shadowed room. With half of his body now in the small closet, Gradyn murmured, "Nice suit."

Devlin didn't look away from Gradyn as he shifted himself

to the head of the bed. "I didn't know what I'd be doing this weekend, so I went ahead and packed it. It's the only one I have."

Gradyn emerged from the closet victorious. With ties in hand, one a two-tone turquoise and the other a deep magenta, Gradyn came back to the bed. He straddled Devlin again, and looked down with a glint in his eyes. "I like that suit a whole hell of a lot." That special light stayed in his eyes, and he never looked away from Devlin as he created a slipknot at the narrow end of the magenta tie. "I think I'm going to have to take you somewhere nice tomorrow night so I can see you in it." He laid the second tie against Devlin's bare chest, as if he wore it with a suit. As Gradyn looked, a rough noise escaped him, and a drop of precum pearled across his slit. "Oh yeah. We're going somewhere. And then I'll bring you right back here and strip you out of it again." He grabbed the knotted tie and rose up on his knees.

Oh shit. Devlin's heart pounded with the knowledge that this thing with Gradyn would last more than one night, and his blood raced as the man's cock poked out in front of his face. *Right at my mouth.* Devlin inhaled the intoxicating musky essence that was Gradyn, along with a hint of Irish Spring soap, and it seeped into his pores. The sight of Gradyn's dick sticking out, the head coated with the sheen of his excitement, lured Devlin to lift up and take a taste.

His tongue touched Gradyn's cock, licked into his slit, and Gradyn hissed and jerked away. "Don't do that." He crushed the knotted tie in his hand. "I need this to be all about you or I'll lose my shit in two seconds."

Devlin shuddered without control. "Please hurry."

"Jesus, man, you're killing me." Moving much faster, Gradyn worked Devlin's hand into the looped opening of the knot he'd created. He pulled, and Devlin sucked in a deep breath as the material tightened around his wrist.

This is it. Gradyn secured the other end of the first tie to the rounded post of the headboard, and Devlin's throat went too dry to speak. Tendrils of chill whipped around his limbs with talons of icy cold, and he felt the blood rush away from his dick and leave him limp. *No! Not now.*

As if he sensed every bit of confusion roiling around inside Devlin, Gradyn pressed kisses to the tips of each of Devlin's fingers. He then pushed Devlin's other hand through the second tie, did the same, and the pinpricks dotting Devlin's arms and legs settled and disappeared. Gradyn tightened the noose around Devlin's second wrist, and then stretched his arm to the other side of the headboard, where he quickly secured the other end of the tie to the post.

Gradyn tested his knots, neither of which gave, and he finally slid back down to settle in between Devlin's legs. His lips came to rest against Devlin's cheek, and he whispered, "Now just close your eyes and breathe."

Easier said than done.

Unable to help it, Devlin tugged against the restraints, and succeeded only in making the bed frame creak. The silk had no give. Devlin pulled against the bindings again, stretching his arms, and in the process made the ties more secure than ever.

I really can't get free.

Right on that realization, blood rushed back to Devlin's cock, and his stiffening shaft pushed against Gradyn's stomach.

Oh hell.

Gradyn kissed his way down Devlin's cheek to his mouth. A chuckle escaped him as he reached down and wrapped his hand around Devlin's rapidly returning wood. "I had a feeling you'd like a little bondage." He rubbed the full length of his body all along Devlin's, and Devlin moaned and pushed his hips into the contact.

Hovering at Devlin's mouth, with eyes still burning bright, Gradyn breathed in deeply. "Let's see what else you like, shall we?" He captured Devlin's mouth in a crushing kiss. Devlin groaned under the force of the taking, and he felt Gradyn's kiss tear through to every corner of his being.

Aching all over, not calmed even a sliver, Devlin fought against the restraints tying his arms immobile. The silk wouldn't budge, but rather than anger or terrify him, the binding fueled Devlin's blood and drove his needs to an unruly place. Without the freedom to move his arms and use his hands, Devlin wrapped his legs around Gradyn's waist and ground his straining cock into a solid wall of muscle. He thrust his tongue deep into Gradyn's mouth, stealing the connection he needed in another way.

In response, Gradyn dug his fingers into Devlin's hair

and jerked his head back, forcing an angle that allowed him complete access and full ownership of Devlin's mouth. He tasted, took, and kissed so deeply Devlin feared he wouldn't be able to breathe … and that he wouldn't care. He only wanted more, *everything*, and he didn't care what kind of damage happened to either one of them to get him there.

Devlin uttered a plea for help into Gradyn's mouth; he bit and licked not only at the man's lips and tongue but also up the side of his face. Devlin laved a trail of saliva, nipped all the way up the swirls and lines of Gradyn's tattoo, and scraped his teeth across the skin, leaving angry red lines in between the blue ink.

"Oh fuck…" Gradyn's mouth fell open, and the shadows turned his features to all hard angles and slashing lines. "You're killing me. Ohhh shit." He shoved Devlin's legs from around his waist and pushed a hand between their bodies. "Sorry, sorry. Need it. One time fast." Gradyn squished their cocks together, making them both jump, and immediately started thrusting his length back and forth, sliding both erections within his hand and creating the most delicious friction imaginable.

"Oh damn it, fucking damn it," Devlin said with a moan. His cock nearly on fire, Devlin tried to throw his hand into the mix, only to snap his wrist against the restraints. He planted his feet into the bedding and thrust his hips up into the hold instead, crying out when his balls slapped against Gradyn's and swelled painfully with seed and need.

The men quickly found a fast, rough rhythm of cock against cock, and Gradyn soon withdrew his hand from between their stomachs. Without relenting in the grind of his body down on Devlin's, Gradyn ran his hands up the sides of Devlin's torso and over his straining arm muscles to his tightly closed fists. Gradyn forced Devlin's clenched hands open, threaded their fingers together, and locked his gaze on Devlin as he scraped their mouths together. "Don't hold back." He gritted his teeth with each full press of their rigid pricks. "Let me feel you come."

Devlin squeezed Gradyn's fingers with all his might and matched the animalistic writhing and grinding Gradyn drove down on him. The rudimentary foreplay abraded the sensitized flesh of Devlin's cock and balls in the ruthless, crushing slide of skin on skin, but Devlin didn't care. Nothing mattered anymore except this man and free-falling over the cliff together.

He locked in on Gradyn's fiery green gaze and didn't blink. "Let me feel you too."

Gradyn fused his forehead to Devlin's, and spat out through clamped teeth, "*Now*."

On command, Devlin's nuts tucked up crazy-tight against his body, and the spiral of oncoming release zipped into his belly and sped up his spine. Devlin bucked his hips, once, twice. On the third wave, he choked out a hoarse shout and shot a load of seed.

As soon as the first jet of Devlin's cum smeared wet heat between their stomachs, Gradyn braced his weight on the link of their hands and reared his upper body in a backward arc. His features twisted and his eyes fell closed. Devlin had never seen anything fiercer or more beautiful than Gradyn's face when orgasm hit him in glorious waves. Thick, hot ejaculate sprayed down on Devlin's stomach; Devlin reveled in the heavenly marking of his flesh and in the intensity marring Gradyn's harsh face.

He calls me beautiful, but good God, he is fucking stunning.

Eventually, Gradyn stopped shaking. He blinked, and the most wonderful cat-got-the-cream smile appeared, matching the twinkle in his green eyes.

"And that was just the appetizer, beautiful," Gradyn said as he dropped down and pecked a soft kiss on the big smile Devlin could not hide. "I haven't even gotten close to where I want to go with you yet." Without wasting a moment, he tilted Devlin's head back and pressed kisses down his chin to under his throat, pausing to suck on Devlin's Adam's apple with a slow pull that stirred Devlin's recently sated cock.

Devlin's dick nudged against Gradyn, and Gradyn looked up, that same smile still transforming his face. "Oh yeah, beautiful." He reached down and caressed Devlin's growing, supersensitive length. "That's right where I'm headed."

Devlin squeezed his eyes shut, and his heart raced with anticipation as Gradyn licked a line down his chest, heading in the right direction…

———

…The combination of an intermittent buzzing noise and banging on wood jerked Devlin upright, throwing him back into reality and the couch in his apartment.

Not the motel room in San Francisco.

Son of a bitch. Devlin glared at his front door as the heavy knocking thundered again. *I was just about to get my first blowjob!*

Someone outside put their full weight on Devlin's doorbell and just let the annoying noise ring without end.

"Hold on!" Devlin grumbled some more under his breath as he pulled himself off the couch, winced, and looked down at the bulge in his jeans. *Fuck.* He untucked his shirt, settled it over the evidence of his arousal, and then scrubbed his face as he made his way to the door and yanked it open.

Wyn Ashworth stood on the other side with a six-pack of beer under one arm and a twelve-pack of cola under the other. "Hey, man." His dark, tall frame towered in the doorway. "I've been standing outside forever; I thought something happened to you. Did I wake you up? You look like you were sleeping."

"Maybe a nap," Devlin conceded. He glanced at his watch and realized he'd been asleep for hours. "Ethan's not here yet. Come on in." Devlin stepped aside and let his giant of a friend, still dressed in his work blues, inside the apartment.

The uniform put Devlin in the mindset of old-school truth and justice. It brought him back to his current situation with Gradyn -- or Garrick -- not their past, and that complication killed what remained of Devlin's erection.

Wyn Ashworth was a cop. And maybe, just maybe, Devlin could figure out a way to pick this man's brain about how and why a person might kill one identity and become another. Not to mention why said person would then turn up in his old lover's hometown but then act as if he didn't know him.

Devlin's soul screamed "Gradyn is a good man! There's a good reason!" but his intellect did battle with millions of questions that needed answers before it could decide how to proceed.

Chapter Four

Garrick leaned the final snowflake rim up against the wall and stepped back to admire his cleaning and painting job. Each of the four shone like new and would look insanely cool when he and Maddie eventually got the rest of the Trans Am refurbished and all its parts in one gleaming finished product. That would take some time but Devlin was absolutely going to flip when it happened.

I'd love to be here to see his face when he looks at the car for the first time.

A band tightened around Garrick's chest, and his thoughts went back to the shock in Devlin's voice when he'd heard Garrick speak yesterday and recognized him as Gradyn. Christ, the confusion and anger that had mapped the man's beautiful face when, somehow, he saw right through the alterations in Gradyn's appearance that had transformed him into Garrick.

You have to be Garrick now; don't ever forget it.

Fuck, though. Garrick couldn't stop reliving yesterday. Having to pretend not to know Devlin… Damn it, he hated himself for doing that to Devlin, even though he knew he didn't have a choice.

He never should have come to Redemption. He'd made the choice in a heightened, panicked situation where he hadn't had time to use anything other than his gut to make a decision, where the only thing that had felt safe and real was the thought of running to Devlin Morgan and finding a way back into his arms.

Devlin, Devlin, Devlin. What am I supposed to say and do now?

Garrick tunneled his hands through his overlong hair and clasped them behind his neck. He exhaled long and low. Jesus, getting shot at hadn't made his heart race as fast as the thought of seeing and talking to Devlin again did.

He stamped down taking his thoughts of Devlin one step further to the memories of them making love. Garrick didn't need the twitch in his cock to become a full-on boner while at work.

The sound of a door slamming at the front end of the garage jerked Garrick's attention in its direction. He saw his boss pause in front of his office door and slip a hand into the pocket of his coveralls.

After withdrawing a set of keys, the stout, gray-haired man looked across the garage to Garrick. "I must go home now," the man said, his Greek accent thick. "My son is waiting for me. Would you like me to leave you the keys? You can drop them off when you are finished working on your project." Mr. Corsini had built his business on the same piece of land as his home, and that house was all of two hundred yards behind the garage.

Before Garrick could open his mouth, Maddie popped up from the other side of the Trans Am. "It's okay, Mr. Corsini." She offered the boss a big smile. "I'm still here too."

"Ah, my darling," the boss's voice softened like that of a grandparent with his favorite granddaughter, "there you are. I didn't see you hiding back there. I will take my leave then." Garrick knew Maddie had her own set of keys. "Do not stay too late."

"I think we'll be right behind you," Maddie replied with a chuckle. "Bye."

Garrick threw in a "Have a good evening," and Mr. Corsini waved as he let himself out through the front.

Maddie wiped her face with a white towel and then shoved the end into a back pocket. "What do you say, G?" She reached toward the ceiling, stretching her back and arms. "You ready to call it quits for tonight?"

"Sounds like a plan. I just finished the rims." He jerked his head toward the wall. "It's a good stopping point."

Maddie came around the car and squatted in front of

Garrick's work. "Wow." She didn't touch, but she ran her fingers over the air in front of one of the rims, as if she could feel its new smooth texture. "They look fantastic." As she stood back up, she whistled. "My brother has no idea how lucky he is that you came across this junker, and that you know so much about the details that are going to make it a perfect mirror of the original." She glanced at him and held his stare. "I really appreciate your help."

Discomfort warmed the back of Garrick's neck. "It's not like I'm doing it for free." He would have, but Maddie wouldn't hear of it. After they were finished restoring the vehicle, and Devlin purchased it, Maddie intended to force Garrick to take a cut of the commission, as well give a piece to Mr. Corsini for allowing them the garage space to work. "Besides, it's not such a big deal for a car junkie like me to have some knowledge about certain classic muscle cars. It's nothing."

She sent an eye roll his way that would have made Garrick's own little sister proud. "Take the compliment, G. And my appreciation."

Garrick just slipped his hands into his coverall pockets and dipped his head.

"Okay, fine." She threw her hands in the air. "If you won't take my thanks, how about taking me up on a meal instead?" As Maddie talked, she peeled off her coveralls and revealed a pale blue T-shirt and mile-long, tan legs in skimpy cut-off shorts. "I'm starving. My brother has a date tonight, so I'm going home to a sad, tasteless microwave dinner unless you come with me and make it worth ordering a couple of pizzas. What do you say? Watch a baseball game together? The TV is high def," she enticed with a sing-song tone, "and honking big too."

Devlin has a date? A noise kept buzzing in Garrick's ears, so he figured Maddie continued to speak, but he couldn't process anything past her throwaway comment that her brother had a date tonight. *If Devlin has a date, maybe he has a boyfriend too.* Garrick froze against the emotional blow; it felt as if someone ran a blade right through his stomach and ripped out his guts.

"Garrick?" Maddie jabbed him in the arm. "What do you say?"

"Um, yeah, sure," he answered, his mind still conjuring images of Devlin eating with, laughing with, confiding in, kissing, and fucking -- *he's mine!* -- another man.

"Great!" Maddie's jubilant tone snapped Garrick out of the nightmare looping in his mind. "Get those coveralls off so we can get out of here."

Great. Wait. What great? What question did I just answer?

Maddie jogged to the back door, slid the double bolts home, and started throwing the light switches. "Come on. Get crackin' on those coveralls. You can wash up at my apartment."

Her voice got him moving, even though he could think of little else except Devlin falling in love and giving his body to someone else.

What did you think would happen when you crushed his heart all those years ago, you asshole? That he would hide his perfection away from the world and wait for you to come back to him?

Intellectually, Garrick knew Devlin had probably been with any number of men in the time since their weekend in San Francisco. Knowing that in his head, though, abstractly, didn't soften the reality of hearing that the man he'd thought about every night for five years straight might very well be involved with someone else.

Maddie pulled a curtain on a rod around the Trans Am, blocking the controlled mess of their workspace from the rest of the garage. He followed her in silence, out of the building to his own truck, and kept an eye on her vehicle as they made their way back to town.

All the while, Garrick raged at himself inside. He couldn't be Gradyn, but he wanted Devlin to be faithful to that person he used to be. He needed Garrick to be a whole new person, with no ties to Gradyn's past, yet he'd run to Redemption, knowing full well that Devlin lived here.

Garrick had prayed, prayed, and prayed some more that Devlin would not recognize him as that man he'd spent two scant days with so long ago; his life could depend on it. Yet something in his soul had wept and swelled yesterday when it appeared Devlin had so immediately connected the two.

Now here Garrick was driving toward where the man lived with his sister.

Good Christ. I'm such an idiot.

Garrick had not clearly thought through relocating to Redemption. In hindsight, it was simply flat-out the dumbest move he had ever made in his life. Then again, in fairness to him, when he'd made it, he'd still had blood on his hands from killing a man.

That tended to scramble ones' ability to make rational decisions.

———

MADDIE PAUSED WITH HER KEY in the lock. "Huh. That's weird."

Years of cautious living had Garrick pushing away from the hallway wall and scanning the empty, florescent-lit walkway. "What's weird?"

"The bolt isn't locked." She pulled a funny face as she slid the key into the lock on the handle instead. "That's not like Devlin."

"Maddie, wait."

Too late, she swung the door open wide. And the second Garrick looked inside, his stomach dropped with a sickening plummet, worse than the first time he'd ridden the big people roller coaster as a kid.

There, in the apartment, emerging from what looked like a balcony, stood Devlin.

With a cop.

Oh shit. Garrick pulled from every acting reserve he possessed and schooled his response to bland. As he stood in Devlin's doorway, his mouth went drier than a drought-ridden California summer, and his heart beat so fast he swore he could feel it throbbing all the way up in his throat.

Why the hell does he have a cop in his home?

"I thought you had a date," Maddie said, answering that question for Garrick. He now knew Devlin wasn't dating this cop. "Is Darren out for good?" Maddie's focus flicked to the guy in uniform, and Garrick couldn't miss the way her left hand clenched into a tight fist. "Are you switching teams, Ashworth? Did you run out of women to date?"

The dark-haired cop smiled in a way that made him look like a wolf baring its teeth. "Not quite all of them, little girl. Could still be one or two."

A blond-haired man came up behind the guy in uniform and smacked him on the back of his head. "Quit being an ass, Wyn. And you," he looked up and winked at Maddie as he crossed the apartment to her side, "stop baiting him."

One glance at the blond, and Maddie's entire face lit up. "Hey, Ethan." She lifted up and accepted a kiss from him. After that, she tugged Garrick inside and shut the door. "Let me introduce you, G." She pulled Garrick to her brother. "You've already met Dev."

Garrick took a breath and braced himself for the contact. He lifted his gaze and found a silvery-gray one waiting for him. One stare from Devlin washed over Garrick in a flood, drenching him in remembered intimacy.

"Y-yes," Garrick said. Goddamn it; he'd been less nervous approaching Devlin in that bar when they were absolute strangers. He wiped his sweaty palms on his jeans. "I remember."

Shit. Of course you remember. It happened yesterday. Damn it, man, you're a professional liar. Pull your shit together.

After another deep breath, Garrick thrust his hand out to Devlin. "It's good to see you again." He focused with every fiber of his being and made sure his arm remained steady as a rock.

Devlin left Garrick's hand hanging between them, unshaken, and didn't say a word for what was probably only a few seconds but felt like an eternity. He didn't blink or look away, and although they weren't touching physically, Garrick remembered what Devlin's hands felt like on his body. His skin heated right where he stood as he relived those fingers digging into his flesh, leaving bruises, as Devlin had taken him with that first rough fucking.

As if he could read Garrick's thoughts, Devlin stared, his pupils flaring, and the black nearly drowned out the silver. He abruptly reached out and engulfed Garrick's hand in his, and the jolt of first contact sucked the air right out of Garrick's lungs.

"I remember too," Devlin murmured. He said nothing more, but he held Garrick to him with a firm grip -- his touch strong, safe, and sure -- and it terrified Garrick down to his marrow.

He's not confused or uncertain. He has no doubt. He knows it's me.

"Dude." Wyn nudged Devlin. "Are you okay?"

Devlin released Garrick's hand and shifted to his friend, his smile predatory. "Oh, I'm fantastic." He crossed his arms and rocked back on the heels of his bare feet. "Never better."

"Whatever," Maddie said. She dragged Garrick from Devlin to the blond man, and Garrick started breathing again. "G, this is Ethan. He's my brother Aidan's partner. And that's Ethan's brother Wyn." She barely gave a flick of her finger in the officer's direction. "Everybody, this is Garrick. He works at the garage."

Three sets of eyes -- one knowing, slate-colored one, one possibly puzzled, curious blue one, and a third one dark with fire -- watched Garrick, clearly waiting for him to say something. Meanwhile, the imprint of Devlin's fingers surrounding his during that prolonged handshake continued to tingle over Garrick's sensitized skin, leaving him unsteady in front of a very intelligent audience.

Say something, damn it.

Ignoring the phantom sensations licking across his palm, Garrick forced his mouth to move. "I've heard good things about all of you from Maddie. It's nice to put some faces with the names."

Ethan was the only one to return Garrick's smile. He offered a "Nice to meet you too," then backed up to the open balcony door and moved into the waning sunlight slanting shadows across the brick floor and glass door.

"Dev, how about getting those steaks started?" Ethan asked. "I haven't eaten anything since breakfast."

"Sure." Devlin kept looking right into Garrick's eyes as

he answered, his gaze hard and piercing. Right when Garrick thought his knees might fold under him, Devlin blinked and turned to Ethan. "I'll get everything and be there in a second."

Devlin joined his sister in the open kitchen, and Garrick let out an unsteady breath.

"Garrick?" Wyn tapped Garrick on the shoulder, and Garrick jerked his head up to find an obsidian stare scrutinizing him. A sensation of exposure tickled its fingers across Garrick's neck, but he managed to only raise a brow at the cop.

Wyn walked backward toward the balcony. "It's a nice night. You want to join us outside?"

"Yeah, sure." Garrick dipped his head. "Be right there."

Wyn stopped at the open door and gave Garrick a second good hard look -- one that re-raised the hackles on Garrick's neck and shot them all the way down his spine. The man finally nodded and moved outside to his brother.

Good Christ. I have to get out of here.

Forget sitting at a table with Devlin and acting as if he didn't possess more intimate details about the man than any other person in this room did -- a task Garrick found he hadn't adequately prepared himself for at all. Forget that nightmare scenario. Garrick's mind raced with one piece of information: *Devlin has a cop friend who is practically related to him!* Garrick more than had to get himself out of this apartment. He had to get the hell out of Redemption. He could not have a police officer poking into his life. Not when Devlin could offer Wyn enough information about who Garrick used to be, enough to light up all kinds red flags to people who wanted Garrick dead.

I never should have given Devlin my real name in San Francisco.

Garrick's mind and body raged with denial the second a thought of tarnishing that weekend with outright lies entered his psyche.

"Hey, G." Maddie pulled his attention to where she stood in the kitchen. "What can I get you to drink?"

"Listen," Garrick rushed to Maddie and pulled her aside, "I appreciate the invite, but I'm more beat than I thought I was." He kept his voice low and half his attention on the men gathered out on the balcony. "You ended up having plenty of company tonight anyway, so you don't need me for pizza and a game. I'm gonna go ahead and get out of here." *Forever.*

"Are you sure?" Maddie held onto his hand. "My brother is actually really good with the grill. There are more than enough steaks to go around."

"I'm bushed. Detailing all those cars from top to bottom today on my own? Killer." He pressed his hand into the small of his back and grimaced. "I just want a shower and a bed."

Maddie immediately furrowed her brow and frowned. "And then I made you stay to help me with the Trans Am."

"No," Garrick shot back quickly, "you didn't make me do anything. I wanted to do that." Shit, running his hands over that car had almost made Garrick feel as if he was touching Devlin.

Stop thinking that way. It's over now. For a second time.

"I'm just tired tonight." Garrick put the mask back on and flashed a wry smile. "I'm gettin' old."

"Doubtful." Maddie snorted and then punched him in the arm. "But if I can't talk you into staying, I'll walk you out."

"Not necessary." Garrick walked to the door and wrapped his hand around the knob. "I can find my way to my truck on my own." With one turn of the knob, he let himself outside, nearly to freedom. "Relax and enjoy your meal."

"All right." Maddie leaned against the door frame. "I'll see you Monday then."

Damn it, he would miss this vibrant young woman. Dipping down, Garrick bussed a fast kiss to her temple and pushed some strands of loose hair behind her ear. "Have a good night." He waved one last time and then turned away so he didn't have to see her shut the door.

As soon as the soft *click* reverberated in his ears, and put a fisting clamp of finality on his heart, Garrick slumped against the wall.

That had been close.

Too close.

Time to go.

Garrick rolled his back against the wall until his forehead came to rest on the white painted door. The clearly close-knit group of people on the other side -- with Devlin smack in the middle of it -- called to Garrick and the desperate loneliness slowly crushing him inside. Keeping all these secrets could drive a man insane faster than a steady diet of psychotropic drugs.

Standing here, Garrick wondered if death was a more welcome alternative.

If someone finds you, and you're with Devlin, it could mean his life too.

Garrick could never let that happen.

"Bye, Devlin." Something deep inside Garrick screamed a denial, nearly doubling him over, but he pushed away from the wood and ran down the overly bright hall toward the stairs.

A door slammed, and the sound of bare feet slapping on tile had Garrick running for what felt like his very life. He didn't have to look back; he didn't have to hear a voice; he *knew* Devlin's presence all the way down to his very foundation. And right now, it scared him to death.

Garrick reached the door with barely a slowdown. He shoved the heels of his hands against the long metal bar, but familiar fingers grabbed him from behind and shoved him face first into the wall.

Caught.

Devlin moved in behind Garrick and put his mouth to his ear. "You left without saying goodbye. Or did you intend to send me an e-mail?" He caged Garrick in and pressed close, until his full front rode Garrick's back like a thick blanket on a cold night. "I seem to recall e-mails are more your style."

"Please." Garrick only had to breathe, and the contact of their bodies drew out a whimper of dangerous need. "Let me go." He still possessed the muscles to overpower Devlin, but right now, a kitten had more strength and self-protection than Garrick did.

With one smooth motion, Devlin spun Garrick around to face him, while still keeping him trapped. He straight-armed the wall, and his slightly shorter height somehow felt like it towered over Garrick. He studied Garrick without wavering, making Garrick feel like a bug pinned to a board.

Then Devlin abruptly leaned in, putting them nearly eye-to-eye. "I don't know what your game is," he hissed, "but you will not to come to my town, pretend to be someone else, and then put the moves on my sister."

"What?" Garrick reared back in horror and smacked his head into the concrete wall. He winced as the sensation of poking pins and needles radiated down his neck and back, but he ignored it, and grabbed Devlin's shirt. "Devlin, no."

Devlin touched Garrick's lips and cheek with the tips of his fingers right then and completely stole Garrick's voice.

He continued exploring Garrick's face, over his forehead, and finally teased the edges of his untamed mane. Devlin's brow crinkled, and his attention drifted up to his hand, as if dazed. "I'm not used to running my hands through your hair." He looked Garrick over from top to bottom. As his focus moved back up, he shook his head, and his voice lost some of its edge. "I don't know what is real about you anymore. Not even your name."

Devlin made eye contact again, and he slid his hand down Garrick's back to his ass. That glint of steel came back to his gaze. "I might not know a whole lot for sure right now, but I fucking know what it feels like to be inside you." He jerked Garrick to him, and his fingers dug into the crease of Garrick's jeans, right over his pucker. "And you damned well know it too."

Pressure from Devlin's touch scraped a shocking wave of concentrated pleasure against Garrick's asshole, and he gasped as his passage sucked in with a powerful spasm. The man dug his fingers into Garrick's crack through his clothes again, and Garrick shot to full life, right there in the hallway, against Devlin's stomach.

Devlin grinned like a man who understood his power. "That's right." He grabbed Garrick's hand and shoved it between their bodies, forcing it over Devlin's equally rigid cock.

Memories of Devlin's shape and physical triggers were embedded in Garrick's hand. His fingers automatically curled around Devlin's shaft to the root, and then moved under and tugged on his nuts. Devlin moaned the second Garrick touched him, and he jerked with the first handling of his balls.

Devlin lifted his head, made eye contact again, and seared them into one being with just a look. "I remember," Devlin said. He moved in until their lips were mere centimeters apart, and he whispered roughly, "And you do too."

Garrick opened his mouth, although he was unsure what to say. With a damning curse, Devlin claimed it with a taking, violent kiss. He slashed his lips across Garrick's and sank his tongue inside, owning Garrick in a dominating manner that had

Garrick opening wider and keening for more. Devlin groaned and swept deeper, tangling his tongue around Garrick's. He sucked it into his mouth, and Garrick immediately thrust back and drank deeply, needing a piece of Devlin too.

Devlin bit Garrick's tongue and lips, and he fought for control of the kiss with a power he hadn't possessed in San Francisco. Garrick cried inside for more of this new Devlin, even as he panicked and pushed back with aggression of his own. Growling, Devlin kept one hand firmly on Garrick's ass, holding him in place for a raw grinding of their bodies that matched the savagery he used to possess Garrick's mouth. Devlin shoved his other hand into Garrick's hair and yanked his head back and to the side, tearing their mouths apart.

Devlin's breath came in sharp pants, and he held Garrick prisoner with the piercing, pale light in his eyes just as completely as he did with the hand he had plastered to Garrick's ass. Devlin scraped their mouths together, made them both shiver, and swore gutturally, "Don't you dare tell me you don't know who I am. Don't you dare claim that you don't recognize the taste of my mouth, or know the shape and texture of every inch of my body." He pushed his face into Garrick's throat and inhaled deeply. "God knows I still remember yours." He licked his way back up to Garrick's mouth. "No matter what you look like now."

Garrick had no voice, and no ability to think ahead to his best course of action. He could only feel this man against him, right now, and plead in silence for forgiveness.

Devlin muttered, "Damn it, Denny," and moved in again for another deep plundering.

The second their lips touched, the slam of a door reverberated and ripped them apart.

Garrick glanced to the left, and Devlin did too. Wyn walked toward them, without pausing, until he stood right beside them. He shifted his attention between Garrick and Devlin, and said, "I suddenly couldn't remember if I locked my car."

Liar. He's a cop, and he came out to check on his friend.

Couldn't have been better timing for Garrick either. He put his full focus on the shiny tile floor, wiped his mouth, and tried not to notice how much his hand shook. "I-I," he didn't dare make eye contact with Devlin again, "I have to go."

Before Devlin or Wyn could say a word, Garrick managed to choke out a quick "Goodbye." Without looking up, he made it to the stairwell door and pushed through it. As the door eased closed behind him, he heard Wyn say, "Is there something you want to tell me, Dev?"

Garrick picked up the pace and flew down the stairs to his truck.

He didn't dare stick around to hear Devlin's response.

TWENTY MINUTES LATER, GARRICK LET himself into his room and made a beeline for the closet. He yanked it open, grabbed his duffel bag, and pulled the handful of shirts and jeans on hangers off the rod. After throwing everything on the couch, he ripped open the top drawer of the small dresser that also served as a stand for the TV. With one sweep of his arms, he scooped up his underwear and socks and tossed them into his bag. One fast trip into the second drawer to grab his T-shirts, and Garrick started shoving as much as would fit into the duffel. For the little bit of clothing remaining, Garrick grabbed a couple of plastic grocery bags from the recycling, filled them, and tied off the handles.

As he went into the bathroom to gather his toiletries, he wondered where in the hell he would run next, and if he could find another new name to answer to when he had just started to find his way as Garrick.

Whatever happened, this time he would have to figure it out completely on his own.

Garrick stumbled on his way out of the bathroom. His knees hit the floor, his gaze landed on his refrigerator door, and he froze. Right in his line of sight was a picture of Godzilla and a monster truck in a battle, something Shawn had drawn and proudly presented to Garrick. The kid had said if Garrick fixed the truck and drove it in the fight then Godzilla didn't stand a chance.

Son of a bitch.

Tomorrow was Saturday. The yellow Post-It note reminder that he had to be down at Grace's house by eight-thirty in the morning glared at him like a beaming sun. If Garrick bailed like a specter in the night, he screwed over Grace's shot at building a new life too.

He couldn't leave that woman in the lurch.

It would crush Shawn if he disappeared without an explanation. Garrick liked the kid; hell, he liked the less trustful Chloe too. He hadn't been in their lives long but he didn't want to be just another guy who didn't say goodbye.

And the truth was, he didn't want to leave Devlin like he had either.

That kiss…

Garrick groaned as he relived tasting Devlin and touching him again. After what had transpired in that hallway, Garrick owed Devlin a private conversation, at the very least, and Christ only knew what else.

He pushed himself upright and unpacked his clothes. Garrick didn't know what in the hell he was going to do tomorrow, but he definitely wasn't going anywhere tonight.

Garrick settled onto his couch for another long sleepless night.

CHAPTER FIVE

A soft knock sounded at Devlin's bedroom door.

In bed after midnight, unable to sleep, Devlin called out "I'm awake," and Maddie opened his door.

Looking like an absolute train wreck in her cut-off sweatpants and a ripped white T-shirt, Maddie studied him from the doorway. "Are you all right?" she asked, as she twisted her long hair into a bun on top of her head and secured it with a fabric-covered elastic band. "You disappeared there for a while tonight, and then you were kind of quiet when you came back."

Damn. Devlin should have known Maddie wouldn't quietly go to bed. After Wyn had come out searching for information earlier, Devlin had found himself brushing aside the man's curiosity rather than prodding him for information as planned. Something about that exchange with Gradyn -- *Garrick* -- in the hallway had kept Devlin mum. Whatever questions Devlin ended up having answered about Gradyn/Garrick, would happen between the two of them.

And no one else.

"Dev?" Maddie stayed where she was and practically bored holes in his forehead with her glaring. "What's going on?"

"I'm fine." He stretched his legs under the thin sheet covering him to the waist, stacked his hands behind his head, and let out an exaggerated sigh. "Just frustrated that I can't get back to work. I'm tired with this lack of activity."

"Uh-uh." She pushed away from the doorjamb, and rolled her eyes. "I've heard that excuse too many times before." With three steps, she was at the foot of his bed, too close for him to hide from her laser stare. "Are you sure this doesn't have anything to do with disappearing tonight right after Garrick left, and with you calling him some other name at the garage yesterday?"

A streak of self-preservation shot adrenaline into Devlin's heart, and he met his sister's gaze with an equally arched brow. "*Are you sure* you're fooling anybody with your biting comments directed at Wyn, least of all Wyn himself?" Maybe it was the kiss he'd shared in the hallway with Gradyn -- Garrick -- *whomever* -- that had left his mind and body humming for hours afterward, but in watching Maddie with Wyn tonight, the truth of his sister's feelings for the man had tumbled into place for Devlin. "You're not feuding with Wyn because you dislike him; you're doing it because you want him, but you don't think he wants you back, and you don't know how to handle it. Up until a few months ago, you guys were civil and even chummy sometimes." He drilled her with an equally probing stare. "Something changed, Maddie. What happened between you and Wyn?"

They didn't need proper lighting for Devlin to see Maddie's face flush with color and her lips to thin down to almost nothing. "Fine." She practically hissed the word, then did an about-face and strode to the door. "Be a jackass. Goodnight."

She slammed his door as she let herself out, and guilt stabbed Devlin in the stomach.

"Shit." When cursing didn't release enough tension, Devlin growled and pulled his hair. He didn't want Maddie sniffing around asking questions about Gradyn -- *Garrick, damn it* -- but that didn't give him the right to take a jab at her in order to get her off his back. He loved his sister. In many ways, with Aidan leaving them for such a long time, it had often felt like him and Maddie against the world. Aside from that, Maddie was younger and more vulnerable than he was, and in a lot of ways Devlin saw himself as her protector.

Shit. Damn. Fuck.

Devlin threw off the sheet, slipped into some shorts and a T-shirt, and treaded to Maddie's room. He knocked softly and then eased open the door, not allowing her the chance to deny him entry. Maddie sat in a chair by her window, her legs folded up to her chest, and her cheek resting on her knees. She wasn't crying. Devlin didn't think Maddie would dare let herself do something as girly as shed a few tears, but he knew the rough edges that made up his sister protected lots of soft places within.

He moved to her side and stooped down until he could see her partially hidden face. "I'm sorry for going at you like I did. It was cruel to exploit your feelings like that, and I'll understand if you don't feel like talking to me for a while."

Maddie kept her arms curled tightly around her legs but shifted her head to rest her chin on one knee. "There was no need to hit back below the belt, Dev. I wasn't trying to start an inquisition about you, or Garrick, or anyone. I was just curious."

"I know, and all I can say is that I've never met *Garrick Langley* before yesterday." A technical truth, at best, but at this point Devlin could offer nothing else other than wild speculations. "But even if I am curious about him, and even if I did disappear to talk to him tonight, that doesn't mean I want to discuss it with anyone, even though I know you only ask because you love me, and I can already see that you like Garrick a lot too."

"I do like him." Her eyes suddenly widened and took over her face. "But not like, you know, *like him*, like him. You don't have to worry about that."

He squeezed her foot. "I know that." He looked past the tear-free eyes to the young woman with a wicked-rough crush on another man. "Now."

The unspoken *"Wyn"* factor stiffened her spine. "I'm not ready to talk about that."

"Fair enough." Using his hand to brace himself against the arm of the chair, Devlin pushed to his feet. "I'm here if you change your mind, and I promise I won't go asking Wyn any questions behind your back." He paused at the door, his hand on the knob. "I'm going to ask you to do the same about Garrick."

She pursed her lips for the longest time, deservedly making him sweat, but finally said, "You have a deal. 'Night."

"Goodnight."

Devlin gently pulled her door closed and went back to his own room. He pushed his door shut with his foot and stripped out of his clothes before crawling back into bed. With an apology to Maddie taken care of, the second Devlin's naked skin hit the cool sheets, his thoughts drifted right back to Gradyn -- *Garrick* -- and what had transpired in the hall. The man had hardly said a word, but his kiss and the way he had touched Devlin felt like a rebranding of the mark of ownership Gradyn had put on his body back in San Francisco.

The sensations of that weekend still deeply imbedded in all of his senses, Devlin closed his eyes against the onslaught of feelings that attacked his body and mind. The memory of the first time Gradyn had taken him was so vivid it had Devlin lifting his arms toward the corners of his bed as he relived the feel of silk binding his wrists immobile, and the hard lips of that near stranger kissing his way toward Devlin's cock…

———

…Gradyn kissed his way down Devlin's stomach, pausing to swirl his tongue in the smear of their combined ejaculate. Devlin's abdomen quivered in response. He'd never been with a man in quite this way before, and Gradyn's reveling in everything they did together went right to Devlin's head.

Both of them.

Devlin's erection throbbed wildly with renewed life, and it pushed against Gradyn's neck, leaving new seed in its wake. Every lick Gradyn flicked or laved over Devlin's lower stomach had Devlin pulling in deep breaths and rocking his hips in anticipation of what would happen next.

Blood flooded his dick as Gradyn inched closer, and Devlin wrapped his hands around the lengths of silk above his bound wrists, searching for a place to cling to that would hold him in this moment. His body buzzed from top to bottom. When Gradyn poked his tongue into Devlin's belly button, Devlin yanked against the restraints, his hands aching to shove Gradyn down to his prick. The bindings held firmly in place; a guttural noise scratched Devlin's throat, full of unparalleled need, and his biceps strained with tension as he pulled and crushed his fingers around the ties.

Gradyn hummed as he finally moved lower and *almost* wrapped his lips around Devlin's erection. He rubbed his face and smooth, bald head all over Devlin's rearing cock, almost like an animal, and delivered hints of contact that had Devlin bucking his hips, searching for an opening to shove his cock inside.

Oh God. Devlin whimpered with the slight touches of cheek, forehead, and nose against the tip of his rigid penis. He spread his legs, silently begging for more. *I feel like I'm going to die without it.*

The teasing went on. Devlin tried to grab Gradyn again, only to have his wrists snap back against the bedposts. He swallowed a cry, whether from the quick sting of pain or the agony of being denied something for so long, he didn't know. He just felt poised at the edge of a dark cliff, barely hanging on.

"Denny..." Devlin's chest heaved with his struggle.

Gradyn lifted his gaze to Devlin's, and the color in his eyes shadowed past the deepest reaches of a forest. "Christ, the way you say my name." He slipped his hand between Devlin's thighs and gently tugged his nuts. "You make me feel like I can't do anything wrong with you." His jaw clenched and his voice became scratchy. "You make me care that I get it right."

"Please..." Devlin heard the frantic rise in his tone but couldn't make himself stop. "I won't know if you get it wrong. Just do it now."

"Breathe through that first punch of need, Devlin." Gradyn kept his fingers wrapped around Devlin's sac, and he didn't break their stare. "Pull it back so you can enjoy this."

Unable to look away, Devlin fed off the certainty in Gradyn's eyes. He let his arms go limp, resting in the restraints.

His legs opened and fell to the bed. He finally inhaled and exhaled a half-dozen times, slow and easy, until the maniacal jittering stringing his nerves tightly to the surface of his skin receded and he felt almost human again.

"There you go." With a soft smile that transformed every brutal line of his face to something breathtaking, Gradyn let go of Devlin's nuts, and stretched himself out between his legs. "Damn, beautiful." He circled his arms around Devlin's thighs, dipped his head down, and poised his mouth so close to Devlin's dick his breath whispered across the slick head like a caress. "You have an amazing cock."

As those words from Gradyn brushed over Devlin, the man's sweet smile lifted to something downright wicked, and he batted his tongue across the tip of Devlin's prick. Devlin barked a hoarse shout as every bit of sensation raced to his penis. His entire frame arched right off the bed with the second flick.

Now that Gradyn had finally given Devlin a hint of what he so desperately wanted, he didn't give Devlin a second to acclimate or breathe. The man held Devlin down and licked all the way down the underside of Devlin's length, igniting thousands of fellatio-virgin nerve endings to roaring life. With barely a pause, Gradyn then kissed and laved his way from the base of Devlin's cock all the way up the shaft. He swirled his tongue around the glans to the sensitive underside, tasting and suckling Devlin all over, as if Devlin possessed the sweetest nectar, and Gradyn a man denied too long what he loved most in life.

Oh God. The magic in Gradyn's tongue worked its way beyond Devlin's flesh and into his core, pulling unfathomably wonderful sensations to the surface from deep within, and drove Devlin mad. *I can't believe I waited twenty-three years for this.*

Gradyn foraged down past the root, took a fast, hard suck on Devlin's balls, and Devlin moaned through the concentrated pleasure and writhed his hips for more. With his head down, and his mouth all over the place, voracious and aggressive, Gradyn contracted his arms around Devlin's thighs and yanked him in even closer to his face. *Yes.*

A rough noise escaped Gradyn, and then he opened wide and went all the way down on Devlin in one hot, wet, swoop. He closed his lips around Devlin's cock and sucked up in one long motion, then went back down again, surrounding Devlin's length in a cocoon of moist suction. The man held on to Devlin's legs with a squeezing grip, keeping them tied together, and moved his entire head back and forth in a semi-circular motion that corkscrewed his lips in a crazy-good twisting that went up and down Devlin's pulsating dick. Devlin couldn't see it, but fuck, he could feel Gradyn's tongue lave flat up and down the underside of his dick and then curl around the width, tasting Devlin all over. Each time Gradyn pushed down and filled his mouth with Devlin's cock, he made deep humming noises that filled the room with the sounds of mating.

Devlin couldn't keep quiet or still. Each time Gradyn

sucked in his cheeks and dragged his mouth up Devlin's cock, Devlin swore he could feel the pressure pulling all the way in his fingers and toes. His sac swelled heavy with seed, and every small brush from Gradyn's chin or jaw, or fast lick with his tongue, made Devlin snap his hips forward, his mind and body confused about what it needed other than an immediate, shattering release.

He must have murmured something because Gradyn lifted his head from his task. "Tell me what you want." His lips glistened with the sheen of saliva and precum, and did battle with the brightness in his hungry stare. "I can make you come like this," he dipped down and brushed the tip of his tongue across Devlin's leaking slit, "or I can ease up and get you ready for my cock while you're still hard."

Fast images of Gradyn's thick cock forcing its way inside his ass had Devlin's chute pulsing in greedy spasms, but the rest of him cried out in protest, spurring his words. "I need to come now." His shaft twitched toward Gradyn's mouth of its own volition, bumping into his lips. "Finish it."

"Hell yes." Gradyn took hold of Devlin's cock and rubbed it all over his face. His eyes glazed more completely with each pass of rigid cock across his jaw, cheeks, forehead, and nose, until finally the tip came back to rest at Gradyn's mouth. He suckled the dark cap like a juicy strawberry, groaned, "Damn, you taste good," and gobbled half of Devlin's prick in one swallow. He went to town in earnest, blowing the upper portion of Devlin's penis with slick up-and-down drags, and used his hand to jerk off the rest with gripping, nearly painful strokes.

Devlin totally lost his mind.

He dug his heels into the mattress and thrust his hips off the bed, crying out as he fought the intensity of sensation centered squarely in his core. It wasn't just his prick screaming with joy, although, God, what Gradyn did with his mouth and hand could turn a saint into a sinner. It was the heavenly and hellatious pull in his balls that, when combined with the mastering Gradyn delivered to his dick, shot lines of pleasure into Devlin's belly and ass and up his spine and then sent it all speeding back to his crotch.

"Shit, Denny, shit." Devlin rocked all over the bed and jerked against the restraints that wouldn't let him touch this insanely perfect man. "Can't…" He gritted his teeth as the tether holding him to earth kept him connected with only one thin strand of thread.

Gradyn spat Devlin out, and looked up into his eyes. "Do it." Command filled his voice. "Fucking do it." He shoved a hand between Devlin's thighs, bypassing his nuts. "Come for me, beautiful." He sucked Devlin's cock back into his mouth, pushed two fingers into the thin skin behind his balls, and pressed hard.

Devlin went stock-still for a few endless seconds, trapped in limbo, and then he came back to life, shouting and shaking as orgasm overtook him. Incapable of pulling back, Devlin spewed in sharp, jerking spurts and poured cum in torrential waves down Gradyn's throat. Gradyn kept hold of Devlin's cock and milked him with his hand and mouth, adding another layer to this release, and had Devlin's dick throbbing within that warm, moist haven and giving up the final droplets of seed.

Devlin struggled against his restraints. "Don't slow down," he ordered Gradyn. "Let me feel your fingers inside me." Spasms rippled through Devlin's chute and shot all the way up to his cock, keeping him rock-solid. "Fuck me. I need it. Please."

Gradyn licked his lips, and that knowing smile of his twinkled right up into his eyes. "I intend to." He climbed up Devlin's torso and leaned over him to the headboard. Gradyn worked the first knot loose and slipped Devlin's hand free. He took a few seconds to massage the red line marring Devlin's wrist before shifting to the other side and repeating the process.

The stinging sensation of millions of pinpricks poking his skin flooded Devlin's hands as blood raced back, but he could hardly process the discomfort as Gradyn scrambled back between Devlin's legs and rolled Devlin's hips right off the bed. Gradyn moved in close and used his thighs to brace the small of Devlin's back, manipulated Devlin's legs apart, eased them upward, and effectively split Devlin open for viewing.

Oh hell. Devlin quaked as he looked at himself spread and on display. *It's finally happening.*

"Christ." Gradyn rubbed his callused thumb right over Devlin's pucker, making Devlin gasp. "I knew your little asshole would be just as pretty as the rest of you." He then dipped down and licked right over Devlin's entrance.

Oh sweet Jesus.

"Ohhh fuck…" Devlin choked on the unexpected shock of contact, and he jammed his ass into Gradyn's mouth for more. Gradyn tongued Devlin's hole with greater pressure, and Devlin grabbed onto his legs and pulled himself open even wider. Gradyn groaned and burrowed his face deeper into Devlin's crack; he switched his flicking and teasing to gentle sucking on Devlin's snug ring, and even threw in a few smacks to Devlin's ass that sent heat rushing to the spanked flesh.

Devlin couldn't look away from Gradyn rimming his pucker, and the sight of it only heated his blood more. His cock remained spike-stiff and his channel flared for a filling. "Shit … shit, Denny…" This kind of intimate preparation -- not at all what Devlin had expected -- had him shaking all over and teetering between begging Gradyn to stop and pleading with him to eat his hole forever.

Gradyn growled and took a bite out of Devlin's buttocks. "Goddamn it, I could feed off your sweet ass all night." His gaze darkened, and he dipped down to lick a fast line from Devlin's cleft all the way to his balls. "But my cock is so fucking hard it's gonna break off if I don't get it inside you soon." He let go of Devlin and stuck three fingers in his mouth. "Hold yourself open for me. I have to stretch you a little bit."

Too far gone, no longer remotely afraid, Devlin reached down, revealed his dark bud, and trembled as he realized he was officially offering himself to a man for the first time.

A low whistle broke the silence. Gradyn shook his head as

he openly stared at Devlin's ring. "Jesus, beautiful." He took a moment to roll a condom down his length. "You have no idea what an enticing sight you are right now." He licked his digits again, put the tip of his middle finger to Devlin's hole, and pushed. Devlin sucked in a breath at the exact same time. Gradyn broke right through the barrier, no resistance, and breeched Devlin's ass.

Gradyn forced his finger deeper, without relenting, and sent Devlin's passage into a frenzy of fluttering.

"Ohhh God…" Devlin moaned through the undeniable pleasure bursting under the burn of discomfort, and he couldn't stop staring at Gradyn's big finger easing in and out of his body. He could feel that disappearing digit twist against his walls on the other side, and it scratched at a need that went much deeper than having something in his ass.

As Gradyn withdrew and ran a finger around Devlin's stretched ring, Devlin rolled his head back and dug it into the pillow. "Give me more," he begged.

Gradyn sank his digit back inside and rubbed right over a sweet spot in Devlin's rectum that Devlin had only read about up to this point. Devlin's toes curled with each tormenting touch on his prostate, and his channel squeezed around Gradyn's finger, holding it inside.

"Oh yeah." Devlin bumped his ass up into the penetration, craving the friction that felt so good it drowned out the pain. "Don't go slow." He lifted his head and bared his teeth, feeling like he imagined an animal in heat did. "Give it to me."

"Damn it, baby." Gradyn shook his head, as if stunned. "I was right." He pulled his finger out and played right at the rim. "You have an ass made for fucking." He lowered his face and flicked Devlin's asshole with his tongue again, making Devlin howl at the flood of pure, raw sensation that raced to his entrance.

Gradyn kept up the licking and sucking on Devlin's relaxed ring, and -- *holy fuck* -- poked his tongue inside the small opening. Soon unimaginable heat swirled into every corner of Devlin's being and engulfed him in an inferno. Perspiration dampened his hair and pooled under his back, wetting the sheets. Just when Devlin wanted to tear out of his skin, and swore he would implode, Gradyn backed off.

A cool, slick coating of lube being applied to Devlin's pucker shocked him back to earth. The reprieve only lasted for a second.

Gradyn pressed a kiss to the inside of Devlin's thigh. "Bear down, baby." He grazed his shiny fingers over Devlin's perineum, causing a quick shiver, and then continued on to his bud. "I'm gonna give you two."

One finger entered Devlin's rectum with only the slightest gasp from him, but even though he wanted it like hell, his body fought the second. He cried out and grabbed onto Gradyn's arms as Gradyn forced him to open and take it.

With his fingers barely an inch inside Devlin's ass, Gradyn froze. He immediately started rubbing Devlin's inner thigh with his other hand, and he looked to Devlin with questions filling his eyes and tension pulling his face stark. "Are you okay?"

Heat and burn and stretching and shivering -- all centered in Devlin's ass -- rendered him immobile and mute. He took a couple of deep, even breaths, and with each one he exhaled, his body relaxed, and Gradyn's two fingers naturally slipped deeper inside. The sting pulling Devlin's ring subsided, and the pleasure of being stuffed so full broke over him in a shivery wave. He pumped his hips up to take more of Gradyn's fingers, needing the friction once again.

"Goddamn it, man." Gradyn kept his fingers buried inside Devlin, but came down on top of him until they were chest-to-chest and face-to-face. "You are so fucking amazing." The green of his eyes nearly eclipsed his pupils, and rosy-red slashes marred the sharp lines of his cheekbones. He dipped down to brush his lips against Devlin's, and Devlin could feel him grin. "You're not getting much longer to get used to this," he moved his embedded digits in and out of Devlin's chute, "before I replace it with my cock."

Devlin kissed his way up the swirls of ink edging Gradyn's face and put his mouth on his ear. "I'm used to it right now." He rolled his hips up as best he could into the invasion, and his passage clenched with delicious tightness around Gradyn's fingers. "Fuck me, Denny. I'm ready." He slid his hands up Gradyn's thick arms and curled them around his wide shoulders. "Please."

In one shot, Gradyn had his fingers out of Devlin's ass and his cock positioned to take their place. He looked down between their bodies, but just as he nudged, he stopped and pulled his gaze back up to meet Devlin's. "I-I don't want to hurt you."

His heart constricting, Devlin lifted up and brushed a kiss across Gradyn's lips. "You won't." He eased his legs down and hooked them around Gradyn's thighs, trying to hold him in another way. "Nothing in my life has ever felt more right than this night, here, with you."

"Shit, beautiful." For a drawn-out moment, Gradyn squeezed his eyes shut and turned his face away. He finally shook his head, as if to clear it. When Gradyn came back to Devlin, his stare held none of the hesitation it had a moment before. "Hold on to me." Gradyn moved his sheathed prick into position again, firmly against Devlin's entrance. "There's no going back now." He rocked up and in with his weight, once, twice, and tagged Devlin's snug ring with ever-increasing pressure. On the third attempt, Devlin grunted through the push of Gradyn's efforts, crazy-ready for this to happen. He gritted his teeth and nudged into the taking again. Gradyn countered at the same time; Devlin's muscle gave way *right then*, and Gradyn's cock broke through and pushed inside Devlin's ass.

Oh, Holy Mother. Holy Jesus. Fucking shit. Devlin's ass muscles clamped down all around the thick, hot invasion of Gradyn's cock. *He's inside me.*

Gradyn pushed his way deeper inside, and with each inch of Devlin's passage Gradyn took, Devlin crushed his fingers into the man's rock-solid shoulders, holding on for dear life.

"Fuck … fuck…" Devlin moaned as the nerve endings in his channel shrieked with a confusion of throbbing pleasure and pain, so bizarrely wonderful. Gradyn continued to invade Devlin's ass and stretch his walls, filling him, all the way to the root, and Devlin hissed through clenched teeth as he struggled to take it without screaming.

Buried balls-deep, his face a twist of savage lines, Gradyn suddenly stopped. He dropped down and put his forehead to Devlin's. "Talk to me, Devlin." His eyes burned green in the blur of their proximity. "Am I hurting you?"

"No, don't stop." Devlin locked his arms around Gradyn's shoulders and fused them together even closer. "Denny… Shit." Gasping with each sensation, Devlin felt his ass pulse around every inch of Gradyn's embedded prick, and it sent repeated shivers into his belly, cock, and spine. "It's so good." His balls pulled up in his sac, competing against the havoc of having another man inside him. The barrage of sensations ripped Devlin in a thousand directions at once and drove him nearly insane.

Without a speck of friction between them right now, Devlin still somehow felt turned inside out. He clutched Gradyn to him tighter. "Shit, Denny." *I don't want this to be over so fast!* "I think I'm gonna come."

Gradyn's soft chuckle warmed Devlin's skin. "No you won't." He scraped their lips together and then licked the tip of Devlin's nose. "Not even a young stud like you is gonna come again that fast." Dipping down, Gradyn claimed Devlin's mouth again. He circled his arms around Devlin's head, whispered, "Hold on," and started to move.

Forget holding on. After the first full out-and-in stroke, Devlin forgot how to breathe. Gradyn flexed his hips, back and forth, slow and easy, and never looked away from Devlin as he showed him how to fuck a man. Each smooth glide of Gradyn's cock stroked the full length of Devlin's channel, creating the most mind-blowing friction in his ass. Out of Devlin's control, his rectum squeezed every time Gradyn withdrew, his body fighting to hold Gradyn inside.

Gradyn bit his lip, and his fingers contracted in Devlin's hair. "You're so fucking tight, beautiful. I want to stay inside you forever." He jerked as Devlin contracted around his erection again, and he suddenly started to knife in and out of Devlin's ass with less control.

"Ohhh goddamn it..." Devlin crushed his thighs around Gradyn's legs and clung to him as if he were a life preserver. "Want you to... Never want this to end."

With a raw growl, Gradyn bit Devlin's forehead, and he drove his cock hard and deep into Devlin's newly breeched ass. He ground his pubes against Devlin's flaming, tender ring, only to pull all the way out amid Devlin's cries not to leave, and then pierce his thick shaft deep into Devlin's chute again.

Devlin growled right back at Gradyn, loving this fiercer mating. He dropped his feet to the bed so he could get better leverage and began pumping his hips up to meet every thrust down from Gradyn, moaning as each drive down from Gradyn pounded Devlin's entrance faster and rougher than the last.

"Oh yeah, fuck me." Devlin scratched at Gradyn's shoulders and back, and surely left torn skin in his wake. "I can take it."

Gradyn reared up and tangled his hands in the bedding. "Oh fuck, Devlin, fuck." He snapped his hips and drove his prick into Devlin in rapid-fire motion. "You're gonna make me come."

Blood rushed back to Devlin's cock in a torrent and shot his prick straight up. "Denny... Denny..." Devlin's passage burned so good with the raw mating. "Come. Ohhh fuck," Devlin strained against Gradyn, begging for everything without words, while looking right into Gradyn's lust-glazed eyes, "come inside me."

Gradyn's jaw dropped, his gaze darkened, and his arms shook as the rest of his frame went taut. "Touch yourself." Fully buried inside Devlin's ass, Gradyn clearly did battle with his body's needs. "I need to see it."

Devlin stared up at the unconventional beauty of the man above him, *deep inside him*, and his tender channel clutched in sharp spasms all around Gradyn's length.

Gradyn jerked, and his lips thinned down almost nothing, matching the harsh lines of the rest of his face. "Hurry." His body glistened with moisture as he rasped out that order. "Come with me. Please."

The open need in Gradyn spurred Devlin to grab his own cock. First contact sliced through him with a line of pure pleasure that raced through to every corner of his being. With his stare locked on Gradyn, Devlin began dragging his fist up and down his sensitized length, and Gradyn started to move in Devlin's ass again.

Each full slide of contact Devlin delivered to his dick increased in speed the next time around, which Gradyn matched with every push in and out of Devlin's chute. Within a half-dozen strokes, Devin had his prick whipped into a painful frenzy, and Gradyn pummeled Devlin's ass with a punishing fucking in return. Devlin didn't care about any discomfort; he only cared about giving Gradyn what he needed in order to come.

"Harder." Devlin bucked up to meet Gradyn's every downward thrust, and he rubbed his hand furiously up and down his own cock as he strained to find a third release. "Fuck me harder and make me come."

A rough curse escaped Gradyn, and he reached down to cover Devlin's hand with his. He closed his fingers tightly, making Devlin gasp with the extra pressure around his dick; then Gradyn pushed lower and fondled Devlin's balls. Gradyn pulled, rolled, and teased Devlin's sac as he drilled his dick into Devlin with a sawing slide, taking him repeatedly to the root.

"Please..." Devlin writhed and whimpered and ground his asshole into Gradyn's thick penetration as pure, gut need consumed him. "I can't..."

Gradyn slid his hand lower. He pushed on the thin membrane of skin between Devlin's balls and hole *just exactly* at the same time he tagged the sweet spot in Devlin's ass, and sparked the most explosive fireball to roaring life throughout the whole of Devlin's body.

"Ahhh!" Devlin split his thighs wide, drove his hips up, fusing cock and ass together as the heat of orgasm ripped through his spine and raced back to his core. Everything tightened inexplicably rigid for a split second, so goddamned solid it iced panic through Devlin, until finally the pulse exploded and hurled Devlin into the stars. He grabbed hold of Gradyn right before it happened and cried out his name as his channel contracted like a vise. He shot a split second later, spraying ejaculate all over Gradyn's stomach.

The second the first spits of cum hit Gradyn's flesh, his entire frame jolted, and his face twisted in a map of base desire. He bared his teeth and surged his cock deep into the furthest reaches of Devlin's ass one more time. He arched his upper body in a way that made him look like an animal howling at the moon, shouted hoarsely, and suddenly the sensation of warmth touched deep in Devlin's passage. As Gradyn came, the tattoos skimming the left side of his face and body made him seem almost otherworldly, but the vulnerability in his eyes, and the way he locked onto Devlin the entire way through his release, showed Devlin exactly how human this man was.

A visible tremble worked its way through Gradyn, and with a deep breath, he finally collapsed on top of Devlin. His weight pushed them even deeper into the dip in the center of the mattress, but Devlin didn't care. He reveled in the perspiration and cum making their skin cling together, and each time Gradyn breathed against Devlin's neck, goose bumps popped up on Devlin's arms. The man still had his cock tucked all the way inside Devlin too, keeping Devlin feeling connected and full. He should probably request Gradyn pull out and dispose of the condom, just in case it tore or leaked. At the same time, Devlin figured he would have felt it when Gradyn came if it had, and he didn't want to separate from the man just yet.

Not sure I ever want to. Fear sluiced through Devlin with that thought, and he clutched his arms tighter around Gradyn's massive shoulders, holding him close. *He's so solid; he feels ... necessary.* A second wave of fear -- that Devlin could be feeling this way about this man so fast -- shivered through him again.

Long minutes passed in silence. Devlin kept holding Gradyn, unable to let him go. Just as he thought Gradyn might have fallen asleep, the man stirred and pushed up to his hands.

Gradyn searched Devlin's entire face before making eye contact. "Are you okay? How does your ass feel?" He reached between them, very slowly withdrew his cock from Devlin's rectum, and then rubbed his hole. "Hurting bad?"

A dull throbbing made Devlin extremely aware of his channel, and lingering tenderness made his entrance tingle. "Feels used." He shifted his weight more to his hip. "A little sore, but in a good way."

The edge of Gradyn's mouth hitched up with a smile. "Nothing you won't get over then. That's good." He scooted backward to the foot of the bed and then got to his feet. "Let me get you a washcloth and a towel. I'll be right back."

Devlin rolled to his side and admired the way Gradyn moved as the man walked to the bathroom and disappeared inside. The sound of the toilet flushing and then water running reached Devlin's ears from through the half-open door, and he closed his eyes to better paint a picture of that sexy hulk of a man standing at the sink wiping Devlin's cum from his belly.

Oh sweet merciful gods. Devlin couldn't keep the ridiculous cat-who-caught-the-canary smile off his face. *I've been fucked.*

And not just for the sake of it, not just to say he'd done it, as had been his original plan when coming to San Francisco. Rather, he'd been fucked thoroughly, properly, and well. By a somewhat scary looking, but sweet-as-hell under the hard exterior, guy.

I can't believe I lucked into meeting him.

Gradyn reappeared right then, glistening with moisture, as if he had wiped himself down all over. "Here you go." He handed Devlin a large towel, one half wet, the other dry. "Housekeeping didn't leave us new stuff like we requested, so go ahead and use that to clean up with the wet side and then dry off with the other. We'll make another call to have something sent up in the morning."

Devlin worried his lower lip as he wiped lube from his skin and gently cleaned his tender hole. He used another portion of the damp cloth to wipe the perspiration from the rest of his body and then patted himself dry. All the while, he couldn't get the implications of Gradyn's words from his mind.

Just bite the bullet, Morgan. You've had the man inside you, for fuck's sake; that allows you some liberties to ask questions.

"So we're going to make this a whole weekend thing?" he blurted as he thrust the towel back at Gradyn. "Is that what you're saying?"

Gradyn paused mid-step to the bathroom; he took a long, drawn-out moment to openly look Devlin over from head to toe. "Oh yeah, beautiful." Devlin could have sworn the man's cock twitched again already. "If you want to."

Devlin's heart fluttered like mad, and he couldn't tear his gaze away from Gradyn. "I do."

"Good." After taking a second to toss the towel into the bathroom, Gradyn crawled back in bed and tucked himself against Devlin's side. They lay in silence for a long time, and then Gradyn murmured, "That might have been your first time, period," his lips brushed against Devlin's shoulder, "but I have to tell you, I've never experienced anything quite like what we just finished doing either."

There went that crazy flip-flopping in Devlin's belly and chest again. "It might not be fair of me," he admitted, "but I like hearing that."

Gradyn settled even deeper into Devlin, snuggling close. It took him all of two minutes of shifting, where he finally draped an arm and leg over Devlin, and then he started to lightly snore.

Devlin stayed awake for a long time afterward, just enjoying the weight of this big man clinging to him. He let the tips of his fingers run up and down the swirling indigo pattern running the length of Gradyn's body, loving the peace and silence of them sharing a bed.

All the while, Devlin wondered how in the hell someone he'd met less than twelve hours ago could so immediately feel absolutely like he was meant to be in Devlin's arms forever...

———

...Devlin awoke with a start to find himself holding his pillow against his chest, mimicking how he'd held Gradyn all night in that motel.

He remembered the quiet combination of confidence and vulnerability he'd constantly witnessed in Gradyn in San Francisco. Then he mentally flipped backward to the hallway outside his apartment tonight, and thought about the absolute fear he'd seen drenching those wrong-colored blue eyes of Garrick's.

He's scared, and he's hiding.

Devlin wanted to know why. He might be able to ignore the stranger Garrick was pretending to be, but no way in hell could he walk away from a frightened Gradyn Connell, no matter that they hadn't talked in four and a half years.

They were the same man. Gradyn -- *Garrick* -- knew that Devlin knew they were the same man. Devlin had a thousand questions, and he did not intend to give up until he had answers for them all.

This isn't over between us, Denny. Not by a long shot.

CHAPTER SIX

Maddie usually works on Saturdays. Garrick reasoned that fact in his mind as he stared down at her home phone number lit up on his cell. *And maybe he won't even be home. You might get a reprieve.* With his finger poised over the button, Garrick still didn't let it drop to make the connection. *Damn it. Stop being a pussy and just hit the damn Send button.*

Garrick cursed himself for the hundredth time since waking up, after going back and forth for the better part of an hour about this call. "Damn it. Shit. Fuck." He finally just did it, and hit the button that would connect him to Devlin.

He had to talk to the guy; he didn't know what in the hell to say, or how much, but he knew he had to set up a meeting so they could have at least one more conversation. He owed

Devlin. The question became: How much? Garrick knew sharing too much information could be detrimental to his own safety. A person like Devlin, who would certainly mean well, might let something confidential slip purely by accident, and set off a chain of events that could lead to Garrick's demise.

This is why I never should have come here. It's messy. And complicated.

However, those were also the reasons he couldn't just cut his losses and run.

Garrick let himself out of his apartment and was in the process of locking the door when a decidedly feminine voice hit his ear with a winded, "Hello?"

Shit.

"Maddie. Hi." Garrick's heart rate kicked up a dozen notches, and he started sifting through his conversation options. "You sound out of breath."

"Just finished a run." Heavy, uneven breathing mingled in with her words. "Nasty habit Aidan taught me." There was a long pause, wherein Garrick swore he could hear Maddie guzzling water. "I'm thinking of quitting. My heart can't take it."

His chest loosening some, Garrick chuckled as he pocketed his keys and traipsed down the narrow flight of stairs. "Only you would say something like that with a straight face, Maddie."

"How do you know my face is straight?"

"I can picture you as you say it, and believe me, I know it's poker straight." Garrick grinned to himself. "But yes, I do know you're actually joking. I can hear the humor too."

"So now that you know I have a love and hate relationship with running," Maddie said, "what else can I do for you this morning?"

"Oh..." *Double shit.* "Um, right." Garrick's heart went right back to Indianapolis 500 level speeding, and his brain spun various scenarios in a fast cycle until one spat out. "I was just wondering if you think I would lose all respect with Mr. Corsini if I ask for a few days off from work. I've only been there a month, and he's such a workhorse, I'm afraid he might let me go after my probation period ends if I start putting in requests for personal days already."

Maddie didn't respond for what felt like eons, and Garrick found himself standing with his breath trapped in his throat.

"Did you really call me on a Saturday morning about that?" she finally asked, her voice rising in pitch. "Or are you wondering if my brother is here, and you really want to talk to him?"

Breathe. Breathe. Breathe. "Why would you say that?"

"No reason; I just don't think you really want time off from work already." Another stretched moment of thick silence fell between them until Maddie said, "He isn't, in case you were wondering."

Garrick stalled in place, halfway up the steps to the Fine's porch. He looked to the floor and pinched the bridge of his nose. "Who isn't?"

"Devlin. He's not home right now. I could tell him you

called, if you'd like."

"No!" Through the panic of dealing with the subtle third degree Maddie was giving him, the hackles on Garrick's spine suddenly shot to attention for an altogether different reason. "Look, I'm sorry I bothered you," he said quickly. "I have to go. See you Monday." Garrick hung up without waiting for her goodbye. He then shifted, stepped up the rest of the way to the porch backward, and took inventory of the neighborhood for the third time in as many days.

He assessed the road from one end of the block to the other but recognized everyone outside as a person who belonged in the area. He studied the cars quickly, one at a time, and again, they all had reason to be on the street or in their respective drives.

Everything looked exactly right, but the tentacles of chill kept tickling at Garrick's back.

Who are you, damn it? And how did you get the skills to blend into the woodwork?

Garrick knew *someone* was out there watching; he had felt it for a few days now. He just didn't know why that person hadn't come for him, since they so clearly knew where he lived. Could it just be Joe discreetly checking up on him? Garrick absolutely could not contact the FBI agent to find out for sure.

He heard the door open and close softly behind him, and Grace stepped to his side. "Something feel out of place again?" Her voice was little more than a whisper.

Garrick crossed his arms and shifted to an at-ease military

stance. "Nothing looks out of the ordinary."

She glanced at him without turning her head. "That's not exactly a complete answer." With a shiver, Grace drew her fitted blazer more completely across her breasts. "Maybe I shouldn't leave the kids after all."

"They'll be fine with me. I promise."

If the person watching Garrick right now wanted to kill him, they would have attacked him already. He'd certainly acted irrationally enough in the last few days and given this person ample opportunity to take him out.

It's Devlin. Garrick suddenly stood up straighter. *Of course. Except, how is someone like Devlin, without the necessary training, disappearing so completely into the shadows?*

"Garrick," Grace's voice pulled him back to her, "be honest with me. Do you really think someone is peeping at us right now?"

"I don't feel it anymore." He outright lied. All of his muscles still sat poised, pulled tauter than a drum. "If anyone was playing Peeping Tom, he or she is gone now. I apologize. I'm feeling antsy, and you're the one who's getting scared. Go. Wow your client and make your first sale. I'll take care of Shawnee and Chloe."

"I don't know…" Grace's left cheek sank in, and even though he couldn't see it, Garrick knew she chewed a hole on the other side.

"Take a look around," Garrick suggested. "You have a couple of guys mowing lawns, a teenager shooting hoops, and three moms three houses down watching one toddler play in the grass. It's only going to get busier as it gets later in the morning; more people are going to be in and out of their houses. We're fine here today, if just due to the safety in numbers."

"I suppose."

Damn it. Garrick hated like hell that he'd put fear in Grace and possibly ruined her big break. "How about thinking about this?" He planted his shoulder against the porch post and put his full attention on her. "Sell that rich son-of-a-bitch a house today and you'll take a good step toward making yours and the kids' life more financially secure."

Grace pursed her lips and sort of shook her head. She glanced from the street to her front door -- Garrick knew she was thinking of her children beyond it -- before finally settling her focus back on him. "Good point. Okay, let me go before I make a bad first impression by being late." She unclipped her keychain from her purse and trotted down the stairs to her serviceable but old car. "The kids are still sleeping but you won't get a reprieve for much longer." As she climbed in behind the wheel and started the engine, she rolled down her window and shouted, "Wish me luck!"

"You don't need it, but you have it anyway. Good luck. You're going to do great." Garrick gave her one final thumbs-up, and he made sure to keep a smile on his face as she drove away.

Then, he couldn't help it, he took one last look around the neighborhood, where the only thing he did was wave back at a guy across the street working on his lawn. Seeing nothing suspicious didn't ease the buzzing wreaking havoc inside him one bit, though.

Garrick went inside to check on the kids and start looking for something to make them for breakfast. All the while, he could still feel the sensation of a target sitting smack center on his back.

———

"OKAY, CHLOE." GARRICK SQUATTED DOWN and cupped his hands in the shape of a baseball mitt. "Let him have it."

In front of him, Chloe nodded and wound her arm to make her pitch. A dozen feet in front of her, Shawn couldn't keep his wrists and arms still, and the Wiffle bat he held waved all about as he stood not-quite-poised to make his swing. Just as Chloe released the ball, all the hairs on Garrick's arms rose straight up on end.

He swirled to face the street, looking for that damned spy again ... and found Devlin watching him from his car parked on the side of the street. Pale gray eyes somehow pierced into Garrick's soul through the distance between them and arrested his heart.

"Devl --" he started.

At the same time, Chloe's voice penetrated Garrick's stunned brain with, "Garrick, catch it!"

Garrick half spun, just in time to catch a streak of white coming straight at him with laser precision, but without a second extra for him to move. The ball *cracked* into the side of Garrick's head with singular speed, stinging the hell out of his scalp with shocking pain, and took his knees right out from under him. Garrick grabbed the side of his head and muffled a string of foul curses under his breath.

Various voices in differing tones shouted "Garrick!" and seconds later bodies swarmed him and dropped to their knees around him. He could *fucking feel* Devlin kneeling, so-very-close, but Shawn's squeaking, "I'm sorry, I'm sorry, I'm sorry!" and the boy's little fingers pulling on his shirt sleeve penetrated Garrick's brain with the quickest sense of urgency.

He grabbed Shawn's hand and stilled the kid's frantic jumping with another hand to the child's shoulder. "Look at me, kiddo." The boy's eyes brimmed with wetness, and it tore at Garrick's heart. "It's okay, Shawn. I know it was just an accident. It's my fault for looking away in the first place while we had a game going on, not yours for hitting the ball. All right?"

Shawn's chin still wobbled. "Do you promise?"

Chloe looked at Garrick too, her eyes wide. "Yeah, are you sure? Cuz the ball made like a cartoon noise when it hit your head. I heard it."

Devlin touched his fingers to Garrick's forearm, drawing Garrick to the concern in his pale gaze. "Do you need me to drive you to the hospital?" He circled his arm around Garrick's waist. "It's smart to err on the side of caution with head injuries."

"It's not an injury." Garrick shook off the lingering throb

on the side of his head and rose to his feet with help from all three of his nurses. "The ball is plastic. It barely left a lump," he probed at his scalp and came away with clean fingers, "let alone broke skin. I'll live."

With his arm still secure around Garrick, Devlin's face was only inches away. "If you're sure?"

Holding eye contact with Devlin, Garrick went a little lightheaded for an entirely different reason than head trauma. "I'm sure, beau --," *shit*, "Dev, I swear." He tore his focus off the black drowning out the silver in Devlin's eyes and put his full attention on the kids. *Where it should be.* "But holy momma, Shawnee," Garrick mussed up the kid's hair, "you pack quite a wallop with that swing."

Shawn went from pale to beaming with one blink of his eyes. "Mom's been teaching me."

"She's doing a good job," Garrick told the boy. Meanwhile, Garrick still couldn't shake the disturbing sensation swirling against his neck and down his spine, even though he had Devlin standing right next to him and knew whose eyes watched him.

I need two minutes alone to get a few things said.

Shit shit shit. This was not how Garrick wanted to talk to Devlin. "Listen, Shawn," Garrick said anyway, "can you run up to my place and get me a bottle of water?" He handed the kid his keys. "Chloe, will you go with him and bring me the bottle of Ibuprofen that is in the first drawer to the left of the fridge? Don't open it," warning laced his tone, "just bring the bottle to me. Can you do that?"

"'Kay," and "All right," came out of Shawn and Chloe respectively. Shawn tore up the stairs to the garage apartment as fast as his little legs would carry him, but Chloe moved with a more deliberate pace, and she kept glancing back at him as she ascended the steps.

Questions. Garrick could see them flashing in her eyes. He could sense them in Devlin too.

As soon as Chloe disappeared into the apartment, Devlin murmured, "Cute kids."

Garrick whipped around and found Devlin studying him. Uncomfortably so. "I'm keeping an eye on them today," he said, determinedly holding Devlin's gaze with a steady one of his own. "They live in the house with their mother, and I rent the apartment above the garage. They aren't my children, Devlin." His tone held strong, and he couldn't look away from this man for the world. "I don't have kids of my own."

Devlin shoved his hands into the front pockets of his jeans and shifted his focus from Garrick to the apartment above the garage. "So I gathered," he said, his voice sounding far away. "I would guess the girl is about ten or eleven, and the man I knew for six months never could have had a daughter all that time and not bragged about her to me. It just wasn't in him." With a blink, Devlin came back to Garrick and penetrated him with one look. "In *you*." He shrugged, and a little light twinkled silver in his eyes. "Aside from that, they don't call you Dad. Kind of a giveaway."

"Right." *Duh*. Jesus, Garrick had to get his mind back in

the game. Speaking of which… "Listen, were you here earlier this morning?" he asked, watching Devlin closely. "Did you drive by the house, or were you in the neighborhood around eight-thirty this morning?"

A frown immediately marred the beauty of Devlin's face. "No." Just as fast, he stiffened to fully alert. "Why? What's wrong?"

Noise of a door slamming and shoes clomping down wood stairs had Garrick lifting his focus to across the yard. Shawn and Chloe elbowed and took verbal jabs at each other on their way down the narrow flight of stairs.

Garrick shouted, "Don't fight on the stairs or we'll go inside!" The kids slowed their steps -- a hair -- and Garrick quickly turned back to Devlin. "Listen to me." He grabbed a patch of Devlin's shirt and crumpled it under his fingers. "My name is Garrick. Please don't challenge me on it today." As the kids bolted across the grass toward them, Garrick's skin felt clammy under his clothes. He implored Devlin to comply with every fiber of his being. "Do you understand?"

Devlin closed half the distance between them. "You're Garrick to them. I understand." He covered the fist Garrick had curled against his sternum and rubbed down each finger with a soothing touch. "I'm not cruel, you know."

"I know." A deep breath released the knot twisting in Garrick's chest. With Devlin's help, he was able to let up the lock-hold on the man's shirt too. "Furthest thing from it."

Shawn and Chloe each skidded to a stop in front of Garrick

and thrust out their respective finds. Garrick grabbed the bottle of water and Devlin intercepted the pills before Garrick could get his hands on them.

"Nuh-uh." Devlin sidestepped Garrick's reach. With a laugh that reached right inside and caressed Garrick's very soul, Devlin shook the bottle of pills in Garrick's face as if it was a maraca. "I'll do it for you. It takes two hands to open these little suckers."

Garrick dipped his head. "Thanks." Jesus Christ, heat burned his cheeks, and he fucking thought he might be blushing.

"Here's your keys too," Shawn said, as he deposited the set in one of the pockets of Garrick's cargo shorts. "And I remembered to lock the door."

"Good job, Shawnee. Guys," Garrick moved and put an arm around each kid, "this is Devlin Morgan. He's…" *Everything I've ever wanted in a man?* Maybe not the right circumstances for such a declaration. "…a friend of mine. Devlin," Garrick's heart skipped a beat as the very best, wonderful result of an accidental meeting in his life officially met the next two down on his list, "meet Chloe and Shawn Fine."

Devlin squatted down and stuck out his hand. "Chloe," Garrick could tell he gave her a good, solid handshake, the very best choice he could have made, "and Shawn," he put his hand up to receive one hell of a high-five from the boy, "nice to meet you."

Chloe responded with one of her half-smiles. "Nice to

meet you too."

Shawn cocked his head and crossed his arms against his chest. "Do you play baseball, Mister?"

"You can call me Devlin, and yes, I know how to play baseball. I'll even do you one better." Devlin propped his fists on his hips and made his voice sound like someone telling a grand story. "I even play on a team with the local police officers because we don't have enough people at the firehouse that can play in order to have a team of our own."

"You're a fireman?" Shawn's eyes grew big and round, and his voice rose so high Garrick thought the neighborhood dogs might hear him.

"Yep."

"So awesome." Shawn grabbed Garrick's knee and started jumping up and down. "Can I go see your fire truck one day, Devlin? Please please please?"

"Shawn!" Chloe clenched her hands into fists and stomped her foot into the ground. "You are sooooo inappropriate."

Devlin shifted his attention to Chloe. "It's okay. I understand Shawn, Chloe. Fire trucks get me hopped up and excited too." He put his attention back on the boy. "I'll have to talk to my boss, and you'll have to talk to your mom, but we'll see what we can do. I think it'll be okay." With his hand cupped around one side of his mouth, Devlin leaned in and pretended to whisper in Shawn's ear. "The chief is my big brother, so I have a little bit of pull."

"So cool." Shawn grabbed Garrick's hand and tugged.

"Don'tcha think it's so cool, Garrick?"

Garrick smiled down at Shawn. "Very cool, Shawnee." His stomach fluttered as he looked at Devlin and said softly, "I think I was just replaced."

Devlin dropped his focus to Shawn's hand firmly latched onto Garrick's. "Doesn't look like it to me." He looked up and made eye contact with Garrick once again, and they shared a smile that felt like an unexpected shaft of sunlight warming his skin on a chilly day.

"Hey," Shawn took Devlin's hand, and also pulled Garrick's attention back down to him, "so Devlin can stay and we can play two on two. Come on, come on." He let go and locked both hands firmly around Garrick's one. "Me and Garrick against Devlin and Chloe."

Devlin shoved his hands into his pockets and raised his brows at Garrick as if to say, *What do you think?*

With brows arched right back, Garrick silently conveyed, *Up to you.*

"Ms. Fine," Devlin began. He paused to study Garrick and Shawn, his lips pursed and stare narrowed. He then nodded and came back to Chloe. "What do you think? Would you like to team up with me and whip their butts?"

Chloe glanced from her brother, to Garrick, and finally to Devlin. Abruptly, she grabbed Devlin's wrist and pulled him a few feet away.

Garrick took a discreet step closer to them and listened in.

"Are you serious about beating their butts?" Chloe asked

Devlin. "Lots of times adults let my brother win cuz they're afraid he's too little and will cry like a baby if he doesn't get his way."

Devlin responded with, "When we were kids, I never let my little sister beat me at anything without a fight. She lived and does just fine today. If we beat your brother and Garrick fair and square, Shawn will live too."

Garrick glanced over just in time to see Chloe thrust her hand out to Devlin. "Then I'll be on your team."

The two of them shook on it, and Shawn yelled, "Come on, come on, come on!" He had his arms outstretched, ball in one hand and bat in the other. "You guys are taking for-ev-er."

Chloe shouted at her brother to be quiet, then ran over to him and snatched the ball out of his hand. She took her position behind the two-by-four serving as their pitching rubber, and Garrick jogged the rest of the way over to Devlin.

Holy hell. The man Garrick wanted more than anything stood in his yard, willingly spending time with him, and Garrick could hardly contain the knocking in his chest. He felt almost shy, but he also couldn't keep a smile off his face. "Let me give you the playing field specs. See that white Frisbee in the grass there?" He pointed to his right. "That's first base."

Devlin sidled up close and followed the line of Garrick's arm. "Got it." As he spoke, his breath rustled against Garrick's ear.

"Right." Shit, heat filled Garrick's cheeks again. Pretending he wasn't blushing, and that Devlin's shoulder wasn't brushing against his arm and driving all of his nerve endings crazy, Garrick shifted and pointed at a silver object partially obscured by the grass. "Now that hubcap straight out, that's second."

"Got it." It seemed liked Devlin pushed his shoulder into Garrick with a bit more pressure. "Where's third?"

Garrick grinned, giddy as a fucking schoolboy, and explained the rest.

———

IN THE KITCHEN, GARRICK PAUSED BEHIND Devlin. The man stood at the counter shaping ground beef and pork into balls that he then handed to Shawn who pounded them into hamburger patties. Garrick stood dangerously close to Devlin, and he tried not to get high on the remnants of sweat left over from their game of baseball clinging to the man's body and clothes. A few damp tendrils still spiked the edges of hair at his nape, though, and Garrick ached to lick them and taste him, and then to push the collar of Devlin's shirt aside and bury his face in the curve of that warm, tan skin.

Garrick dipped down; just as he breathed in deeply, maybe even hummed with pleasure, Devlin shifted out of kissing range and shot a pointed look at Garrick from over his shoulder.

Shit. Garrick's heart almost stopped. Shawn stood on a stool right next to Devlin, and Chloe was spreading mac-n-cheese into a baking pan only a half-dozen feet away. *That was too close.*

Devlin bit his lip and his shoulders shook. "Do you need

something, Mr. Langley?" he asked, laughter in his voice. "Shawn and I have this part of our lunch covered, and we're doing a good job, thank you very much."

"Damn good!" With his declaration, Shawn slammed his hand down on a defenseless ball of meat.

The crack of sound hurled Garrick the rest of the way back to reality. "No damning anything, buddy." He tugged the kid's shaggy hair. "It's 'darn good.' Got it?"

"Got it," Shawn said, without turning around.

Devlin met Garrick's gaze. "Seriously, go ahead and relax for five minutes," Devlin said. He bumped his hip to Garrick's in a way that made the contact feel like a hand soothing his back. "We have this covered here."

Feeling restless, Garrick clasped his hands behind his back and strolled over to Chloe. "How about you, Miss?" He leaned forward and rested his elbows on the kitchen island. "Do you need any more help?"

Chloe nudged the foil-covered glass cookware in his direction. "If I open the oven, can you put that in? It's kinda heavy now with all the noodles and cheese."

The second Garrick touched one finger to the dish, Chloe raced to the oven and whipped open the door.

"You want it to get all bubbly on the top, right?" he asked as he slid the dish onto the top rack. "That's what we're going for?"

"Yeah."

"Okay, so to do that I think we need to let it cook for a

little bit longer, then remove the foil and switch the oven to broil." With his hand on the oven controls, Garrick looked to Chloe at his side. "Sound about right to you?"

She sucked her lower lip between her teeth. "I think so."

"Then that's it for us for now." As Garrick double-checked the oven settings one more time, he said to Chloe, "Grab us a couple of juice boxes and let's go kick our feet up."

By the time Garrick was satisfied they wouldn't burn the mac-n-cheese, Chloe already had their drinks and was tucked into the booth table in the corner of the kitchen. Garrick slid in next to her, and she handed him a drink. They both stabbed their straws through the small seals, took a sip, and settled into watching Shawn wrangle condiments out of the fridge as Devlin grabbed a frying pan and asked Shawn to get him some butter or cooking oil.

Chloe squished her juice box, clearly testing her ability to get the liquid as close to the tipping point through the straw as she could without spilling it over the edge.

"Can I ask you something?" she asked, her voice almost a whisper.

Garrick could feel the vibrations of her heels kicking into the base of the booth seating. "Shoot."

She looked up at him and then back to the body of the kitchen. "Are you and Mr. Morgan gay together?"

Holy shit. Garrick's hand compressed. Juice shot out of his straw and rained down on the table. *Where's her mom?* He grabbed napkins out of a holder and busied himself with wiping his mess.

"Well?" She looked up at him without blinking. "Are you?"

Careful. Be careful. "That's a word a lot of people think of as being for adults." Garrick chose each word deliberately. "Do you understand what gay means?"

The kid rolled her ever-loving eyes at him. "I'm eleven, Garrick." She sat up straight and tipped her chin up high. "I even know what transgender and transvestite means."

Garrick propped his elbow on the table and put his chin in his hand. "Do you now?" Better to let her lead this conversation.

"Yes, I do," she shared. "I heard these two ladies whispering in the grocery store one day. They sounded so nasty, and I didn't know why, so I told my mom what they were saying and asked her why it was making them look so mean." Little furrow lines appeared between her eyebrows. "She said transgender would be like if God put my soul in Shawn's body, but I still felt like me, like a girl. When I got bigger I could maybe even have an operation to change it so that my outside matched my insides. She said that's what transgender means."

"That's a good way to explain it. Your mom is very smart."

"Uh-huh, she is. She said transvestite is like if Shawn might sometimes like wearing my clothes or her clothes when he gets bigger, but he still feels like Shawn on the inside, like a boy, then that's transvestite. Or the opposite with me, she said. Like if I wanted to look and dress like a boy sometimes, but still know I'm a girl inside."

She tapped Garrick's wrist and then pointed toward the

kitchen. "I think Mr. Morgan wants you to look at him."

His mind swirling, Garrick glanced up at Devlin, his thoughts still on Chloe, her intelligence, and her one, pointed question that had started it all.

Devlin jerked his thumb toward the oven, and mouthed, *Uncover mac-and-cheese for you?* Garrick nodded and offered a little smile.

Chloe poked Garrick in the arm again, and didn't even wait for him to put his full attention back to her before going on. "My mom said people sometimes don't understand stuff like boys dressing like girls, and they get afraid so they act mean to people who are different." Clouds filled Chloe's eyes and her mouth turned down. "I'm different cuz nobody knows me every time we move, and I have to go to a new school, and I have to wait for the teacher to introduce me to see if the other kids are gonna want to play with me when we go out for recess. I don't like it," twin dots of color spotted her cheeks as she spoke, "so I don't think it was nice of those ladies to be mean to someone they don't even know yet."

"I agree." Garrick covered her hand and gave it a light squeeze. "You're a pretty thoughtful young person, Chloe, you know that?"

Chloe narrowed her gaze. "I know being gay means you wanna kiss and marry Mr. Morgan more than you do my mom." Her tone remained low, but it didn't lose a bit of its firmness. "I know cuz you stare at him like Edward looks at Bella in *Twilight*. It doesn't matter to me, cuz I know you're just Garrick, but you should tell Shawn cuz he's still little. He thinks you're gonna marry my mom and move into our house and be our dad. I never thought that. Even if you didn't want to be gay with Mr. Morgan, I didn't think you would be our dad, but Shawnee's different." Chloe stopped and looked to her brother a dozen feet away, where he unwrapped a slice of cheese and handed it to Devlin, the boy all the while yakking a mile a minute. Her focus remained on Shawn, and Garrick detected the tightening in her voice. "He's gonna keep thinking you're gonna be our dad and wanting you around more and more until someone tells him to stop."

Garrick closed his eyes as his heart lurched right up into his throat. That he might have misled that little boy for one second, no matter how innocently, churned bile in Garrick's stomach.

He forced himself to look at Chloe, then Shawn, and find his voice. "Have you told your mom what Shawn is thinking?"

She shook her head, her dark hair swishing back and forth as she did. "He said it today while we were brushing our teeth. I think it's cuz you made us breakfast, and Mom's not here, so it kinda felt like you live here and were the dad." When Chloe came back to him, she didn't have a tear in her eye, but her chin quivered just a smidge, and her lips were pale. "Even to me."

"Jesus, kid." Garrick leaned in and pressed a kiss to the top of her head. "I'm so sorry." *Fuck. Fuck. Fuck.* He knew these kids didn't have a father, but with absolutely nothing even hinted at between himself and Grace, it had never hit him that someone Shawn's age would still think they could all live together as a family. "I'll talk to your mom when she gets home, and we'll let her decide what needs to be said to your brother. Can we keep this conversation between us until after something is settled?"

Chloe nodded, but Garrick still felt like he'd ripped a puppy out of her hands and stomped all over it. He dipped down until they were on eye level. "Hey, I do like spending time with you and Shawn," he told her. "Whatever feelings I have or don't have for Mr. Morgan don't have anything to do with me being in your life, as long as it's okay with your mother. You know?"

"Yeah." Chloe looked down at the table, started fiddling with her juice box, and began kicking the seating again. "Until we move again. Then we'll be new somewhere else and just the three of us like always before."

Pushing back deeper into the booth, Garrick exhaled and curled his hand around the back of his neck. "Maybe this was your last move." Shit, was this conversation in confidence? Or should he tell Grace about Chloe's dejected acceptance at the thought of moving again? "Could be this one sticks to you all like glue."

"Maybe."

"You've been here a year now," Garrick pointed out, remembering Grace telling him that when he'd rented the garage apartment. "And your mom is getting this whole real estate thing going here in Redemption. Has that ever happened before?"

The kicking stopped. "No."

"Well, there you go." Garrick found himself staring at Devlin's strong back. He couldn't help the small grin that lifted his lips or hold back the sensation of mini fireworks popping in his chest and stomach. "Things might be looking up for all of us," he said, his voice as soft as hers had been earlier. "Can you hope for that? With me?"

Chloe scooted closer to him and leaned her head against his arm. "I'll try."

Shawn suddenly screeched, and he shouted, "The cheese is burning! The cheese is burning!"

Garrick looked up just as Shawn yanked open the oven door.

"Shawn!" Garrick flew out of the booth, and panic scraped his voice raw. "Don't touch that!"

Devlin spun in a flash, grabbed Shawn by the back of his shirt, and hauled him away from the open oven door just as the kid had begun to stick his hand inside. Devlin moved Shawn well out of the way, turned off the oven, and then used two hand towels to remove the mac-n-cheese.

Garrick stalled out at the island, his legs feeling like jelly the second he processed that Shawn was okay. "Shit." His heart raced too fast, and he could not breathe properly to slow it down. "He would have been badly burned."

"That's why mom always uses the latch and locks it," Chloe said, now at his side.

Rookie mistake. "I should have done that too," Garrick

replied, his throat still tight.

"I should have thought to tell you," Chloe murmured. "No matter what mom tells him or takes away to punish him, he gets too excited and still tries to take stuff out of the oven all the time."

A hand curled around Garrick's shoulder, and Garrick followed the line of strong, tanned arm up to Devlin's eyes. "Everyone is fine. Okay?" Devlin's touch and voice steadied the buzz of adrenaline speeding within Garrick. "Disaster averted." He pulled Shawn to his side and gave the kid a noogie. "Maybe it just means Shawn is going to be a chef one day. He likes the kitchen."

With a snort, Chloe said, "Maybe it just means he's dumb."

"Am not!" Shawn whirled on Chloe and jabbed her in the leg with his little fist. She shoved him right back with an open hand to his shoulder.

"Hey!" Garrick pushed his way in between the flailing arms. "Both of you stop it now."

Devlin and Garrick ended up in the middle of the kids, strong-arming each of them, and acting as a divider wall.

"How about we end this round as a draw and sit down to eat?" Devlin asked.

"I vote for Devlin's plan," Garrick said. He eyed Chloe first and then swung the other way so Shawn got a piece of his stink eye too. "And if you both want to go back outside to play when we're finished, you'll agree to it too."

They both grumbled, but they divvied up the task of

carrying the condiments and paper plates to the table without further complaint.

Once Garrick saw the kids playing nicely again, he lifted his gaze to Devlin's. The man had the most enticing light sparking silver in his eyes, so full of knowledge, and Garrick couldn't create enough saliva to do more than whisper, "Thank you."

"No problem." Devlin handed Garrick the plate of burgers. The grazing of their fingers as it traded hands rippled a gentle wave of awareness under Garrick's skin, making him feel as if they'd been comfortably touching forever. Devlin winked, and said, "Let's eat." He left Garrick standing there with his jaw on the floor.

Chloe giggled behind him, and Garrick knew she'd witnessed the little moment too.

Great.

GARRICK WINCED AS SHAWN SCREECHED from his bedroom, "I can't find my Transformer!"

Chloe rolled her eyes and sighed dramatically. "Why does he need to bring a stupid toy with us?" She pushed open the door, let herself out onto the porch, and looked up at Garrick and Devlin through the screen. "Tell him to forget about it or we're gonna leave without him."

With lunch finished, Garrick had promised the kids a trip to the ice cream shop if they helped make the kitchen sparkle as clean as their mother had left it this morning. They'd completed that task a few minutes ago, but after everyone took a turn using the bathroom, Shawn had declared he needed his Transformer.

After glancing at his watch, Garrick joined Chloe on the porch. "Come on, Chloe, let's give Shawn a break. He's only been looking for two minutes."

Still on the other side of the screen door, Devlin *ahemed* and raised his hand. "Why don't I go see if I can help him find it?"

Another easy smile pushed up the corners of Garrick's mouth, as had been happening all damned day. "Tell him he has three more minutes." Garrick's finger brushed against the soft screening as he pointed at the too-sexy man inside. "Don't let tears sway you into more."

Devlin jogged backward across the living room, pointing right back at Garrick. "I'll have him on the porch in two!" He spun as he said that and disappeared down a hallway.

Dropping down to sit on the steps, Chloe mumbled, "I bet he cries and we never get to the ice cream shop."

Garrick lowered himself next to her and clasped his hands between his spread knees. "I bet Shawn and Devlin are standing on this porch in under three minutes *with* Shawn's toy in hand." He watched her out of the corner of his eye. "What are you willing to put on it, Miss?"

She raised her brows at him. "How about, if I win, you have to buy me a new computer game."

Grace had mentioned with pride that Chloe had a way

with technology. "I think I can handle that," he told her. "And if I win?"

"Let me think." She pursed her lips and drummed her fingers against her chin. After just a few seconds, she perked up and looked at him. "I don't have enough money to buy something good for you, but I'll help you wash your truck the next *three* times you do it."

"Three?" Garrick reared back and put his hand over his heart. "Well, that's way better than anything you could buy me." Laughing, he reached out his hand. "It's a deal."

Just as he and Chloe shook on it, a familiar car pulled into the drive.

"Mommy's home!" Chloe shot to her feet, and Garrick stood too. Grace climbed out of the car, briefcase in one hand, purse in the other, and a smile as wide as the whole United States lit up her entire face.

"Well, what do you know," Garrick said, his voice soft. "She did it."

Chloe jerked her attention up to Garrick and then swung it back to her mother. "You did it?" The girl bounced in her little pink sneakers. "Seriously?"

After dropping her bags on the walk, Grace nodded and whispered back, "I did it." Suddenly, she started moving, her stride growing wider and gaining speed with each step. "I did it! I did it! I did it!" She scooped Chloe into her arms and swung the girl in a big circle. "I sold a house." With a big, smacking kiss planted on Chloe's cheek, Grace made eye contact with

Garrick and smiled somehow even bigger. "I started the process anyway. I put a bid in for my client, and the seller immediately accepted. There are potentially still tons of things that might derail it, but this guy's credit is gold." Excitement took over Grace's voice more and more with each word. "The house is in fantastic shape too, so I think everything is going to work out just fine."

Feeling a little choked up, Garrick reached out and squeezed Grace's forearm. "Congratulations."

Grace wiped the corner of her eye. "A big part of this is thanks to you, Garrick." With Chloe still clinging to her side, Grace pulled Garrick into their embrace and hugged him. "Thank you so much." She pecked a kiss on his cheek. "I couldn't have done this without knowing my kids were safe with you."

He dipped his head. "It's truly my pleasure."

"We found it!" Shawn shouted as he burst through the front door. "Oh, Mommy! Look!" The kid thrust his hand up in the air, a shiny, metallic red toy in hand. "I found my Transformer."

"Great," Grace said.

Garrick pulled away from Grace. The second he'd heard Shawn's voice, Garrick looked up and saw Devlin through the screen. The man had clearly witnessed the kiss, hug, and words between Garrick, Grace and Chloe. Devlin's expression and body language held none of the openness or ease he'd conveyed all day long.

Garrick's stomach did a sick dive. *Oh fuck.* He took a step toward the door. "Devlin…"

Still in the shadows of the living room, Devlin shook his head. Then he joined them outside. He smiled and stood still long enough for Garrick to make introductions. After an exchange of "Nice to meet you," Devlin informed them that he had to leave.

Shawn looked up at him, a frown marring his normally mischievous face. "You don't want to get ice cream with us?"

"I'm sorry, Shawn." A frown altering his face too, Devlin squatted down next to the boy. "I wish I could, but I just remembered I have plans tonight, and I can't break them. It would be rude to cancel at the last minute."

Devlin's date. Garrick had managed to wipe that out of his mind the whole day today.

Before Garrick could say a word, Devlin hopped up from his kneeling position. "Here." He pulled out his wallet and handed Grace a card. "That's my number. The kids want to talk to you about taking a trip to the firehouse where I work." Devlin shifted his focus completely to Shawn and Chloe. "You guys tell your mom all about it, and I'll talk to the boss." He started walking down the porch steps backward, and then crossed the yard, away from Garrick, without even looking at him.

Stopping at the edge of the lawn, Devlin's entire frame looked rigid, as if he fought stepping onto the sidewalk and then crossing the street to his car. "I had fun today, guys." He finally lifted his hand in an abbreviated wave. "Bye."

Garrick took the steps two at a time, bounding off the porch. He raced across the yard, grabbed Devlin's arm just as he hit the street, and spun him back around.

"Please," Garrick heard a funny crack in his voice, "don't go like this."

For the longest minute in eternity, Devlin stared right into Garrick's eyes, his slate gaze softening it seemed. Garrick didn't look away, and he held so still he didn't even breathe. Devlin finally blinked, and his line of his sight shifted to beyond Garrick's left shoulder.

"You have things you need to figure out and get settled that are more important than me," Devlin said, his voice solemn. "I think you know that." The edge of his mouth lifted just the slightest bit, and he grazed his knuckles across Garrick's jaw. "Goodbye." He dropped his hand and jogged across the street to his car.

Garrick couldn't make himself move. He stood on the sidewalk, locked in place, and watched Devlin drive away.

Something brushed against his arm, and Garrick finally realized Grace had joined him. "Do you need to go?" she asked, staring in the direction Devlin had driven away.

Garrick shifted and caught a glimpse of Shawn and Chloe sitting close together on the bottom step, pretending not to watch him. "No." He understood what Devlin meant. More, he agreed with the man. "I need to stay."

Shit. Where am I supposed to begin?

"I promised the kids ice cream." Garrick's chest pained him, more than he would have thought with just one short month knowing these people, but he got it said. "When we get back, we have to talk."

Chapter Seven

Twenty minutes later, Devlin's hands still shook as he pulled his car into the designated slot in front of his apartment building.

I can't believe I found him -- not only in Redemption a few days ago -- but where he lives now, and then I just drove away.

Devlin hadn't thought there could be anything that would make him walk away from Garrick without a bloody, drag-out fight, but he hadn't counted on two kids who maybe needed a father more than Devlin needed a lover.

Garrick. I started thinking of him as that person today.

For a little while, Devlin had even slipped seamlessly into the role of playing house with the man. He'd completely blocked out of his mind, until Grace Fine had shown up on her porch looking so beautiful, happy, and well-loved, that there was a mother attached to those kids. To Garrick, it seemed, too.

Not that Devlin thought Garrick was sleeping with the woman. If he were, Devlin figured the kiss Grace had given Garrick would have been more intimate than the one she'd pecked on his cheek. That didn't mean they didn't have a relationship of some importance and intimacy, though; they clearly did. That woman so obviously trusted Garrick; she liked him, she respected him, and Devlin could tell it went both ways.

Devlin couldn't categorically say Garrick would never have sex with a woman, or that even if he chose to do so that he wouldn't enjoy it. Devlin could only say that the person he'd known in San Francisco had a wild passion for other men and a sexual appetite for his own sex that Devlin could certainly attest to firsthand. Conversely, the man Devlin had corresponded with toward the end of their e-mail and phone relationship had not only hinted at women, but then in that final goodbye had out-and-out stated he'd been in a long-term relationship with a woman and intended to marry her. Devlin supposed it could be possible that Garrick was bisexual.

No. I would have sensed it. He's not. He flirted with me. Today. And I think he almost kissed me. He didn't want me to leave.

Holy Mother of God, up until Grace had come home and their family vibe had knocked the wind right out of him, Devlin hadn't wanted to leave Garrick or those kids.

Today had been amazing. Devlin could only remember one Saturday in his life being better…

———

…A soft thud followed by a light scraping noise tickled in Devlin's ears and tried to pull him from sleep. He mumbled and hugged his pillow tighter to his chest as he burrowed deeper under the snuggly protection of the covers and tried to slip back into the most wonderful dream.

"Good morning, sleeping beauty." The man in his dreams manifested in real life and spoke from somewhere in Devlin's room. "Well, almost good afternoon now."

The sound of that voice, so new yet already recognized by Devlin, spread warmth through his insides and brought forth a secret smile.

Oh right. I'm not in Redemption. And last night wasn't just another jerk-off fantasy.

He had a new awareness of his rectum to prove it.

Opening his eyes, Devlin turned his head on the pillow and found Gradyn sitting in one of the two chairs at the table in the far corner of the small room. He was dressed in the jeans and flannel shirt he'd worn yesterday, and he had his booted feet kicked up on the table next to a handful of paper and plastic bags. The man looked intimidating as hell with his shaved head and tribal tattoos, yet humor and clear intelligence sparked his green eyes, and he smiled in a way that invited a person closer to taste and feel. Devlin's body hummed as it slowly came out of its slumber, and he knew he'd never seen a sexier human being in his life.

As Devlin's staring went on, Gradyn shifted and adjusted himself. "You're very cute when you're not quite awake," he said, his voice a little gruff.

Speak, Morgan. Clear the fog and open your mouth. "Um, thanks." Feeling his face heat, Devlin stretched his arms and legs toward the top and bottom of the bed, groaning as each muscle slowly woke up. "What time is it?" He scrubbed the sleep out of his eyes and rolled toward the nightstand. "Shit." The big red eleven and thirty-seven on the digital clock loomed large and bright. "I never sleep past eight."

"I think today you can be forgiven. You have a good excuse. I'm sure you're exhausted." The green in Gradyn's eyes darkened, and his lips thinned to a tight line. "And probably more than a little sore too."

Even though Gradyn had tasted and touched every centimeter of Devlin's body so very recently, Devlin experienced a strange sense of shyness right then. "Did you go somewhere?" he asked, and then immediately cursed himself. "I mean, you obviously did." He eyed the bags on the table. "Where did you go?"

Gradyn pointed toward the top of the bed, and Devlin looked up to find a note folded on the other pillow. He grabbed the tiny square of paper and opened it.

Need a change of clothes. I'll pick us up some food too.

Be back soon. -G

Devlin went to tuck the note into his pocket and then remembered he didn't have on a stitch of clothing. Shoot. He didn't want to lose it.

Trying for casual, Devlin curled his hand around the square of paper and got to his feet. "I guess you didn't drive home, huh," he asked as he made his way to the bathroom, "or you would be wearing different stuff right now." Over dinner last night, Gradyn had mentioned he had an apartment in Oakland and did work with gangs in that city.

"Didn't want to be gone from you that long." Gradyn's answer stalled Devlin in place with his hand on the bathroom door.

Fuck. Devlin's balls and cock stirred, and it pulled a funny line of nervous excitement in his belly. "Oh." Devlin squeezed the paper in his fist and pressed it against his stomach.

Another soft chuckle took over the room. "Go take your piss, beautiful. I'm not going anywhere."

Somehow, Devlin got his legs moving. Before relieving himself, he unzipped his shaving kit and slipped the little note inside an interior zipper compartment lined in plastic. As soon as he emptied his bladder, his stomach grumbled. Loudly. It also clenched with enough force to make him grimace.

No wonder. You burned off every calorie and more from that dinner you only picked at more than fifteen hours ago.

Devlin turned the water in the sink on low, and called out,

"Denny, can you get a pair of jeans out of my bag for me?" After washing his hands, Devlin quickly brushed his teeth, sighing as the grit went away and the toothpaste left his mouth minty.

The door creaked as it swung the rest of the way open. Gradyn stood in the doorway with dark denim hooked on the tip of one finger. Dangling the pants just out of reach, he said, "I don't mind you naked, you know."

"But you're dressed." Devlin delivered an exaggerated glare as he snatched the jeans off Gradyn's finger. "It would feel weird."

With his shoulder planted against the doorjamb, Gradyn let his gaze drop briefly to Devlin's cock. He held just long enough to pull an involuntary physical reaction from Devlin, and then he made eye contact again. "Are you asking me to get naked with you?"

Down, boy.

Devlin waited the two ticks it took for his prick to comply with his orders, and then pulled his jeans up to his waist. Leaving the button undone, and feeling a little more on equal footing now that he had some clothing on, Devlin sauntered up to Gradyn. "Maybe you can take everything off again after you feed me." He brushed up against the bigger man, pausing with their chests, stomachs, and dicks nearly grazing each other. "For some reason," Devlin licked Gradyn's chin, "I have an incredible appetite today."

He went to slide past; Gradyn grabbed his arm and hauled him right back close to him. He tucked Devlin against his front, and descended. "I'm fucking hungry too," Gradyn said, just before he took complete possession of Devlin's mouth.

Like a freaking stick of butter on a hot stove, Devlin melted into Gradyn's taking. He opened his mouth and let Gradyn inside with only the slightest flick from the man's tongue. Gradyn explored deeply and then sucked Devlin's tongue into his mouth. Devlin dug his fingers into the man's back through his shirt, insatiable in his need to fuse their bodies into one again. The noise Gradyn released in response vibrated all the way up from his core and rumbled through Devlin too. Gradyn kissed Devlin as if he needed the contact to sustain his very life, and he curled his hands around Devlin's hips and back to his ass, then shoved his hands under the waistband of Devlin's jeans to grab his ass. The rough calluses on Gradyn's palms scratched against Devlin's bare flesh with every knead of his fingers, and Devlin gasped with pure, unadulterated pleasure. Pushing at Devlin's sanity more, Gradyn rubbed the blunt tips of his fingers down and up Devlin's crease, and Devlin slipped past the point of control into voracious, unskilled animal. With a raw keen of need, Devlin writhed his ass into Gradyn's groping hands, seeking and begging for more.

Gradyn groaned and jerked against Devlin, but after taking another nipping bite, he broke the kiss. "Christ," he leaned his forehead to Devlin's, "you have the perfect ass." One more squeeze that shoved Devlin to past half-hard, and Gradyn removed his hands from Devlin's jeans. "Jesus, man," Gradyn stole another fast kiss and then straight-armed Devlin out of touching distance, "you respond to my mouth like no one I've ever known." He pointed back at Devlin as he walked to the table and took a seat. "You're damned lucky I'm starving for actual food too -- and know that you need a little bit of recovery time -- or I'd have those jeans around your ankles and you bent over the side of the bed in two fast moves."

A fluttery sensation went all the way through Devlin, making him slump against the wall. His eyes on Gradyn, unable to break the desire for any kind of contact, he murmured, "God knows I'd let you."

Gradyn burned Devlin all the way through with the stare he delivered back. It looked as if he was going to push out of his chair but he abruptly sank back down and grabbed a white paper bag off the table. "Come and eat before I lose my better judgment and we test the resiliency of your ass after all. I bought us sandwiches." He withdrew two giant wax-paper-wrapped squares from the bag. "I hope that's okay. I didn't want to worry about food being cold by the time I got back."

"Yeah, that's fine." Devlin took a seat and folded his hands between his knees. His stomach still felt like it had a mass of excited butterflies flapping around inside it, and he offered a small smile. "Thanks."

"Ham or turkey?" Gradyn held up his left hand and then the right, one wrapped sandwich in each. "I noticed there was ground beef in the pasta sauce you ordered last night, so I didn't worry about picking something vegetarian."

"Ham is good." Devlin accepted the sandwich and a bottle

of cold water. "Thank you."

Gradyn stretched out his legs and trapped Devlin's between them, stilling a jittery tapping Devlin hadn't even realized he'd been doing.

"Stop saying thank you, beautiful," Gradyn said. "It's just a sandwich. It's not like I went out and bought you a car."

"Right." Devlin busied himself with unwrapping his sandwich and pressing the folds of the paper flat. "I'm sorry." As soon as those words left his mouth, he lifted his hand before Gradyn could say a word. "I don't mean 'I'm sorry' I'm sorry, like an apology. Those were the wrong words. It's just that you excite me and confuse me and make me nervous, but I also feel safe at the same time, and all of that going on inside me makes me fall back on manners and apologies out of habit because I don't always know what to say."

Devlin could see Gradyn hiding a smile behind taking a sip of water, and Devlin wanted to run back into the bathroom to hide. *Shit. Every time I open my mouth he sees how un-cool and inexperienced I am.* "Never mind," Devlin blurted. "I was just babbling and … whatever. Don't listen to me."

"It's all right," Gradyn said. "I think I followed what you were saying." He swirled the remaining water in his bottle and studied Devlin with an intensity that made Devlin's breath catch. "You're refreshingly open, Devlin." For just a second, something within Gradyn seemed to pull all the stark lines in his face to jutting prominence, and his jaw clenched visibly under the design of his tattoo. "You have no idea how attractive a quality that is to me."

Devlin swallowed down the sudden lump in his throat. "And now you've forced me into having to say thank you again." Sensing a subtle dark shift in Gradyn's demeanor, Devlin forced lightness into his voice and a smile to his lips. "After all, it would be rude of me not to."

Over the course of just a few seconds, every bit of tension eased from Gradyn's body, and the glint that had temporarily taken over his eyes dissipated. "Then I'll be equally polite and say you're welcome. Oh, before I forget," animation suddenly filled Gradyn's voice, "let me show you something." He put his sandwich down and got to his feet. "While I was out looking for a pair of jeans, some underwear, and a shirt, I passed by this big secondhand store that donates its proceeds to a local children's shelter. I decided to run in really fast to see if they would have anything decent that would fit me."

As he walked backward toward the closet, his step was almost a childlike skip. "Listen to this. It just so happens I stumbled into a favorite charity of the wives of the Forty-Niners. They donate all their husbands' clothes to this store. So," he reached into the closet and came out with what looked like a dry cleaning bag, "ta-da!" He tore white plastic covering off the hanger and revealed a charcoal-gray suit jacket. Hanging beneath the jacket was a matching pair of trousers. "Not only was I able to find a pair of jeans and a couple shirts that fit me, but now I can also wear a suit when I take you out later." He rushed over and held the suit in front of Devlin. "What do you think?"

I think I'm somehow half in love with you already. Devlin's chest hurt with that impossible truth. He stuffed the swell of improbable emotion deep down into his gut and soaked himself in Gradyn's sweet excitement instead. "You're going to look incredible in that color, Denny." The rich fabric lured Devlin to reach out and run the back of his hand down the front of the jacket. It was so finely woven Devlin barely resisted pulling it to his face to rub against his cheek. "It feels amazingly luxurious too. I can't wait to see you in it."

"The pants are a few inches too long but the waist is doable and the jacket is a perfect fit." Gradyn returned the suit to the closet and hung it up. "I figured a hundred bucks for a suit that probably cost close to a thousand was a good deal." After sitting down again, he took a bite of his sandwich and swallowed it down with a swig of water. "You know, I can't remember the last time I wore a suit. I guess if you do it every day as part of a job then it's not a big deal, but for someone like me, it's nice to feel like there's something worth getting cleaned up for every once in a while."

"I guess working with gang kids wouldn't be conducive to getting decked out in a suit and tie every day, huh?" Devlin suddenly sat up straight. "Or am I making an ignorant assumption by saying that?"

"Um," Gradyn scrubbed his hands over his scalp and down the back of his neck, "what I do doesn't often require that I wear a suit, no." He licked the edge of his lower lip and then pulled it between his teeth. "How about you? Any mandatory dress codes?"

"At the bookstore and coffee shop?" Devlin had told Gradyn about his two part-time jobs over dinner last night. "Nope, both places are pretty casual." He chewed down a bite of honey ham and swiss cheese with mayo while thinking about it some more. "I suppose I could suit up every day if I wanted to. I doubt the owners would care, but I'd stand out like a sore thumb."

"You don't talk about either of your jobs with a lot of passion." Gradyn's comment immediately shot a line of adrenaline into Devlin's bloodstream. "I know you said you took business courses, but you also more than hinted that they didn't get you juiced up." A long pause enveloped the room in a thick silence wherein Gradyn studied Devlin in a way that made Devlin feel sick to his stomach and hard behind his zipper at the same time.

"Is there something specific you want to do with your life, Devlin?" Gradyn asked, his tone making it sound like the most important question in the world. "I don't see you as a guy who wouldn't excel at something you loved. It makes me curious about what kind of job might really get you psyched to get out of bed every morning."

Think, Morgan, think. Oh right. Some of the knots building inside Devlin started to loosen, and he affected his easiest smile. "Do you mean after I got over my crushing disappointment that driving across the country in a cool Trans Am while eluding the law wasn't a real job?"

Water spat out of Gradyn's mouth with his bark of laughter. "What the hell are you talking about?" he asked as he wiped spittle off his chin.

Devlin started breathing normally again. "I'm talking about *Smokey and the Bandit.* I watched that movie with my brother and dad when we got our first VCR, and I thought the car in that movie, and driving it way faster than you're supposed to, was about the coolest thing in the world. I probably watched it at least a hundred times by the time I turned sixteen and got my learner's permit. Unfortunately, I've only ever owned a used Tempo and Corolla." He shrugged, and then took a bite out of the second half of his sandwich. "I guess I'm never gonna be the Bandit," he said around a mouthful of food.

"That's about the cutest damned thing I've ever heard, beautiful." The twinkle of humor left Gradyn's eyes with one blink, and the pinpoint focus of the man that remained made Devlin shiver. "It's also a nice way to make me forget about the question I asked. What do you want to do, Devlin?" His voice held command, and Devlin could not ignore the palpitations it incited in his core. "And why would you rather make me smile with a sweet story than talk about it?"

With difficulty, Devlin swallowed and finally forced down the ham and cheese lodged in his throat. "It's not that big a deal, really. I don't want to become an astronaut or the president or anything. It's just..." He'd never uttered his secrets to another soul in his life. "I think I want to be a firefighter."

"Okay. Not strange at all. So why aren't you?"

Having to share his reasons for staying away from that career was why Devlin had never allowed himself to talk about his dream. In this moment, he found he couldn't look away or shut down in any way with Gradyn Connell.

"My brother is a firefighter," Devlin exhaled an unsteady breath, "and I don't know if I want to be anything that he is."

Gradyn frowned, and furrow lines creased his brow. "I don't understand."

That's because it's stupid.

"Tell, me, beautiful," Gradyn pressed softly.

"My brother," Devlin found his lips moving and words spilling out of him in a way they never had before, "he's older. His name is Aidan, and he's the reason we had to move to Redemption, where I live now. We used to live in Texas, but Aidan got into a lot trouble there, so my parents moved us to Maine so Aidan could start fresh somewhere new." All these years later, Devlin still got cramps when he remembered staring out that plane window and watching everything he knew get smaller and smaller as they flew away. "I was ten and, God, I hated moving. I hated Aidan for being such a jerk that we had to move away from our cousins and friends and the school where I knew everybody, and all of them already knew me." Devlin looked at Gradyn without blinking and let his anger and eventual guilt from that time come back to the surface. "Back then, I couldn't understand that if we'd stayed in Texas Aidan probably would have ended up in juvenile detention, and maybe eventually much worse."

"That's serious stuff."

"Yeah." Devlin nodded. With the outreach type of work
Gradyn did, Devlin figured he was probably one of the few
people who could say those words and actually understand the
depths of trouble Aidan could have drowned in all those years
ago. "I didn't even want to look at Aidan let alone speak to him
for a long time after we moved. Eventually, I started to come
around. Aidan was nicer in Maine than he was in Texas. There
was a lot less yelling in our house. Aidan was home a lot more
too; he would come knock on my door and ask me if I wanted
to play a video game with him or shoot some hoops in the
backyard. It was finally like having a real big brother, when while
we were in Texas it was more like having this teenage stranger
living in our house." Devlin leaned his elbow on the table and
tapped his fingers against the smile forming on his lips. "Aidan
really did become a different person in Redemption," he said,
his voice softening with the nicer memory.

"I was so proud of Aidan when he graduated," Devlin went
on. "I was only twelve, but by then I understood how hard he'd
worked to change his life. Then the next day, he was gone, just
like that." Devlin slammed his hand on the table, creating a
resounding *crack*, all traces of sympathy gone from his voice.
In this motel room, Devlin's emotions ran a spectrum in just
minutes that had taken years to occur in real life. "He left a
note saying he was moving, and he said he would eventually
call, but that he was fine and not to go looking for him. He

didn't say goodbye to any of us or try to explain why he was going away. Shit," Devlin felt his mouth twist in a harsh line, "he didn't even tell his best friend. The guy came over that morning and I had to tell him Aidan was gone. Ethan -- that was his name -- was totally stunned. I could tell he didn't know a damned thing more than we did."

"His disappearance must have been a blow to all of you." Gradyn kept his voice gentle.

"Yeah. I remember feeling betrayed more than anything else," Devlin admitted for the first time. "Aidan eventually contacted my mom from Arizona. We have an uncle there and learned that Aidan had moved in with him. I don't know." Devlin's shoulders, neck, and back ached, and he realized he'd been holding his body tight, as if he needed to be ready to run at any moment. He rolled his neck and shoulders to work out the stiffness and then forced himself to sit back, his limbs loose. "Maybe I feel like if I become a firefighter then Aidan will think I'm doing it to be like him, and then that'll be like I'm saying I admire him or that the choices he made were okay and that it didn't hurt me like hell when he left." Devlin blinked away the burn of tears that wanted to fall. "It did. I *was* actually starting to want to be just like him when he suddenly went away. I thought he was really cool and smart and funny, and then he just up and left without even saying goodbye." A band constricted Devlin's chest today with as much power as it had that day, and his hand opened and clenched repeatedly at his side as he re-experienced the days, weeks -- hell -- months

188 | Cameron Dane

after Aidan disappeared. "I cried so much after he left; it made me feel like such a pussy little girl, and that only made me even madder at him for going."

Gradyn leaned across the table and pressed a kiss to Devlin's forehead. He held his lips to Devlin's skin, and also rubbed the back of Devlin's neck, working out the final kinks. "You're not ready to forgive him," Gradyn said, his voice brusque as he pulled away and took a seat again. "That's okay."

Devlin snapped his head up and homed right in on Gradyn. "What? No. I forgave Aidan a long time ago. My mom, Maddie, and I would go visit him in Arizona a couple of times a year after he left. We still do. My hesitation isn't about forgiving him."

"Then why are you so concerned he might think your becoming a firefighter is the same as saying to him the choice he made to leave was okay?"

"It's not." Devlin stopped cold. "Shit." New thoughts swirled in his brain like a tornado as Gradyn's blunt observation slammed smack into him. Devlin looked up, and he felt almost dizzy. "Maybe I haven't completely forgiven him."

"I'm not trying to tell you that you should forgive him. I don't know the guy at all to offer an opinion about it."

"No, Aidan is a good man now." Devlin spoke to Gradyn but felt almost like he was explaining this to *himself* for the first time. "He's been a firefighter since he moved away when he was eighteen. He never fell back into trouble with the law. Once he finally contacted us that first time, he always called me, Mom, and Maddie at least twice a month to see how we were doing. He still does," Devlin mused, "to this day."

"How old is your sister?" Gradyn asked.

"She's fifteen." As Devlin thought about Maddie, he shook his head and raised his brows Gradyn's way. "Going on about thirty."

"Oh." Gradyn's face fell into a combination of a wince and a grimace. "That could be worrisome."

"No no." Devlin swiped his hand across the surface of the table with a decided chop. "Not in *that* way. At least I don't think so. We got real close after Aidan moved away, so I think Maddie would tell me if she'd gone down that road already. God," he clenched his teeth, "she'd better not be having sex."

Gradyn went back to grinning behind his water bottle. "Now you sound like a father."

"Maybe." Devlin shrugged halfheartedly. "Our dad isn't really one for confiding important things to. It doesn't matter. I only meant that Maddie seems older because she is very organized and focused and knows how to make a plan to go after the things she wants. She's a good kid. I admire her a lot.

"Geez," Devlin suddenly muttered. The nature of everything he had revealed suddenly penetrated his brain and pulled him up short. "When did this become a Devlin Morgan therapy session? Enough about me. What about you?" Curiosity about this muscle-bound, inked man raised Devlin's blood to a buzzing simmer. "Do you love what you do?"

"Yeah," Gradyn answered immediately. "I love my job." He

fell silent then, and his mouth slowly flattened to a narrow slash. The tips of his fingers traced the lines where his tattoo edged his jaw down to his neck, perfectly skimming the ink pattern as if he had the design memorized. "It's tough, though, and it's lonely sometimes." The light in the room didn't change, but he turned his head just a hair and shadows concealed his eyes. "There aren't a lot of people to trust…" He looked and sounded a million miles away.

Devlin started to reach out, but Gradyn abruptly swung back to face Devlin, and that hint of melancholy Devlin had thought he'd seen and heard was gone. "Anyway," Gradyn said, "it's rewarding and I like it, but we'll have to shelve the rest of that conversation for another time. I have big plans for us today." He got up, yanked Devlin out of his seat, and started guiding him toward the bathroom. "If we're going to have time to visit a few places before we eat dinner then we have to shower and get ready to go. I'm all for doubling up and conserving water." He dipped down and skimmed his lips across Devlin's as he fumbled out of his flannel shirt. "How about you?"

Devlin helped Gradyn work his shirtsleeves over his wrists and then went for the man's belt. "Where are you taking me, Denny?" Between kisses, Devlin let the belt fall to the floor, and they stumbled into the bathroom together.

"You'll find out," Gradyn murmured, arousing Devlin with the rich texture of his voice. "I did a little asking around while I was out today, and think I heard about some interesting places. They're not fancy," he held Devlin's stare with the heat in his, "but I think you're a guy who would be cool with that."

"You do, huh?"

"Oh yeah." Gradyn kept his hand tangled in Devlin's hair; he tugged and tilted Devlin's head back, holding him in place. "Just like I think you'd do really well as a firefighter. You're strong and have good stamina and you're smart. And goddamn it," he whistled low as he openly took his visual fill, "you'd be amazing in the gear."

Devlin's insides hummed with Gradyn's words, making him feel as fucking giddy as a kid being chosen first for the kickball team in school. He hooked his fingers in Gradyn's open jeans and tugged him closer. "Would you like to fuck a firefighter?" With that question, Devlin shoved Gradyn's jeans and underwear down to his knees, revealing his thick, semi-erect cock.

Gradyn sucked on his lower lip as he looked Devlin up and down, and then glanced down as his prick grew some more. "If it was you," he licked over Devlin's jaw and cheek to whisper in his ear, "hell yeah, beautiful."

The man stuck his tongue in Devlin's ear, and Devlin gasped and sank his fingers into Gradyn's hips in reaction. "How about a bookstore clerk?" Devlin asked. Excitement and new power stripped his voice to raspy. "Would you press your face into the shower tiles and let a man who can show you where to find *The Ultimate Guide to Anal Sex for Men* fuck you under the warm spray of a shower?"

A shudder resonated within Gradyn. "I'm hard for him

already." He grabbed Devlin's hand, worked it in a snug squeeze down the rigid length of his cock, and scraped his teeth over the sensitive skin of Devlin's temple to his hairline. "Grab a condom and show me what you've got."

Thank you, God, for making me walk into that techno club.

Devlin spun Gradyn into the wall and covered him from behind. He leaned in and inhaled the natural musk that clung to this man's flesh, and his prick shot to full attention. Smiling against Gradyn's shoulder, Devlin reached back blindly and snagged his shaving kit off the counter.

He forced the black case into Gradyn's palm so he could shove his jeans down his legs. "Find what we need." Aroused as hell already, Devlin rocked his erection slowly back and forth between the hills of Gradyn's ass.

"Mmm… Yeah." Sounding breathless, his cheek plastered to the wall, Gradyn fumbled with the small leather bag. "Here." He pushed a travel tube of lube and a condom into Devlin's hand. "Hurry."

Using his teeth, Devlin pried open the plastic cap. "Maybe we won't make it into the shower quite yet after all."

Gradyn's chuckle turned into a low, stunningly arousing moan as Devlin cupped the man's balls, rubbed slick lube into the crease of his fine ass, and fingered his hole…

———

…The blast of a horn jerked Devlin back into his car in his apartment building's parking lot. He darted his attention all around, didn't see anyone, and belatedly realized he had his hands wrapped around the center of his steering wheel and that he was the one honking a horn.

Good God. Devlin rolled his eyes at his sappy mentality as he climbed out of his car and pocketed his keys. *You never could stop thinking about that weekend, even when you didn't have the very man in your hometown.*

That had been one amazing Saturday. After taking Gradyn -- *Garrick* -- against the bathroom wall, to the most incredible cries from Garrick urging him on, Devlin did finally drag Garrick into the shower and clean him up. Afterward, Devlin remembered Garrick standing behind him in front of the bathroom mirror and knotting his tie from over Devlin's shoulders, and then Devlin turning around and tying Garrick's for him. Devlin had been right. The man had looked stunning in his new-used suit.

Garrick had treated Devlin to an afternoon at a little museum that showcased cartoon art. Then he'd taken Devlin to a park to enjoy a free outdoor concert. They didn't have a blanket to sit on, and there wasn't an empty square of bench in sight, but it hadn't mattered. They'd just wandered along the paths listening to the music rather than watching the musicians play. Finally, they caught another cable car to an awesome family-style restaurant. They'd had to wait close to an hour to get a table, and not a single other person in the place was dressed up like Devlin and Garrick were, but it hadn't bothered them because the food was beyond delicious and the people were friendly. Devlin got to sit across from Garrick and just bask in his company and enjoy the atmosphere.

Then it was back to the motel. Into their cocoon again. They'd stripped down to just their underwear, crawled into bed, and watched some horrible comedy movie. They laughed at every lame joke and then got quiet and held hands when the guy, of course, got the girl in the end. Without a word, Garrick had turned off the TV and fucked Devlin with a slow, raw intensity that had felt dangerously close to what Devlin imagined making love must feel like. Garrick had stayed inside Devlin for a long time afterward, and had even made Devlin come a second time without either of them ever moving. When they finally did separate, they cleaned up together, again, without any conversation, and tucked right back into bed, sharing the dip in the center as they fell asleep.

The perfect night.

Even sitting side-by-side in the cable car that night, as they went from one destination to another, being with Garrick, had made the day and evening enchanted and special.

Garrick. He's slowly becoming Garrick to me now. Even in my memories.

That special day today -- like that Saturday back in San Francisco -- was what changed everything for us.

Devlin's heart lurched as he exited the stairwell and headed for his apartment. He recalled how special Shawn and Chloe thought Garrick was too, and how very clearly Garrick adored them.

I don't know --

"Devlin, hi." A familiar voice stopped Devlin in his tracks. "No wonder you're not answering your door. You're not inside."

Oh no. Devlin's heart plummeted for a second time in less than a minute. "Darren, hi." Devlin raced to where the man stood at his door, and shoved his key into the bolt lock. "I apologize. I got caught up in my own head and lost track of time." He clicked the second lock open and kicked the door wide.

"And I had to cancel on you yesterday, so I guess we're even." The blond grabbed Devlin's shoulders and studied him through a narrowed gaze. "Where have you been? You look like you've been running a marathon or something. Never mind. Go shower and change. Go. Go. Go." Darren walked inside, flopped down onto the couch, and grabbed the remote. "I'll find something on TV to entertain me while you get ready."

Shit. Damn. Fuck. Devlin looked at the impeccably dressed younger man. The guy was so attractive, and Devlin could see that he would be incredible out of his clothes. Devlin stared, but Darren's body registered as nothing more in Devlin's head, heart, or cock than a catalogue of lovely male features. *What am I supposed to do?*

Darren popped up from the sofa and turned Devlin around one hundred and eighty degrees. "Get moving, Dev." He slapped Devlin on the ass in a way that nudged him toward his bedroom. "You promised me pizza, and I'm starving."

"Okay." Devlin plodded to his bedroom. "Give me fifteen

minutes and I'll be ready to go."

Before Devlin shut his door, he lingered on the image of the sexy young thing relaxing on his couch. Not until it morphed into a dark-haired guy, frantic over a little boy possibly getting burned, did the unease within Devlin dissipate and allow him to breathe freely.

It ultimately didn't matter what choice Garrick made; tonight, Devlin knew what he had to do.

CHAPTER EIGHT

Dusk settled over Crawford Street, and the chirping songs of crickets in hiding danced across the air. From his position sitting on the top porch step, Garrick looked over his shoulder as Grace stepped out of the house.

"Chloe is across the street at Shelby's," he shared, as soon as she made eye contact. "She asked me for permission. I figured you'd be okay with it, so I told her to go ahead."

"That's fine." Grace ran her hands through her hair and let out an audible breath. "Thank you for keeping an eye on her."

"You know it's my pleasure." Garrick's thoughts immediately raced back to the other kid somewhere inside this house. He gave Grace a moment to sit down next to him and then somehow managed to talk through his held breath. "How'd it go with Shawn?" Garrick had told Grace about Chloe's concerns … as well as about his being gay.

Just let that little boy be okay. I'll live with anything else that comes.

"Shawn is feeling like he wants to play by himself for a little while right now," Grace said. "But he'll be okay. He's not mad at you; he doesn't hate you." She gave his knee a quick squeeze. "Don't worry about that."

Garrick's throat grew tighter, and he felt his mouth pull down at the edges. "I don't care about me. He can hate me if he wants, as long as he's all right."

"Shawn is resilient, Garrick. Chloe is too. He's definitely bummed out; I won't lie about that. Shoot," she reached a step down and grabbed one of the boy's little action figures, "he thinks you're Batman, Superman, and Wolverine all rolled into one." After straightening the toy's plastic legs, Grace balanced it on the porch between them. "What kid wouldn't wish a guy like that could be his dad?"

"Motherfucking shit." Garrick's lungs burned a line right up through his esophagus, and he felt like he might hyperventilate. He'd never been important to someone who *needed* him in exactly this way. He'd never mattered to an impressionable sponge-like kid. With a sharp as a tack sister too. "Motherfucking shit."

"Don't lose your cool on me." Grace's words held the same even tone she often used to keep her kids in line. "I told Shawn the next best thing is having an awesome guy like that as a friend, and that your being his friend isn't going to change. I promised him you weren't going anywhere, and that just like before, all he has to do is go knock on your door if he wants to hang out. Nothing has changed." She put her chin in her hand and pierced Garrick right through with one steady look. "Was I right in telling him that?"

A pitter-patter sensation grew in Garrick's chest, paining him and kicking up his heart rate as he recalled his frantic urgency to hightail it out of town.

You hadn't spent almost an entire day with Devlin when you were packing your bags last night. Hadn't had an adult conversation with an eleven-year-old, wise young woman either.

Garrick scrubbed his face, and with one sentence, sealed his fate. "I'm not going anywhere."

"Good."

The scratch in Chloe's voice as she'd talked about moving all the time reverberated in Garrick's head, and he studied Grace just as hard as she did him. "How about you?"

She stayed quiet for an eternal heartbeat, first looking at him, and then letting her attention wander the houses surrounding them, before coming back to him. "Don't much feel like packing up the car and moving again. I'm tired. Ready to stop."

"Me too." Garrick wondered about her story but figured she had just as much a right to privacy and a chance to start over as he did. Probably more.

Grace rested her head in her hand, and Garrick could feel

her checking him out from the corner of her eye. She suddenly smiled and laughed in a way that lit up her whole face. "So what freaked you out more?" she asked, turning fully to face him. "That Shawn was starting to see you as a father? Or that you took the next step in your head and worried that meant I was starting to see you as a potential husband?"

"What? I didn't…" *Fuck.* "Maybe I did for a second." A heavy ache sat like lead in Garrick's gut, weighing on him with a pain he could not ignore. "I worried more that you might not want me around your children anymore when you found out I was gay."

"Got news for you, Langley. I already knew you were gay." Grace covered his mouth before he could protest. "Let me clarify," she said as she took her hand away. "I suspected you might be."

"No way." Garrick's blood rushed too fast, making him feel unsteady. "You've never even hinted that you thought I might be."

She shrugged. "I figured you might be in the closet. It wasn't my place to ask."

Garrick sucked in a breath that burned his throat and lungs, and his hand shook as he held it against his mouth. "I tried not to think about it," he said, the words muffled. "I don't think I even realized how scared I was until my talk with Chloe today. You can never be sure how people will react."

"Look at me, Garrick." Grace paused, waiting him out in silence until he pulled his head out of hiding. When he did, she offered him a small smile. "I am tired a lot and it shows on my face, I'll admit that. But if there's one thing I can count on with a heterosexual man, it's that he's going to look at my breasts." She raised a brow, and her lips twisted as she added, "And that he's going to stare more than once. I don't dress provocatively but I can't hide my shape or that my size is noticeably above average. You gave my breasts a cursory glance when you first came to look at the garage apartment, and your gaze hasn't drifted back to my chest since. I figured you were gay or asexual. Either way, I knew you weren't interested in me physically."

"Motherfucking shit." Garrick couldn't seem to pull more than that one phrase from his vocabulary.

"It has been nice having a guy around without having to worry about fending off moves." Grace curled her hand around his forearm, warming his skin with her touch. She didn't break eye contact as she spoke. "I'm not worried about you and my kids, Garrick. I'm grateful for your patience with them, especially Shawnee, and that you care about them and want to be in their lives."

"I do." He blinked and blinked and blinked, and could not fucking believe he was fighting the pressure of tears threatening to fall. "Yours too, Grace. I like you, and in a short amount of time, you've become one of the most solid friends I've ever had. It's just not a sexual interest." *Christ, I can't believe not ogling her boobs gave me away.* "For what was to you an apparently obvious reason."

"What was obvious to me was that you didn't want that

guy to leave earlier."

Garrick chuckled, the sound husky. "I'm that far gone, huh?" He wiped his eyes to make sure everything was still dry. "It didn't take your daughter more than a few hours to pick up on it either."

"And what about the guy?" Grace asked. "Devlin. Is he aware you have feelings for him?"

"It's complicated."

"You're a smart guy. Find a way to make it simple."

Garrick couldn't control the grin or burst of pride that took him over whenever he thought about Devlin. "He's smart, and he makes me laugh, and I don't think I've ever met anyone sweeter. And he's sexy too." He could feel himself blushing like a fool and didn't care. "Isn't he?"

Grace nodded and smiled back at him. "He definitely has something that makes you look twice. You're no slouch yourself, though, mister. Could use a haircut, maybe." She pushed strands that had come loose of his elastic band behind his ear. "But other than that, very attractive. If it wasn't for my daughter, I'd say you have the prettiest blue eyes I've ever seen."

Garrick plummeted. *Yet another thing that isn't real. Something else that isn't the same as the man Devlin found so attractive in San Francisco. I don't even have my name anymore. My career. An identity that I can claim truly belongs to me.*

He wavered, and his shoulder hit the porch railing as the yard swam in front of his eyes. "I don't have anything to give him."

Garrick hadn't even realized he'd spoken aloud until Grace rubbed his shoulder. He turned to her, and sympathy filled her gaze. "Give him you," she said. "Believe me, I've learned the hard way that everything else is just noise."

He opened his mouth, curious once again about where quiet wisdom like that came from, when that buzz of awareness simmered under his skin again. Garrick glanced into the oncoming darkness of night beyond the front yard, finding it hard to see in the shadows. Instinct said to shoot to his feet and do a thorough search of the neighborhood, but then the softest scuffing noise pricked his ear, and Garrick whipped his head around to look behind him.

Shawn stood on the other side of the screen door, Transformer in hand.

"Jesus, buddy." Garrick pressed his hand to his heart, as if that would control its speeding pace. "You're getting as quiet as a ninja."

The boy perked up straight. "Yeah?"

"Definitely."

"I didn't hear you one bit, sweetie," Grace added.

"Cool." The kid none-too-gently kicked the screen door open and stepped outside. "I'm hungry. Can we have pizza?"

"Good idea," Grace said. "I don't feel like lifting a finger to cook tonight. Shawnee, bring me the phone."

"No, wait." Garrick stalled the boy with a hand to his arm, but looked to Grace. "Why don't Shawn and I go pick something up?" He needed some time with the kid to not only assure Shawn they were okay but to make sure they were still cool for himself.

"Please, Mom?" Shawn grabbed Garrick's shoulder, nodding while he jumped up and down like a baby bird trying to achieve flight.

Grace exchanged a *see-I-told-you-so* look with Garrick. "I guess I don't have to ask him what he thinks," Grace said. She shifted her attention to her son. "Bring me my purse instead, baby."

Garrick touched her hand. "I have it covered."

"Thank you. That's very sweet, but I'm actually talking about the fact that you need to drive my car. Shawn still has to sit in the backseat." She turned Shawn in the direction of the front door and gave him a little swat on the tush. "Get going."

Shawn tore into the house, and Garrick looked back to Grace, stricken. "I swear I would have remembered that the second I went to put him in the passenger seat of my truck. We were going to take Devlin's car for our ice cream run earlier. I promise."

"Relax. I believe you."

Garrick reined in his burst of nervous panic just as Shawn busted out of the house with an enormous black purse dragging from his shoulder. "Here you go, Mommy."

"Thank you, sweetheart." Grace pecked a kiss to her son's cheek, undid the keys from a metal loop holding the strap, and dropped them in Garrick's hand. "Have fun, you two."

I can do this. Grace is right. It's no different than what I've been doing for a month already.

One look at Shawn, seeing the excitement vibrating through the boy over such a small excursion, and everything shifted into place inside Garrick, calming him.

I need him. Them. Chloe and Grace too, just as much as they need me.

His heart constricted as a picture of Devlin flashed in his mind.

Hopefully he will understand.

Shaking off that uncertainty, Garrick pointed over his shoulders to his back. "Climb on, kid. Let's go."

As soon as Shawn latched on securely for a piggyback ride, Garrick loped down the steps, laughing as Shawn egged him on to go faster.

———

GARRICK KEPT TIGHT HOLD OF Shawn's hand as they jogged across the parking lot to the restaurant's entrance. "Watch your step." He pointed at the sidewalk lip a foot ahead.

Shawn made an exaggerated leap onto the raised brick walkway. "Can I get a dessert while we're waiting?"

"Ah, how about you can pick a dessert to take back to the house for later?"

"Maaaaannn." Shawn tugged against Garrick's hold. "I want to eat it now."

"Not gonna happen." Garrick sympathized; he remembered wanting sweets as a first, second, and third course, but he would lose points with Grace -- not to mention Chloe for shortchanging her a pre-meal treat -- if he caved. "You can pick something for your sister and your mom, though." Garrick murmured an "Excuse me" to a small group milling in front of the door, then pulled Shawn in front of him, keeping the boy close as they entered the restaurant. "But you have to pick ones you think they'll like," he added as soon as they were inside. "I think I'll know if you're trying to pick three for yourself."

"Chloe likes anything chocolate."

"All right. What about your mom?"

"She likes stuff with fruit. She makes lemon bars a lot."

Garrick took a moment to explain to the hostess that they just wanted to place a To-Go order, but that with the little one with him Garrick didn't want to sit at the bar to wait. The place had the best pizza in town, but it also boasted the largest variety of beer on tap, and it drew a bar crowd on weekends just for that. It was a little early in the evening for anything too boisterous but the noise level and potential conversations would still be too much for the ears of a six-year-old.

The hostess handed Garrick a couple of menus and guided them to a small round table with tall-leg chairs that just skirted the area between the bar and the restaurant. They had already decided on their pizza topping choices on the car ride over, so Garrick went ahead and placed that order with a request that the hostess return in a few minutes after they had a chance to look over the dessert menu.

Shawn swiveled one way in his barstool, wide-eyed, and

then slowly circled in the other direction, his focus traveling the area of the restaurant.

"Never been here before, huh?" Garrick asked, biting down a chuckle.

"Uh-uh." The boy's shaggy blond hair swished into his eyes as he shook his head. "It's big. Look at all the stuff everywhere. Is that a real boat?" He pointed to the center of the wall on the other side of the room, in which it looked like the front end of an old ship with a mermaid figure attached to the hull protruded from the wall.

Garrick covered Shawn's hand and brought it back down to the table. "I don't know," he replied. "We'll have to ask the hostess when she comes to take our dessert order. Let's decide what we want so we'll be ready when she returns."

He discovered Shawn didn't yet have the reading skills to decipher a menu that didn't have pictures, so he pulled the boy's chair closer, put their heads together, and between them came up with desserts for everybody. The hostess swung back by their table to give them an ETA on their pizza, and Garrick relayed the rest of their order, as well as went ahead and gave her a tip as a thank you for letting them have a table while they waited.

"Your son is a cutie." The young woman winked at Shawn and bumped his fist. "I couldn't say no to him. A server will be out with your food soon, and he'll take care of your tab. Ya'll have a good night."

Garrick watched Shawn suck his lower lip between his

teeth, and his heart dropped like a fifty-pound dumbbell straight into his stomach.

"You okay?" Garrick asked, his voice low. He kept a steady eye on Shawn, searching for a second quiver in his lip or a tear he might try to hide. "With what that girl just said, knowing what your mom talked to you about earlier?"

Shawn suddenly focused intently on his Transformer, and his little eyebrows pulled together. "You don't love my mom the way dads are supposed to love moms, and Mommy said she doesn't like you that way either, so you won't live in our house." He chewed some more on his lip but eventually looked up at Garrick again. "But she said you still like me the way other dads like their kids, only you're not my dad so I call you Garrick."

"That's true." Garrick treaded carefully for Shawn's sake, but the truth was, he thought it might crush him more than it would the freaking kid if he got shot down. "Are you okay with that?"

"I might feel better if you let me eat my strawberry cake first."

All the tension drained out of Garrick into a puddle on the floor, and he fell back against his chair. "Nice try, Shawnee. I don't think so."

"Maaannn." Shawn pulled the most petulant face. "That sucks."

Resilient. Garrick had to laugh. *Grace definitely knows her children well.*

A young man carrying a large paper bag and two pizza boxes stopped at their table. "Okay, guys." He put everything down. "Here we go."

He handed the bill to Garrick, and Garrick pulled the appropriate amount from his wallet. After handing the money to the guy, he added, "Keep the change."

Garrick assessed the overlarge bag with their desserts and garlic bread and then shifted to study the extra large pizza boxes. "All right, how are we going to do this?" He'd never wondered how a parent held onto children and packages and navigated public spaces with large vehicles pulling in and out and driving around at the same time.

"I can carry the bag," Shawn said.

"Shawn, the thing is half as big as you are," Garrick told him. "You're not quite tall enough to keep it off the ground. And it's dark out; there's no way I'm letting you walk outside without holding my hand." The pizza boxes were much too large for the kid to handle too. "Here's what we're going to do." Garrick lifted Shawn into his arms and situated him on his hip. "Hold on tight, please." The boy squeezed his legs around Garrick's stomach and his arms around his neck. "That's plenty. Thank you."

Garrick then maneuvered the pizza boxes onto his free hand and finally grabbed the bag's handle while using that arm to anchor Shawn to him. "Ready?" The boy nodded, and Garrick started to wind his way through the tables to some strange looks coming at him from left and right. "I suppose

I could have just asked for help, huh?" he asked with a laugh. "That's probably what your mom does."

"Nah." Shawn pounded Garrick's shoulder with his hand, giggling. "This is more fun."

"For you, sure." Garrick looked at the boy sideways and raised one eyebrow in an extremely exaggerated manner. "I'm the one doing all the heavy lifting. It's like a ride at Disneyland for y…" Garrick skidded to a halt.

Straight ahead, Devlin entered the restaurant. And the guy wasn't alone. He had a wildly attractive younger man at his side. Garrick couldn't process any more than that because right then Devlin laughed at something the guy said, and it crushed Garrick's soul.

"Garrick, look at Devlin!" Shawn shouted right into Garrick's ear.

Clearly having heard Shawn say his name, Devlin snapped his attention up to them, locking on Garrick.

"Hey," Shawn nudged Garrick, "who's that other man?"

"I don't know." The ringing echoing in Garrick's head from the volume of Shawn's voice couldn't compete with the slamming in his heart and the difficulty he suddenly had breathing. He knew he shouldn't stare but he couldn't blink or turn his head. Devlin didn't either.

He's on a date. He went out on his date. He's fucking spending the evening with another man.

"Devlin! Devlin!" Shawn let go of Garrick's neck for a second and waved wildly.

Devlin whispered something to his partner for the evening; the guy nodded and took a step to the side while Devlin approached. Devlin slipped his hands into his pockets, and smiled at the boy. "Hi, Shawn. It's good to see you again."

The kid bounced against Garrick's side. "I talked to my mom!"

If Garrick had a free hand, he would have rubbed his ear. "Take it down a couple of notches, kiddo. All right?"

"Sorry." Shawn dropped his voice to a whisper. "I talked to my mom. She said since you know Garrick that it would be okay to go see the fire trucks with you as long as he's there too."

"Right," Devlin murmured. He lifted his gaze to Garrick's, glanced back and forth between him and Shawn, and Garrick watched his lips pale and his throat convulse.

Oh no. No no no no no. It's not what you think.

Garrick went to grab Devlin but remembered he had too much going on to make it happen. "Wait," he said instead.

Devlin shook his head. "It's all right. I understand." Garrick could hear the strain in Devlin's voice. Then Devlin put his full attention on Shawn, and covered every tumultuous emotion with a smile. "I haven't had a chance to talk to the chief yet, Shawn, but I'll be sure to get in touch with him very soon. Sound good?"

Shawn beamed. "Cool."

"Cool." Devlin's smile back looked forced.

Sick to his stomach, Garrick felt gagged and tied. "Cool," he said dully, all polish gone from both good patches of this day.

Devlin looked to his date a dozen feet away and held up one finger. The blond smiled and nodded, and Devlin turned back to them. "Can you do me a favor?" Devlin directed his question to Shawn. "Will you cover your ears and hum Spiderman's music for just a minute? I have to say something private to Garrick."

"'Kay." Shawn let go of Garrick's shoulder and clamped his hands to his ears. "*Spiderman, Spiderman...*"

Garrick beseeched, damn it, he fucking begged Devlin with his eyes. "Devlin, listen to me."

"Please don't." The sharp sting in Devlin's tone shut Garrick up. Devlin then glanced at Shawn, and his entire face softened. He moved to Garrick's side, and he leaned in, speaking softly in Garrick's ear. "He looks right in your arms. Like he's supposed to be there." Devlin shifted, and the tips of his fingers lingered against Garrick's hip. "When we talked that whole night on the phone, I remember you telling me how badly you wished you had a father. I could feel your pain even though we were three thousand miles apart. I understand your choice." Lips brushed with shivery softness against the skin behind Garrick's ear. "Goodbye," Devlin whispered. Before Garrick could find his brain and utter a word, Devlin pulled Shawn's hands from his ears, said goodnight to him too, and joined his date.

"But..." Garrick spun. The pizzas burning his hand tilted, and another patron grabbed them, righting them before they fell.

Garrick thanked the man, but he was still half focused on Devlin and the cute-as-hell blond being shown to a table. He just knew by looking at him that Devlin's date would be one hell of an enthusiastic bottom. Garrick ached to put everything down, chase after Devlin, explain everything, and promise to bend over for him forever, if that's what he now wanted.

Instead, Shawn poked him in the shoulder and pointed out that the nice man who had saved their pizzas from disaster now stood holding the door open for them. Garrick noticed Shawn chewing on his lip again in that way he did when he got nervous, and Garrick knew he wasn't doing anything but going home and eating pizza -- as he'd promised.

CHAPTER NINE

Garrick tore into the garage apartment three hours later still ready to rip something apart. He'd kept a lid on everything through dinner and a kiddie movie, and even managed to focus on Shawn and Chloe's friendly bickering for a little while, but the second their eyes started drooping from their busy day, Garrick excused himself, and everything flooded back to him in a torrent.

Devlin. And his date.

He couldn't believe Devlin would still go on that date after the day they'd shared together. And to give up on them as a couple, just like that? To turn Garrick over to the Fine family as if Devlin and Garrick hadn't shared the most incredible intimacy two people possibly can?

214

And Garrick wasn't talking about all the fucking they'd done in San Francisco either.

Not that the sex itself that weekend hadn't shifted from a hook-up designed to relieve an itch into an act Garrick could honestly swear he'd never done with anyone else. He'd lost himself not only in the stunning male body, but in the man himself, and Garrick had never let that happen with any person before Devlin. Shit, he hadn't intended it to happen with Devlin either, but from the moment Devlin's sweet, nervous energy had taken over that cheap motel room, Garrick had found himself drowning in a place from which he did not want to be saved.

Now he's out with another man. Maybe falling into bed with him too.

"No way." Garrick growled and paced his apartment, a living space not much larger than that motel room he would never forget. He clenched his hands into fists again and again, trying to contain the desire to maim one hot young blond with a sweet behind.

Better not be tapping that pretty ass tonight, beautiful, or any other while I'm still breathing.

Garrick groaned, slipping back to the last time he and Devlin Morgan had made love…

———

…Gradyn ignored the band tightening his chest as he folded his flannel shirt and set it on top of his other dirty clothes in a plastic bag.

Almost time to say goodbye to him. Don't be a wuss about it when it happens either.

He listened to the water running in the bathroom and didn't have to turn around to know steam would be pouring out of the half-closed door. Gradyn couldn't believe how much in just forty-eight hours together he'd gotten used to having another person underfoot. Someone his gut said was one of the good ones, a person worthy of trust.

Someone easy to love.

Gradyn fell into a chair and buried his face in his hands. "Don't even think about that, Denny." He spoke the denial aloud a second time, determined to force it down his throat and into his brain, into the cold light of reality. He had to talk himself out of envisioning a future with this man, especially since he didn't even know what his own life would bring tomorrow.

My normal life again, maybe. Definitely no more living with looking over my shoulder. At least for a while. No more daily lifting weights either. Gradyn looked up and caught his tattooed, menacing reflection in the mirror. *In time, hopefully no more image looking back at me that I've had for so long now I can't remember if it's the real me or not half the time anymore.*

I won't have Devlin anymore, that's for sure.

Gradyn's insides coiled tight on that thought, and his mind gutted him with fast-moving pictures of Devlin in Gradyn's bed at home or sitting at his side at his friend Jimmy's annual barbecue that Gradyn always attended alone. Gradyn moaned and turned in his chair, as if facing away from the mirror could stop the barrage of images tormenting and tempting him with scenarios he could not let be.

Devlin deserves the world. And I can't give him that. Not right now. Maybe never.

Christ, his job wasn't even technically complete yet. Just because they had Kressley and most of his people behind bars right now didn't mean Gradyn wouldn't have to go back inside the motorcycle club if some aspect of the case went to shit and that butchering, human-trafficking SOB Kressley got released on a technicality. Gradyn didn't fool himself that a weekend pass as part of a job well done meant he was actually free of this case that had eaten up the last two years of his life.

Fucking might never get the full stink of it off me.

"You look far away, Denny." The sound of Devlin's voice pulled Gradyn back into the motel room. He shifted, lured by the gentleness of it, and found Devlin leaning against the bathroom door frame, still glistening from his shower, wearing nothing but a towel.

Good Christ. Gradyn's breath caught in his throat. *You're everything I need right now.*

"Are you okay?" Devlin asked.

Gradyn forced an easy smile. "Just listening to the water and picturing you naked in the shower."

Devlin stayed where he was, watching Gradyn so intently that Gradyn's skin heated and tightened under his clothes.

Furrow lines appeared between Devlin's brows, and he softly said, "I don't think so."

Please don't make me outright lie to you, Devlin. "Let's just say I was, okay?"

It took a moment, but Devlin eventually nodded. "If that's what you want."

With an uneven, deep breath, Gradyn held out his hand. "Come here, beautiful."

Devlin moved to Gradyn with an easy grace and fluidity that defied the jittery, untried enthusiasm he'd exhibited just two nights ago. Gradyn swallowed hard as he took in the taut, tanned skin encasing perfectly defined muscles that didn't tend toward too lean or too thick. Gradyn could happily kiss and nibble on Devlin's chest and down to his flat stomach for years and not grow bored with it or what that narrow line of hair led to below the towel.

The body was damned amazing but it was Devlin's eyes that did Gradyn in. Holy Mother, Devlin's pale stare, that didn't waver under the scrutiny of a much larger man, and in fact held Gradyn locked in place right now, sucked Gradyn into a place in which he would happily drown.

"Jesus." Falling fast, Gradyn tore off his shirt and tossed it aside. He then captured Devlin's hand and drew the younger man between his spread legs. "I can't walk away while we still have an hour on the clock before you have to go." He splayed his hand across Devlin's stomach and trembled when he felt it quiver under his palm. His pinky finger caught on the damp towel knotted around Devlin's waist. Gradyn wanted to tear the white terrycloth aside to get at more of that wonderful warm skin, but their activities of the past two days nagged at his conscience. He commanded his hand not to move, and looked up into those mesmerizing gray eyes. "Can you take me one more time?"

"Yeah." Devlin swayed into Gradyn's open palm, pressing with his weight. He stared down, his eyes full of languid lust. His cock jutted, tenting the towel. "If you go slow."

"Baby," Gradyn slid his arms around Devlin's waist and tugged him closer, "we can set whatever pace you want." He pressed his face to Devlin's stomach, closing his eyes as he inhaled the mingling scents of woodsy shower gel and a natural spicy musk that was purely Devlin. Blindly, Gradyn rubbed his cheeks, forehead, and nose across Devlin's skin, sipping at droplets of moisture still clinging to the man from his shower.

With every nip and taste he took, Gradyn's prick thickened and pushed harder against the confinement of his jeans. He clung to Devlin, digging his fingers into the man's back as he sucked on the firm skin above his hipbone and pulled blood to the surface. *I could feast on him forever.*

Needing more, he turned Devlin to the side and bit his way around his waist to the small of his back, leaving red tracks in his wake. Gradyn swirled his tongue into the dip at the base of Devlin's spine and then teased down to the line of the towel, suckling right above the cleft of Devlin's ass. The man whimpered and pushed back for more, but Gradyn licked the other way instead, up Devlin's spine as far as he could go without standing, and pushed his hands under Devlin's arms to his chest. He scraped across Devlin's nipples with his trimmed-to-the-nub fingernails, quickly stiffening the peaks to tiny eraser points.

"Ohhhh shit…" Devlin covered Gradyn's hands and helped him scratch deeper welts into his flesh. "So fucking hard already." He shoved one of Gradyn's hands under the towel to his cock, knocking the fabric to the floor.

Scorching heat seared Gradyn's palm at first contact, but he welcomed the fire; he wrapped his hand firmly around Devlin's swollen penis and pumped the full, rigid length. Devlin hissed and jerked his hips, and Gradyn reached with his middle finger to smear the early pearls of cum Devlin released. Devlin let out a needful little hum and pushed Gradyn's other hand down to join the first, bypassing his cock and curling Gradyn's fingers around his heavy sac.

Oh yeah, he's already primed to shoot.

Gradyn delivered what he knew was an agonizingly slow pull and too-soft rub to Devlin's prick and nuts, and made the man standing in front of him moan and writhe like crazy. Gradyn couldn't stop the grin he stamped against the small of Devlin's back … or from slipping two fingers further between his legs to tease the sensitive patch of his taint.

"Oh God, Denny…" Devlin gasped as if someone had stolen all the oxygen from the room. "So good." He pushed Gradyn's hands away, and then spun around, putting his erection in front of Gradyn's face. "Suck me." Looking down through eyes like mirrored glass, Devlin took his cock in hand and guided it to Gradyn's mouth. "Please."

The smell of precum took over Gradyn's nose and had him growling. A bead formed on the tip of Devlin's cock, right in front of Gradyn's eyes. Gradyn darted out his tongue, savoring the faintly bitter drop with a lick across Devlin's slit. Devlin moaned and rubbed the moist head over Gradyn's lips, cheeks, and chin, leaving streaks of slick heat, and in doing so toyed with what little restraint Gradyn had left in him.

Devlin slid his penis over Gradyn's lips again, lingering. This time, Gradyn opened wide and sucked almost half the stiff length down in one swoop. Hot, throbbing flesh burned Gradyn's tongue, cheeks, and roof of his mouth, but he just relaxed his jaw and went down for more, swallowing as much of Devlin as he could take.

As he neared getting Devlin to his throat, Gradyn slowed, working diligently to get the extra length and thickness into his mouth. Once he got there, stuffed so fucking full, Gradyn grasped onto Devlin's hips, held him in place, and sucked in his cheeks for all he was worth. He dragged all the way up Devlin's shaft and then filled his mouth to the brim with hard cock again as fast as he could, swished his tongue back and forth on the sensitive underside, and pulled up with every bit of suction in him a second time.

"Shit ... shit." Devlin stared down as Gradyn sucked him off. He sank his fingers into Gradyn's scalp, and his beautiful face twisted to stark, harsh lines. "Fuck, you're gonna suck me inside out."

Gradyn spat Devlin out and looked right into his eyes. "Don't warn me." Gradyn's entire body hummed as his world slipped to a place of pure lust. "Come wherever you want when you can't hold back."

Not waiting, Gradyn licked down the underside of Devlin's cock, latched onto one of his balls, and sucked it into his mouth. He tongued and tugged gently while continuing to tease his fingers ever-more-closely toward Devlin's asshole, to the man's moans of encouragement and delight. Gradyn murmured around his mouthful of nut, gave the smooth, hot orb one more swirl with his tongue, let it go with a wet *pop*, and eased the other into his mouth for similar ministrations. He sucked and breathed in the scent of aroused man, and rubbed the pad of his middle finger over the star pattern of Devlin's tight pucker. Gradyn loved feeling the contractions of the small muscle as Devlin relearned the intimate contact, and he savored the moment of power and victory when the man finally whimpered and pushed down against the digit playing with his asshole.

Gradyn tongued Devlin's sac one last time, and withdrew his finger without penetrating Devlin's ass.

Devlin cried out and tried to force Gradyn's head back to his balls and hand back to his snug entrance. "Please..." He ground himself into Gradyn's face and fingers.

Gradyn grunted and bit the inside of Devlin's thigh. He

licked deeper between Devlin's legs, not stopping until he found the tangle of their hands; he anointed Devlin's fingers with saliva. With a quick move, Gradyn then reversed the hold between Devlin's legs, reaching from behind instead, and forced Devlin's own finger against his hole, with Gradyn holding it there.

Devlin shuddered. "Oh God."

Gradyn kissed his way backward until he had his lips poised once again at the head of Devlin's cock, and then looked up into his lover's eyes. "Help yourself, baby." Gradyn pressed against the back of Devlin's hand, nudging Devlin's ring. "Let me feel you do it."

The flare in Devlin's pupils told Gradyn everything he needed to know. *He's never fingered himself before. He's unsure.* Gradyn held frozen, for just a couple of heartbeats, as Devlin stood locked before him statue-still.

His chest hurting again, Gradyn pecked a kiss to Devlin's cock. "Whenever you're ready, beautiful." He kept his hand on top of Devlin's but stopped applying that gentle pressure. "It doesn't have to be with me." Gradyn licked the sensitive rim of Devlin's cock; he smiled and growled with pleasure when the red length jutted straight out before his eyes.

"Christ." Gradyn's mouth automatically filled with saliva. "You are something to see." He opened up and took another deep pull of hard cock, moaning as Devlin filled his mouth to capacity.

Devlin jerked, stilled, and then started pumping his hips

at Gradyn's face, fucking his mouth with shallow thrusts that didn't choke. Gradyn relaxed his jaw and took the gentle assault, reveling in an act that could be incredibly crude or completely intimate, depending on the man thrusting his cock. Devlin didn't shove -- although Gradyn thought he could come to love a forced throat full of dick from this man.

With each brief pump of his hips, Devlin's hand slowly moved under Gradyn's, fingering his own ring, as if learning and searching. Gradyn stayed with Devlin, his palm lined up on the back of Devlin's hand, piggybacking passively. His cock leaked inside his jeans every time he felt a hint of more aggressive movement and thought Devlin might push his own finger into his ass.

Devlin picked up the pace of fucking Gradyn's mouth, and Gradyn needed more too. He curled his free hand around the base of Devlin's erection and started twisting his fingers and mouth in separate directions, squeezing and sucking with more power, taking charge again. Gradyn ate up and down two thirds of Devlin's cock with wet, sucking pulls. Scorching-hot, salty, rigid flesh burned his tongue with every lick, providing everything Gradyn craved in giving a blowjob to another man.

"Denny... Denny..." Digging his fingers into Gradyn's scalp, Devlin scratched the smooth skin, and his thrusts lost any hint of gentleness. His finger moved harder against his bud, and he begged, "Fuck me." Devlin suddenly shoved his finger into his own ass, and Gradyn's pointer finger went right along with him, breeching Devlin with two simultaneously.

"Ohhh fuck…" Devlin's rectum clamped down with moist heat around his and Gradyn's fingers, drawing the invasion deeper into his passage. "Can't… Ahh!" Devlin drove his dick into Gradyn's mouth as he shook from top to bottom. A moment later, hot, bitter ejaculate poured down Gradyn's throat in jetting bursts, each consecutive pulse losing a little of its strength as Devlin came.

Gradyn swallowed down every sharp-tasting drop of Devlin's cum, craving this taste of man again. *No, not just any man.* Gradyn milked Devlin's cock with his throat and hand, stealing as much seed as he could. *The taste of this one man.*

He growled around Devlin's length as he struggled with that truth; Devlin hissed in response. Right then, Devlin withdrew his cock from Gradyn's mouth and their fingers from his ass. Gradyn, still full of desperate need, yanked Devlin down and savaged him with a kiss meant to seal ownership.

Devlin groaned and kissed Gradyn back just as deeply. He curled his hands into Gradyn's shoulders, crushing the muscles, tangling tongues, and then abruptly tore his mouth away. "Oh fuck, Denny." He breathed heavily against Gradyn's mouth, clearly needing to catch his breath as much as Gradyn did. He then licked across Gradyn's kiss-swollen lips, up to his nose and forehead, where he pressed a small kiss. "I love tasting myself inside you." Silver flecks danced in Devlin's eyes. He darted his tongue inside Gradyn's mouth again with a fast, tormenting lick. "Feels right. Like I'm supposed to be there."

"Damn it, beautiful." Gradyn wiped his mouth, and found

his hand unsteady. He struggled to breathe through the haze of desire and the acute discomfort pushing against his jeans.

Without looking away, Gradyn dug into a bag on the table and unearthed one of the few remaining convenience packets of lubricant he'd purchased yesterday. "Turn around." He handed the lube to Devlin and then started fishing for a condom. "Get yourself ready to sit on me before I lose my shit and this never happens."

Devlin shifted and presented Gradyn with a straight-on view of his ass. The hills of his buttocks sat high, firm, and so smooth Gradyn just barely resisted the urge to lean forward and rub his face all over them. Devlin tore open the lube just as Gradyn's fingers brushed across a condom.

After slicking up a couple of fingers, Devlin reached back, pulled a cheek aside, and rubbed his hole with the tips of two shiny digits. Gradyn heard Devlin suck in an almost inaudible gasp at first touch, and Gradyn swallowed hard on the enticing visual. Unable to look away, Gradyn got his belt and jeans open blindly, his fingers fumbling as if frozen, and got the fabric down to his hips. He tore the condom package open as he watched Devlin learn to get comfortable with his pucker; Gradyn grew somehow harder as Devlin finally broke through and forced a finger up his ass.

Jesus Christ.

Devlin moaned and pushed his hind end into his own taking. It took him a minute, but he pushed a second finger in, clearly stretching himself. Gradyn bit the inside of his cheek with a groan of his own, practically able to feel that snug channel clutching the penetration.

"Oh God." With his voice sounding strained, Devlin thrust his ass out and worked his fingers in and out of his hole. "I'm getting hard again already."

Gradyn's dick reared upward and dropped a line of precum onto his belly. "It's fucking pushing me to the breaking point just sitting here watching." He rolled the condom down his cock on instinct, tucked the end to the base, and pinched the tip. "Give me some of that lube," he ordered, stretching out his hand. "I don't want this hurting you one bit."

Devlin reached back with his free hand and squeezed the rest of the clear stuff into Gradyn's hand. Gradyn quickly transferred it to his sheathed prick and stroked his length a couple of times, moaning as he watched Devlin withdraw his fingers from his hole and leave that opening pulsing for something to fill it.

Holy fuck. He's beautiful all over.

Gradyn took hold of Devlin's waist and pulled him closer. As he did, perspiration beaded on his flesh, making his chest slick and shiny. With Devlin facing away from him, Gradyn guided Devlin between his spread legs, and then curled the man's hands around the arms of the chair. "Now ease down onto me." Gradyn let go of Devlin and took hold of his own erection, pointing it straight north. "Take however much you want, however fast or slow you want it."

His hands braced on the chair, Devlin slowly lowered

himself; his biceps bunched and veins popped on his forearms as he inched closer, and he stopped when the head of Gradyn's cock *just* kissed his entrance. He rocked back and forth, moving barely enough to graze Gradyn's tip up and down the line of his crack. Gradyn gritted his teeth with every slight touch that didn't give him what he wanted. Gradyn's prick screamed for full penetration, for a smothering of every nerve ending up and down his length, but he held still and let Devlin feel him out, one brush of skin against skin at a time, and find his own way.

Then -- *oh fuck* -- just when Gradyn thought his head would blow clean off from unadulterated, denied need, Devlin lined himself up with Gradyn's cock and sank down. He slowly took one inch at a time with his fucking beautiful ass, and eventually encased most of Gradyn's prick in an amazing, suffocating fire. Both men moaned through the joining. Gradyn rubbed his hands up and down Devlin's glistening back, needing to touch, and Devlin crushed the arms of the chair under his fingers as he pushed down, his upper body angled slightly forward as he forced his rectum to fully accept the mating.

Burning, tight-as-hell heat enveloped every bit of Gradyn's prick. "Oh yeah, that's so fucking good," Gradyn murmured. He hissed as Devlin wiggled on his lap, the move stretching and opening his passage for more of Gradyn's length.

"That's it," Gradyn said. "Get it all in." He slid his hands down to Devlin's hips and held on. "Relax that ass and sit all the way down on my cock."

A thick chuckle escaped Devlin. He pressed his back into

Gradyn's chest, and laid his head to rest on Gradyn's shoulder. "Thought you said this was at my pace." He turned his head to face Gradyn, and the color of his eyes deepened to slate. All of Devlin's muscles tensed at once, including those surrounding Gradyn's buried cock.

Out of his control, Gradyn's prick swelled inside Devlin's chute, pushing at the hold. He sucked in a gulp of much-needed air, breathed through the fierce concentration of pleasure, and spoke through clenched teeth. "I'm sorry."

Devlin smiled against Gradyn's neck; Gradyn could feel the imprint. "I was just teasing." He stuck his tongue into Gradyn's ear and drew out a tremble. "I like that you can't help talking dirty when you fuck me."

Gradyn pulled Devlin's face out of his nape and fused their foreheads together. "Listen to me." He sounded winded, and knew it was because his throat was so tight with unchecked emotion. "It's my dick in your ass, but you're the one in total control." He looked into the blur of Devlin's eyes, losing himself in a way that should not be possible. "Fuck my cock, beautiful." His chest felt crushed, panicking him, and he closed the distance between their lips. "Make it good enough to last." He seared his mouth to Devlin's, desperate for every bit of connection he could achieve, and kissed Devlin with all the foolish things he could not afford to feel but already did.

"Yes…" Devlin latched onto Gradyn and kissed him back with equal hunger. Every deep or soft lick Devlin pushed into Gradyn's mouth housed a rough noise that vibrated right through Gradyn and into his core, infecting him even deeper with everything of this man.

Aching all over, Gradyn whimpered under the tension straining his legs in his effort not to move. Devlin caught the message, and he twined their hands together, palm to palm. He used Gradyn as an anchor for the first roll of his hips that slid him up Gradyn's cock, almost to the point of separation, and then back down, enveloping Gradyn's shaft fully again. Gradyn moaned, and Devlin did it again, sighing against Gradyn's lips as he took Gradyn to the root.

Devlin set up a concentrated pace of rocking all the way up and down Gradyn's invasion, one that nearly slipped Gradyn out each time, but Devlin always eased back down, smothering Gradyn's cock in mind-altering throbbing heat just in time, keeping them connected. Gradyn wanted to close his eyes and just *feel* but he couldn't break away from the brightness in Devlin's gaze or the hard lines and angles of his face that telegraphed everything he felt right as it was happening. Gradyn memorized each small gasp Devlin made as he undulated his hips and lifted himself off Gradyn's prick, and every bite to the edge of his lip as he took Gradyn inside him again. Gradyn filed each shift and movement away for tonight and every other night when he wouldn't have Devlin sleeping beside him in bed.

You'll never see him again. You can't.

"No." The denial slipped out of Gradyn, his voice stripped raw. He surged up under Devlin, driving his cock fast and deep into Devlin's scorching tight ass.

Devlin cried out at the rougher spearing but shoved back down on it with just as much desperation. "Again," he said. He let go of Gradyn's hands, shifted clumsily, and hooked his legs wide over the arms of the chair. The move split him open; he grabbed the chair and braced his back against Gradyn's chest, grappling for a new hold. "Take more…" Devlin struggled to glide up and down Gradyn's cock in his new position. "Do it hard." Gradyn knifed up and took Devlin's steaming passage again, and Devlin jerked and moaned, "Oh yeah." His chute clamped down, grabbing onto Gradyn's dick as Devlin pounded his ass down onto the mating. "Fuck me."

Gradyn curled his hands around the underside of Devlin's thighs, holding tight, and stabilized him for repeated, snapping-fast pumps from his hips that sawed his length into Devlin, not stopping each time until he ground the base of his cock into Devlin's stretched hole. Devlin let his head fall back to Gradyn's shoulder, and he writhed his seat into Gradyn's lap; the man keened for more and squeezed his ass around Gradyn's taking with each thrust, and every little and big response from Devlin stripped away a bit more of Gradyn's control.

Sweat poured off Devlin and onto Gradyn, drenching him. The smells of sex and perspiration thickened the air and sank both men into a world where just the two of them mating in a furious rhythm existed.

Devlin twitched like an open-ended live wire on top of Gradyn in a way that Gradyn could barely contain. The man buried his face in Gradyn's neck and bit down, stinging the hell out of Gradyn and surely breaking skin, then reached down and wrapped both hands around his cock. "Shit, Denny, shit." Devlin pulled hard on his rigid length, wincing, and shoved his ass down against Gradyn's dick with every up-stroke. "Don't stop. Oh God." His breathing grew more and more erratic with the pounding Gradyn gave his ass. "I'm gonna come."

Gradyn moved with lightning speed; he wrapped his arms around Devlin's waist and chest and pulled him in tightly to his body. "Do it." He held Devlin locked to him so close it felt as if their skin fused together. No longer moving, Gradyn kept his dick tucked all the way up in Devlin's throbbing ass, and said at his ear, "Now."

On command, Devlin's entire body shook in racking waves. He whipped his hand up and down his erection like a man possessed, and then he suddenly jerked and shouted, his voice hoarse as orgasm overtook him. He spewed all over his stomach, spraying lines of milky-white cum. His chute squeezed and squeezed, putting a chokehold on Gradyn's cock. Gradyn clamped his teeth, fighting coming with every ounce of willpower he possessed, and rode the blinding pleasure of Devlin's release.

The second the final ebb of Devlin's orgasm waned, Gradyn bent him over double at the waist. He pulled out, tore the condom off, and put his dick on the small of Devlin's back. Gradyn trembled, and he didn't dare touch himself. Instead, he leaned over and pressed his mouth against Devlin's spine. "Say my name." The request came from such a deep, needful place inside him that Gradyn wasn't sure he said it loud enough to be heard. "Say it. Please."

"Gradyn. Denny…" The sound was muffled due to Devlin's folded position, but Gradyn heard it. Devlin rubbed his hands down the lower half of Gradyn's legs, almost petting him through his jeans, and whispered, "My Denny."

Without touching himself, without even breathing, Gradyn opened his mouth in a silent cry, and spilled himself on Devlin's back. He held Devlin around the middle and watched himself mark the man, desperate for an honest connection, a tie to another human being, even if it was just this person saying his real name aloud and momentarily wearing his seed.

They sat still and quiet for long minutes afterward, Gradyn folded over Devlin, holding him, breathing together. Gradyn would have stayed there forever but when he turned his head to press his cheek into the warmth of Devlin's upper back, he got a glance at the clock on the nightstand out of the corner of his eye.

Almost time for Devlin to go.

His chest ached and his head screamed in protest but Gradyn commanded his body into an upright position and let Devlin out of his scrunched hunch. Instead of getting up, Devlin turned sideways and curled himself against Gradyn, not letting go.

Jesus Christ. Gradyn draped his arms around Devlin and held him close. *How is letting go of him harder than walking into a chop shop with a viper pit full of drug dealing, human trafficking, murdering bikers?*

Gradyn rested his head against Devlin's temple and breathed in his scent. "I want to come with you to the airport," he said, changing his thought about the situation from this morning. "I don't want to say goodbye in this place and ruin the memories of what we had here for two days."

"Then come," Devlin said, his voice soft. He ran the tip of his finger over the swirls of tattoo covering Gradyn's shoulder, silent for a handful of heartbeats, and then somehow snuggled in even tighter against Gradyn. "I've never had an airport goodbye."

The timbre of Gradyn's voice went well past rough. "Me either."

"I've never said a real goodbye anywhere, except to family," Devlin added, playing with the pattern on Gradyn's arm now. He suddenly shot to his feet, furrow lines pulling his brow, and poked Gradyn's chest. "Don't make me cry like a pussy in public or I'll do something to your balls that you won't like nearly as much as what I've done to them in this room."

"Ooh." Gradyn wiggled his fingers toward Devlin's face, while inside breathed easier at the sudden laughter in Devlin's eyes. "Is that a threat or a promise?" He moved between leering suggestively at Devlin and glancing down at his cock. "Maybe a challenge that it's up to me to issue?"

Devlin delivered an exaggerated sideways glare. "Get your mind out of the gutter, Connell." He walked backward in the direction of the bathroom, still pointing. "I might have had a lot of firsts this weekend," he raised his voice as he disappeared into the other room, "but sucking you off in an airport bathroom isn't going to be one of them!"

"Damn." Gradyn laughed to himself. He jumped up and stalked Devlin into the bathroom, finding him at the sink. "How about we double up for one more record-fast shower instead?" He moved in behind Devlin and buried his nose in the man's nape, growling as he inhaled. "I love that you smell like my cum but the other red-eye flight passengers might not take to it so kindly."

Devlin found Gradyn in the reflection of the mirror, and his eyes deepened smoky-dark in color as he stared. "How about we wash up instead," his voice licked across Gradyn's flesh and made him tremble, "and I leave a little bit to carry home with me?" He smeared his finger through the lines of ejaculate streaking his stomach, turned within the sliver of space Gradyn left between their bodies, and marked a shiny X over Gradyn's heart. "How about you do the same?"

"Christ, beautiful." Gradyn's heart beat a furious rhythm that clogged his throat. "You are something incredible." He slid his hand down Devlin's back and rubbed his thumb through the stickiness he'd left behind. After coating his thumb in his seed, he slashed two intersecting lines to Devlin's chest. "How's that?"

With a fast spin, Devlin paused and studied himself in the mirror, his eyes clearly focused on the shiny new X adorning his flesh. "Perfect. You know," he turned back to Gradyn, and a cheeky smile appeared, "I've never sealed anything with a kiss before either."

Gradyn buried his hand in Devlin's hair, tipped his head back, and brushed his lips across the other man's, to his sigh and smile. "You have now."

Gruff didn't even begin to describe how Gradyn's voice sounded scratching out those words. Devlin looked so fucking dreamy right in front of him, and so to ensure Gradyn didn't lose his shit right there in the bathroom, he slanted his lips across Devlin's again and released every bit of coiling, raw emotion inside him in a breath-stealing kiss...

———

...Garrick came back to reality and found himself leaning against his bathroom sink in the dark, struggling to catch his breath. Remnants of his memory swirled before his eyes, snapshots of their bodies merging on that chair in such a guttural, intimate way, drowning Garrick in the incredible connection he and Devlin had so briefly shared.

A picture of a too-sexy smiling blond from this evening intruded on the mental images. Garrick snarled and bared his teeth at the image, instinctually protecting what was his.

Devlin.

You can't have him, pretty boy. You can't give him what I do when we're together.

Except -- Garrick raced out of the bathroom and grabbed up

his discarded watch -- Devlin might let the blond try. Garrick certainly hadn't given Devlin a lot of honesty since showing up in town, or any real reason to think he even wanted Devlin back. Looking at the time, Garrick felt sick to his stomach as he realized Devlin could still be on that date right now, maybe even moving toward a more intimate moment. After all, at the apartment the other day, Maddie had implied this wouldn't be Devlin's first date with Darren.

If he isn't there already, he could be close to crawling into bed with that hot young thing right now.

Garrick's legs went out on him and he stumbled to his knees. *No.* Everything inside him twisted and pulled, ripping at him from the inside, and he grabbed for the coffee table. *Devlin is mine.*

Keys sitting on the coffee table winked with the glint of the moon and pulled Garrick's attention to the scrap of paper sitting beneath them.

Devlin's cell phone number.

During dinner at the Fine's, Garrick had noticed Devlin's card attached to the refrigerator. He'd repeated the number in his head every time he looked at it. As soon as he'd gotten a moment to himself, he'd torn the corner off a newspaper, jotted it down, and tucked it in his pocket for safekeeping.

The paper called Garrick to it; once seen, he couldn't pretend it wasn't there. He reached out, unable to withdraw his hand or stop his fingers from closing around it. His cell sat on the table too. The moment Garrick pulled it to him and punched in the first number, he thought he might throw up.

He hit the second, third and the rest anyway, clicked Send, and held his breath.

Devlin picked up on the fourth ring. "Hello?"

"I know you're probably still out with Darren, and I know it's rude to interrupt, and I know I don't even necessarily have the right to do it and, goddamn it, I wanted to kill the blond when you walked into the restaurant with him, but I had Shawn, and you thought something, but it's not what you think. It wasn't a choice, beautiful. It wasn't you or them, I promise. You're everything to me. I don't want you to be with him. I want you to be with me. Please tell him you have to go, and come be with me. I'll wait all night. Forever, if that's what it takes. I'm not ever saying goodbye to you again." The words poured out of Garrick, one on top of the next, through a throat that barely let him make sound.

Oh Jesus. Garrick's chest banded too tight for comfort. *Jesus. Jesus. Jesus.*

A long, silent pause -- too fucking long -- sucked the rest of the air right out of Garrick's body.

He hung up the phone as if it had a disease, without Devlin ever having said a word.

Garrick didn't dare risk hearing a rejection. If he did, he might never get up from the floor again.

CHAPTER TEN

Devlin leaned against his headboard, in total darkness, listening to the drone of a dial tone buzzing in his ear.

Garrick's heartbreaking run-on confession reverberated in his ear, all of the words mingling for a moment in a confusing cacophony until a handful sorted themselves out and rang loudly, as if someone shouted them into his very being.

It wasn't a choice between them and you; it's not what you think.

And, he called me beautiful.

Devlin's heart squeezed, and he stifled a ridiculous sob. His muscles protested the tension that had held his entire body in rigor from the moment Garrick Langley's name had shown up on his cell phone's LCD screen. Devlin forced himself to breathe, but the second the tightness within him released, he hissed through a concentration of pleasure as the thick silicone dildo lodged halfway up his ass slid out of his body and dropped to the mattress.

His passage throbbed as if it were a pair of hands reaching to pull something into its clutches again. Devlin fitted the rounded head of the toy to his pucker once more and nudged it against his rapidly closing entrance. He closed his eyes and pushed the black silicone against his ring. As he did, he tried to conjure the image that had helped him relax enough the first time to get the dildo inside him. Pictures of the same man immediately came back into Devlin's mind, but instead of the tattooed, bald, muscle-bound images of Gradyn that had kept Devlin company in his dreams for five years, a chiseled, sleeker, raven-haired Garrick appeared. The desperate longing in Garrick's voice from just minutes ago filled Devlin's head, along with a picture of the frightened man in Devlin's hallway the other night, which then morphed to the sexy-as-all-get-out memory of him laughing with Shawn as he carried the boy out of the pizza joint.

Devlin's cock stirred and pushed against his belly but his channel would not stop clenching long enough to ease the toy back into his ass.

Come be with me. I'll wait all night. I'm not ever saying goodbye to you again.

Devlin's body already knew what his once-broken heart feared to risk again.

He tossed the dildo aside and grabbed his sweats from the foot of his bed. He crashed against his wall with a *thud* as he hopped his way into them, then grabbed his T-shirt, and finally his keys off a table by the door as he tore out of the apartment.

———

DEVLIN'S BARE FEET SQUISHED IN the mist-damp earth as he ran across the Fine's front lawn but he didn't dare slow his steps through the slick grass or up the narrow flight of white-painted steps that led to Garrick's apartment. Devlin hadn't thought to grab sneakers in his frantic race down to his car and then hadn't wanted to waste time going back up to get them when he realized he didn't have on shoes.

Didn't matter. He only cared about getting to Garrick.

Garrick ripped open the door the second Devlin hit the small landing. He stood before Devlin so beautiful, clad only in the cargo shorts Devlin had left him in earlier that day, and everything about this newer, leaner, dark-haired man made Devlin's mouth go dry.

Devlin cleared his throat; he tried to smile but it felt tight. "Hi."

Garrick reached out and put his hand on Devlin's chest, as if feeling him out. "You're here." His unfamiliar blue eyes glistened with brightness for a split second, and then he grabbed a fistful of Devlin's shirt and tugged him over the threshold. "I couldn't stop thinking about you. I stare out the window when I can't sleep, and when I saw your car my stomach started to flutter. When you opened your door I didn't know if I was seeing you just because I wanted it so badly." Garrick's fingers shook as he shut the door, and the trembling didn't let up when he took Devlin's hand in his. "But here you are."

Devlin wasn't entirely steady either. He wanted to remain strong and get Garrick's secrets out in the open right away, but that became less and less important with every second Garrick's vulnerability hit at him in drenching waves.

Garrick pawed at Devlin's shirt, as if afraid to stop touching him. "Devlin…"

"Promise me we'll get this sorted out and be okay together," Devlin said, his voice as shaky as Garrick was all over. He wanted to throw himself into Garrick's arms and learn him all over again. At the same time, the man's reemergence in Devlin's life had dredged up a heavy ache whose weight had almost crushed Devlin once before. "I can't survive having my heart ripped out by you a second time."

Garrick's face crumbled, and his voice cracked. "I'm so sorry I hurt you." He tugged Devlin to him with their linked hands, pulled him into his wonderful warmth, and held him tight. "I ran to Redemption because of you, beautiful." He slid his hands down Devlin's back and knotted them into fists against the slope of Devlin's ass. Choppy breathing warmed Devlin's neck. Garrick kissed his way up Devlin's skin, stopping with his mouth at Devlin's ear. "I love you." Garrick's chest heaved unevenly as he said it. "I promise."

Oh sweet Jesus God. Devlin's knees went wobbly, his chest

burned, and his throat clogged as he stifled down a stupid, hopeful sob. *He said he loves me.*

"Stay with me," Garrick added quickly. He clung to Devlin, half holding him up, and his voice slipped to something well past raw exposure. "Please don't go out with that other guy again."

Garrick's plea sank into Devlin's flesh, hurting him physically. He pulled out of hiding, looked, and saw clear torment mapping Garrick's face into harsh lines of need. Easing his pain slipped Devlin the rest of the way home.

"I wasn't with him, baby." Devlin caressed Garrick's cheek, almost tearing up when the man nuzzled into his hand. "It wasn't what you thought either. I was home when you called, not out with Darren." Heat burned up Devlin's chest and neck. He could feel it suffusing his cheeks too, but Garrick stood before him, naked longing shining in his too-blue eyes, and Devlin could not leave him hanging, wondering about the rest. "I have this toy, and I tried to make it feel like you. But then you called, and I couldn't trick my body when it knew you were so close by." Devlin pushed his sweats down in the back and guided one of Garrick's hands to his hole. "I'm still slick inside from what I was doing while thinking of you."

"Really?" Garrick asked.

Looking into each other's eyes, Devlin nodded, and Garrick pushed his middle finger into Devlin's ass. Devlin sucked in a deep breath at the breeching of his bud.

"Jesus," Garrick whispered gutturally, and kept delving

until his finger slipped into Devlin past the second knuckle. He went right for Devlin's sweet spot, and Devlin bumped his ass back into the taking, requesting more. Garrick forced a second digit in right alongside the first and worked them in a shallow thrust to Devlin's low moans of delight.

Garrick probed Devlin's chute with one hand, and with the other rubbed at his own bulge pushing full and visible against the light tan color of his shorts. "You're fucking primed already," Garrick said, "and I feel like I've been hard since you walked into the garage two days ago." Garrick held his two fingers just inside Devlin's entrance. He teased the sensitive ring, stretching Devlin just enough to pleasantly sting. Never once, as Garrick did it, did he look over Devlin's shoulder or break their gaze. "You swear you really weren't with Darren after the restaurant?" Clear fear continued to live in his eyes.

"I wasn't. I promise." Devlin ran his hand down Garrick's arm, trying to soothe, and ended by threading his fingers through the backs of Garrick's, over the heat of Garrick's fully erect cock. "What you saw was friendly acquaintances who'd made plans for dinner and were hungry. I talked to Darren at my apartment before we went out. After the day I spent with you…"

Devlin took an unsteady breath as the swell of elation and then the debilitating crush of a possible second rejection worked its way through him where he stood. "It didn't matter if you ended up feeling like you needed to create something with Grace for those kids; it didn't change what I knew *I* felt, how

I've always felt, about you. It wouldn't have been right to let Darren think I could ever develop the kinds of feeling for him that I already feel with you."

Devlin let go and stripped off his shirt. As the shock of white cotton drifted through the shadows to the floor, Devlin lifted Garrick's hand, put it against his heart, and let Garrick feel the beat that pounded inside Devlin just for him. "I love *you*, Gradyn, Denny or Garrick, no matter what your name is." Husky thickness coated Devlin's words. "And I don't see that ever changing."

A hoarse noise that almost didn't register as human escaped Garrick. He pulled his fingers out of Devlin's ass, and clutched his face, dragging him close. Garrick's eyes burned too bright, breaking Devlin's heart, but Devlin swore he could see the green hiding within the watery blue.

Garrick dipped down and grazed his mouth across Devlin's, and then did it again, and again, clinging each time, as if unable to let go. Devlin dug his fingers into Garrick's arms, squeezing into the solid, warm flesh, and moaned at the first flick of their tongues. Heat surged straight down to Devlin's prick and pushed his length out to poke against Garrick's thigh. The greedy nerve endings on his cockhead demanded more, and as Devlin licked his way into Garrick's mouth for a deeper taste, he shoved his sweats down to his ankles, kicked them off, and seared himself to Garrick from top to bottom. He rubbed himself all over the other man, needing skin-to-skin on more than just his stiff dick.

"Oh shit." Garrick gasped and stumbled backward, hauling Devlin with him to the door. "You feel so good." He tunneled his fingers into Devlin's hair, jerked his head back, and descended, taking Devlin with a rougher kiss. What started out with a nip that drew a pinch of blood only increased in brutality as Garrick's deep kiss of complete ownership consumed Devlin inside and out.

Devlin groaned and threw himself against Garrick with equal fervor, kissing him back in a way that scraped and hurt, but that he knew they both needed to feel right now. His entire being flamed inside, hungry and achy. Devlin ground himself against Garrick's body with everything he was worth, searching for relief. He shoved the man's hand back down to his asshole and tried to force a taking. Any taking. "Please." He licked at Garrick, and the sharp metallic bite of his own blood assaulted his taste buds.

Garrick drew back just a sliver. He kept his hand curled tightly around Devlin's neck as he looked into his eyes; his breathing was uneven and his lips were red from a combination of aggression and a tinge of Devlin's blood. Choppy tufts of Garrick's long, dark hair fell across his face, the strands brushing against Devlin's skin.

"Christ, I love you, beautiful." Garrick's pupils sparked black ice, and a flash of feral grin appeared. "I want you forever." He brushed his lips across Devlin's again, tormenting Devlin with just a whisper of contact. With his other hand, Garrick pushed his finger an inch into Devlin's passage. He maintained constant eye contact, watching, almost uncomfortably so, and then without quarter tripled his penetration into Devlin's channel with another two fingers at the same time.

"Ohh yes…" Devlin hissed as his body worked to accept the extra thickness. "Me too." His rectum closed in tight on Garrick's buried fingers and pulsed in a fast pattern that milked the length, making Devlin bite his lip to hold back a scream. "About you."

Garrick eased his fingers deeper inside Devlin, just a hair, and Devlin felt the slight caress all the way in his fucking toes. A brushing glance slid over his prostate, almost a phantom sensation, but Devlin groaned and rolled into the invasion as if it were a full-on assault. Garrick massaged Devlin's neck and anal muscles at the same time, murmuring explicit words of encouragement with each touch, and Devlin rocked into him like an animal denied his loving master for too many years.

The masterful fingering of Devlin's ass; Garrick's constant, brushing kisses against Devlin forehead; the way Garrick plied the tendons in Devlin's neck that went all the way down Devlin's spine, straight to his chute, drove Devlin quickly to the brink. "Holy fuck," Devlin bit down the urge to come, "you always knew how to kill me."

Slipping too fast, Devlin hooked his hands around the waistband of Garrick's shorts, ripped the material open, and tore them down his legs. Thick, hot cock fell right into Devlin's hands, scorching his flesh with a wonderful, familiar burn. Devlin closed his fingers tightly, taking Garrick's prick and sac in his hands, and gave both a good rub and tug.

Garrick sucked in a deep, sharp breath, and he dug the back of his head into the door. "Oh shit. Reality feels too good, beautiful."

Devlin ran a trimmed fingernail into Garrick's slit, and Garrick bucked and gritted his teeth. Devlin did it a second time, and Garrick jerked again as he produced a fat bead of seed. "Devlin," Garrick sounded winded, "you're gonna make me come."

No! Devlin nearly buckled as an onslaught of denial tore through him.

"Control it." Devlin reached back, ripped Garrick's fingers out of his asshole, and shoved him fully into the door. "Just like you once told me to do." Devlin tried to climb up Garrick's body, frantic and losing control too. "Fuck me." He looked into Garrick's eyes as desperation roughened the texture of his voice. "Right here." He wrapped his arms around Garrick's shoulders and pulled himself up, locking his legs around Garrick's waist. "Right now."

Blue fire flared in Garrick's eyes. "Christ, yes." Garrick hooked his arms under Devlin's thighs, and fused their mouths together. "Hold on." His words went into Devlin between tantalizing licks of their tongues that quickly turned into a voracious, raw kiss. Devlin clutched at Garrick, clinging with his thighs and arms, kissing him back. Garrick started moving, and he blindly bumped them into something that stabbed cold metal into Devlin's back, making him "Umph" and Garrick mutter, "Sorry."

Devlin smiled against Garrick's lips. "It's okay." The man's cock rode *right* against Devlin's balls and taint, though, and pushed Devlin disastrously close to the edge. "Just put me down somewhere and fuck me now."

Just as Devlin demanded that, Garrick hoisted him onto a counter, stole his breath with a biting kiss, and drove his cock deep into Devlin's ass.

Both men cried out, shuddered as one, and then went absolutely still.

Sweet Mary. Devlin's passage squeezed in a series of exquisite throbbing waves around Garrick's rock-solid *bare* cock. *He's not wearing a condom.*

Garrick's jaw dropped, his eyes closed, and his hands curled into fists against the edge of the counter. He looked like he fought through an epic battle before opening his eyes and facing Devlin again. "Jesus Christ," Garrick whispered. Devlin moved, just an inch, and Garrick abruptly bit off a curse, his jaw clenching. "I didn't even think."

Devlin locked his ankles around Garrick's back and held him fully buried inside. "Me either, but I'm okay." He brushed the tips of his fingers against Garrick's jaw, reveling in the rough stubble. His thumb caught the edge of Garrick's incredible mouth. The man's gasp of response brought Devlin's attention up to his eyes and pulled another confession out of his soul. "There hasn't been anyone since you."

"No one?" Those blue eyes somehow swirled green

throughout again, and the light within Garrick's gaze took away the last remnants of fear in Devlin's heart.

Devlin shook his head. "Not like this. I've only made love with you."

"I'm good too. I couldn't be with anyone after you," Garrick told him. "My life didn't allow it." His jaw tensed visibly again, stopping him. He uncurled his fists from the counter and dropped his focus to watch himself rub his palms up and down the outside of Devlin's thighs. "It doesn't matter, though. Even if I could have, I don't think I could have settled for less after what I had with you."

"Then don't stop." With a couple of fingers under his chin, Devlin drew Garrick's face out of hiding, and offered him a gentle smile. "We've both waited too long to stop now."

Garrick darted out his tongue and delivered a fast lick to the inside of Devlin's wrist. His eyes danced with humor and heat, and he yanked Devlin's ass right up to the edge of the counter. "Put your feet up on the counter. Spread for me, beautiful." Garrick helped Devlin unwind his legs from around Garrick's waist, plant his feet on the scratched Formica, and in doing so put the connection of their bodies on full display. "Christ," he looked down, and added another curse. "I needed to see us like this again." With that, Garrick sent a shiver through Devlin's chute as he slid his thick cock out of Devlin's ass completely, left him open and bereft for a pair of heartbeats, and then pierced Devlin's hole again, and slowly, oh-so-fucking-slowly, filled Devlin to the root.

Devlin gasped as Garrick pulled out and teased the head of his prick over Devlin's perineum and stretched entrance, rubbed the shiny red tip up to Devlin's balls, and then returned to Devlin's opening and sank his length back through the snug hold of Devlin's fluttering passage.

On the third penetration, Devlin bit his lip and reached out, searching for a toehold, and latched his fingers into the cabinet handles on his left and right sides. Watching Garrick take him with such precision heightened the mating for Devlin. As Devlin lifted his backside off the counter and tried to thrust his asshole into the drive of Garrick's cock, desperate for a rawer mating, his arm muscles popped and strained under his weight.

Glancing up, Garrick had a wildness in his eyes that matched the predatory flash of his smile. He looked back down at where they were one body, and clutched at Devlin's hips with digging strength, holding him in place for the sudden roughness of his fucking.

"Still the most incredible thing I've ever seen." Garrick snapped his hips and jabbed his cock into Devlin's ass in rapid order. "You're so beautiful all over."

"Please..." Devlin's thighs and back screamed with the strain of vigorous use, but he didn't give a damn about the consequences of ignoring his rehab rules right now. "Fuck me." He cried out at the fast, deep drives Garrick pummeled his passage with in response, yet still it wasn't enough. "Jerk my cock." His balls swelled heavy and painful with seed for this man. "Five years..." Devlin choked under the tidal wave of unearthed emotions. Garrick's gaze suddenly snapped up to his. Devlin couldn't look away from the intensity in Garrick's stare, and he couldn't swallow down truths he hadn't been able to share with anyone else. "I missed you every day. I loved you just as long."

Garrick surged into Devlin full-force and simultaneously claimed Devlin's mouth as savagely as he took his ass. He released his crushing hold on Devlin's hips and put an equally bruising one on Devlin's head, angling him for a deeper plundering of his mouth. "I'll make it up to you, Devlin." His vow washed over Devlin's lips as he spoke it. "I loved you the whole time too." He let go with one hand, caressed his palm down Devlin's throat to his chest, and drew an X over Devlin's heart with the tip of one finger. "I promise."

San Francisco. The motel bathroom. Their cum.

With that move, Devlin knew Garrick remembered too. "You knew in the bathroom that night?" Devlin asked.

Garrick shook his head. "Before. From the second I saw you sitting alone in that club something inside me knew I was meant for you." The rasp in his delivery echoed the sheen filming his eyes. "I think it's why I gave you my real name that night." He pulled Devlin's mouth to his again and whispered, his voice breaking, "I know it's why when my life was in danger, and I couldn't think clearly, my instincts brought me to Redemption and you."

Devlin found he didn't need Garrick pulling on his cock after all. He pressed his forehead to Garrick's, touched their lips together, and got lost looking into a sea of blue that wasn't that of a stranger anymore. "Garrick…"

The man kissed him while murmuring words of love, and Devlin trembled as his body pulled tight all over, and then released every contracted muscle at once. He gasped as his rectum repeatedly clamped and let go of Garrick's deeply-tucked cock, and he keened an inhuman sound when, without any hint of internal warning, he came, spilling his seed onto his stomach in spurting streams.

While Devlin rode the wave, he didn't blink or break away from Garrick's burning gaze. "Let me feel it," Devlin said, brushing his breath over Garrick's lips. He let go of the cabinet handles and grazed his fingertips over Garrick's cheeks and forehead, down the bridge of his nose, and over his reddened mouth, memorizing every inch with touch as well as sight. "Come inside me."

Garrick's pupils flared and took over the ring of blue. "Yes." He burrowed his hands under Devlin's thighs, took hold of his buttocks, and lifted him right off the counter. He moved fast and shoved Devlin into the refrigerator with the force of his bigger frame, nailing Devlin there with a driving stab of his cock that felt like it went right through Devlin's tender ass straight to his heart. Not letting up, Garrick took possession of Devlin's mouth and staked a claim with his tongue just as aggressively as he did with his dick. "Yes." He panted the word with each thrust of his hips. "Yes." His fucking rocked the refrigerator and sent magnets and slips of paper dropping to the floor. "Yes."

Devlin held onto Garrick, gloried in the pounding, and even bumped his passage up into it, all the while looking into Garrick's eyes. Devlin squeezed his thighs and rectal muscles, trapping Garrick within on a deep in-stroke. He licked his man's nose, and said, "Yes."

Garrick shuddered, and it looked like he struggled to breathe. Distress seemed to consume him, but suddenly he jerked, shouted hoarsely, and fused his forehead to Devlin's. "Mine," slipped past Garrick's lips with breathless softness just as a spurt of wet heat filled Devlin's ass. Garrick held absolutely still, Devlin in his clutches, with his back fused to the fridge door, both men pulsing where they were connected as Garrick warmed Devlin's channel with endless lines of cum.

Afterward, they might have stayed there tangled in each other for five minutes, or it might have been an hour, Devlin didn't know. He didn't want to be the first to look or break away. Eventually, though, his thighs and lower back did make their displeasure at his cramped position painfully clear. He winced, and Garrick acted the second it happened. One step backward on Garrick's part peeled Devlin off the fridge. Garrick pried his fingers from Devlin's buttocks, gently lowered him to the floor, and in doing so, his cock slipped out of Devlin's tender ass.

"Sorry." Red slashed across Garrick's cheekbones. "I got a little carried away."

Devlin twisted side-to-side and then walked the length of the one-room apartment, working out the kinks in his muscles.

"It's okay," he said, and grinned at a stunning, naked Garrick from over his shoulder. "I liked that you did."

"What do you need?" Garrick rushed to Devlin's side. "I can run you a shower." In two big strides, Garrick reached inside a darkened space and flipped a switch, flooding the smaller room with harsh light, revealing a sink and what had to be the bathroom. "Or I could give you a heating pad to use." Garrick broke away quickly and tore open a door. "I found it in the closet when I first moved in."

Devlin put a hand on Garrick's arm, and the man turned to face him, empty-handed.

Now comes the hardest part.

Devlin tried to make his smile an encouraging one, but he didn't take a step back and give this man any running room. "What I need right now, more than anything, are some answers. Who are you Gradyn Denny Garrick Connell Langley?" He squeezed the man's forearm, begging in more ways than one. "I think it's time I know the truth about what the hell happened five years ago, not to mention what the fuck has you running so scared right now."

The man visibly trembled, but he took a breath, and held in place. "Today, I'm Garrick Langley, and I'm a mechanic," Garrick answered, his voice bland. "But Gradyn Connell used to work for the San Diego Police Department and then was recruited and did undercover work for California's Bureau of Investigation and Intelligence. Shortly after our weekend together, he got a gig working with the FBI. That's when everything slowly went to shit," Garrick's Adam's apple moved in a visible wave as he swallowed, "and Gradyn Connell had to die."

CHAPTER ELEVEN

Police? CBI? Fucking FBI too?

Devlin's head spun with the new information ... and the matter-of-fact way this man looked and sounded as he delivered it. Devlin glanced at the stony, still nearly blank expression shaping Garrick's face, and he stuffed down a scream that would wake up the entire neighborhood. As an antidote to his frustration, he started to pace.

"I don't understand." Devlin scrubbed his face and tunneled his fingers through his hair, pushing the damp stuff off his forehead. "You told me you did outreach work with gangs in Oakland."

"No," more of that careful, even tone droned out of Garrick, "I made a vague statement about working with gangs and that I

257

lived in Oakland. You drew your own conclusion."

Devlin whipped his head around to face Garrick at that.

"And I let you," Garrick added with a shrug. "It's what you do when you work undercover; you don't tell people the facts about your job." His lips thinned to a pale, hard line. "You don't even tell your family, let alone a guy you picked up in a bar for a quickie."

"Undercover?" Devlin couldn't care about the quickie comment coldly mixed in with so much other jaw-dropping information. A fast, easy lay was the unvarnished fact of being in that bar, for both of them. "So all that stuff you told me about the gangs was a lie?"

Garrick made a face that looked like a wince. "Not precisely, but only for the fact that I didn't really tell you anything. You just think I did. Look, this is going to take a while. Why don't we get cleaned up and get into bed?" Garrick walked into the bathroom without breaking that fingernails-on-a-chalkboard annoying monotone commentary. "You look like you're about to fall over."

Devlin rushed to the bathroom door and talked to Garrick's reflection in the mirror above the sink. "The guy I love just told me everything I've thought about him for the last five years wasn't his real life." When Garrick started wiping down his cock -- easy as you please -- Devlin almost reached between the man's legs and ripped his balls off. "You'll have to pardon my lack of cool, but I think I should be forgiven if I need to take a few minutes to digest and adjust to the new information."

"Hey, look at it like this," Garrick said as he reached back and handed Devlin a wet washcloth, "that means the stuff I told you about having a girlfriend and you being a weekend fling to get men out of my system wasn't real either."

Devlin narrowed his stare to slits as wildfire ripped through his core.

"I apologize." Garrick broke his gaze from the mirror and busied himself with a handful of items lining the back of his sink. "Bad time for humor."

"Yeah, it is." Devlin was treated to the sight of Garrick's back and ass. God, he looked, and wished to hell he cared one bit about the stunning view right now. "How about you cut out the flippant shit and start showing me some emotions so I know this matters to you and that I'm not just the butt of a nasty joke."

Still looking down, fiddling with God knew what, Garrick murmured, "Can't."

Son of a bitch. Devlin shoved in between Garrick and the sink, forcing himself directly into Garrick's line of sight. "Talk to me. Why?"

Garrick finally lifted his gaze and -- *Holy Mother* -- it was once again the pure green Devlin remembered from so long ago. Only this time, it was drenched in a layer of moisture.

"Why, Garrick?" Devlin asked again, this time gentling his tone.

Garrick blinked repeatedly and looked up at the ceiling for a handful of seconds before coming back to Devlin. "Because if you can't accept my former life and some of the things I've done..." He breathed shakily. "If you can't forgive me, it's going to annihilate me, and I need to start armoring myself against that possible outcome right now."

"Hey." Devlin grabbed Garrick's face and forced him to stay connected. "Do you see me running? I think you can safely assume that if I were going to ream you a new asshole and then walk away I would have done it a few days ago when you looked me in the eyes and pretended not to be who I damn well knew you were."

"But it wasn't entirely a lie." Garrick's voice, stripped bare of any machismo or detachment, echoed against the bathroom tiles with the sounds of despair. "I *have* to be Garrick now. With the exception of taking out the contacts before I go to sleep, Garrick Langley has to become real to me, and to everyone around me. He's the new me."

Garrick took a moment, looked like he swallowed a few times, and when he started again his voice was a little less hoarse. "I've been other people in between our time together, Devlin -- people who were complete fabrications and nobody I would want to be in real life -- but this guy -- Garrick -- is okay, I think. The man you were with in San Francisco -- Denny -- who was the same man who loved hearing your voice on the phone and seeing your e-mails in his Inbox, he is in every way that matters the same guy who is standing in front of you right now. Every bit of that man in that motel room, except for the tattoos, bald head, and the extra bulk, is who I am at my core.

He is who I am trying to be here in Redemption, only with a different name, a new job, and no family anymore."

He drew Devlin to him and pressed a kiss to his hair. "I never lied to you about my family, or ever showed you anything different than who I really am inside. Everything we talked about that weekend, and later on with the phone calls and e-mails -- except for that last one -- is the real me."

Devlin clutched at Garrick's forearm as the nausea that came with reading that last e-mail a thousand times over spiraled through him again. "So you never had a girlfriend, and you didn't get married."

"No. I hated doing it, but I knew it was the only way out of something I never should have let start in the first place, which was a relationship with you." Garrick took a step back, and this time he looked like the one who might throw up. "I did it to maximize your hurt and betrayal so that you'd never want to go sniffing for anything about me again. The truth is, there's never been anybody I've ever even thought about marrying." His attention slid Devlin's way. "Unless you count all those nights I was sleeping somewhere I didn't want to be and couldn't escape without detection; on all those nights in the dark, I thought about what it would be like if you knew the truth, could forgive me, and I was allowed to spend the rest of my life with you."

Fuck.

Devlin's knees suddenly turned to the consistency of Jell-o. "You've already sweet-talked me out of my pants," he said with a rough chuckle. "There's no need to pile it on."

Garrick closed the distance between them and caged Devlin against the sink. "Now who's nervous about the truth?"

Devlin exhaled a shaky breath. "Why don't we get this thing back on the rails?" His cock automatically stirred and sent testosterone pumping to all four corners every time this man looked at him for more than a heartbeat, but Devlin wouldn't allow himself to leave this apartment in the morning happily sated and sore but without answers. "Start at the beginning, and tell me how it all ended up with you here in Redemption."

If you want a future with him, you have to trust him with your secrets.

Familiar adrenaline that normally served to save Garrick's life by signaling it was time to run for safety suddenly coursed through his veins, making him jittery. For the first time in his life, he refused to heed the warning mechanism that had saved his ass more than once.

Garrick looked down again, needing a minute to get his shit together. The sheen of dried cum still stuck to Devlin's belly caught Garrick's attention and tugged a response in his balls. *Christ, it doesn't take much with this man.*

"Garrick?" Devlin's prompt yanked Garrick back to reality. And to the fact that he still didn't know where to begin with his history.

"Excuse me." Garrick moved Devlin a step to the left. As he busied himself turning on the water and wetting down a new washcloth, he closed his eyes and relived what it had felt like to spill himself inside Devlin's body -- a first for him. He bit down a moan as he wondered what it would feel like to bend himself over the sink and let Devlin do the same to him. His ass throbbed for it, and he half reached back to spread himself and beg for it, but abruptly whipped his hand back to the sink.

Pull yourself together and start talking or he's going to walk. "Here." Garrick thrust the new washcloth at Devlin's stomach. "The water on that other one is probably cold by now." He grabbed the first out of Devlin's hand. "You clean up, and I'll unfold the bed." *While I figure out what I'm supposed to say.*

Garrick left Devlin standing in the bathroom and made a beeline for the couch. He'd already pulled the coffee table aside hours ago but hadn't been motivated to unfold the bed. He did so now, tossing aside cushions and fluffing up the two pillows, and then taking care to fold back the thin plaid blanket and white sheet. By the time he finished doing that, he'd listened to Devlin take a piss, flush the toilet, and the water turn on and off again. Garrick crawled into bed and folded an arm under his head just as the bathroom light went out, throwing the room into deeper shadows again.

He held his breath, almost as if he'd never had a man in a room with him before, and didn't exhale until Devlin exited the bathroom and walked toward the bed. Garrick watched Devlin and openly admired the fluid grace of movement and the beautiful lines of his fit, naked body.

Don't try to finesse him, Langley. If you do, this time you'll lose him for good.

Devlin climbed onto the foldout bed, but rather than taking the second pillow, he stretched himself perpendicular to Garrick and used Garrick's stomach for a pillow. He looked up at the ceiling, and said softly, "Just start somewhere, Garrick." He reached out and pulled Garrick's arm across his stomach, then twined their fingers together in a hold, so gentle, yet sure, it burned tears behind Garrick's eyes. "It's going to feel like an impossible task until you do."

Garrick let out a shaky breath. "Okay, well, I was living in Oakland when we met. That wasn't a lie. I was involved with gangs too, just not the kind you were probably thinking. And when I used the term 'worked with them' I let you think I was a counselor of sorts for at-risk gang kids when actually I was undercover in one." Garrick fiddled with Devlin's fingers and focused on controlling his breathing. "I'd infiltrated a biker gang -- a club is what it's called. I was in for two years, living a completely fabricated life under a different name, gathering evidence of the many criminal enterprises this new club controlled. We had just brought them down the week before I met you in San Francisco. The weekend we met was my thank you from the CBI; a brief gift of freedom where I could relax and let go of the facade I'd been living with for two years before I had to get back to work."

Devlin shifted to his side and looked up at Garrick. "That's why you were so frantic that first time we were together." Understanding lit his pale eyes. "You weren't able to be with a man while you were undercover."

"No, I wasn't." Garrick grimaced and automatically rubbed a protective hand over his balls. "You are not gay in a biker club, open or otherwise. Not unless you want to get killed."

"So the tattoos, and the shaved head, and the extra muscle mass, were all part of the undercover work?"

"Yeah."

A furrow pulled between Devlin's brows. "But those tattoos were real. I licked them; I took showers with you." He reached up and ran his fingers down the side of Garrick's face to his shoulder. "And now I don't see or feel a trace of them on you anywhere."

"The CBI tapped the assistance of some scientists and doctors who are experimenting with new tattoo ink technology," Garrick explained. "They were real tattoos. Before I agreed to have them put on, I talked to the creators, and they believed that I would have success in fully removing them with lasers once the gig was finished. It wasn't one hundred percent guaranteed -- they'd never done anything that big -- but I felt good enough about the data they showed me to risk it."

"Wow." Devlin sat up next to Garrick. He studied the invisible line the previously tattooed side of Garrick's body had taken, and he trailed his fingers right behind. "You put a lot of faith in them. You could have easily ended up living with that ink for the rest of your life."

"It was worth it." Images of missing children assaulted Garrick's mind's eye and brought up a growl. "The CBI hadn't had any success getting an agent into this club and keeping him or her there for any length of time. Then they came across me -- a hotshot all high on some success I had working an undercover operation as part of my job with the San Diego police department. I already knew cars and bikes inside and out from being half raised by my Uncle Chris, and that was a good way for me to nudge my way into the club. The CBI thought I was a good combination of raw and focused and could get the job done for them. They couldn't afford to have another failure, and we all agreed to go balls-to-the-wall to make it a success."

Devlin met Garrick's gaze again, while his fingers traced an *exact* pattern the tattoo artists had put on Gradyn all those years ago. "Still…"

"This club was running some nasty shit." Heat burned straight through Garrick as he remembered, and his hands curled into bone-crushing tight fists at his sides. "Forget the drugs, chop shops, and weapons you would normally associate with organized illegal activity -- although they did that too. These guys were going into Mexico and other Central and South American countries and working as coyotes. They would take the money from desperate families and transport illegals over the border, only to kill the adults and sell the young ones. They made money off them twice, first from the families for entry into the US and then trafficking the children into brothels here in the United States and Canada, as well as other parts of the world."

The color fled from Devlin's face. "Shit."

"Yeah. You don't say no to that, and you don't refuse any weapon that might sell your character and help get you inside the club. The tattoos were part of that weaponry." Garrick's lips twisted into a frown. "I hate that word 'club.' Makes it seem like a weekend social where you discuss your favorite books or movies rather than an organization neck-deep in illegal activities. Anyway, that's why I agreed to the tattoos. I was willing to live with them forever, if I had to. I was already bulked up from the work I'd done on the San Diego job, and shaving my head wasn't a big deal." Garrick scratched his fingers through the overlong, dark stuff on his head now, and the reality of living with yet another new facade -- this one for the rest of his life -- settled an oppressive weight on his chest. He sought Devlin, met his gaze, and some of the tightness went away. "You got to see the outer shell of another person, but everything else I gave you that weekend, including my name, was the real me."

"You must have succeeded in bringing down the biker club or I never would have met you in a gay bar that weekend." Devlin's voice was hushed. "Am I right?"

Garrick nodded. "We'd already busted the head guys. The CBI pulled me out so they could grumble about my 'escaping' arrest. They were busy rounding up the few remaining lieutenants when I got my weekend of freedom. I was prepared to have to go back undercover, or at the very least testify at trials but, in a race to save themselves, these guys turned on each other faster than I've ever seen." A dry laugh escaped Garrick. "The CBI had one hell of a closer, and when the biker club lieutenants found out the death penalty was on the table, they tripped over themselves trying to be the one making a deal to stay off death row." Garrick clenched his teeth so hard he could hear his jaw clicking. "Thinking about those kids, and the horror these monsters sold them into, made everyone involved real motivated to do their jobs. I didn't have to do anything other than make my statement and sign off on the record of my time inside the club." With an audible exhale, Garrick then rolled his eyes heavenward. "Then, the FBI came knocking on my door, and I was primed and ready for plucking."

Devlin's brows pulled inward, and he cocked his head to the side. "What does that mean?"

"They tapped me to work a tight-knit family organization out of Indianapolis, believe it or not." Garrick nodded at Devlin's comic disbelief. "Yeah, I swear. Close-knit clan of Irish descent, which because of my own heritage -- my mother and uncle being very proud Irish folk -- I also knew something about. The FBI had a man and a woman inside, but they weren't sure the guy would make it the duration without breaking. They gave me the laundry list of illegal shit these people were involved in, and as I'm reading it, there's a healthy amount of my ego being stroked that the fucking FBI want *me* to be the one inside on their behalf."

Garrick owned his youthful conceit, along with a healthy bit of cynicism for the government officials who could spot the mix of intelligence and brash ego in its recruits and use it to their advantage. "There is an incredible adrenaline high that comes from taking down the bad guys, and when you're in your twenties, like I was at the time, feeling invincible and important, and you've had success, you think you've got the world by the tail, and you're David defeating Goliath. You don't say no. Hell, you don't want to say no." Garrick reached up and brushed his thumb across the fullness of Devlin's lush mouth. "Even if you've just met the most amazing guy and think you might be half in love with him."

"That's why you broke up with me," Devlin murmured, his body going still. "Because you went undercover again."

Garrick flattened his lips into a hard line, but forced out a nod. "It wouldn't have been fair to ask you to remain faithful to me. I knew I could have no contact with anyone from my real life once I went undercover again. I couldn't say 'Devlin, I won't be able to see or talk to you for anywhere from a two to five year period, and by the way, that's only if I don't die during that time and you simply never hear from me again.' I couldn't do that. You were a young man just getting the feel for your sexuality. It wouldn't have been right to put you in a place of limbo.

"I should have ended our relationship right away," Garrick said, his throat tightening with regret and loss, "but you were this wonderful truth in a new sea of lies I was about to dive into, and I couldn't make myself cut off the contact with you. For those six months we were together long distance, I was having the tattoos removed, and the FBI was also drilling information about this new organization into my head. Almost every second of that six months, I was learning to live in the skin of the new character I was about to play."

Garrick suddenly surged upright and sank his hand into Devlin's hair to pull him close. Clinging to the fact that Devlin hadn't walked away yet, Garrick scraped his mouth across Devlin's, and he drowned himself in the honesty and openness in his eyes. "And each day, in secret, I ached for that time we would talk on the phone or when I'd check my e-mail to find something from you. I craved every moment I had with you. But at the same time, each day, I hated myself more and more because I knew what we had couldn't go on. I would have to break things off with you." Garrick swallowed the bile wanting to rise inside him. "And I'd have to make it something so shitty you wouldn't want a damned thing to do with me ever again."

Devlin withdrew. He untangled Garrick's hand from his hair but kept their fingers connected against his thigh. "I could feel you pulling away toward the end," he said, his voice scratchy. "I knew something was wrong. You seemed less and less open, less and less like the person I thought I knew. Then when you told me you were getting back together with a girlfriend, and getting married, it all fell into place for me. It made sense." Devlin looked at their linked hands, and his mouth pulled down at the edges. "Even though I couldn't picture that self-assured man I knew in San Francisco as a person conflicted about his sexuality, I still believed what you said in that final e-mail. During our time in San Francisco, I never once thought you were deceiving me, yet the *second* I felt that blow of rejection," he snapped his fingers, "I discounted everything I believed in my gut and accepted that you were dumping me for a woman."

Garrick's gut twisted with nausea. "Hey," he lifted Devlin's face and tried to wipe away the harsh lines around his mouth, "*you* don't have any reason to feel bad about yourself. You were supposed to believe me. The e-mail was supposed to hurt you, and make you angry, and make you hate me. It had to. I couldn't tell you the truth. It's forbidden. Anything less than you despising me and thinking me the worst kind of coward and liar might have left you with some hope. That would have been worse, at least to me. I didn't want you thinking 'what-if' forever." Garrick wiped at what he thought might be a tear forming in the corner of Devlin's eye. "Okay?"

Devlin swiped at Garrick's arm. Then, with a surprising burst of strength, he shoved Garrick onto his back. He grabbed one of Garrick's wrists, pinned it to the mattress, and planted his other hand on Garrick's chest as he crawled on top of him and straddled his waist. Garrick yelped and put up a struggle … just not much of one. He loved being under Devlin too much to risk actually shoving him off, and his chest swelled with too much love at the laughter he saw lighting Devlin's pale gaze.

With his thighs squeezing against Garrick's hips, Devlin looked down with a smile that went all the way up into his eyes. "Ego much, mister?" he asked. "Who says I would have pined for you forever?"

Garrick's heart beat a furious rhythm under Devlin's palm, but he didn't break away from Devlin's stare. "I already knew I would for you. Maybe I was projecting a hope that you felt the same." Not an ounce of humor colored his voice.

The twinkle in Devlin's eyes dimmed. "I did feel the same," he said, his voice rough again. "That's why it hurt so much. I hated that my instincts could have been so wrong. I didn't trust myself for a long time after you."

Pressure bore down on Garrick's heart, and he almost couldn't breathe through the pain. "I am so sorry about that. Not sorry I did it -- I had to -- but I hated causing you pain." He reached up and cupped Devlin's smooth jaw. "My instinct to push you away was right. I was undercover in that job for over four years, and it did almost get me killed." The memory of the moon reflecting off the barrel of a gun flashed before Garrick's eyes, and he used his other hand to rub his chest. "Twice."

Devlin pressed a kiss to the center of Garrick's palm. "I read Gradyn Connell's obituary online the other day." He dropped down on his side beside Garrick and curled his hand under his head. "What happened?"

Garrick wiped a hand over his mouth. Christ, this part still pumped insane amounts of adrenaline through his system … and then ripped his heart right out of his chest. He turned on his side too, facing Devlin. "I made it inside the new organization. I met up with the other agent and together we climbed our way up to the second-in-command's inner circle.

We were so fucking close; I could taste the leader's trust. I knew we were going to bring them down." Garrick bit back a snarl and a howl of renewed rage. "Then one day I get a text. Two words: Breach. Run. Clarissa -- she was my partner -- got the same message. We got the hell out of there just as the whole operation imploded. Four years of work gone. She went one way and I went another in order to make ourselves more difficult to track. It took me a week to get back to my FBI handler, but I made it. Turned out the organization had obtained classified information about Clarissa and me and put hits out on both of us. That was when Gradyn Connell had to die." Garrick's chest constricted anew with the loss. "It was the only way to protect my mother, sister, and uncle."

Devlin gasped, and his eyes grew wide. "They really believe you died in a car accident?"

"They have to." It still rubbed Garrick's throat raw to think about his family, let alone speak of them. "It's the only way."

"God, Denny."

Garrick slapped his hand over Devlin's lips in a snap. "It's Garrick. You can never call me Denny again. If you call me that in private it increases the risk of you slipping up and saying it in public."

Devlin pried Garrick's fingers off his mouth. "You're right. I apologize." He offered a sweet smile. "*Garrick.*"

Grinning back, Garrick leaned in and pecked a quick kiss to Devlin's upturned lips. "Thank you."

Devlin snuggled back into the pillow, his hands tucked

under his cheek. "So how did you end up in Redemption? Are you in witness protection?"

"No." Garrick chuckled but it sounded brittle to his ears. "Witness protection couldn't protect me. The FBI set me up with a new identity in a home fifty miles north of DC. It lasted about two weeks." His Adam's apple bobbed as he swallowed a lump in his throat.

You have to tell him everything, man.

Feeling as if he might throw up, Garrick said, "Thirty-nine days ago a man broke into that house and tried to kill me."

The blood flooded from Devlin's face again. He grabbed Garrick and pulled him into a suffocating hold as he whispered, "Shit."

Garrick clung too, needing this warm body, desperate for someone to know everything and care. "I wasn't sleeping." He rasped the words out deliberately, one at a time. "Hadn't done much of that in years; it was hard to break the cycle. The intruder was good, but I heard him breaking in, and I was ready. We fought. The element of surprise allowed me to kick his gun away, but like I said, he was good, and we tussled around for a long while." Garrick's body tensed, as if ready to do battle right now. "Until I finally dropped him and sliced his neck clean through with a steak knife. I killed him, Devlin." Garrick pulled back. He needed to see Devlin's eyes -- study him -- while he told the rest. "I don't know if I had to, but it doesn't matter because from the second he broke into my house, before I was even certain he was a hired killer, I knew it would be him or me, and it wasn't going to be me."

Every line of Devlin's face and body remained loose and open, while Garrick was just the opposite.

"Hey," Devlin caressed Garrick's cheek with his knuckles, "it was reasonable to assume someone breaking into your house, whom you quickly assessed had a weapon, was connected to your undercover work and there to murder you."

Jesus Jesus Jesus. He doesn't understand.

"You have to listen to me." Garrick grabbed Devlin's shoulder and shook him. "I didn't know it was an assassin when I first heard the noise." Stirred up fears and old emotions seized Garrick's insides and cramped his belly. "It could have been a kid breaking in on a dare. It didn't matter to me. I'm so dialed into paranoia from living undercover for so long that I think every noise I hear, or every stranger who looks out of place, is someone watching me while thinking about how to kill me. In DC, I had already decided to take the intruder out, no matter what. It could have been a completely random stranger not out to harm me at all, for all I knew. Shit," Garrick's chest heaved and his voice broke, "if it had somehow been you, I wouldn't have stopped to look before I gutted you open and let you bleed out on my floor."

Devlin's eyes welled with wetness. He grabbed Garrick into the circle of his arms and held him close. "Baby, you don't know that." He rocked Garrick against the solid frame of his body. "You can't say for certain how you would have responded if it hadn't become a life or death situation."

Garrick buried his face in the crook of Devlin's neck and clung to him with every ounce of his strength. "I don't know." Uncertainty -- about everything -- lived inside Garrick all the time now. "I can still remember how I felt that night. Primal. Like an animal protecting its cub, only I didn't have a baby anywhere; it was just me."

Big hands rubbed up and down Garrick's back, soothing the stirred demons within. Devlin waited, as if sensing when Garrick had settled. He then withdrew, took Garrick's face in his hands, and held Garrick's attention with his piercing, pale stare. "It's called survival instinct." Devlin's tone brooked no room for argument. "You've worked law enforcement, so I know you understand it. It's pretty powerful stuff. I've smelled a whiff of it once or twice during tight spots inside a burning building."

Devlin's eyes softened; he brushed the pads of his thumbs back and forth across Garrick's cheeks -- *so fucking loving* -- and Garrick's breath caught as he fell under Devlin's spell.

"I understand that it's going to take some time for you to get your perspective back, and to learn to live every day without believing someone is out there trying to kill you," Devlin went on. "But know this: You are not a murderer. You did what was necessary in order to survive. That is all. Nothing more. Nothing less. Those are the facts. And that is what I believe. Okay?"

He's not afraid of me. Nothing had terrified Garrick more than worrying that Devlin would fear the man living inside him who could kill without mercy when needed. The violence that *had* to remain inside Garrick in order to maintain his ability to kill in case someone found him one day again. *But he's not afraid of me.* Tears burned behind Garrick's eyes, threatening to fall once more.

Garrick exhaled and then inhaled deeply as he fought through an overwhelming wave of love that pushed to burst a floodgate he was working with everything in him to keep intact. "I'm glad you became a firefighter." He desperately needed to change the subject so he could regain his equilibrium. "You seem so comfortable in your skin now." A smile came naturally as Garrick thought about the man with enough balls to come looking for his former lover who had denied being that. "It makes you even more attractive than you were before."

"Thank you." Even in the shadows, Garrick could see the pink flood Devlin's skin. "I don't know if I ever would have let myself go for it if we had not had that talk." He ran his fingers down Garrick's shoulder to his chest, and that sweet little smile appeared as he teased the tips in a circle around Garrick's nipple. "You remember that one?"

"Yeah." Garrick's voice was strained as Devlin scratched his trim nails over the already stiffened peak of Garrick's nipple. The man brushed the pad of his thumb over the sensitized area, and Garrick grunted as his cock twitched. *Not right now.* He clamped a hand over Devlin's, halting his arousing play. "I see your big brother is home too. From what Maddie says, you're all pretty close now."

Devlin nodded. "Aidan came back three years ago to take over as chief of the Redemption fire department. He came back for Ethan too." Shadows suddenly filled Devlin's eyes, putting Garrick in mind of a stormy sky. "Turns out my mother sent him away. That's why he disappeared."

Garrick forgot all about foreplay in a second. "I wish I could have come help you when your mother died." He dipped down and pressed a kiss to Devlin's shoulder, holding the connection for a moment. "I was having the tattoos removed and prepping for the new job when you called and told me she'd passed, and there was no way I could have up and left."

"It's all right." Devlin dug his fingers into Garrick's hair and moved him so they were facing one another again. "I got your sympathy card. I still have it." The dark slate swirls continued to churn in Devlin's eyes. "Turns out my mother wasn't as open-minded as she claimed to be. On his graduation night, Aidan told her he was gay and in love with Ethan, and that Ethan wanted him too. He said he was so fucking happy, and her first question was if he'd ever molested me."

Garrick's heart stopped and then broke for the younger Aidan. "Jesus Christ."

Devlin's lips pulled downward, creating harsh brackets around his mouth. "My mother held Maddie and me over his head. Told him he'd never have contact with us again if he chose Ethan and a gay lifestyle. Aidan walked away from what he had with Ethan so he could keep his relationship with us. Tough to hold a grudge against him after we found out about that."

"But Aidan ultimately ended up with you, Maddie, *and* Ethan after all, so that ended well." Garrick cupped Devlin's jaw and rubbed his palm against the beginnings of stubble. "Right?"

Devlin reached out and duplicated the way Garrick held him. "It could end well in Redemption for you too," he said softly, "if you decide to stay."

The floodgate inside sprung a leak, and a rush of adrenaline pumped through Garrick's veins worse than wildfire. "With someone still possibly after me, and after I killed that guy in cold blood... I don't know."

Devlin clamped his hand over Garrick's mouth. "That *hired assassin* who would have done the same to you." Passion infused Devlin's voice. "That is who you killed, Garrick, not some innocent on the street."

Garrick pried Devlin's hand away as the need to purge himself overtook any previous vows. "I left that man on the floor of that house and I ran. I had nothing but the cash I had stashed in the house. I trusted Joe -- he was my FBI handler -- but it was obvious to me that someone else in the FBI who had access to the undercover operation and my relocation status was on the take and selling us out."

"That would be my uneducated guess."

"I bought a disposable cell phone and placed one call to Joe. I told him what happened, and he agreed that someone on the inside was bad. He told me he would take care of it, but that he would only be able to call me one more time, so to give him a few days to put something together. During that time -- I don't even think I realized I was doing it at first -- I was making my way north, to you." Garrick could hardly get the words out through the clog in his throat. "I didn't know what in the hell I would do when I got here, I just knew I needed to find you."

Devlin squeezed Garrick's hand, and it gave strength to Garrick's voice so he could finish this.

"Joe called me five days later. I was already hiding out in a motel on the outskirts of Redemption by then. He wired me ten thousand dollars from a dummy account; he had a new identity for me -- Garrick Langley -- that he trusted one person to create, someone not part of the FBI." Hearing this surreal story aloud for the first time, when previously Garrick had lived with working things out in his head, drove the insanity of it all home for him. "Joe quietly did his magic at my crime scene too. By the time he was finished, there was a record of *two* dead bodies found in that home, charred from a fire that got out of control. As part of his ruse, Joe said he was going to kick up a good amount of internal fuss about one of his operatives being murdered and demand to know what the hell had happened. He knew nothing would come of it. The government rarely admits to a fuck-up, but Joe figured it would make the mole believe I really was dead, along with the assassin, and that Joe was fucking pissed about it."

Devlin had a rapt look on his face that put Garrick in mind

of someone watching a terrifyingly intense thriller.

"I'm scared to ask how this Joe guy came up with another body," Devlin said.

"Don't know." Garrick shrugged. "My guess is a John Doe from a morgue somewhere in DC." He rolled onto his back and tunneled his fingers into his hair. "Shit, I don't even know if the ruse Joe created was successful because I can't have any further contact with him. It's too big a risk. I can't dig too deeply for information via the Internet, because who the hell knows who might be tracking for patterns or particular word searches? Whoever wants me dead might be tracking key words and come looking if they see enough of them strung together by one person." He rolled his head on the pillow and met Devlin's gaze. "I'm still close enough to Gradyn Connell in physical appearance that if I were scrutinized by someone who wants me dead, they would see through my new name and altered appearance and know who I used to be."

"These people can do that?" Devlin now looked like he had slipped into watching a horror flick. "People can monitor random Internet activity?"

"It's not probable," Garrick admitted, "but it's not impossible either. Nothing done via the web is truly secret. That's why this is all still so up in the air."

Devlin took Garrick's hand and tucked it against his heart. "I'm glad that when you didn't know where to go, you came to me."

"Christ," Garrick chuckled softly, "I didn't know what the

hell to do when I got here. My two marketable skills are law enforcement and mechanic, and I definitely couldn't get back into law enforcement." He shook his head and rolled his eyes. "You should have seen me when I walked into Corsini's and saw the girl who was going to interview me. She didn't have to introduce herself as Maddie Morgan; she lifted her gaze, said hello, and fuck, it was almost like looking into your eyes. I didn't know shit about what your sister did for a living, but I knew it had to be her."

Garrick sobered as he relived the moment he came face to face with Maddie Morgan. "Meeting your sister scared me," he confessed. "It drove home how unprepared I was to see you again. I didn't know how I was going to deal with having to be a different person, on top of knowing that you would be mad as hell at me as Gradyn. I went back and forth in my head between praying that you wouldn't recognize me, and desperately hoping that I was important enough to you that you would know it was me the second we met again." Garrick's heart hurt as he faced Devlin and unloaded all his heavy, crap-filled baggage on a man he wanted to have love him and admire him more than anything in this world. "I admit that I hid from you. I wanted to see you and be near you more than anything, but I was spinning from everything that had just happened, and I didn't know if I could handle anger from you. I thought it might break me, when more than anything else I needed you to embrace me, and even to hold my hand while I got these new feet under me."

Devlin continued to clutch Garrick's hand, encouraging him without words. Garrick could feel the steady beat of Devlin's heart under the connection, and Devlin's heartbeat pumped new life into this new man, Garrick Langley.

"During this last month," Garrick went on, "as much as I was terrified of your reaction to me, there was also this big piece of me that was terrified Joe's cover-up wouldn't fool anybody, and that another assassin would find me. And if he did, and if I was with you, you could be killed too." Garrick's core screamed a line of white-fire pain through his being with just *speaking* words of losing Devlin. "You're the only one in this whole world, other than Joe, who knows who I really am. If you had changed, and if you'd decided to be spiteful… I knew showing myself to you could expose me as a fake. You could have insisted on calling me by my old name, and that would have brought hell down on me. Fuck," Garrick sweat bullets right here in bed, much as he had a few days ago under that Accord, "I was not even close to prepared for you to walk into Corsini's the other day. You didn't even have to look at me to know who I was. One sound of my voice, and you knew it was me."

"I would know you anywhere." Not even a sliver of hesitation inched into Devlin's voice. "I'm amazed I didn't *feel* you the second you stepped foot in Redemption. When you pretended not to know me," Devlin's chin suddenly wavered, and Garrick wanted to cry for him, "I felt played for a fool all over again."

"No." Garrick surged forward and kissed the tremble in Devlin away. "Not a fool," he promised. "Not you." Chagrin burned slashes of heat across his cheeks. "What you saw is what I look like when I panic. It doesn't happen often, but you've managed to see it a couple of times now."

"I was so pissed when I walked out of the garage that day," Devlin said. "Then the more I started thinking about it, the more I knew it couldn't be a coincidence that you had suddenly shown up in Redemption. I became determined to find out the truth." He quirked a brow Garrick's way. "I drove around town and half the neighborhoods looking for your truck before I came upon you playing outside with the kids."

"I'm so glad you did. Shawn and Chloe are important to me; Grace is too. But not in a romantic way," Garrick added quickly. If Garrick could see himself this second, he knew his entire body would be flaming red. He faced Devlin anyway, and finished. "She knew I was gay even before I told her."

Devlin's brows went even higher. "Oh yeah?"

"I didn't look at her tits enough."

Devlin threw back his head and let loose a sharp bark of laughter. "Classic dead giveaway."

Garrick threw himself back on his pillow. "Apparently."

"You're good with Shawn and Chloe. A blind man could see how much they love you."

"I already love them too. I don't know…" Garrick was so unused to sharing himself with people that he had a hard time formulating his thoughts. "Maybe they're just good kids and

I like them, or maybe I'm working out some absentee father issue of my own with them, but I can't help feeling like they need me."

Between their prone bodies, Devlin tapped his open hand against Garrick's in a comforting rhythm. "And you need them. Grace too."

"I don't have my sister anymore. I can't ever get her back. We were close before I started taking undercover assignments. Grace reminds me of her a little bit," Garrick shared. "A fighter."

Devlin stopped toying with Garrick's hand and linked their fingers together instead. "I'm so sorry you can never have them in your life again."

"Me too." Garrick's emotions swayed the pendulum again, and he fought the wetness that wanted to fall. "I knew the risks when I started taking undercover assignments. On an intellectual level, I knew I might have to change my identity, lose my family, and start over again on my own. But when you're young and filled up with your own talent, the potential lifelong sacrifices don't quite penetrate your brain. There's a part of you that thinks you're invincible. And in truth, to do that kind of work, you have to believe you are indestructible, or you'll get made. It gives you the swagger to step into a dragon's den and believe you can slay them." He turned his head and latched onto the comfort of Devlin's presence beside him in bed. "It also blinds you to the long-term consequences of a case going bad. It was my choice to do the job. My only regret is that my family is mourning someone who isn't really dead," his voice cracked, "and I can't do anything to make it better for them."

"Oh, baby." Devlin rolled himself into Garrick and tugged him close. "You've been living so many different lives for so long that it must be tough to know who you really are anymore."

"I know myself when I'm around you." Garrick held Devlin's face. He pulled it so close his lips snagged on Devlin's with each guttural word he confessed. "Your presence settles something inside me. I can feel the instincts and the ingrained things that Gradyn Connell understood and believed in still alive in me when I talk to you. He's in this body, with this longer hair. He has blue eyes instead of green, and he has a new job, and a different name, but his *identity* is still intact, and can exist because you know it too."

The very deepest of Garrick's fears, that he had refused to let himself examine and mourn, broke down the damaged gate inside him and roared through his being. "Otherwise, how can Gradyn ever have been real if I'm the only one who knows him, and he always has to stay inside me? He would fade away, and I don't want to forget him." Tears that Garrick had successfully suppressed finally won out and filled his eyes. "I don't want to forget his family. I don't want to forget that he was a good person." Ugly tears streamed down Garrick's face, and thickness coated his every word. "I don't want to forget that Gradyn had a dog named Turbo who slept in his bed for ten years. I don't want there to be no one who ever knows that when Gradyn was seventeen, and the dog got sick, he had to put him to sleep. I don't want to never be able to tell anyone that Gradyn had to pretend to his buddies that he was cool about losing his dog but that he really cried himself to sleep every night for two weeks afterward, and he still gets teary if he sees a chocolate-colored Lab."

Devlin brushed the mess of Garrick's hair away from his face, and moisture filmed his eyes too. "You don't want Gradyn to disappear forever as if he never existed."

Garrick heaved an uneven breath. "I know I need to but --"

Devlin stopped him with a kiss. "You don't need to, baby." He touched their foreheads together, and Garrick swore he could see past the blur of pale eyes right into Devlin's soul. "You'll tell me stories when we're alone, and I'll listen. You don't have to worry about keeping Gradyn buried so deeply all the time that you begin to question if those memories are real or figments of your imagination. It's going to be okay. You're safe with me." He pressed lingering kisses to Garrick's cheek, temple, and into his hair. "I promise."

"Thank you." Garrick breathed Devlin in, and the acceptance within this man made him shudder. "For everything." Old Gradyn memories surged through Garrick. Suddenly stricken, and understanding that Devlin needed to know so he could make an informed decision, Garrick said, "You have to know, I've killed other people, Devlin. In my old job, as Gradyn --"

"Shh, shh." Devlin put two fingers to Garrick's lips and masterfully shut him up. "Save it for tomorrow. I'm not going anywhere. No matter what you tell me," more of that strength coated Devlin's voice, "I'm still going to love you and want you in my life. You don't have to get it all out in one night." He rolled onto his back and pulled Garrick with him. Devlin tucked Garrick into his side and tilted his head back with a fistful of his hair until their gazes connected. Softness and full acceptance shone clear and bright in Devlin, turning the color of his eyes silver. "You have to be exhausted. Why don't you try to get some sleep?"

"Yeah?" Garrick croaked the word. He didn't think he could get another out just then.

Devlin put Garrick's head against his chest, kissed the top of his head, and brushed his hair as he whispered in return, "Yeah."

Maybe Garrick actually could close his eyes for more than a few minutes at a time tonight. Devlin held him so tightly, and he continually grazed his hand back and forth over Garrick's hip and ass, soothing Garrick and settling his breathing more completely than Garrick had experienced in years.

He won't leave me. He won't spill my secrets. I can trust him with my life.

Shit.

I just did.

The truth of everything Garrick had just spilled punched him right in the chest … yet it didn't speed up his heartbeat or make him sick to his stomach one iota.

Everything is going to be okay.

Garrick snuggled in closer to Devlin's warmth, blanketed

by their bond, and comforted himself with the steady beat of Devlin's heart pumping under his ear. "'Night, beautiful." He pecked a kiss to Devlin's chest. "I'll see you in the morning."

Devlin squeezed him in return. "You absolutely will."

CHAPTER TWELVE

Devlin stirred, roused by a siren somewhere in the distance. *Police car, not a fire truck.* Not that he would get a call if it were a fire.

Soon, Morgan. Soon.

Heat rode Devlin's front, not quite a crackling blaze, but still damned toasty. He smiled against the shoulder of the man in front of him, pleased to see that Garrick was still asleep.

He needs this peace.

Devlin scooted in somehow closer to Garrick and kept his arm wrapped tightly around Garrick's waist. He attached himself to his man from top to bottom, closed his eyes against the moonlight peeking in through the edges of the curtains pulled across the window, and drifted back to sleep...

...The softly lit airport and smattering of people milling about reflected the lateness of the hour. His hand linked in Gradyn's, Devlin felt his legs grow heavier with each step that got him closer to his flight ... and to a goodbye. Devlin's stomach twisted, and he crushed Gradyn's fingers, as if fusing their hands together would change the outcome of this weekend fling.

I don't want this to be the end.

Devlin took another step, and met with resistance. He glanced back, and a foot away, Gradyn stood motionless, their hands twined in the middle.

Gradyn's lips flattened to a thin, pale line, and his tattoos suddenly seemed stark and prominent, as if they took over his whole face and head.

"This is the stopping point for me," Gradyn said. He looked up, over Devlin's head, and Devlin followed his stare to the sign PASSENGERS ONLY BEYOND THIS POINT. "I can't walk with you any farther."

The end of this weekend punched Devlin fully in the gut, right where he stood. *Damn it, Morgan.* Devlin forced his back straight. *Don't you dare pussy out and cry.*

Gradyn tugged Devlin to him, speared his fingers into Devlin's hair, and tilted his head back. "We had fun, beautiful." He grazed his thumb back and forth along Devlin's jaw, and a softer smile took over the hard lines previously shaping his lips.

"At least I know I did."

"Me too." Devlin's voice caught, and he covered it by throwing his arms around Gradyn and burying his face in the man's chest. The feel of muscular arms immediately circling him sucked Devlin back into the raw places he had gone with this man this weekend, and he tried to drown the goodbye with levity. "It's going to take weeks before the imprint of you inside me goes away," he murmured with a thick chuckle. With just speaking those words, Devlin's ass throbbed. His sore passage reached for Gradyn again, and his chest constricted with loss. "I wish I could feel it forever."

Gradyn exhaled, and his breath washed over Devlin's ear. "Don't do this, Devlin." Even as he said that, Gradyn clutched Devlin to him in a suffocating embrace. "Please." He dug his chin into the top of Devlin's head, and his voice sounded rough. "I can't handle tears."

Suck it up, Morgan. Quit being a needy little bitch.

Devlin took a couple of deep breaths, and pulled away. "I apologize."

Gradyn's face fell, and he reached for Devlin. "Devlin, I didn't mean --"

"No." Devlin lifted his hand. "I'm fine. I promise." He took a step backward, prepared to leave this tryst in the unspoken way they'd somehow agreed it should end, but he couldn't make himself move another inch away from this fierce, harshly-attractive, sweet, funny, generous, patient, kind man. Devlin's body would not process and act on the commands his brain sent his limbs to move.

It's because this isn't right. You don't turn your back on an amazing weekend and an incredible person just because it's not supposed to become something special.

Devlin's entire being rejected the idea of never seeing Gradyn Connell again. That was why he could not move.

No guts, no reward, Morgan. Sometimes you have to step onto the ledge and risk falling without a net.

Right.

Devlin prayed for bravery and extra balls as he reached into the outer flap of his carry-on bag and unclipped the pen he had attached to his travel portfolio. His throat felt a little tight, his heart sped like crazy, but Devlin picked up Gradyn's hand, his own shaking, and put ink to skin. "This is my phone number and e-mail address." He wrote both ways to contact him on Gradyn's palm. "Before you say anything, I know that wasn't how this weekend started when you picked me up in that club, but it's the way I have to end it." He clicked his pen closed, and looked up into Gradyn's eyes as he curled the man's hand into a fist. "Think about using them. I can only speak for myself, but I don't want this to be the last time I see you or speak to you." His chest heaved, and he worked like the devil not to lose what was left of his cool. "You've already become too important to me to say goodbye."

Piercing brightness shone in Gradyn's pure green gaze, and his mouth gaped for a moment, without sound. "Devlin..."

"It's not goodbye. I hope not anyway." Devlin rushed to

speak over Gradyn, frantically drowning out what might be a rejection. "How about, see you lat --"

Gradyn made an inhuman noise, and he crushed his mouth down on Devlin's, stealing his breath and voice. He dug his fingers into Devlin's head and held Devlin in place for a scorching, devouring kiss. Right in the airport -- Devlin was acutely aware of other patrons not far away -- Gradyn pushed down on Devlin's jaw, forced his mouth open, and kissed Devlin with an intensity and desperation it hurt to feel. Devlin clung to Gradyn with hands twisted in his shirt and gave himself up to the mating with equal fervor, fearing that he needed this show of affection from Gradyn as much as he needed air to breathe.

Devlin slashed his mouth across Gradyn's, and strained up into him with all of his weight. Gradyn abruptly tore his mouth away, making Devlin keen a needy, "No."

Gradyn wrapped his hands around Devlin's wrists and pushed him a measure away. With his fingers crushing bone under their hold, Gradyn breathed heavily, his chest rising and dipping in waves. He looked at Devlin in a way that Devlin felt brush against his soul.

"Please know these were the best two and a half days of my life." Gradyn's voice sounded like he'd abraded his vocal cords. "But it can't go on." He released Devlin's arms, and whispered, "Goodbye." He turned and walked away, taking long, fast strides, out of Devlin's reach.

Out of his life.

Standing there watching Gradyn get smaller and smaller, Devlin rubbed his fingers across his swollen mouth, still able to feel Gradyn's kiss, and mentally willed the man to turn around and look at him one more time.

Devlin stood rooted to the floor for long minutes, his heart cracking inside. People moved around him; he didn't know what they thought about what they had witnessed, and he didn't care.

As the time ticked away, and Devlin knew he needed to move or miss his flight, he kept praying Gradyn would come running back to him and admit he felt something that meant more than a weekend of fucking too.

He never did.

Devlin finally turned, his soul crying inside, and got in the proper line to fly home to Maine. All the while wishing he had a tattooed man by his side, and wondering how a person could disconnect from their feelings the way Gradyn Connell just had...

...Devlin came awake with a start, his heart beating a furious rhythm as he lived inside the remnants of his memory. He reached out for Garrick, only to find him not there.

"I'm over here." Garrick's familiar voice reached him in a hushed tone.

Devlin whipped around and found Garrick sitting on a stool situated just to the right of the window. The man used the side of the microwave as a brace for his back. He wore only a white pair of cotton briefs, and the streak of moonlight streaming in through the sliver of open curtain highlighted the paler tone of his skin. It also put the definition of his sleeker muscles on one hell of a display.

Thank God. Devlin started breathing again. *He's still here.*

"That must have been some dream," Garrick said as he glanced over at Devlin. "You were twitching your way through it."

"I was remembering when you said goodbye." The second Devlin answered, his stare narrowed, and he perked up. "Hey, when did you wake up? You were asleep," Devlin searched for the time and found it on the microwave, "less than an hour ago."

"I woke up when I heard the siren," Garrick replied, "just like you did. You got comfortable right away again, though, and I didn't want to disturb you. Once something wakes me, I don't fall back to sleep." His Adam's apple suddenly bobbed visibly. "I'm sorry that e-mail is still hurting you. God knows I hate myself for it."

"What?" Devlin scrubbed his face, trying to wake up, as confusion overtook him. "Oh." Garrick's comment suddenly hit him. "I didn't mean *that* goodbye. Not the e-mail. I was dreaming about when we were at the airport together. I was thinking about the way you kissed me." He felt himself smile but then it fell away. "And then how you walked away without looking back."

Garrick chuckled, the sound without humor. "That's about the only successful thing I did that night. I managed to walk away, when all I wanted to do was stay with you. I successfully pulled away and started walking, and I told myself the whole time not to glance back." Garrick held Devlin to him right now with the rough texture of his voice and the intensity of his stare. "I knew I'd run right back to you if I did. I could feel your phone number and e-mail address burning my palm," he curled his hand into a fist, "like a fucking brand, so I went into the first bathroom I found, determined to wash it off. Instead, I stood in front of that sink, staring at my hand, and I memorized the information rather than wiping it away. Right then and there," he shook his head as he tipped his head back and turned his gaze up to the ceiling, "I understood I wouldn't forget you. I ran out and back to you, but by then you were already gone." Garrick rolled his head and found Devlin in the shadows again. "I thought that might be fate -- a sign that I wasn't supposed to see you again after all -- so I went back to the motel, got my stuff and my bike, and I drove back to CBI headquarters. Through the entire ride, I tried to memorize numbers on signs, and did my best to dislodge your contact info from my head." He shook his head and laughed. "But what did I do the second I walked inside that federal building?"

Devlin found himself perched at the end of the bed, as if he didn't already know the answer. "You sent me an e-mail," he said, his voice soft.

"Yep." Garrick had a look on his face that seemed to mingle

humor and annoyance. "I knew it wasn't smart to instigate contact with you. At that time, I thought for sure I would have to go back into the biker club. At best we'd only have time to trade a couple e-mails and phone calls before I had to disappear again, but the thought of never hearing your voice again..." Garrick pursed his lips, his eyes unnaturally bright. "I couldn't live with you believing that you were just a fuck for me. I think I knew from the beginning you would be much more than that." Garrick turned his head toward the window again, and his voice dropped to a hush. "Then I had to go break your heart anyway. Maybe it would have been better to let you believe what we did together was just about relieving a physical need."

"Don't say that." Devlin's chest squeezed and his throat hurt. He went to the sink, taking a moment to fill a glass with water and drink it. "If we hadn't shared those six months together through phone calls and e-mails," he leaned against the counter and stared at Garrick's stark profile, "would you have come to Redemption when your life fell apart?"

Garrick finally pulled his attention off the wedge of uncovered window and put it on Devlin. "That six months took us from lovers to partners, I think. Ass backward, but no less powerful, if that makes sense."

"It does." The small room, along with the wee hours of the night, cloaked each word they spoke in an additional layer of intimacy. "That makes the pain worth it for me. The time we spent getting to know one another is ultimately what brought you back to me." He looked right into Garrick's eyes, and he did not let his voice waver even a hair. "I forgive you. I think maybe you need to hear that."

"I do." Garrick nodded, and he clearly worked hard to blink some of the sheen from his eyes. He averted his head, and his voice dropped, but Devlin still heard him say, "Thank you."

Devlin got up to go to Garrick, when suddenly Garrick narrowed his stare through the crack in the curtains. "Oh, sweet merciful God." The man shot up off his stool, ripped open the door, and then tore out of the apartment at a breakneck speed.

"What the fuck?" Devlin picked up his sweats, shoved himself into them, and snatched Garrick's shorts up off the floor. He flew out of the room and took the steps two at a time after Garrick, but Garrick was already halfway across the lawn, heading for the Fine's backyard.

Someone is breaking into the house.

Garrick's first thought: assassin.

He ate up the grass under his feet and sped around the house to the Fine's kitchen door, knowing he could kick that lock in a shitload easier than the front door.

Thank God Devlin had almost fucking brought him to tears, forcing Garrick to avert his head so the man wouldn't see them. If Garrick hadn't sought the safety of his nightly ritual of peeking out the window when he couldn't sleep, he would have missed the dark shadow jumping over the side of the Fine's front porch and disappearing around the far side of the house.

If someone hurts Grace and the kids in order to get to me...

"Shit." Garrick couldn't even contemplate that. He might not be able to recover.

A scream shrieked through the house just as Garrick leaped up the steps to the kitchen door. The sound pierced Garrick's skin and sank into his bones, horrifying him to his core. Pure adrenaline flooded his system, charging him with superhuman strength. He put every ounce of his weight behind his shoulder and slammed into the door, cracking the wood right off the frame, and sent the door flying open.

Garrick ran through the darkened kitchen and dining room, through the living room, and found the kids screaming "Mommy, Mommy!" in the hallway outside their mother's open bedroom door.

Shit.

"In your room; get in a room!" Garrick came up on them and shoved both kids none-too-gently away from their mother's door. "Right now!" His voice went hoarse as he saw Grace and a man dressed in camouflage doing battle out of the corner of his eye. A knife and a gun were on the floor. He yelled back at Chloe and Shawn, "Lock the door and don't come out!"

Devlin appeared at the end of the hall. "I got 'em!" he shouted, grabbing each kid by their arms and dragging their little kicking bodies to safety. "Go!"

Garrick dove into the fray just as Grace rammed the heel of her foot back into her assailant's knee. The man roared a foul word and let go of her, but then threw himself onto her back the second she moved, and he took them both to the carpet. Garrick hurled himself onto the man's back, and he burrowed his arms under the guy's armpits, chopping at his hold on Grace.

The man reared and elbowed Garrick in the jaw with near bone-crushing force. He turned on Garrick and threw a punch to the center of Garrick's chest, knocking the wind right out of him.

Fuck. He's had special training. Gotta be after me. Garrick kicked the man's leg out from under him and took him to the ground again. As Garrick gasped for breath, he threw himself at the assailant who had shot to his feet with lightning-fast moves, who lunged for Grace again.

Grace grabbed the knife and plunged it into the man's shoulder -- or at least she tried to. She cried out as the blade didn't sink in deeply -- as it should have -- and she grabbed her wrist as the knife fell to the floor.

Kevlar vest. Garrick processed that the man had on some sort of protective gear under his fatigues while simultaneously tackling him from behind and shoving him face first into the wall. The man surged with much the same strength Garrick had possessed when knocking down the door; the guy rammed his head backward and head-butted Garrick's skull with brain-shaking power and precision.

"Ahh!" Garrick clutched the side of his head as white-hot pain snaked through every part of his body. He lost his knees and dropped to the carpet.

The assailant went for Grace again. Through the dizzying

hit Garrick's head had taken, he managed to lunge and yank one foot out from under the attacker. At the same time, Grace kicked her leg out at the guy in a karate move and jammed him in the stomach hard enough to send him flying out the door and into the hallway.

Still seeing two of everything, Garrick jumped to his feet and raced out into the hallway after the man, unsteady as he chased a blurry figure streaking toward the front of the house.

The attacker yanked the front door open without incident. *He must have unlocked it before going after Grace.* The man flew through the opening and down the steps, shouting, "You got lucky, bitch." He pointed as he sprinted across the street and threw himself into a car. "I'm coming back for you!" Wheels spun, creating smoke, as the car, clearly already running, chewed up the pavement, and the guy got away.

Garrick chased the car halfway down the street, and he managed to get color, model, and the first half of the license plate number, but no more than that before the car turned out of sight.

"You got lucky, bitch." The words reverberated in Garrick's head as he jogged back to the house. *This guy wasn't here for me.* Still, even as Garrick wondered what the hell this man wanted with Grace, he couldn't stop shaking as scenarios of how easily that could have been an assassin coming for him hit his psyche.

It could have been for me.

The bastard could have taken out my family in the process.

Right on the front lawn, Garrick doubled over and threw

up what was left of his dinner. Bile burned his throat as he coughed and retched up everything in his stomach while his arms and legs shook like a newborn foal.

I have to get out of here. I can't do this. It's not safe. I might as well kill them all myself.

"Here." Devlin's deep, familiar voice burrowed into Garrick's being, and his warm hand rubbed the tension knotting the small of Garrick's back. "Put these on." Devlin dangled a pair of shorts under Garrick's downturned face. "Let's start with that."

Garrick took his shorts, and Devlin held him steady with a hand around his upper arm while Garrick struggled into them. Garrick didn't have to look up at his mate to know that Devlin understood every bit of fear coursing through Garrick right now. Garrick could hear the knowledge in the gentle nature of Devlin's tone.

He forced himself to look up into those pale, knowing eyes anyway. "It wasn't a hired killer here for me this time," Garrick said. "But it could have been. Jesus, Devlin," Garrick spat the horrid taste out of his mouth, "they all could have been butchered before I even had a chance to step one foot in that house."

Devlin's features turned ruddy and hard. "So you're going to pack up and run." He snapped his fingers, the sound cracking in the night. "Just like Grace is frantically doing inside right this second."

Garrick narrowed his gaze on Devlin first and then to the

home behind him. "What?"

Devlin nodded, and Garrick ran for the house, taking the steps two at a time, and bounding across the porch. He pushed open the half-closed door and found Grace rushing her kids into their bedrooms, telling them to pack a bag and their most special toys.

Grace moved toward her bedroom. Garrick grabbed her arm and drew her into the living room before she got half a dozen feet away. "Where are you going?" he asked, as she tugged against his hold.

"Don't know yet." Her dilated pupils nearly drowned out the rim of brown, and through Garrick's hold on her, he could feel that her jitters matched his own. "Anywhere far away from here."

Garrick replayed not only the professional moves of the assailant, but also Grace's battle technique, which had gone toe-to-toe with a bigger foe. "What the hell went down here tonight?"

Grace's delicate hand shook as she covered her mouth. "That was my ex-husband. He's obviously out of prison. Now that he knows where I am, I have to leave."

Running from an abusive ex. Of course. I should have known. She immediately took my fears about someone watching the house seriously; any other time in my life that would have set off my radar in a shot.

Grace stopped pulling against him. She looked up at him, and frown lines marred her forehead. "Your eyes are green."

"Shit." Garrick turned away and cursed under his breath again. Not that it mattered. She'd already seen the color. Stupid mistake. It was exactly the kind of rookie move he couldn't afford to make.

"I don't care why." The lulling softness in Grace's voice drew Garrick's attention back to her. "You've been good to me." She squeezed his hand. "Even if I could stay in Redemption, I wouldn't make trouble for you."

"Thank you."

"I still have to get the kids and go." The shakes took Grace over once again. "My ex doesn't make empty threats. He will come back."

Garrick snatched Grace's hand before she took one step toward her children. "You're not going anywhere."

Suddenly, a manacle-tight hold circled *Garrick's* wrist. "And neither are you," Devlin said, his hand bruisingly strong on Garrick's arm.

Garrick whipped around to his mate. "Devlin --"

Resolute determination filled Devlin's eyes and tone. "Neither one of you is leaving this town. Not tonight." He dragged Garrick, who by virtue of the fact that he still had a hold on Grace, pulled her too. Devlin shoved them both onto the couch, and transferred his grip to their shoulders, keeping them seated.

"And you," Devlin turned a hard gaze on Garrick, "not ever without me. Not anymore."

Grace struggled against Devlin. "But --"

"Dev." Garrick bit down a curse. "This is serious. Stop it."

Devlin didn't loosen his hold on either one of them in the slightest. "I know it's serious. So here's what's going to happen," he said, his tone reminiscent of some of the sharpest, hardened, lifer law enforcement officers Garrick had ever known. "You're both going to sit tight. I'm going to make a call," Devlin eyed the phone on the end table, but didn't yet move, "and for once, you're both going to have to trust that someone else loves you enough to make things safe for you."

He eyed Grace first, and then switched to Garrick. Devlin's mouth lost some of its hard lines, his grip switched to a soothing caress, and he offered a small smile that tugged right at Garrick's soul as he said, "Got it?"

CHAPTER THIRTEEN

Trust me.

    Devlin held his breath and waited for someone to speak.

Grace snatched the phone off the receiver and hugged it to her breast.

"No offense, Devlin," she said as she shielded the phone from him, "but I don't know you well enough to trust you. I have to think about my children." Her focus darted to the hallway, and presumably to the rooms of her children beyond. "You can make whatever call you want, but we'll be gone by the time you're done dialing."

It will kill Garrick to lose another family. Devlin saw the man flinch as Grace delivered her decree. *That means it will crush me too.*

Devlin put a hand to Grace's knee. Not a controlling grip this time, just a human connection. He waited for her to settle and make eye contact with him before he spoke. "Do you trust Garrick?"

She studied Garrick's stiff profile, and a small smile appeared. "With my life. With the lives of my children."

Devlin turned to Garrick. He ached to pull the bigger man into his arms and hold him all night, as long as it took to take the fear away, but he forced himself to remain seated on the coffee table.

"Do you trust me?" Devlin asked Garrick.

Garrick exhaled, and his pure green eyes deepened with shots of deep-forest. "I love you," he said, the sound thick in his throat. He curled his hand around Devlin's neck, drew him close, and pressed a kiss high on Devlin's cheek. "I couldn't love you if I didn't trust you completely."

Devlin dipped his head and grazed his lips against the inside of Garrick's forearm, and took a moment to nuzzle into the warmth. "Thank you."

He brushed another soft kiss, and then shifted back to Grace. "So you trust Garrick, and he trusts me. Ergo, you trust me too." Devlin nodded, and tried to nudge the woman along with his logic. "Grace," he let go of Garrick, took both of Grace's hands in his, and dangled them between their legs, "I don't know your entire situation, but I'm going to say this to both of you because I think it applies: you have got to stop running."

He put one of their linked hands against her mouth before she could open it. "You say your ex is dangerous? Okay, I saw him tonight, and I believe you. But I also believe it would be a wise move to make a stand against him here, in Redemption, where you have neighbors who likely care very much about you and your children."

"They do," Garrick said. He put his arm around Grace's shoulder and hugged her to his side. "I've seen it."

"Okay," Devlin went on, "so you let your neighbors know about this son of a bitch, and they will be on the watch for any suspicious car or person in this neighborhood until the cops track your ex down and put him behind bars again. I know a cop." Devlin let go of Grace and put his hand on Garrick's knee, knowing the man would hit red-alert upon hearing Devlin's suggestion. "His name is Wyn Ashworth. He's a good man. With your permission, I'm going to call him here to take a description of your ex, put a warrant out for him, and alert the local force that he is dangerous and that you and your kids need protection from him.

"And you," Devlin put his attention back on Garrick, and stilled the erratic beat of the man's leg as he tapped his heel into the floor, "*you're* going to trust that I know this cop very well. Then you're going to keep trusting me and believe that I can talk to Wyn on your behalf without revealing information that I know needs to remain between only us. You're going to trust that Wyn will take me at my word, and that you will be all right."

Garrick's pupils widened like a sun flare, and he frowned at Devlin.

"It's okay." Grace answered before Devlin could. "I don't need or want to know what Devlin is talking about. You're one of the good ones, Garrick. That's all I need to know."

Garrick shifted on the couch and fully faced Grace. "What do you think? Do you want Devlin to call his friend? Yesterday you said you don't much feel like moving anymore. You said you were tired and ready to stay in one place for a while."

Grace hugged herself, and her gaze strayed to the now closed front door. "But Randy..."

"That's your ex-husband?" Garrick asked.

"Yes."

A sigh escaped Garrick. He tunneled his hands through his dark hair and shoved it off his face. "Maybe Devlin is right, Grace. Maybe it's time to stop running. Maybe it's okay to ask for help against your ex. You don't have to fight Randy on your own."

Grace turned a pointed stare back on Garrick. "Are *you* going to stay?"

A long pause filled every corner of the room with heavy silence. Garrick stared over Grace's shoulder in the direction of the hallway, came back and held on Grace for a handful of heartbeats, and then settled on Devlin for what felt like eons. He finally nodded sharply, and said in a rough voice, "Yeah, I'll be here."

Devlin doubled over, his forehead falling to rest on Garrick's knee, as relief flooded his system. *He's staying.* Devlin covered his mouth, stifling a sob that wanted to break free.

Garrick ran a hand through Devlin's hair, offering the sweetest simple contact, and Devlin nearly wept all over his lover's leg.

Grace cleared her throat. "Then call your friend, Devlin. I want Randy captured as soon as possible."

Devlin jolted back up straight. *Shit.* "Right." This wasn't over. Convincing them was only half the battle. Devlin scrubbed his face, and his gaze lit on Garrick's as he pulled his act together. *Damn it.* "Garrick, you go take care of," Devlin pointed at Garrick's eyes, "while I make this call."

"Oh." Garrick shot to his feet. "Right." He glanced down at himself as he walked backward to the door. He then moved his focus up Devlin's bare stomach to his chest and finally back up to his eyes. "I'll get us some shirts while I'm at it."

"Good idea."

As Devlin watched Garrick open the front door and disappear onto the porch, he couldn't help his heart lurching and his throat seizing as the man slipped out of grabbing distance.

Trust him. It goes both ways. He will come back.

Grace put the phone in Devlin's hands, jerking his attention back to her.

"I'm going to talk to my kids," she shared. "Let them know we're not going anywhere. At least not tonight."

The woman's skin was still pale as a ghost against the navy

blue color of her T-shirt and pajama shorts. Her obvious fear and exhaustion tugged at Devlin's heart. He could understand why Garrick had taken to her so quickly.

"This is a nice place to raise kids," Devlin said. He squeezed her arm, pleased when she attempted a smile in return. "It's going to work out. I have a good feeling, and I've recently learned I can trust my gut, after all."

"Thank you again." She dipped her head and moved down the hallway, out of sight.

Devlin picked up the phone. Not even a siren in the distance -- *definitely a fire truck this time* -- pulled his attention away from dialing Wyn Ashworth's number.

DEVLIN MET WYN ASHWORTH AT the door. The guy had on sneakers, wrinkled jeans, and a Bruins T-shirt that had a tear in the shoulder. It didn't look like he'd taken the time to run a comb through his short, dark hair, and Devlin thought he saw little crusts from sleep in the corners of the man's eyes.

His friend's intimidating frame dwarfed the doorway. "I got here as fast as I could." Wyn withdrew a small spiral pad from his back pocket. "Where is Ms. Fine?"

Devlin put a hand on Wyn's stomach and eased him back over the threshold. "Can I have just a few words with you first?" He closed the door behind him. "In private?"

Wyn crossed his thick arms over his wide chest. "Make it fast. I want to get this asshole's information into the system as fast as possible."

"Believe me, I do too." Devlin took in the solid stance of his friend, and looked him in the eyes. "Here's the deal. I was with Garrick when Grace's ex-husband broke into her home. Garrick saw the guy run around the side of the house, and he immediately bolted out of his apartment above the garage to help." Devlin swallowed past his own discomfort and matched Wyn's stalwart chin with one of his own. "What I need you to do is keep that part of it out of your report. I need you to keep *Garrick* out of the report."

Wyn's entire face went stony. Then his mouth twisted as if Devlin had forced shit down his throat. "I'm sorry. You fucking want me to falsify a report for your boyfriend? Why the hell would I do that?" He narrowed his gaze to black slits. "Why the fuck would I need to, Devlin?"

"Not falsify." Devlin jumped to correct Wyn. "Just don't poke holes in the statement Grace gives you."

Wyn ran his hands through his hair and tufted it up in even thicker clumps. "What the hell, Dev?" He clasped his hands behind his neck and tipped his head back. "You have to give me something more to go on here. I don't understand what kind of shit you're asking me to do for you."

"Look at me." Devlin grabbed Wyn's arms and shook him, forcing the man's gaze back down to his. "I am your friend. You know I would not steer you toward covering up someone with a record, or anything bad, or wrong. But I need you to hear me." His throat tightened and his mouth went dry as the need for speed and success grew within him. "Garrick Langley is a good man. He is on the right side of every single law you believe in and work to uphold. But I need you to not only keep him out of this report, I also need you to promise me you aren't going to put his name or image into your system and start looking into his life on my behalf. That would be *very* bad." Devlin pried his fingers out of Wyn's biceps, but his voice shook with the emotion he worked like the devil to contain. "I'm trusting you with the life of the man I love. Grace wanted to run. They are both trying to build new lives here in Redemption. Grace is trusting me because Garrick trusts me, and Garrick is trusting you because I told him I trust you. He cannot be put under a microscope." Devlin looked right into Wyn's eyes and didn't shield the secrets he could not speak aloud. "Do you understand what I'm saying?"

Wyn delivered a hard stare, and Devlin watched his jaw tic a mile a minute. The man threw out a colorful bevy of curse words that would have made any of his fellow cops proud. He finally bit off, "I can only write in my report what I'm told." He didn't look one bit happy or pleased. Devlin thought resigned was probably a better word. "What I will tell you is that a story with questions and holes in it that might normally make me want to dig deeper won't rouse my suspicions in this case. That's all I can promise you."

"I would never ask for anything more." Devlin locked his legs in place to stop himself from leaping into Wyn's arms and hugging him to the point of embarrassment. "Thank you."

A dastardly chuckle escaped Wyn, and a dark glint suddenly flashed in his eyes, transforming his intimidating frame. "Damn it, Morgan. I fucking knew you had a history with that guy the second he walked into your apartment the other night. Then when I saw you pin him to the wall in the hallway... Shit, you owned him, man. I could feel it."

Right now, Devlin could feel heat rushing to his face. "He's someone you will come to admire and respect. I know it." Devlin's heart slipped back inside the house, to the man sitting on that couch *trusting* in Devlin, and Devlin's tone went soft. "Thank you, Wyn. You won't regret this."

In one blink of his eyes, Wyn slipped fully into cop mode. "I'm not doing anything but taking a statement from a woman whose ex-husband broke into her home. There's nothing to regret." He jerked his head toward the front door. "Now, how about you introduce me, and let me get to work on putting this ass-wipe back in jail where he belongs?"

Devlin led him inside. "Let's do it."

WITH HIS BACK TO THE group of three sitting at the dining room table, Wyn said, "Thanks," and ended his phone call.

So far, Grace had quickly given Wyn an updated physical description of her ex-husband, including his choice of army garb, and Garrick had shared what he could recall of the car and license plate number. Grace had also told Wyn about the gun, which Wyn had photographed with his cell phone and taken as evidence using a Ziploc bag Grace had provided. While Wyn took care of the gun and photographing the window in the bathroom Randy had broken in order to gain entry into the house, Devlin had watched Garrick speak softly to the kids once again, quietly assuring them that everything was okay.

Now Devlin, Garrick, and Grace were back in the dining room, where they could talk while keeping an eye on Shawn and Chloe in the living room. The kids were sitting so close together they were almost on top of each other, huddled up tightly as they watched a movie.

Wyn moved back to the table and sat down. "All right. That call I just made will get a BOLO created so that we can officially start looking for Randy and his car. We'll also have the black and whites make a point to check out parking lots of area hotels, as well as motels off the local interstate ramps. That's just to get us started." He shifted his attention and put it fully on Grace. "You said Randy was wearing military gear. Is he retired Army or part of the Reserves?"

"No." She rubbed her bare arms, and Devlin saw her shiver. "He was one of yours, though." Her voice scratched some as she shared. "A police officer, out of Boise."

Garrick's lips twisted in a snarl, and Devlin knew his green eyes sparked fire under the blue of his contacts. "Son of a bitch," Garrick swore viciously. "That is not what going into law enforcement is about. It's a fucking abuse of power. That's how he was able to find Grace so quickly after being released from prison."

Grace nodded, and Wyn turned a sharp glance on Garrick. Just a quick second's worth of a look from Wyn, but it was clearly enough for full understanding of Garrick's former life to slip into place for the man.

Wyn made a blink of eye contact with Devlin, and then moved on to Grace. "I'm going to take a look into why the parole board didn't contact you the minute he was granted an early release," he said. "That is a serious error on their part."

"Randy didn't get sent to prison for assaulting me," Grace shared. "I couldn't make that happen. He had too many friends on the force willing to believe I was hysterical, or a bitch, or out for revenge because I'm a woman, and of course men can never do enough to please a woman." The waver she'd started out with left her voice. She sat up straighter, and her chin lifted higher, but she kept her tone low enough not to be heard by small ears one room away. "But when Randy attacked a man in a bar and took a stab at him with a skinning blade, his brotherhood couldn't turn a blind eye to the crime. The second they arrested him, I packed up Chloe and got the hell out of Idaho, just in case he wormed his way out of the charges." Grace's gaze strayed to her children. "I was pregnant with Shawn, but I hid it. I didn't show with either one of them until I popped in the seventh month. Randy is Shawn's father, but for obvious reasons, I never wanted him or anyone in his family to know about the baby. His mother thought I was overreacting to normal marital scuff ups."

"What about Chloe?" Garrick asked. "Didn't Randy's

family hire people to come after you for rights to see her?"

Grace's entire face transformed, and it was as if light emanated from her golden skin. "Chloe belongs to my first husband. Matt was a wonderful man. Sweet and funny and generous," the twinkle left her eyes, "and just as alone in the world as I was. I lost Matt to a freak pulmonary embolism when he was only twenty-five. Just like that." She snapped her fingers. "His death sent me reeling. I was taking care of Chloe by myself; I was working two jobs, and I wasn't sleeping. Then this guy comes along, and he seems steady and safe and friendly; he was a cop for goodness sake."

Grace seemed to turn inward, her voice so soft it almost couldn't be heard. "He could have been anything, though, truthfully. I wasn't even close to thinking clearly; I know that now. I was deeply mourning Matt, and my decision-making skills were not intact. I let myself get sucked into Randy's world, and he slowly morphed into this brutal, belittling person. It was so subtle," lines marred her brow as she spoke, "I didn't even know it was happening at first. And he very cleverly stayed away from Chloe." Grace looked toward the living room, very likely studying Chloe's profile. "I think he knew putting a finger on my child would snap me out of my fog. By the time I woke up from my stupor, I didn't have much money of my own to speak of, and none of his buddies would take my abuse claims and turn them into charges. They just gave him 'warnings'." Red lines burned across Grace's cheeks as she said that. "I started secretly saving every penny I could. I didn't know what I was going to do; he was still harassing and threatening me, but when he attacked that guy, I knew I had to run. I didn't have nearly enough money to do me any good, but I knew this was my one chance to disappear, and I took it."

Devlin's head spun. "How in the hell did you make it?"

Grace shrugged. "When you finally look in the mirror and realize it's potentially your very life on the line, and you're about to have a second child depending on you, you just do it. I kept tabs and knew Randy hadn't escaped the charges. He eventually got out on bail, but it took a while and he wasn't allowed to leave the state. I didn't trust that, though. I got into a mode of moving, always feeling like I needed to get us a bit farther away from him geographically. I even kept it up when he went to prison. Then we hit Redemption." Her lips turned up at the edges. "Something about it felt right. My kids seemed to breathe easier. I felt less jumpy. Eventually I felt completely safe." She turned to Garrick. "At least until you started getting vibes a few days ago."

Garrick looked beaten too. "Christ, Grace, you should have told me. I would have moved in here with you in a shot."

"It wouldn't have mattered. Randy obviously spent his time in prison thinking about coming to get me. If he saw you living in the house, he just would have changed his strategy. He wouldn't have given up wanting to grab me or kill me or … or … God knows what. If he'd been successful… If he'd hurt Chloe or Shawn." She grabbed at Garrick's arm, and her face drained of all color. "What if Randy saw Shawn and figured out he's his son?"

Garrick rubbed at the hand Grace had embedded in his forearm. "I don't think you have to worry about that. If Randy cared about taking the boy, he would have attempted to grab Shawn before going for you. It doesn't make sense to go for the adult first, who will fight back and likely create a scene. As a former cop, I'm sure Randy understood that. If he realized Shawn is his, I don't think he cared."

"I'd agree with that assessment," Wyn added.

Grace took a deep breath, and then another. "Thank God."

Wyn's phone suddenly vibrated and bounced in a circle on the table. "Excuse me." He tilted the device and looked at the screen. "That's the station. I need to take this."

Getting up again, Wyn put the phone to his ear, and wandered into the kitchen. Devlin heard him say, "What's up, Shue?" before pulling his focus off Wyn and putting it on Grace and Garrick.

"You're both doing great." He reached out and squeezed their hands. "How are you feeling?"

Garrick turned his hand over and put his palm flat against Devlin's, linking their fingers. "You were right about your friend," he said. His mouth was still set in a hard line, but less so than when Devlin had come to him on the sidewalk a bit ago. "I can see in Wyn's face that we can trust him. He has your back, which means he has ours too."

"I think this must be what therapy feels like," Grace said, her pitch still high. "I've never shared so much about my history at once."

Devlin's heart squeezed as he studied this woman who appeared to be the same age as himself. *She's been through so much.* "I'm sorry about your husband. The first one, I mean. About Matt."

"Me too," Garrick murmured.

"Thank you. Matt was another one of the good ones." A wistful smile that reached her chocolate-brown eyes transformed her into a lovely woman.

The first shoots of dawn fought against the darkness outside, and to Devlin it felt as if the battle for daylight lifted the weight of the house too. As the shadows slowly started to recede, Grace watched her children with a returning sparkle in her gaze. "There's a lot of Matt in Chloe," she shared. "And I know it's not biologically possible, but I see him in Shawnee sometimes too."

Garrick followed her stare to the children. "Maybe it's Chloe rubbing off on Shawn, and the osmosis is happening that way."

"Probably," Grace replied.

Wyn returned, and Devlin almost asked the man if someone had sucker punched him.

"You're not going to believe this," Wyn said. He looked at his phone, still in his hand, as if it had sprouted horns, a tail, and wings. "We don't even have an official BOLO out yet, but a patrol car just responded to the preliminary information that our dispatcher shared over the radio. I can't confirm it this second, but a car matching Garrick's description of Randy's plowed into a garbage truck at full speed a bit ago. The driver flew through the windshield. The guys on the scene say it doesn't look good."

The fire trucks I heard.

"Call Aidan," Devlin told Wyn. "He's on duty right now. His emergency crew would be called to the scene of an accident like that."

Wyn raised a finger as he stepped away, his phone already once again at his ear. A murmur of unrecognizable words floated to Devlin as the man moved into another room.

Grace looked back and forth between Garrick and Devlin. She stared at the wall that had Wyn on the other side, and then back to Garrick. She started sawing down on a thumbnail with her teeth. "I know it's not right to wish someone dead…"

"I don't think anyone would judge you in this situation," Garrick said. "We're all hoping we hear the same thing when Wyn hangs up that phone."

"Agreed," Devlin said in a hushed voice.

All three of them sat in strained silence, listening to indecipherable murmurs coming from Wyn in the kitchen. When he returned, they all leaped out of their seats in unison like Jack-in-the-boxes.

"Take a seat." Wyn gestured them down with his hand. "I talked to Ethan. I thought he was doing his overnight last evening, and he was. I figured I'd have a better shot getting through to him than I would Aidan." Ethan was part of the volunteer fire brigade; twice a week he was part of the volunteer rotation that slept at the firehouse as part of the official crew.

"Ethan was still at the scene doing cleanup," Wyn told them. "He confirms the make and model of the car Garrick described. While I waited on the line, he took a look at the plate and confirmed the first three numbers too." Wyn took a seat and focused solely on Grace. "It was Randy. The physical description, as well as the clothing of the driver, is what you gave me. They didn't find any identification on the victim or in the car, but it has to be him. A coincidence in this situation wouldn't jive. He's DOA, Grace." Wyn nodded, as if to help her believe it. "He wasn't wearing a seatbelt. The speed with which he was driving propelled him out of the car and into the back of the garbage truck. He died instantly. You don't have to worry about him hurting you or your children ever again."

Grace covered her mouth and stifled a moan. She started to tilt to the side, and Devlin and Garrick grabbed her arms to situate her upright.

A minute passed in silence, in which Grace gathered herself and blinked away tears. "I can't believe it's over," she whispered, clearly dazed as hell.

"It'll take some time to sink in," Garrick said. "That's natural."

"I already put a hold on the BOLO when Shue called to let me know about the accident," Wyn offered. "Here's the deal. I've canceled it. As far as I'm concerned, I never came here." He kept his attention on Grace. "Unless there's some reason you want me to file a report, I'll just say the BOLO was in reference to something illegal I got a tip on, and I'll leave it at that."

"No need for a report," Grace answered. "If that really is Randy in that car then there's no reason to file anything." Grace pushed her hair off her face and twisted it into a knot. "I'd just like to go back to my life and try to get my kids past what happened tonight."

"I understand that," Wyn said.

"Thank you so much for coming here in the middle of the night." Grace reached across the table and shook Wyn's hand. "You've been very kind. I don't know what we would have done without your willingness to help."

Wyn dipped his head. "It's all right. Just so you're aware, when the victim is formally identified, it's possible an eager reporter with the local paper will connect the dots and come ask some questions. How much or little you say is up to you." His gaze slid to Garrick. "There's definitely no reason to mention anything about your tenant. Which is a damned good thing," Wyn narrowed a stare at Devlin, "because I would have had a hard time ignoring a kicked-in back door in my report when I already had a broken bathroom window as my perp's point of entry." The stare turned to a full-on glare. "You didn't mention that little detail when we talked, Morgan."

"It wasn't deliberate." Devlin held up his hands. "I honest-to-God didn't even think about it."

Open worry shone in Grace's eyes. "Are you sure someone won't get nosy and put Garrick's picture in the paper, should they come questioning me?"

"Highly unlikely," Wyn answered. "It's a sad statement of our priorities, but your domestic abuse history and stalker ex-husband isn't that unique. The second something more scintillating happens -- and it always does -- what little interest anyone might have about you and your ex will disappear." He shifted his focus to Garrick. "I can't promise you anonymity, man. Keep your eyes and ears open for a while, just in case, but I think everything will be okay."

Garrick reached out and shook Wyn's hand. "Thank you. I always do."

"Yes, thank you, Wyn." Once again, Devlin could have smothered the guy with slobbery kisses. "For everything."

"It's my job," Wyn said. He pushed his chair back and got to his feet.

Devlin walked around the table and pulled the man into a suffocating hug. "It's a whole hell of a lot more than that to me."

Wyn thumped his hand against Devlin's back, and murmured, "No problem." He quickly broke contact and palmed the bagged gun off the table. "I'll take care of this." He tucked it discreetly against the side of his body. "You guys take care of getting that back door and window fixed. I don't want to have to come back and file a report of a crime of opportunity."

Garrick held out his arm and led Wyn to the front door. "I'll hit the home improvement store the second it opens and take care of the door. We'll call someone in to replace the window ASAP."

"I'll get on the phone and get someone here today," Grace said. "I don't mind paying extra for Sunday work. I want it taken care of right away."

"Good deal." Wyn stepped out onto the porch. "I think you're all set. Garrick, it was good to see you again. Grace," he shifted to her, "I'm sorry it was under these circumstances, but it's nice to meet you. Try not to let this keep you awake for days on end. Goodbye."

From inside the open door, Garrick and Grace each offered Wyn a wave goodbye. Devlin took the opportunity to walk his friend to his car. "I can't say thank you enough," Devlin said. He had to give his appreciation one more time. "You came through for me, and I owe you one. Let me know when you want to cash it in, and I'm there, whatever you ask."

Wyn chuckled, and it was that reckless sound the man sometimes let escape him. "That's a dangerous offer, Morgan." He opened his car door and then planted his hand on the roof. A dangerous darkness deepened his eyes to pitch. "Someone you love might put your balls in a vise when I collect."

Maddie.

Devlin's heart raced on behalf of his sister. He loved Garrick with everything in him, but physically, Wyn Ashworth was sexy-as-hell and something to behold. "As long as it's not physically or emotionally damaging to," Devlin caught himself, "*whoever*, I will help you."

"Something to consider." That flash of fire flared in Wyn's

eyes again, but he quickly banked it. "Get some rest." He climbed in behind the wheel of his car. "You've all had a trying night."

Devlin chuckled. *You don't know the half of it.* "Will do." He closed Wyn's car door for him and banged the roof a couple of times. "I'll talk to you soon."

Wyn lifted his hand in a small wave. Devlin stayed on the walk, watching as the man backed his car onto the street and drove away.

Just as Devlin turned to head back inside, Garrick emerged from the house and jogged down the steps, meeting Devlin halfway. A sudden, sharp breeze brought a gust of cold. It swept right through Devlin; he rubbed his arms, but he wasn't sure the shiver racing down his spine was from the chill in the air.

Garrick didn't hold eye contact with Devlin for more than a blink as he said, "Listen, I'm going to shower and start making myself a to-do list before I head into town for supplies."

"I figured you would." Devlin curled his hand around Garrick's upper arm. "Come on. I'll help you."

"No." Garrick's refusal came at Devlin bullet-fast, and Devlin's hand fell dead to his side. Garrick backed away until a half-dozen feet of what felt like a bottomless chasm existed between them. "You've had to process a lot of information in the last few days, Devlin. Shit, in the last ten hours, I've rewritten part of your history. You don't even have shoes or a change of clothes, and you look exhausted." Excuses flew from Garrick's mouth in rapid order. "Why don't you go home, get cleaned up, get some food, and try to catch up on some sleep." Garrick didn't form his suggestion as a question. "I'll talk to you later."

Devlin put a hand to his stomach in an effort to control the pain of the blow. "Is that what you want?"

With his focus somewhere to the left of Devlin's face, Garrick murmured, "I think you need some time. I'll call you tonight. Bye." Garrick spun and sprinted across the front yard to his garage apartment before Devlin could take even one step and attempt to grab him back.

With difficulty, Devlin swallowed down a shout that would have woken up this entire neighborhood. He scratched his fingers through his dirty hair, and breathed in Garrick's scent still clinging to his skin. He stood perfectly still for one moment and took in the beauty of the sun twinkling through the trees in the early morning sky.

"Thank you." Devlin basked in the sunlight that didn't yet bear down on him with muggy heat, and let the invigorating vitamin D sink into his pores. "I needed that."

Soon enough, baby, it will be time for round two.

CHAPTER FOURTEEN

Garrick looked up from replacing part of the frame for the back door to find Shawn and Chloe watching him work. Chloe chewed on her lip; Shawn scuffed his dirty sneakers into the linoleum, and Garrick's chest hurt for them all over again. As it had been doing all morning long.

"It'll be fixed soon, guys," he told them. "I promise. Just a couple more nails to hammer in and the door will be good as new. Better than new." He beckoned them closer, and Shawn immediately trotted over to look. "See?" Garrick pointed at some shiny hardware. "It has new locks and everything."

Shawn's face twisted, and he cocked his head to the side. "But then how will we get in?"

Garrick stifled a laugh and tousled the kid's hair. "We have new keys to go with the new double locks, Shawnee. *We* can all get in just fine."

Chloe rushed across the kitchen to join them. "You too?" she asked. Her voice and body language seemed almost … hopeful, and Garrick slumped into the door frame a bit. Chloe had always been more subdued around Garrick, which Garrick now understood better. The main concern of Grace's and Garrick's when discussing his accepting a key earlier had been Chloe's reaction more than Shawn's.

"Me too." Garrick tried to keep his voice even and smooth when in fact her acceptance of him had his throat clogging tightly. "I'll still live over the garage, but your mom and I talked about it, and she thought it would be a good idea for me to have keys. That way I can get in to check on you, or just hang out with you guys, whenever I need to."

Shawn threw his arms around Garrick's leg and gave him a quick squeeze. "Cool."

"You sure you don't want to go to the movies with us?" Chloe asked. "You can, you know."

"Thank you for the invitation, sweetheart, but I'm going to stay here and finish this project." He hammered another nail into the frame, then let Shawn do one when the kid grabbed the hammer the second Garrick put it on the floor. "After doing this --" Garrick stopped as Chloe pushed her way in too. He lined up a nail in its proper place and let her slam one into the wood as well. Maybe it would make them feel safer in their home. "After this, I'm going to stay close by so there's someone here when the repair guy comes to replace the window in the bathroom."

Grace appeared in the arch that led to the dining room. "The window guy said he would be here between two and three." As she walked into the kitchen, she pulled an elastic band off her wrist, moved in behind Chloe, and pulled her daughter's hair back into a ponytail. "But the kids and I really can come straight home from the movie and beat him here. You don't have to hang around. We can go to the park another time."

"Absolutely not," Garrick replied. The kids had remained close to Grace's side all morning, and Garrick knew they needed this time together, just the three of them. "You won't get a more beautiful day to take advantage of being outdoors. And the puppet show won't be there next week."

An exasperated *tsking* noise escaped Chloe. "Puppet shows are lame. They're for little kids."

"I don't know." Garrick pretended to shield his mouth from Chloe, and fake whispered to Grace, "One of the guys at work told me they have it every year, and that it's good stuff. There are pyrotechnics involved."

Chloe perked right up straight. "Really?"

Shawn pulled a comical frown. "What's pyrotetnis?"

"Pyro*technics*, nimrod." Chloe rolled her eyes at her brother. "It means there are special effects that could have fireworks, or smoke, or maybe even fire in them."

Garrick once again marveled at Chloe's vocabulary and

intelligence.

Shawn started doing his little happy dance. "Awesome," the kid said. "We need to get in the front row."

"Please don't call your brother a nimrod." Grace spoke to her daughter over her son's enthusiasm. "I don't like that word."

"Sorry, Mom." Chloe all of a sudden looked like she wanted to cry.

Grace pulled Chloe to her side and kissed the top of her head. "It's okay, sweetie. I just don't like you calling your brother names any more than I like him doing it to you." She shifted her focus up to Garrick. "Thank you for taking care of the door."

"I'm the one who broke it down."

"That's neither here nor there. But I swear to everything holy that if you pay the window repair guy yourself, I will --" she snapped her lips shut, and Garrick watched her mentally rework her threat for the ears of children, "-- twist something until it hurts. Do you hear me? Have the man send me the bill."

"Will do." Garrick had no interest in taking over Grace's life, or in trying to strip her of her independence. She was far too strong now to let any man, romantic interest or not, do that to her ever again. "Go." He shooed them out of the kitchen. "You don't want to be late and miss the previews. I'll see you later."

"Bye." Chloe waved.

"See you later, Garrick!" Everyone winced as Shawn lost

control of his "indoor" voice again.

Grace mouthed *Thank you*, and Garrick shared an understanding smile with the woman. He took a moment to watch them as Grace put an arm around each child and steered them out of the kitchen. A heartbeat later, he heard the front door click closed, and then the sound of metal against metal as the bolt slid into place.

As soon as a car engine started, and he knew Grace and the kids had gone, Garrick fell to his knees and put his face in his hands.

I love them already. Garrick had spent the entire morning running around and fixing things, as if he had some great right to belong here. *What if I'm not doing the right thing?*

"I wasn't sure you'd be here when I got back." A voice that had grabbed Garrick's heart from word-one drifted to him on a perfect warm breeze. Garrick spun to find Devlin leaning his shoulder against the back corner of the house. Devlin stared at him, and Garrick suddenly found breathing a challenge.

Devlin looked stunning in jeans that appeared as if he'd lived in them forever, and a Redemption Fire Department T-shirt pulled oh-so-sexily across his chest, shoulders, and upper arms. The man looked beautiful, but it was the silver taking over the gray in his eyes that held Garrick riveted in place.

Not moving an inch from his position a dozen feet away, Devlin added, "When you didn't want me to help you, I half figured you might make a run for the home improvement store and just keep driving."

Garrick's stomach leaped right up into his throat, and he thought he might throw up.

I don't know if I like someone knowing me so well.

Devlin wouldn't look away. When it felt like Garrick might collapse if he stared into those knowing eyes another second, he spun and put his full attention on the door.

"I won't let you walk away like I did last time," Devlin said. He moved closer; Garrick could fucking feel his heat without looking, and he started to sweat. "And I won't buy that you're not freaking out on the inside, right this second, so it might be a good idea to eliminate any bullshit you're thinking about telling me and start getting the truth off your chest."

Garrick squeezed his eyes shut, but the rawness swirling around inside him would not be shoved down anymore. "I thought about leaving," he said softly without facing Devlin. "Still thinking about it, if you want the full truth."

He palmed the new keys out of his pocket and tested the strength of his work, all the while fully attuned to the man now standing next to him. "Grace and the kids don't have to worry about Randy being a threat to them anymore, but that doesn't do them a damned bit of good against anyone who might come for me." The frame and new bolt held up well against Garrick's attempts to force the door open after locking it.

With nothing else to do until the window guy showed in a few hours, Garrick forced himself to make eye contact with Devlin. He stared, and so much love hit him at once, it almost buckled him where he stood.

"Jesus, beautiful." Garrick cupped Devlin's cheek, needing to feel his warmth and life. "It doesn't put you out of danger either."

Taking a step closer, Devlin held Garrick's stare while covering his hand. "I'm not scared."

Fire burned through Garrick, and he ripped his hand out from under Devlin's. "Then I don't know if you're still painfully naive or just stupid." He pushed past the man and flew down the back steps, heading for his apartment.

Devlin caught up in a flash and strode step-for-step at Garrick's side. "Don't throw insults at me. I know you don't mean them; they won't make me leave." He stomped up the steps behind Garrick; Garrick could feel him on his heels. "Saying I'm not scared doesn't mean I'm not aware or cognizant of what could happen if someone finds you. It just means that I'm trying to apply reason, and assessing that I don't see any real threat right now that should send you reeling in this way."

Garrick spun around on the landing and found himself right in Devlin's face. "You don't think someone could find me tomorrow?" Escaping panic raised his voice. "How are you all of a sudden the expert when I'm the one who has been working law enforcement since I was twenty years old?"

Devlin smacked his hands into Garrick's chest and shoved him into the railing. "Because I'm taking my cues from you!"

Garrick reared at the storm brewing in Devlin's eyes. "What?"

"I'm sorry." Devlin immediately stepped back and held up his hands. "I didn't mean to shove you." He straightened Garrick's T-shirt and then his own. Taking two steps down on the stairs, he made room for Garrick to open the door. "All I'm saying is that I'm using the fact that you're still here to tell me there isn't an immediate threat."

"That doesn't make any sense." After letting them inside, Garrick pulled the curtain wide open. "Obviously, I think there is a danger or we wouldn't be having this conversation."

Devlin's sigh encapsulated the entire room. "Stop looking out the window, Garrick. This conversation deserves your full attention."

With his hand clutched around the curtain, and his heart racing with Devlin's proximity, Garrick pinpointed his focus on his truck in the drive. "I promised I'd keep an eye out for the repair guy."

"Who I overheard Grace telling you isn't scheduled to arrive for a couple of hours," Devlin shot back quickly.

Shit.

Garrick commanded his hand to let go of the fabric, and moved to pace the short length of his kitchen. "I don't know what you want me to say." He walked and walked like a caged animal, unable to remain still. "I ripped myself open for you last night. Isn't that enough?"

On Garrick's third attempt to circle the tiny kitchen table, Devlin grabbed his arm. He eased Garrick into one of the two kitchen chairs, and then kneeled down in front of him, filling

Garrick with his presence. "Baby, I can't even begin to imagine how difficult this all is for you." Devlin smiled, something soft and welcoming, and the sight of it started stripping away protective layers Garrick hadn't even realized he had anymore.

Devlin pushed in between Garrick's spread legs, took his hands, and looked up, right into his eyes. Garrick started to shake. He had never felt so naked, but also completely safe, in his life. Devlin dipped down and pressed his lips to the backs of Garrick's hands, lingering for a moment. As if Devlin's touch was a special sedative, Garrick settled inside and stopped trembling.

"You've already essentially lost one family," Devlin began as he made eye contact again. "I get that you're scared about losing another, which is why you're all over the map with what you think is the right thing to do right now. But you're also still alive," passion infused Devlin's every word, "so I know you must have been good at your job. I am sure a sixth sense kept you alive more than once while you were undercover."

"That's not the same as this." Garrick tried to pull away but Devlin wouldn't let him go. "That was just me on the line, not," his voice broke, "*you.*"

Devlin tunneled his fingers through the thick mess of Garrick's hair and pushed away the fall hiding his eyes. "Look past the fear of losing me, and Grace, and the kids that is ruling you right now, and answer me this: Would you really still be here if you truly sensed the new identity Joe had created for you had been compromised?"

Garrick's chest heaved and banded tight. "But --"

Devlin clamped his hand over Garrick's mouth. "But, nothing." He immediately soothed away the force of his hold with a brush of his fingers over Garrick's lips. "Tell me again how long after you went into the witness protection program it took for that assassin to find you?"

"Less than two weeks."

"And how long have you been in Redemption?"

"Five weeks today."

With a nod, Devlin nudged Garrick with a squeeze around his waist. "So what does that tell you?"

Devlin's line of questioning clicked into place for Garrick. "That Joe picked the right person to trust with creating this new Garrick Langley identity, and that's why right now I'm still safe. Or, Joe found the mole, and so the threat to undercover and witness protected agents is gone, which also means I'm safe now." Garrick spoke the logical words that made sense even though it frightened him to death to believe it.

"So why aren't you trusting your ability to assess risk?" Devlin grabbed Garrick's forearms and tugged him to the edge of the seat. "Tell me why you don't trust your gut anymore."

"Because my gut told me someone *was* watching us." Garrick bolted up and rushed to the window, needing to check the perimeter. "I was right, but something held me back, and look what happened."

"That's because you didn't have full information." Devlin ran to Garrick and spun him around. "You didn't know that Grace was hiding too." He jammed his finger into the windowpane. "You sensed that something wasn't right, but on some deeper level -- that gut of yours -- you knew it wasn't a hired killer contracted to find you. That's why you stayed."

A hitch grabbed Garrick's heart and choked his voice. "No. I stayed because of you, beautiful. And because of them."

"No." Devlin shook his head. "You stayed because something inside you knew it was safe for you here. You wouldn't have risked yourself, and us, if you really thought someone was gunning for you."

"Even if you're right about that, what about the newspaper now?" Horrible scenarios spun in Garrick's head, as they had been doing since seeing Randy breaking into Grace's home. "Wyn said there's a chance someone might come poking into Grace's life when they learn Randy's identity. What if they somehow get interested in me?"

"Baby," sympathy filled that one word from Devlin, "I think you're over-thinking this because *you* know you have something to hide. No one else does." Devlin took Garrick's hand, tugged him away from the window, and pushed him down onto the couch. "But if one day down the line, that happens, or your gut starts talking to you again, and you *know* you've been made, and it's time to run, all you have to do is say the word and I will run with you."

"What if I can't?" Garrick shot back to his feet and took Devlin's face in his hands, his fingers digging in hard. "What if I feel it too late and someone dies because of me?"

Devlin matched Garrick's hold and pulled him in until their foreheads touched. "You won't, Garrick. I believe in you. I trust in your training, and I have faith in that extra sense you have that cannot be taught. Do you think Grace will feel any different than I do? I can tell you right now, just from being with you guys, she won't. She and those kids love you just as much as you love them. Last night, when you and Grace agreed together not to run in your own directions, that was tantamount to making a commitment to being a family. When she trusted me to help her that made me a part of it too."

He brushed kisses against the slashes of Garrick's cheeks, and his eyes shone bright. "We're in this together now. All of us. Even if the two 'dads'," Devlin made a funny face that actually drew a rough chuckle out of Garrick, "share a bed in the room above the garage." He pushed his hands into Garrick's hair and brought him in for a scraping of their mouths. His lips clung to Garrick's, and Garrick whimpered at the intimacy swirling around them. "A family, Garrick." Devlin put the words, a vow, right into Garrick's being. "A real one again. For you. Can you promise me you'll stay and believe in yourself the way we already believe in you?"

Garrick cracked inside, opening another gap, wider even than the one Devlin had chiseled in him last night. Unconditional love and acceptance rushed into him through the break, filling in all the tiny chinks and fissures, making Garrick a whole person again.

He clung to Devlin, raw and exposed, everywhere. "I

promise." Garrick whispered it again, needing Devlin to know he was in for good.

Devlin held Garrick's head back with a fistful of hair. "Good choice." He winked as he said it, and Garrick fell for this sweet, clever man all over again.

"I love you." Garrick attacked Devlin, raining kisses all over his perfect face. "I love everything about you."

Devlin pulled a frown as redness rushed to his cheeks. "You haven't been around me when the Red Sox or the Patriots lose."

Something between a laugh and a sob escaped Garrick. "I'll still love you anyway." Garrick suddenly became very aware of their bodies rubbing against one another, and desperation took over his voice. "Make love to me." He ripped at Devlin's shirt, then dove for his belt with one hand and his cock with the other. "I need to feel you." Garrick rubbed at the bulge already hardening behind Devlin's jeans as he tore the belt out of its loops.

Devlin gasped and jerked in Garrick's hand. "Yeah." His prick thickened, and he ground himself into Garrick's touch. "I want inside you again too."

Garrick shoved his hand into Devlin's jeans, unable to wait the extra few seconds to tear them down Devlin's legs. He curled his fingers around scorching hot flesh and tugged hard on the velvety-smooth length. Devlin winced and covered Garrick's hand, stilling his hand job. Garrick murmured an apology against Devlin's lips, sipping at the tense line of the man's mouth, while forcing his hand to release the death grip it had on Devlin's prick.

Keep it cool and steady, Langley. You have the rest of your life to mate with this man.

Garrick breathed and slowed everything down. He grazed whisper-soft kisses back and forth across Devlin's mouth and teased him with barely-there darting licks in between. Devlin flicked his tongue out to meet Garrick's, tormenting Garrick with hints of something deeper, and adrenaline pumped into Garrick's bloodstream again with dizzying speed. Everything inside Garrick ached. He wanted to shove his way into Devlin's mouth and devour, and his fingers itched to own the thick cock burning a stamp into his hand, but Garrick exerted will over his body and forced his impulses back under his control.

A chuckle washed warmth across Garrick's lips. He pulled back and caught a glint sparking in Devlin's eyes.

"I didn't mean you have to stop completely," Devlin said. He guided Garrick's hand into a rubbing motion up and down his growing cock, moaning as Garrick once again took the lead and teased his fingers over the head, gathering precum as he did it. "Doesn't mean you can't give me something rough either." Devlin bit Garrick's lower lip and tugged at it, creating a wonderful sting. As it slipped from between his teeth, Devlin soothed with a lick, and added, "I just might need some spit or lube first if you're going to go full guns blazing at first pull."

Garrick touched his own mouth, fingering the extra sensitivity Devlin had put there with his love bite. At the same time, he found himself riveted by the millions of as yet unknown stories and desires living right behind the light in Devlin's eyes. "It's strange to accept that we still have this learning curve between us when we spent two and a half days fucking each other." Touching the tips of his fingers over Devlin's cheeks, Garrick studied this face he already knew so well, and committed a few new laugh lines and cutting edges to the memory. "In so many ways I feel like I know you more completely than any other single person in this world."

Devlin's gaze deepened in time with an accompanying arousal below, and Garrick watched the part of this man's personality that liked to laugh and play naughty emerge. Devlin pulled off his shirt and tossed it aside. He shoved his jeans and underwear down to his hips, exposing Garrick's hand steadily working its way up and down Devlin's long cock. Devlin kept contact with Garrick's stare as his dick stiffened to granite-hard, rearing under Garrick's ministrations.

"Oh God … yeah." Devlin bit his lip and pumped his hips into Garrick's handjob. "I have a feeling we'll be moving in unison like a pair of finely tuned race horses in no time at all."

A real, honest-to-God grin took over Garrick's lips. "I think they pair up the race horses with the mares, beautiful."

"Maybe…ahh, yeah, that's so good…" Bead after bead of early ejaculate pearled at Devlin's slit. As Garrick ran his finger across the opening, Devlin hissed, and his eyelids slid to half-mast. Devlin suddenly shook his head and opened his eyes, as if trying to clear the growing fog. "Maybe," his voice sounded strained, "maybe most. But there have to be one or two studs out there that see another stallion and get just a little too worked up about another sleek male horse in top form, you know?"

Garrick swallowed down another laugh. "Gotta be a few, I imagine." He loved the twists and silliness mixed in with the core of strength and honor in this man. "I remember how you like your blowjobs. Giving and getting them." Watching Devlin, Garrick withdrew his hand from Devlin's erection and licked his palm and fingers. He transferred Devlin's precum onto his tongue and savored the light taste of salt and man. "Do they still make you lose your mind?"

Devlin swallowed visibly as he stared at Garrick eating his early seed. "You don't have to tie me up anymore." He cleared his throat and lifted his gaze back to Garrick's. "Unless you just want to do it for fun."

Garrick snaked his hand around Devlin's neck and jerked him in close. "Maybe another time." He sealed his lips to Devlin's, pushed inside and kissed deeply, and let the man taste himself inside Garrick's mouth. Devlin opened up and tangled his tongue with Garrick's, moaning and fighting for as much dominance as Garrick did. Devlin ran his hands down Garrick's back and shoved his hands under the hem of Garrick's shirt, pushing the fabric up in the back. He scratched his trimmed nails up Garrick's spine, taking the shirt with him, and Garrick shivered. He fucking felt the light scrape shiver over every nerve ending in his body.

Their mouths broke apart as Devlin lifted the T-shirt over

Garrick's head. "Naked," Devlin said. His eyes burned bright, even in the shock of sunlight pouring in through the open window. "I want you naked now."

"You too." Garrick kicked off his shoes and toed off his socks, his motions clumsy, his focus riveted on Devlin. "I've missed your body."

A quick grin flashed in Devlin. He took a second to drag Garrick in and smash a hard kiss on his mouth. "I'm gonna choose to think that's a really sweet thing to say."

Fuck. Heat burned red right down Garrick's flesh. *I'm no poet.* "I meant for it to sound nice. Christ." Garrick's breath caught as Devlin stripped out of the last of his clothes. Garrick took his fill of the specimen before him; Devlin was perfect everywhere he looked. "You were solid before," he ran his hands all over Devlin's upper body, mapping ropey lines in a way he'd been too frantic to do last night, "but five years has turned your body into something exquisite."

Twin dots of red in Devlin's cheeks mirrored back to Garrick. "Thank you. It's the firefighter training." He looked openly too, studying Garrick all over, making Garrick's cock twitch toward his belly button under the scrutiny. "I loved that massive guy in San Francisco." Devlin ran the flat of his hand down the centerline of Garrick's torso, and then back up to curl around his biceps. "But I love this man too." He held onto Garrick's arms and swayed them together. "He definitely feels like someone I can put my arm around when we're out getting groceries, or someone whose shoulder I can rest my head on when we go to the movies." Devlin wiggled against Garrick's front, rubbing their cocks against one another in a way that flooded Garrick with seed. "Or just someone I can burrow in real close to in the winter when it's freezing cold."

"Jesus." Garrick didn't know whether to come or cry. His dick pushed with purpose into Devlin's stomach and answered for him. "The thought of grocery shopping has never made me so hard."

That mischievous twinkle reentered Devlin's eyes. "I remember all the other ways to get you rock-solid too." He walked them backward to the couch and shoved Garrick down onto it. "I believe you said something about my loving to give a blowjob?" Devlin dropped to his knees and yanked Garrick's hips to the edge of the couch. "Never gave better head than the first night I brought you back to my motel room."

"I don't know." Garrick remembered any number of award-worthy moments in San Francisco that involved Devlin's mouth on his prick. "There was that time in the shower that was pretty good too."

While looking right up at Garrick, eyes open wide, Devlin went down on Garrick and swallowed the full length of his cock in one swoop, stealing Garrick's voice. And his mind too.

Garrick bucked and then grabbed his balls, but Devlin batted his hand away and took over the job himself. Only, Devlin fucking *massaged* the incredible, tormenting weight pulling at Garrick's nuts, rather than put a clamp on it, and it drove Garrick nearly insane with the heightened sensation.

Devlin bobbed up and down Garrick's shaft with wet suction, and each time he circled up and teased the rim with the tip of his tongue, he gently squeezed Garrick's balls at the same time.

"Damn it… Damn it…" Garrick prayed for the willpower not to come and end this perfect act so fast. "Jesus, beautiful." He buried his hand in Devlin's hair, and through half-slitted eyes watched the man blow and fondle him. *So fucking beautiful.*

Devlin had the sexiest mouth Garrick had ever known; seeing it stretched wide around his cock, working full, strong, mind-altering pulls from root to tip, had Garrick spreading his legs even wider and pushing his hips up for more. Devlin swirled his tongue around the tip and across the slit, moaning as he did it, and shimmered the most glorious vibrations straight down Garrick's prick to his nuts.

"Ohhh fuck." Garrick twisted the handful of Devlin's hair he gripped in his hand, and hissed as his cock disappeared all the way into Devlin's mouth again. "You're amazing."

Devlin sucked even harder, and Garrick clenched his jaw against the pleasure, focused on the pale eyes watching every reaction he gave. Unable to look away, Garrick grew painfully rigid and thick with each swipe of Devlin's mouth or tongue. Sweat filmed Garrick's flesh and soaked the hair at his nape, and he thought he might pass out if he didn't let himself come.

His muscles went tight, and the tingling in his balls started pulling and creeping up his spine. Garrick whimpered and his voice went raspy. "Devlin…"

Devlin grabbed Garrick's sac, and whipped his mouth off

Garrick's cock. "Not yet." He openly looked up and down the length of Garrick's body, which in turn heated Garrick's skin and turned his cock harder still. "Turn over." Devlin helped Garrick shift to his knees, facing away from Devlin. Garrick braced himself on the back of the couch and pressed his cheek into the cool plaster of the wall.

A strange vulnerability attacked Garrick as Devlin's body heat went away. Cool air grazed his scorching skin, leaving him chilled.

Just when Garrick didn't think he could take the loss a second longer, Devlin covered Garrick from behind, creating a human blanket for Garrick that chased away the cold. The man dipped down and put his mouth at Garrick's ear. "You're not coming until every inch of my dick is smothered deep inside you." He sank his tongue into Garrick's ear as he wedged a soft plastic tube under his palm. "Keep that for me."

Garrick opened his hand and glanced down. *Lube.* He hadn't even thought about that.

A whispery-soft brush of lips moved down the side of Garrick's neck to his shoulder and stayed there for a moment to suck on Garrick's skin.

"I didn't see any stuff in your medicine cabinet last night." Devlin offered that explanation as he kissed his way across Garrick's upper back, inducing more shivers. "I went out and bought a new one before I came back. I hoped we would need one here."

"I hope we'll need lots. Ohhh yes…"

Devlin licked right down the center of Garrick's spine to the small of his back, and Garrick groaned low in his throat in response. Each licking kiss from Devlin, that went back up Garrick's spine in reverse, and then traced every point across Garrick's back, conjured additional throaty noises from Garrick, and soon had him thrusting his ass backward, searching for Devlin's cock. Devlin kept just out of reach; he tormented Garrick with continued kisses against his back, and he brushed the tips of his fingers over Garrick's hips and down his outer thighs, always keeping contact just shy of Garrick's ass.

Sparks lit under Garrick's flesh everywhere Devlin grazed his lips. Garrick's cock leaked a wet spot into the couch cushion with every soft lick from Devlin, and his passage already throbbed like mad for someone to plug it deeply.

Not someone. Devlin. It has to be Devlin.

When Devlin's mouth came within millimeters of tasting the curve of Garrick's left buttock, Garrick shrieked inside with denied need.

"Please," Garrick whispered roughly. He reached back and shoved the lube into Devlin's hand. "Get me ready. Fuck me."

Devlin paused with his lips against the cleft of Garrick's ass. "Open that for me," he pushed the lube back into Garrick's hand, "and I will."

Garrick took the small tube and put the sealed cap to his mouth. The second he did, Devlin spread Garrick's ass cheeks apart and licked right down his crack to his hole. His nubby tongue teased and poked at Garrick's ring, and Garrick bucked back into the shock of intimate contact. Devlin held him wide open and nuzzled his full face into Garrick's crease, making hungry, voracious noises as he laved and sucked on Garrick's pucker. Each press with the flat of Devlin's tongue on Garrick's sensitive asshole alternated with a gentle suckle on the tight muscle and then a dart of his tongue into the tiny opening to fucking *lick* inside. Each rotation spiraled Garrick deeper and deeper into a place where only raw pleasure and need existed.

"Oh yeah…" Garrick pressed his forehead into the wall, and he gritted his teeth through the base, heavenly kiss Devlin delivered to his hole. Garrick's passage and dick pulsed in unison. Without thinking, Garrick shoved his hand down to his cock, tunneled the length between his spread thighs back to Devlin, and ordered roughly, "Suck that too." He growled and pushed his ass into Devlin's face, feeling primal to his core. "Eat me everywhere."

Devlin dipped down; he tongued the rim of Garrick's cock, licked into the slit, and then took the first few inches into the warm cavern of his mouth, surrounding Garrick in wet, wonderful heat. The abbreviated blowjob squished Garrick's balls up against his body, but he continued to rub the base of his cock while Devlin sucked the other end, together creating the sweetest kind of pain. Garrick squeezed his eyes shut and suffered through the perfect agony of this mating. He didn't think anything could make this moment better … and then Devlin started thumbing Garrick's pucker and oh-so-gently eased the blunt tip into Garrick's ass.

Oh yes. More.

Garrick tried to push back and steal something more than just a phantom touch, but Devlin pulled away and bit the inside curve of Garrick's buttocks, surely leaving marks. He spanked Garrick's hip and flank, not quite gently, but not with violence either. The sound cracked through the room as Devlin's hand made contact with Garrick's flesh again, and it drew a sharp cry from Garrick at the same time it pulled an arousing sting to the surface of his skin.

"You like that, huh?" Devlin rubbed the flesh he'd just reddened with his hand.

"Yeah." Guttural emotions and fears still churned inside Garrick, and he needed something equally powerful and coarse to take it all away and make it better. "Do it again."

Devlin smacked the flat of his hand across Garrick's buttocks, one, two, three, four times, delivering stinging hit after hit that smarted and had Garrick grunting in time with each firm spank. As quickly as Devlin warmed Garrick's buttocks with his hand, he delved two fingers down Garrick's crack to finger his hole. He pressed just a bit, enough to start a little burn, but not enough to break through and penetrate Garrick's ass.

Garrick moaned, and he wiggled his ass and rubbed his prick, turning himself into a wanton who would take anything from this man. "Please." He pushed back for those fingers again. "Push them in. Take me."

Devlin murmured words of patience as he kissed his way

up Garrick's back to his nape and rested his mouth just inches from Garrick's ear. "I thought you wanted my cock." He rubbed over Garrick's hole, and then reached further down to tease a couple of fingers around the head of Garrick's dick, stirring those ultrasensitive nerve endings all over again.

Garrick's chest moved in big waves, and his throat felt like he hadn't taken a sip of water in weeks. "I fucking want that too." He ripped the plastic off the lube with his teeth and bit down on the cap until it popped open. Turning his head, Garrick looked right into the stormy blur of Devlin's beautiful eyes. "I want everything with you."

"And you'll get it." His pupils flaring, Devlin closed in and seared his lips to Garrick's, stealing a rough, invasive kiss. He took Garrick's mouth with something close to violent savagery as he palmed the tube of lube out of Garrick's hand. Garrick accepted every punishing thrust of Garrick's tongue and scrape of his lips -- that sometimes involved teeth -- with equally aggressive enthusiasm, and very likely bruised Devlin just as much as Devlin did him. Garrick kissed Devlin as if he'd never tasted the man before and wasn't sure he would ever get the chance to do so again.

Cool slick suddenly coated Garrick's asshole, and just a second later Devlin slipped one long finger up Garrick's chute, offering a heavenly hint of taking. Devlin twisted his finger inside Garrick's channel, greasing the walls of Garrick's ass, and Garrick gasped as his rectum sucked in to hold Devlin's finger inside.

Devlin withdrew his digit but quickly rubbed the tips of three fingers around Garrick's sensitized entrance. "Relax, baby, so I can get a couple more in this time."

Garrick panted, and he let all the desperation inside him slip into his voice. "I'm so ready you could drive a truck straight up my ass and I would bend over and push back until it was in to the rear bumper."

His gaze softening, Devlin pressed his lips to the side of Garrick's head. "That's quite the image."

Everything inside Garrick screamed for Devlin to consume him completely. "I'm just that horny for you." He nuzzled into Devlin's face until their mouths touched again. "Take me, beautiful." He whispered the plea. "Please."

"Shh ... shh." Devlin replaced his fingers with the head of his cock, kissing the excited nerves surrounding Garrick's bud with the tip. He wound an arm around Garrick's waist, held him steady, and burned a brand right into Garrick's soul with the intensity in his stare. "Now." Devlin latched his mouth to Garrick's just as he surged forward, and Garrick shoved backward, straight into Devlin's cock, and made them one. Garrick shouted, his voice stripped bare as Devlin took him in one driving thrust all the way to the root.

Oh Jesus. Skin on skin. This is what it feels like to trust someone in every way.

Devlin immediately stopped; he shoved Garrick's hair out of his face. "Are you okay?" Devlin's cock throbbed with its own heartbeat in Garrick's ass, Garrick could fucking feel it, but Devlin gritted his teeth and didn't move. "Do you need a minute?"

Garrick reached down and covered Devlin's hand on his stomach. "Don't stop." He didn't break their gaze as he eased forward, nearly separating them, and then pushed his ass back into Devlin's invasion, demanding friction again. "Please don't ever fucking stop."

Devlin remained still for a heartbeat, his eyes on Garrick. But it was then as if he found the permission Garrick had already told him he had, and he slammed into Garrick again, taking his mouth and ass in one rough shot. He covered Garrick like one animal does to another and pummeled Garrick's channel with fast, shallow hits. He bit at Garrick's lips and then down his cheek to his shoulder, sinking his teeth into skin as he attacked Garrick's tight ass with the sweetest kind of pain. It was everything Garrick begged for and craved, and he thrust himself back to accept each deep piercing from Devlin's long cock.

Soon Devlin put a bruising hold on Garrick's hips and angled him for a drive down of his cock that rode right over Garrick's kill spot with every thrust. With each spearing into his rectum from Devlin's shaft, Garrick braced himself against the wall and shoved back to steal every inch of Devlin he could.

"Is that good, baby?" Devlin growled the question. He let go of Garrick's hips for a second, smacked his buttocks again with a couple of sharp stings, and then dove in deep with his dick once again. "You want more?"

"Do it." Garrick arched his spine inward even more and created a straight shot for Devlin into his hole. "Oh yeah... Ahh shit!" To Garrick's cries of delight, Devlin pulled all the way out and sank back in to the hilt. Garrick looked over his shoulder, and he bared his teeth at a glistening Devlin. "Fucking do whatever you want."

Devlin flashed his teeth like a fighting animal right back; he grabbed Garrick around the torso and shoved him sideways until Garrick was face-down on the couch. Devlin banded his arms around Garrick's lower belly and came down on top of him, pushing his way in between Garrick's legs, and then drove up and deep into Garrick's flaming entrance. The man's breath panted in sharp bursts against Garrick's ear with every knifing of his cock into Garrick's chute, and Garrick grunted and bumped his ass up for more each time Devlin took ownership of his tender, fluttering channel.

Garrick bucked and jerked under Devlin, his muscles straining as he pushed against the arm of the couch and tried to fuse himself to the man on top of him. His body rejected finding a rhythm in this mating; he just ached for a taking. Devlin kept it rough and out of control too, owning Garrick's ass in a way that should hurt but instead spurred Garrick on to beg for more.

He reached back and grabbed onto Devlin's hips, sinking his fingers into the solid flesh. "Fuck me, beautiful." Garrick pushed the side of his head into the couch cushion and made himself an immovable object for Devlin to penetrate. "Oh

Jesus," he gasped as Devlin plunged deep and up in response, "take me harder."

Devlin reared up to his knees, using his arms around Garrick's waist to drag him like a ragdoll upright in front of him. "You feel so incredible," Devlin said with a moan. He held Garrick to him and kissed him all over his neck, shoulders, and cheek, scraping with his teeth as much as his lips. "A thousand times better than I remember." Devlin shoved one hand up to Garrick's chest and the other down to rub his spike-stiff cock. "I can't stop touching you."

Garrick reached down and covered Devlin's hand on his prick. "Don't want you to."

Devlin squeezed his fingers around Garrick's cock with unforgiving pressure, and then whipped his hand up and down Garrick's penis in fast drags, making Garrick hiss and jerk and moan.

"It feels too good. Ohh shiitttt…" Garrick moaned as his ass channel squeezed around Devlin's invasion with each swipe of the man's hand over his cock. He jerked his hips back and forth without control, trying to grab for pleasure at both ends. "Fucking make me come." Garrick dug his fingers into Devlin's thighs, and leaned his head back on his shoulder. Whimpers of base, ugly need married with the erratic thrusts of Garrick's body. Garrick turned his face in to Devlin's neck, burrowing and searching for a safe place to die. "Please."

Devlin snatched Garrick's head out of hiding and fused their foreheads together. The pale blur of his gaze captured Garrick in its hold, keeping him prisoner. Devlin watched Garrick intently as he thrust his hips in miniscule pumps, tormenting Garrick by pushing just the thick head of his cock past Garrick's stretched, ultrasensitive pucker, and then withdrawing it, only to invade him with that teasing tip again. The *pop* of Garrick's ring, again and again with that shallow penetration, was soon joined by Devlin slowly stroking Garrick's prick, and then pressing the tips of his fingers into Garrick's sac, drawing a moan and a tightening of Garrick's muscles every time Devlin did it. Garrick felt like his entire body hung over a cliff, with only the head of Devlin's cock in his ass and his hand on his dick holding him safe from falling into a bottomless abyss. Garrick kept looking into Devlin's eyes, though, into a steadiness that never wavered, and his chest clamped so tightly tears sprang into his eyes.

Just as the slugging of emotion walloped Garrick, Devlin plunged his cock into the furthest reaches of Garrick's ass, fucking ripping a piercing cry right out of Garrick's soul as Devlin ordered, "Now."

The man took complete ownership of Garrick's ass, claimed his mouth with a fierce kiss that went as deep, and Garrick shouted right into Devlin as orgasm slammed through him harder than an avalanche. Garrick's entire body shook in deep, convulsing waves; release tore up through his rectum, into his spine, and raced through to every corner of his being, touching each nerve ending along the way. It punched Garrick in the gut, yanked his balls halfway into his body, and finally shot out of his cock. Devlin was right there too; he held onto Garrick's dick, aiming it straight out, as Garrick came. He held Garrick's body upright as Garrick screamed, his hips jerking with each streaming jet of cum he shot over the arm of the couch and onto the end table. Each spurt stole energy from Garrick's body, but filled his heart to bursting, making Garrick believe he could fucking do anything with this man.

When the last drop of seed dripped onto the couch, and Garrick clearly had nothing more to give, Devlin let go of Garrick's cock. He tunneled his hand into Garrick's hair and yanked his head back until they could see each other's faces again.

Devlin's gaze swirled with more shades of gray than the foulest sky on a rain-filled day, and his face was stark and full of sharp, hard angles. His voice, all rough edges, cut Garrick up inside as he said, "Say it, Garrick."

"I love you, beautiful." Emotion clogged Garrick's throat, but he somehow managed to get out the words he knew Devlin needed to hear. "I'm never running anywhere without you again."

Devlin's chest pressed against Garrick's back. He squeezed his eyes shut, and he clutched Garrick to his front, holding them connected as he shuddered and came. Wet heat warmed Garrick's passage, shocking a gasp out of him as he felt the man he loved spill inside him. Devlin opened his eyes as he bucked and shot within Garrick again, filling Garrick with a second wave of cum. Devlin's features twisted with the pleasure of his release, and he had never looked more beautiful in Garrick's eyes.

They both stayed still for a dozen heartbeats, kneeling on that couch, with Devlin tucked inside Garrick. As their breathing returned to normal, it synced up, and they fell into a rhythm they'd both so aggressively fought just moments ago.

With his arms still around Garrick, Devlin fell backward onto the couch, and Garrick landed on top of him, his back glued to Devlin's chest.

"Damn," Devlin said. He exhaled as he settled himself into the cushions and Garrick into him. "We've never done anything like that before."

Not with this much trust. "Not quite like that." Garrick turned his head on Devlin's shoulder and tried to see his face. "You've developed a dominant streak in the time we've been apart."

"I don't know about that." Devlin rubbed his hands over Garrick's stomach in soothing circles, and kept his tone low. "Something in me felt like you needed someone to take command of you, so I went with my gut."

Garrick's heart started hurting with the best kind of pain. "You have good instincts," he murmured. "I did need it. Thank you."

"You were... I don't know ... all raw inside or something. I could feel it, even if I don't know how to describe it." Devlin strained his neck and managed to make eye contact with Garrick. "Do you feel all right now?"

"A little sore." Garrick's rectum still pulsed around Devlin's embedded shaft. "But I think I needed that too."

"Shit. I'm such an idiot." Devlin's mouth drew down at the edges. "Do you want me to pull out?"

Garrick twisted his arm up and rubbed the pale line of Devlin's lips, easing away the tension. "Want you to? Not a chance." He already knew he'd be walking a little bit sideways tomorrow, though. "But it's probably a good idea."

Devlin rolled them both to the side, and they both gasped as Devlin slowly withdrew his cock from Garrick's wonderfully abused ass.

Garrick hated to roll the rest of the way off the couch, away from Devlin's warmth, but he did it anyway. "I'll get you a washcloth," he called out as he hobbled to the bathroom.

"Hey!" Devlin's sharp tone stopped Garrick at the door.

Garrick turned, his heart suddenly in his throat. "Yeah?"

From over the arm of the couch, a big, cheeky smile lit up Devlin's entire face. "You still have the sweetest ass I've ever fucked."

Flames burned all the way up Garrick's body. *Damn it. His cock tried to stir. There's no way he's making me hard again already.* "According to you," Garrick delivered his best eye-roll Devlin's way before moving to the sink and turning on the water, "I have the *only* ass you've ever fucked."

Devlin appeared behind him, his nudity stunning in the mirror's reflection. "True enough." He slipped his arms around Garrick's waist and snatched the wet washcloth out of his hand.

Their gazes collided in the reflection of the mirror as Devlin rubbed the cloth down Garrick's belly, inducing a tremor, and cleaned his cock for him. "But there's no point in looking for sloppy seconds when you've already had the best." He trailed the damp cloth around Garrick's hip and wiped away lube and cum from his ass. "Right?"

This man had an uncanny way of making Garrick feel as if he was ten feet tall and could walk on water. His heart about as full as it could possibly get, Garrick turned in Devlin's arms, and linked his hands at the small of Devlin's back. "Are you trying to remind me why I love you so much, beautiful?"

Devlin pursed his lips and cocked his head to the side. "Maybe just trying to show you how great a boyfriend I can be." He pecked a fast kiss to Garrick's lips. "How am I doing?"

Garrick drew Devlin in and pressed his lips to the man's forehead. He held there, eyes closed, and tried his damnedest not to lose his shit all over again. "You locked in the job the second you didn't let me push you away." He breathed and breathed, working like the devil to maintain his cool. "First at the airport all those years ago, and then when I wanted to keep my secrets from you here, and finally just now when you came back on your own and pushed me after I told you I'd call you tonight." Garrick opened his eyes and looked into the brightness of Devlin's, knowing something similar existed in his own. "Thank you for fighting for us every time I got scared."

Devlin nodded, and his Adam's apple moved visibly. "Thank you for picking me up in that bar when you had to sense I didn't have any kind of experience with men or sex. Thank you for showing patience and turning a one-night fuck into a whole weekend together, and then for e-mailing me and keeping it going even though you knew you shouldn't." He moved his hands up and down Garrick's arms, as if gently petting a skittish animal. "Thank you for believing in what we had, and for making your way to me when you didn't have anyone else to trust. I'm going to keep you safe, Garrick Langley." Devlin rubbed their fronts against one another as that infectious smile of his appeared again. "Just you watch and see."

"I have no doubts about that." Garrick buried his hand in Devlin's hair. He tilted the man's head back and descended, brushing their lips. "You take them away every time they try to creep in."

Devlin smiled against the connection of their mouths. "Good. I --"

Bzzz. Bzzz.

"Oh shit." Garrick untangled himself from Devlin and dove for the clothes strewn about the floor, searching for his pants.

"What the hell is that?" Devlin asked. From the corner of his eye, Garrick could see Devlin wiping his cock clean.

"Doorbell," Garrick answered as he struggled into his underwear and jeans. "The previous owners of the house rigged it so that it makes a noise up here every time it rings." He pulled on his T-shirt and ran to the window. "That has to be the window guy." One look at the logo-emblazoned truck in the driveway confirmed his suspicions. "He's early." Garrick shoved open his window and stuck his head halfway outside. "Hello! I'll be right there!"

A grizzled guy walked to the end of the porch and looked up at Garrick.

"Two minutes!" Garrick lifted a couple of fingers in the man's direction. "I'm coming." The guy gave him a thumbs-up and moved out of sight. Garrick turned back to Devlin. "I have to go."

In the short time it had taken Garrick to gain the attention of the repairman, Devlin had donned all of his clothes. He now sat on the couch, tying his sneakers. Garrick's were sitting neatly on the cushion right next to him, laces untied, and shoes ready to go.

"Thanks." Garrick took two strides to the couch. Without sitting, he lifted one foot up to the cushion at a time and put them on.

Devlin, fully dressed, folded his hands on his lap. He looked up at Garrick, the edge of his lower lip tucked in between his teeth. "Do you want me to come with you?" he asked, his voice soft.

Oh, baby. Garrick almost crumpled to his knees at the hesitation he heard in Devlin's voice. *No fear. Never again.* "Yeah, beautiful. I do." Garrick stuck out his hand in offering, wiggling it. "You're part of this too."

Devlin dipped his head, smiling as he took Garrick's hand, clasping it into the warmth and strength of his. *As it should be.*

364 | CAMERON DANE

"Let's go." Garrick led Devlin out of the garage apartment, pausing for just a moment to lock the door. "We have work to supervise."

Hand in hand, Devlin and Garrick loped down the stairs and across the lawn.

Epilogue

Devlin's world went black as Garrick tied a strip of stained white fabric across his eyes.

"Oooh."

Devlin spun in surprise as his sister's voice came at him out of the dark.

"Kinky," she added.

Devlin started to topple, but hands whipped out and righted him before he tipped over. "Careful, babe," Garrick said, his warm breath brushing Devlin's ear. "I don't want to spend the night at the ER having you treated for a broken limb."

The scuff of footsteps and the sounds of metal things sliding and clanging -- noises Devlin associated with his visits to see

Garrick or Maddie at the garage -- reached Devlin's ears. Then he heard Maddie say, "Here are the keys. I'll be out of your hair in just a few seconds."

"Thanks, Maddie." His voice low, Garrick's rich, deep tone still carried to Devlin where he stood. "I appreciate your letting me do this."

"No problem." That was Maddie again. "Maybe one day I'll care enough about a guy to want to do something special for him too." A wistful quality filled her voice, and Devlin wanted to shake his stubborn sister.

"You already do," Devlin reminded her from his position in the dark.

"Shut up." Maddie's voice snapped around the room, cracking against the walls like a whip. "I only tolerate Wyn for Aidan's and Ethan's sakes."

"I didn't say Wyn." Devlin flashed a smile. He probably looked like an idiot with half his face covered by a blindfold, but he couldn't help it. "You did."

"He's right, sweetie," Garrick added. "You're the one who mentioned him first."

"You shut up too, G." In his mind's eye, Devlin could see his sister whirling on Garrick and getting right up in his face. "Or I will decide I have a lot more work I can do here tonight after all."

Garrick immediately responded with, "Wyn who?"

"Thank you." Maddie's voice sing-songed, and now Devlin could mentally see her with a smile of satisfaction at having made her point.

More scuffing noises echoed in the big garage. Moments later, the lightest wafting scent of peaches and cream tickled Devlin's nose, and a brush of soft lips caressed his cheek. "Have fun." That was Maddie again. She squeezed his hand. "I'll talk to you tomorrow."

"Bye, sis." Devlin waved in what he assumed was the direction of the exit where his sister headed.

"See you, Maddie," Garrick called out too.

The click of a door closing, and locks turning and sliding into place, echoed into Devlin's ears, and then silence filled the air.

But just for a moment. Garrick's heat suddenly crowded Devlin's back, and he dipped down to press a kiss into the curve of Devlin's neck. "Finally. You're all mine." He curled his hands under Devlin's elbows and nudged his cock against Devlin's ass. "Walk forward with normal steps until I tell you to stop."

Devlin shuffled forward one cautious step at a time, acutely aware of his balance, even with Garrick guiding him. "You've been very mysterious ever since you called me," Devlin said. Garrick had called him at the firehouse and instructed him to come to the garage as soon as his shift ended.

"It's a boyfriend's prerogative. Stop right here." With Garrick's hands on Devlin's arms, Devlin came to a halt when Garrick stopped moving. "Just wait where you are." Garrick let go of Devlin, and his heat left Devlin's backside. "Keep the blindfold on until I tell you to remove it."

"You're lucky I love you and trust you." Devlin put his hands on his hips and cocked his head to the side, as if he could see whatever the hell Garrick was doing. "Normally I'd demand my lovers keep the blindfold play confined to the bedroom."

"Oh yeah?" Garrick's tone was light, and Devlin could feel him flash one of those glances he liked to give from the corner of his eye. "How many more lovers have you had since the last time we talked about it?"

"None." Devlin's heart and belly fluttered, and he felt himself blush. "But if I had, that's what I would tell them."

"Glad to hear that I would at least still be special."

"You're not just special, Garrick." Devlin tried to look through the blindfold to where he imagined Garrick would be standing. "You're everything."

A *thud* hit Devlin's ears, and then a wonderfully colorful curse filled the garage. "Damn it." Garrick mixed in a sharp whistle with another four-letter word. "You make me trip over my feet when you say shit like that."

God, he's so fucking sweet.

Devlin swallowed down a swell of love that wanted to take him over and make him bawl like a pussy. "I'd tell you to strip me naked, bend me over and fuck me where I stand, but I don't want to spend our evening taking *you* to the emergency room."

"Thank you for the courtesy." The Sahara desert had nothing on the dryness in Garrick's tone. "Okay. You can take off the blindfold."

Devlin stripped the piece of fabric off over his head. He

blinked a half-dozen times to adjust to the shock of light suddenly attacking his eyes, and then everything cleared, and an absolute vision filled Devlin's gaze.

Sweet mother. It's perfect.

Devlin blinked and looked again, but his eyes did not deceive him. Before him, Garrick had himself laid out across the hood of a car -- his ass probably leaving an imprint on the windshield because he didn't have on a stitch of clothing. The man was insanely sexy, as always, but he fucking had himself draped over a cherry specimen of a '77 Pontiac Trans Am Firebird, exactly in the pristine shape Devlin had always dreamed of owning, and Devlin couldn't much process anything more than that. Shiny black in color, with the *exact* gold trim along the sides, firebird design beautifully depicted on the hood, and snowflake rims recreated with the right color of paint and everything.

It's everything I've always wanted. And more.

Garrick swept an arm across his front like a game show model. "So? What do you think?"

Devlin rushed to the car and ran his hands along the side of its perfect, sexy shape. "Whoa," he whispered. Maddie had never mentioned the car again after showing it to him that first time. With everything that had happened since, Devlin had totally forgotten she'd found it and was restoring it to its original state.

He opened the passenger side door and leaned a knee on one of the custom seats, inhaling some spray she must have used to recreate a new car smell. He looked to the back, and whistled. The car fucking even had the specialty bucket seats in the back. Then Devlin looked toward the front, and his attention caught on the shine glinting right in front of his eyes. "Oh, damn it." He reached out and fingered the shiny, raised pyramid, stamped metal running across the front of the instrument panel. "There's a diamond design panel and everything."

Garrick rolled over on the hood and looked in at Garrick through the windshield. "Yep." Pride infused his voice. "It's the perfect recreation. Every detail is right. Straight down to the CB radio."

Son of a bitch. Devlin shot out of the car. *Our talk.* He rounded the open door to Garrick and stooped down so they were at eye level. Everything was right there in the man's eyes. It didn't matter that they were blue; Devlin could see the truth filtering through. *Of course.*

"You did this," Devlin said, his voice choked. He flipped back through those few conversations he'd had with Maddie about the Trans Am and it hit him that she'd never actually said she found the car herself. "Maddie didn't find the car to refurbish. You did."

Garrick shrugged. "I brought it in. Your sister knows you well, though. The second she saw it, she said she had a buyer and wanted to do the work herself. I volunteered to lend a hand." He shifted upright and reached out to caress Devlin's cheek. "It was a way I could be close to you, even though I didn't have the nerve to face you yet."

Devlin turned his head and kissed Garrick's hand. "It's beautiful, Garrick."

The sweetest damned smile, something Devlin got the privilege to see every day now, tilted Garrick's lips at the edges. "Not as beautiful as your face the second you laid eyes on it," Garrick told him softly.

Flashes of eating sandwiches while sitting across from a tattooed man in an ugly motel room filled Devlin's head. "I can't believe you remembered that silly thing I said that day."

"I remember everything you tell me. If it's important to you, it's important to me."

"Yeah," Devlin agreed, his tone a bit gruff suddenly, "me too. So…" He let his gaze wander down the length of Garrick's enticing physique, pleased to see the man's cock respond with a visible jump. "What's with the nakedness? Not that I'm complaining." He arched a brow as he looked some more. "But you can't have thought I'd need extra incentive to love this car."

With a deep breath that expanded his chest, Garrick blurted, "How would you feel about parking this cock-on-wheels next to my battered old truck every night?"

Devlin jerked his attention away from Garrick's growing prick and shot right up to his face again. "What are you saying?"

Garrick didn't blink or look away. "I'm saying I want us to live together."

Oh Holy Mother.

Devlin grabbed the open car door to his left as his legs went weak on him.

Two months had passed since the night Randy had broken into Grace's home and changed all their lives. A reporter had indeed come to ask Grace some questions about Randy, about his presence in Redemption, and if Grace had known about it. However, Wyn had also been right in his guess that the reporter wouldn't have any interest in the tenant above the garage. Garrick had not even been mentioned in the article that ran a few days later.

Devlin and Garrick had spent almost every night together since then, the only exceptions being when Devlin had gotten the okay to go back to work and had to do his overnight shifts at the firehouse. Garrick's room was cramped with two people, and Devlin's place had Maddie, so what exactly was he suggesting?

Maybe... Devlin's heart leapt right into his throat. *No. Don't get ahead of yourself.* Devlin couldn't help it, his chest started to pound at the possibilities, even though he told himself not to hope.

"Damn it." Garrick smacked his hand against the hood of the car. "You're looking completely shell-shocked, Devlin, but hear me out." He grabbed Devlin's hand and pulled him around to the front of the car. He slid there too and braced his feet on the front fender. "Shit, I'm kind of springing this on myself as much as I am you, beautiful. You know the people who live one house across and to the left of Grace? The Sheridans?" At Devlin's nod, Garrick went on. "The wife told Grace today that the husband found out his work is moving him to Virginia in two months. She asked Grace if she would list the house for them. Grace was telling me about it," Garrick took Devlin's hands in a loose hold, "and I told her to hold off for a day."

"You did?" So much hope filled those two words that Devlin barely choked them out.

Garrick drew Devlin between his legs. "I know it's a big step, and happening very quickly, but what do you think? Do you want to buy it with me?" He fiddled with the buttons on Devlin's shirt, darting his focus between them and Devlin's eyes as he spoke. "It's a bigger step of trust for you," Garrick said. "We'd have to work it so that yours is the only name on the paperwork. I still don't feel like I can risk too much scrutiny."

He looked up into Devlin's eyes, and his hands went from playing with Devlin's shirt to grasping it in a twisting hold. "But I promise I love you and want to live with you all the time, in our own place. This is close to the Fines, so we can still check in with Shawn and Chloe every day. I promise you can trust me with your credit score. I would never leave you ever, period, and I swear I would never renege on my half of the mortgage payment and bills. Whatever you need me to do to make you feel safe taking this risk, I am willing and want to do it for you." Earnestness shaped every line of Garrick's being, and his eyes shone with just as much love as Devlin was sure his own did. "Will you buy a house and build a life together with me?"

Oh Holy Mother. Devlin gulped down a grapefruit-sized lump lodged in his throat. *Jesus, Mary and Joseph.* He could not break from the brightness in Garrick's gaze. "I-I…"

Garrick's face fell as quickly as his hands did from Devlin's shirt. "It's too much too fast. I knew I shouldn't have put you on the spo --"

Devlin clamped his hand over Garrick's mouth. *Snap the fuck out of it, Morgan, before you ruin this moment and kill every damned thing you've always wanted with this man.* "Yes." Devlin laughed out loud, filling the garage with the joyful noise. "Yes!"

Garrick's eyes burned bright, and the green once again somehow magically beamed through the blue. "Yes?" he parroted. The word came out muffled around Devlin's hand.

Devlin shoved Garrick back onto the hood of the car, and crawled up on top of it himself, stalking his man with each scoot Garrick took backward until the man's spine hit the windshield and he could move no more. The second Garrick could go no further, Devlin settled in between the spread of his legs, rubbed their cocks together, and let his mouth descend and brush against Garrick's.

With each graze and scrape of his lips across Garrick's, Devlin whispered another "Yes." He ran his hands down the sides of Garrick's body, reveling in the warm, firm flesh burning with life under his palms. "You can tell me all about the specs of the house right after we put your nakedness to good use in celebration."

"Mmm…" Garrick pushed the flat of his hands down Devlin's back, and then kept right on going, slipping them into the back of Devlin's jeans to caress and knead his ass. "I stocked your glove compartment with lube."

"I always thought you were a smart, prepared man. Maybe you can take me on a full tour of the car a little later." With their gazes fully connected, Devlin reached between their bodies and closed his hand around Garrick's rigid shaft. "Right after I show my thanks."

Garrick rocked up into the contact, his chuckle warm against Devlin's mouth. "Will do, beautiful." He spread his legs and locked them around Devlin. "It's a deal."

No coherent words were heard after that. Just the sound of Devlin's clothing rustling as it was removed and hit the concrete floor. Then nothing but the sounds of sweat-slick bodies rubbing against one another and across the smooth metal beneath them, and finally the cries of pleasure as two beings merged into one and found completion in one another's arms.

Hours later, after Devlin got that tour of the car, and Garrick filled him in on all the specs, Devlin declared the hood of his new Trans Am his favorite part of the vehicle.

Funny. Garrick was partial to it too.

AUTHOR NOTE ABOUT DEVLIN AND GARRICK

Disclaimer: The tattooing in this story, as well as its removal, is a fictionalized interpretation of emerging tattoo ink technology and in no way reflects the actual results of any known testing or trial research happening in this field.

ABOUT THE AUTHOR

I am an air force brat and spent most of my growing up years living overseas in Italy and England, as well as Florida, Georgia, Ohio, and Virginia while we were stateside. I now live in Florida once again with my big, wonderfully pushy family and my three-legged cat, Harry. I have been reading romance novels since I was twelve years old, and twenty-five years later I still adore them. Currently, I have an unexplainable obsession with hockey goaltenders, and an unabashed affection for *The Daily Show* with Jon Stewart.

FIND ME ON THE WEB AT WWW.CAMERONDANE.COM